Against the Wall

by Alexa Land

a M/M love story

Book Seven in the Firsts and Forever Series

Books by Alexa Land Include:

Feral (prequel to Tinder)

The Tinder Chronicles (Tinder, Hunted and Destined)

And the Firsts and Forever Series:

Way Off Plan

All In

In Pieces

Gathering Storm

Salvation

Skye Blue

Against the Wall

Dedicated to the

M/M Community on Facebook

It's a wonderful thing

when a reader or a fellow author

becomes a friend.

Thank you, each of you,

for the love, support, and

encouragement!

Table of Contents

Chapter One

It was time to go.

It was past time, actually. I knew this. But even as part of my brain was chanting *come on, come on, come on,* another part was thinking *almost there, just one more minute, that's all I need.* The part of my brain that promised one more minute was a liar. One minute always turned into two, then five, then ten.

I shook the can of pink paint in my hand. According to the label, it wasn't actually pink. It was *Ferocious Fuchsia.* Who named these things? I stretched up as high as I could, the pile of pallets beneath me swaying just a bit, and brought my arm around in a wide arc as I pushed the nozzle with my index finger. The oh-so-familiar smell of spray paint flooded my senses and with my free hand, I tugged the black bandana that was wrapped around my face up an inch, so that it covered my nose completely.

With a few quick movements, I used the pink paint to highlight the enormous face of a young girl, just beginning to take shape on the back wall of a condemned apartment building. Then I leaned back a bit to assess the mural, which was tough to do in the dim light. It didn't help that I was wearing sunglasses, both to protect my eyes from the paint and to hide my face from the security cams that dotted the city. My unsteady perch wobbled, and I crouched down a bit to lower my center of gravity.

Leave it, Christian, you can come back later. You know you've been here too long. The rational part of my brain always lost out to the adrenaline junkie though, the 'one more minute' part of me that needed to be here, painting, creating, all while on high alert, just waiting for the police or some random street thug to roll up on me.

That adrenaline rush was as much a part of this as the need to make art. I knew this about myself. I probably could go through legal channels and get permission for my murals, but where was the thrill in that? I absolutely lived for this. I *really* didn't want to get caught, though. Jail was so not part of the plan.

Given that, it was incredibly stupid that I was out here so early on a Friday night. It wasn't even one a.m. The city wasn't asleep yet, not fully, but I'd been obsessed with this painting all week. I saw it so clearly in my mind's eye, this little girl in a field of daisies, and I needed to make her real. Well, *little* wasn't quite the right word. By the time I was finished, she'd be almost twenty feet high.

My phone vibrated in my pocket and I pulled it out and glanced at my best friend's name on the screen. I hesitated for a long moment, considering letting it go to voicemail. But then I felt like a douche and answered the call with, "Hey, Skye."

"Hey yourself, Christian. You haven't been returning my texts."

"I know. I got busy but I was just about to text you." I stifled a sigh. Liar. I really was a douche.

"What are you doing? Feel like going on an art supply run with Dare and me?" Skye was a metal sculptor, and what he really meant was dumpster diving, probably on private property. Normally, I enjoyed scavenging with him. But since he'd gotten engaged, I felt totally obsolete around him and his fiancé.

"Thanks, but I'm actually working on one of my projects right now."

"You're painting already? Isn't it kind of early?"

"Yeah, a bit. This part of town isn't exactly party central, though."

"I miss you, Christian," he said. "Promise me we'll get together sometime this weekend."

I wanted to make excuses, but instead I said, "Are you going to be at the warehouse tomorrow? If so, I'll come by and see how the boys are doing." He'd already completed what could have been his senior project, an absolutely amazing sculpture of a male dancer in mid-leap, inspired by his fiancé. But then he got incredibly ambitious and decided to make two more sculptures, showing the same dancer beginning and ending that leap. Each piece stood ten to fifteen feet high, and I knew he was going to stress

9

himself out trying to get the two additional sculptures completed by June. Still though, I admired what he was trying to accomplish.

"Yeah. Dare, Benny and I are spending tonight at the warehouse and plan to work all day tomorrow." Benny was their dog.

"Alright, I'll be by tomorrow then. Not early." After we disconnected, I sighed as I slipped my phone back in the pocket of my jeans. I really had to get a grip on the fact that my best friend was engaged.

I'd been attracted to Skye when I first met him. We'd even gone out a couple times before some things happened that redefined our relationship as firmly platonic. But when he'd started going out with Dare I'd gotten kind of panicky and, in a rash moment I wasn't proud of, I'd kissed Skye. It had felt really wrong and we both knew even as it was happening that it was a total mistake. But that was how desperate I'd been not to lose him.

That was crazy on so many levels, though. His relationship with Dare was a really positive thing. It made him happy, which was what I wanted for my best friend more than anything. Besides, I was going to have to say goodbye to him when the school year ended, so it was great knowing he wouldn't be alone.

When the police cruiser pulled into the south end of the alley, it took me a moment to notice since I was lost in thought. My heart leapt in my chest when I saw it, even though I totally knew that would happen tonight. I quickly capped the spray paint and dropped it into the backpack I was wearing, then pressed myself against the part of the brick wall that didn't have fresh paint on it. Sometimes, the police drove right past me. The stack of boxes and pallets under me was more than ten feet tall, maybe they wouldn't glance up. My heart was pounding in my ears. I swallowed hard.

The police car slowed, then stopped just a few feet away. I held my breath. I was dressed all in black and the alley was pretty dark, so maybe I'd get lucky.

In the next instant, a powerful spotlight mounted to the police car blinded me and a deep voice started barking orders over the P.A. system. Yeah, no, I really wasn't going to surrender. I grabbed the safety rope attached to the harness around my chest and began to climb. The cops were out of the car now, yelling at me. One of them even threatened to shoot me, which was not going to happen. I'm sure he wanted to, but he wouldn't really do it. The paperwork for shooting an unarmed graffiti artist in the back was a bitch.

I made it to the top of the building and hoisted myself over the edge, then pulled the rope up after me. Working quickly, I stripped off the harness and my hoodie. I crammed these inside the backpack along with my sunglasses and bandana, then jogged across the roof in a crouched over position (as if the cops could see me from six stories below) and hid my backpack inside an old vent that I'd scouted ahead of time.

The question now was whether to leave through this building, or some other way. I ran to the front of the rooftop and took a quick peek over the edge. The police car was double-parked in front of the building, so they were probably already heading up the stairs. I'd thought to barricade the door to the roof before I began painting, so that was going to slow them down.

I ran to the side of the building so I could use the fire escape, but another police cruiser was parked beneath it and a cop was already starting to climb the rusty ladder. Shit, really? They'd called in reinforcements, just for little old me? Were there no actual crimes being committed in the city right now?

Alright, time for Escape Plan F, for fucking crazy. I pressed myself against the half-wall framing the top of the building, then took off at a dead sprint across the rooftop. The building to the left of this one was one story shorter, with a six-foot-wide alley in between. Piece of cake, as long as I didn't stop to think about what I was doing. Just as the cops started rattling the door I'd barricaded, I reached the edge of the building, leapt up onto the half-wall and pushed off with my legs, propelling myself forward as my heart almost exploded in my chest.

For just a moment, I was airborne. I flew across the alley and dropped ten feet to the neighboring building. The landing was jarring, but I knew to take it at a roll. Immediately I was back on my feet, running across the roof and jumping over one more alley. Fortunately, the building I landed on this time was the same height as the last one.

I'd planned ahead, like always. The door to the rooftop was still ajar, just the way I'd left it. I stepped into the hotel and clicked the door shut behind me as quietly as possible, then paused and listened. The only sound was my ragged breathing and the pounding in my ears. I leaned against the wall for a couple minutes as I caught my breath, mopping at my sweaty face with the cuff of my long-sleeved black t-shirt. Then I detangled the elastic band that was holding my hair back in a stubby ponytail and ran my fingers through my brown curls. There was nothing identifying me as the person in the alley now, but the police might still stop me and question me. They did things like that.

I headed for the stairs, taking in my drab surroundings. The paint was peeling and the carpet was so stained I couldn't even guess its original color. It had been a nice place once, just enough ornate plasterwork remaining to suggest an opulent past. But that had been a long time ago.

A door to my right opened and a thin young guy with dark hair and pale skin stepped out, shutting it behind him. He was obviously a prostitute, even though he was dressed simply in a t-shirt, jacket and jeans. I could always tell, though. It was something in the way they looked at you, assessing you in an instant: friend? Foe? Possible john? That wariness seemed to be part of the job.

He acknowledged me with a nod and headed toward the stairs, a couple paces ahead of me. We descended in silence, but when we reached the mezzanine, we both stopped dead in our tracks and he whispered, "Damn." There were three cops below us in the lobby of the building. They must have reached the rooftop of the building where I was painting in time to see me duck inside this hotel. "They're raiding this place? Really?" the guy murmured. "What are they planning to do, go door to door and drag all of us out from under our tricks?"

I told him, "I actually think they're here for me."

He turned to me, his blue eyes assessing me more thoroughly. "Why?"

"I broke the law."

"Well shit, who hasn't?" He crossed the few feet between us and frowned a little. "Were you painting graffiti?" I nodded and he sighed. "Like this neighborhood isn't bad enough." He raised a slender hand and rubbed the bridge of my nose with the pad of his middle finger.

"Paint?"

He rolled his eyes at that. "No. I have a nose fetish and suddenly got this urge to feel you up." He pulled his hand back and looked at me, then said, "Alright, Basquiat, you're good to go." I raised an eyebrow at that and he frowned at me, totally reading my mind. "Yes. The hooker was able to make a cultural reference. Shocking, I know. Really though, I missed the mark. Upper-class white boy like you only wishes he was Basquiat. More like WASPiat."

"Are you done?"

"Pretty much."

"Let's get out of here."

We joined hands without discussion, and the guy started talking animatedly about something or another, like we were two lovers out for a stroll. He kept this up as we trotted down the remaining stairs and cut through the lobby. The cops eyed us suspiciously, but for a moment it seemed like they were going to let us go without harassing us.

Not quite.

"Hold up." That came from the biggest cop in the bunch. The man was built like Optimus Prime. "What are you two doing here?"

Before I could launch into a speech about violating our civil rights by illegally detaining us, my companion clicked his tongue and put on a shrill lilt as he exclaimed, "We're *staying here*. What a dump! Are all your hotels like this? And here I thought San Francisco was supposed to be all luxurious! This place should be condemned, isn't that right, honey?"

He turned his gaze on me and I jumped in with, "I told you we needed to spend more than fifty dollars a night in the big city, or we were going to end up in a shit hole. Did I not tell you that?"

"You guys are tourists?" The cop asked.

"We're here on our honeymoon. This was supposed to be our dream vacation." The guy sounded choked up and actually managed to look a little misty-eyed. "But instead, we got this!" He waved a slender arm to encompass our surroundings.

I fought back a smile and said, "Come on baby, we still have an hour before the clubs close. You know you always feel better when you're shaking your cute little ass on the dance floor. I'll even ask the DJ to play your favorite song."

"Achy Breaky Heart?" he asked. I had to bite my lip to keep from laughing as I nodded. He sniffed and murmured, "That *would* make me feel better." The guy was good. He gave me a little apologetic smile and slipped his arms around my neck. "I'm sorry I got all emotional, pookie. I know this place isn't your fault. It looked nice in the picture on the internet."

"I'll make it up to you, baby. I'll bring you back to San Francisco for our five year wedding anniversary and I'll book us at the Best Western. I promise." My companion covered a laugh, turning it into a sob as he hugged me tightly.

"I love you so much, pookie," he exclaimed.

"I love you too, sugar butt."

That was the police officer's breaking point. He said gruffly, "You two get out of here and for God's sake, next time read Trip Advisor or something!"

"Yes, officer," my companion said sweetly, picking up my hand again and leading me out of the building.

"Pookie? Really?" I said when we were on the sidewalk.

"It's all I could think of. Besides, you did far worse! Sugar butt? What a terrible nickname!"

"What's wrong with it?"

"You basically just called your husband a candy ass."

"True, but it got us out of the building. The cop wanted nothing more to do with us after that." We were no longer holding hands, but we'd fallen into step with each other as we headed down the street. "I'm Christian, by the way," I added with a grin. "You should know that, as my husband."

"Hi Christian. Chance."

"Really?"

He rolled his eyes. "Yes really. My hooker name is Slutty McFuckmahbutt."

"Nice to meet you, Slutty."

We both chuckled at that, and then I pointed across the street and said, "That's one of mine, by the way, so you don't think I'm just out here adding to the urban blight." I'd painted a series of life-size dancing people across the top of an out-of-business department store. It had been one of my most challenging murals, since it actually faced the street. Most were tucked out of the way.

He looked at the mural, then turned to me with wide eyes. "You're Zane?" That was the name I used for my artwork. I was really surprised he'd noticed my signature. When I nodded he said, "Well, damn. I'm sorry about all the shitty things I'd thought about you."

"Likewise. You're actually a good guy."

"For a rent boy."

"I didn't say that."

"Didn't need to."

We'd reached an intersection and I turned to Chance, gesturing over my shoulder as I said, "I'm parked this way. Can I buy you a drink as a thank you for helping get my ass out of that situation?" There was that look again, another assessment. I added, "Just a drink. No hidden agenda."

He mulled it over for a few moments as I shivered a bit in the brisk December air. Finally he said, "Okay, but there are two ground rules. Number one, I'm not sleeping with you. Contrary to popular belief, sex workers aren't constantly looking to give it up to absolutely everyone. Number two, you can't ask me the question."

"What question?"

"You know. 'What's a smart guy like you doing selling his body?' I really fucking hate it when people start scrutinizing me like I'm a sociology study."

"You're in luck," I said as I fished my car keys from my pocket. "I have no interest in sleeping with you and I don't care why you're a hooker." I flashed a smile and added, "Come on, I need about five shots of whiskey after this evening."

He fell into step beside me again and said, "Just so you know, I only have an hour."

"You have someplace you need to be at two a.m.?"

"Yeah, bent over with some guy's dick up my ass. It's Friday night and people start to get desperate as closing time draws near. When they fail to pick up any of their fellow bar patrons, they start looking for options."

I stopped at the passenger door to my black Jeep and unlocked it for him, then said, "For someone who doesn't want to talk about being a prostitute, you're certainly candid about it."

He paused in front of me. He was a couple inches shorter than me, so he looked up and held my gaze as he said, "I'm not ashamed of what I do. I just don't want to explain the why of it to anyone."

"Got it. Any preference on where we go?"

"Someplace like Freddy B.'s or Rounders would be great." He'd named huge night clubs that were popular with tourists, both gay and straight. I'd never set foot in either one.

"Seriously? There would be plenty of horny guys at any bar in the Castro, too."

Chance smirked at that. "No shit. Most of those club owners can recognize a prostitute a mile away though, and they really don't want to incur the wrath of the SFPD by letting us work their customers."

I considered that for a beat, then said, "Well, whiskey is whiskey," before getting in the car.

Chapter Two

Rounders was located off Market Street, in a neighborhood that a realtor might ambitiously describe as Castro-adjacent. But while it really wasn't far from San Francisco's gay neighborhood, it was a world removed. While the Castro was vibrant and interesting, this little wedge of shops and restaurants was just sort of generic. The club itself somehow came across as the equivalent of a chain restaurant, clearly owned by some anonymous out-of-town interest and lacking the soul of a small, local business.

The big club was in a boxy white building that had been outlined and accented with hot pink, blue and yellow neon. It looked like the 1980s had thrown up all over it. I was always up for new experiences though, and going to a tourist bar with a prostitute certainly qualified.

Chance held on to my arm as we pushed through the crowd. The place was packed. It was a shame, really. Tourists came from all over to see and experience San Francisco, and then they ended up in a place like this, bypassing all that made the city unique and interesting.

We lucked out, because a couple happened to get up from the bar just as we arrived and my companion and I took their seats. We were in a prime location, in a corner overlooking the entire bar area and dance floor. Chance scanned the room as I ordered us a round. "You certainly cover a lot of territory," I said, "from the Tenderloin to tourist traps."

"And everything in between." He pulled a business card from the pocket of his jeans and slid it over to me. It was sheer white vellum and was inscribed simply, Chance, along with a phone number. "I usually work by appointment and believe it or not, a lot of businessmen like that hotel in the Tenderloin. That's because they don't ask for a credit card or ID, so there's no paper trail afterwards." He toasted me with his drink and after he tossed back the shot he gestured at the card with his empty glass. "Keep that if you want. You never know when you might need a fake husband again." I grinned at that and slipped the card inside my wallet.

His eyes were scanning the room, so I asked him, "Anyone look promising?"

"They *all* look promising," he said loudly over the pulsating techno music. "A sea of horny men. What's not to like?" I downed my shot and gestured to the bartender for two more as Chance turned to me and said, "So, the Artist Sometimes Known as Zane, tell me. What's your story?"

"Don't have one." I finished my new drink quickly and he did the same.

"Sure you do. I mean, look at you. You're running around the mean streets of San Francisco under the cover of darkness, your weapon against all that's wrong with the world a can of spray paint. Anyone who's paying attention would notice the messages of hope in your work. I sure as hell did. You're like the Robin Hood of the Tenderloin, only instead of spreading wealth, you're leaving little gifts of beauty. I'd love to know what's behind it."

"That's really overstated."

"What can I say, I'm a fan. That's why I agreed to come and have a drink with you, because I find you interesting."

"I'm just an over-privileged art student with too much time on my hands."

"Well," he said, "you may be that too, but it doesn't change the fact that your work's profound."

I grinned at him. "Thanks. It really isn't, but it's nice that you noticed my murals at least. Aside from a couple of my friends, it feels like no one ever actually sees them."

"You'd be surprised." He gestured to the bartender and bought the next round. We both watched the crowd for a while, until he leaned in and said, "There's a seriously hot guy staring at you. Did you notice?"

"No. Where?"

"Diagonally across the dance floor. Royal blue polo shirt, shoulders and arms like Atlas."

I spotted the guy in question. Talk about gorgeous. He was totally built, with short, dark brown hair and eyes so blue I could see their color even at a distance. He was talking to three other guys. They all seemed to be about the same age, mid-twenties, but his three companions were all shorter and skinnier than him, and not to be unkind, but they were clearly dorks. The two white guys were a perfectly matched set (except that one was blond and the other brunet) who'd worn long-sleeved dress shirts along with their jeans, totally buttoned up and stiff. Their African American companion wore a bright t-shirt with the word Bazinga splashed across the front of it, along with a fedora. I had to wonder what Captain America was doing with the nerd herd.

"How would you know who that guy was looking at? This place is wall-to-wall people," I yelled to Chance.

"You're directly in his line of sight. Just watch him for a minute and you'll see I'm right."

The guy appeared to be having some sort of debate with his buddies. His friend in the fedora pointed across the bar, directly at me, and yelled something to his hot friend, who shook his head emphatically. Then one of the buttoned-down white boys took him by the shoulders, spun him toward me, and tried to give him a push. The hottie dug in his heels.

He did look up though and saw me watching him. Maybe. I still wasn't convinced that I was the focal point of his attention, though he did suddenly turn a shade of red so vivid that it was noticeable even among the club's bright, flashing lights. Chance leaned in and said, "Why don't you go talk to that guy? Ask him to dance or something."

I glanced at my companion. "First of all, I don't dance. Secondly, why would he be looking at me, out of all the people in this place? Maybe he's looking at you, you're right beside me and pretty damn hot."

"He's not looking at me. Watch." Chance got up and made his way to the center of the dance floor, then held his arms over his head and moved his slender body provocatively to the music. This got the attention of a half a dozen men around him, but not the guy in the polo shirt. Captain America was still glancing my way every few seconds while his friends appeared to give him some kind of pep talk. It involved a lot of hand gestures, yelling over the music and emphatic pointing.

I was still skeptical that any of that had a thing to do with me, but I had just decided to go say hello to him anyway when the pep talk finally worked. Captain America took a drink from the tall glass in his hand, then spun around and took a few steps in my direction, cutting across the dance floor. In the next instant, his arms were flailing over his head and he fell like a tree that had been chopped down, tripping over God knows what and landing flat on his belly. Oh man, the poor guy was dance floor road kill.

He knocked over at least ten people on his way down in a domino effect. The slippery ice that had flown out of his glass took out another dozen, most of them knocking down even more people as they fell. Chance was fairly nimble and managed to remain standing, but he was in the minority.

I leapt up to go help the guy in the polo shirt, but he was back on his feet in a flash. He darted toward the exit with his buddies in hot pursuit. Chance appeared beside me, somehow having navigated the wreckage on the dance floor, and said, "Aren't you going to go after him?"

"I still don't know if he was even coming to talk to me."

"He was, trust me."

"And what am I supposed to say to him?"

Chance grinned at me. "Try 'hi'. Works wonders." When I turned to look at him, he added, "That guy's having the worst night ever. I bet he could really use some happy right about now."

"You're right. It was good to meet you, Chance."

"Keep in touch, Christian," he said with a smile before directing his attention to a couple guys at the bar.

I looked for the boy in blue as I cut through the club, but he was nowhere to be seen. He wasn't in the crowd milling out front, either. I stood out on the sidewalk and looked in both directions, and finally spotted him and his little group halfway down the block. I went after them, and saw as I got closer that they were still debating. They had their backs to me and didn't notice me as I approached. "Let's just go back," the guy in the fedora was saying. "It's your birthday, we're supposed to be celebrating!"

"Yeah somehow, after humiliating myself in front of *him* of all people, I don't feel all that festive, Leo," the guy in blue said.

I was just a few feet away by now, so I stopped walking and said, "So, you probably don't mean me, which is going to make me feel like such a dumbshit for coming after you."

The foursome turned to face me, the nerd herd beaming ear-to-ear as the boy in blue went full-on deer in headlights. I noticed he still clutched the empty bar glass. "Oh, he *definitely* means you," Fedora Guy said. He glanced at his friend, then took a second look and poked his arm. "Isn't that right, Shea?"

I hadn't quite caught that so I asked, "Sorry, what was your name?"

Cricket, cricket.

His friends stared at him in anticipation, and finally the buttoned-down blond boy answered for him. "His name's Shea. Rhymes with gay."

His dark-haired counterpart added, "Today's his birthday, he just turned twenty-five."

I stepped a little closer and looked into those wide blue eyes, noting that he and I were the same height, six-one.

"Happy birthday, Shea. I'm Christian." I tried giving him a friendly smile, but that just seemed to freak him out more.

"Dude," the buttoned down brunet told his friend in a loud stage whisper, as if I couldn't hear that, "say something."

"I...um...hi," Shea finally managed.

I smiled cheerfully. "Hi."

His posse took that as their cue. Fedora Guy chimed in, "Our work here is done! We're going over to Bas's apartment, Shea, so you'll have the whole house to yourself if you know what I mean. Nudge nudge, wink wink!" *Everybody* knew what he meant, and Shea once again turned a vivid shade of pink. Or maybe it was *Ferocious Fuchsia.*

I stepped a little closer and carefully extracted the glass from his hand. It was surprising that it hadn't broken in the fall. As I handed it to one of his friends, my eyes never leaving Shea's, I murmured, "You are absolutely beautiful."

"*Awwww yeah,*" buttoned-down blond boy said with a huge smile, throwing his hands in the air and swiveling his skinny hips. "It's *on*! Have fun, Shea! But don't forget dude, no glove, no love!"

The guy in the fedora grabbed the blond's arm and started dragging him down the sidewalk as he called, "Bye,

Shea. Bye, hot guy. We'll be out late. *Real* late! Y'all will have plenty of time to get it on!"

"Oh God," Shea whispered, still staring at me. "I'm so sorry about that."

"Don't be. What's life without perfectly certifiable friends?" My gaze drifted to his full, luscious lips. I slid my hand around the back of his neck, pulled him to me and kissed him gently. Every part of me came alive, my pulse quickening and my cock swelling. I wanted this guy, no doubt about it. He was absolutely terrified though, and I was a little concerned that he'd throw up on me out of sheer panic.

A chorus of cat-calls came from his friends, who by now were down the block but apparently still watching. I ran my hand down his arm and asked, "Do you want to go back to your place?"

He nodded but remained rooted to the sidewalk. Maybe he'd only recently come out and wasn't used to being with guys yet. That might explain the terror. I draped my arms around his shoulders and kissed him again, lightly. Then I rested my forehead against his and told him softly, "I'd love to go home with you and fuck you all night, Shea. But that won't happen unless we actually start walking." That was, of course, the only reason anyone ever went to a meat market like that club, to hook up.

He swallowed hard and whispered, his voice shaking a little, "Yeah. Okay. It, um...it's that way." He pointed behind me, in the opposite direction his friends had gone.

I picked up his hand, pretending not to notice how sweaty it was. He noticed though and let go of me, dragging his palm across his denim-covered thigh before taking my hand again. We started walking and as we passed the club, Chance came out, his arm linked with a baby-faced guy in his mid-twenties. My new friend smiled and winked as we crossed paths.

After another block it became clear that it was going to be up to me to make small talk, even though I wasn't usually the chattiest guy in the world. "Those guys are your roommates, huh? They're an interesting bunch."

"We...uh...we've been best friends since seventh grade. After college we bought a house together since none of us could afford one on our own." His voice was still shaking a bit, poor guy.

"Makes sense. This city's really expensive."

He nodded at that but didn't say anything. After a while, I swung him into the alcove of a closed spice shop, pushed him against the wall, and kissed him deeply. His hands came up hesitantly and rested on my back. I kissed my way to his ear and whispered, "Don't you know how incredibly beautiful you are, Shea? I wanted you from the moment I laid eyes on you. You don't have a reason in the world to be nervous."

"How I look doesn't matter much, though. As soon as guys start talking to me, I freeze up and blow it."

"You're doing just fine."

"I'm not. You're just kind."

"No I'm not." I nuzzled his neck as I said that. He reached up and touched my hair, lightly, experimentally. "You sure you want to do this, Shea? No pressure."

"Oh God, please don't change your mind!" He pulled back and stared at me, his eyes pleading.

"I'm not," I said gently as I cupped his face in my hands. "I just want to make sure this is what you really want."

"It is."

"And you understand it's just sex, right? No expectations beyond tonight." Normally, I didn't feel the need to point that out. Gay men in this city knew the score. But it was pretty obvious that the bar scene wasn't Shea's thing, so I wanted to make sure there was no confusion.

"I know," he murmured.

As long as I was listing disclaimers, I added, "I should also mention that I only top. Is that going to be a problem?"

"That's what I want you to do." He couldn't look at me as he said it.

When I hugged him I could feel him tremble. I wondered how many times he'd done this and how his previous sexual encounters had gone, given how nervous he was. I found myself suddenly determined to give him the best birthday sex of his life.

We held hands as we walked the remaining four blocks to his house. It turned out to be a quaint little craftsman with some nice details and a great period color scheme of dark blue, brown and forest green, exactly what I would have chosen for this place. I wondered which of the roommates had an eye for color.

That palette was carried through in the living room, where tasteful, deep green walls complemented the dark wood trim. But then I decided the house must have come like that, based on the fact that it was decorated in Comic Con meets Pee Wee's Playhouse. Six overstuffed chairs were clustered around a big, square coffee table, which was covered in some kind of board game. It looked like they'd walked away mid-game, judging by all the cards and tokens still in place.

The walls were lined with classic monster movie posters, but they were obscured by a whole host of characters, all life-size, photorealistic cardboard cutouts. I spotted at least three doctors from Doctor Who, a Dalek, Luke Skywalker (who'd been positioned in a passionate embrace with Han Solo), Thor, Iron Man, and a bunch of other characters that I wasn't dorky enough to recognize.

"Do you, um, want a drink?" I dragged my attention away from the cardboard crowd and focused on the gorgeous guy fidgeting nervously beside me.

"Sure. Thanks." He darted from the room while I wandered over to the fireplace. The attractive dark wood mantel was completely cluttered with all sorts of miscellaneous wonders, including a couple Rubik's Cubes, a little plastic Godzilla battling Bender from Futurama, and dozens of action figures. It made me smile.

Funnily enough, in a place of honor among all the toys were three framed photographs of Hunter Storm, a gay porn star that was actually a friend of a friend. The photos were all the same publicity shot of Hunter from the waist up, grinning back at the camera over his bare shoulder, and each photo was autographed but made out to a different name. I assumed Cas, Ridley and Leo were Shea's roommates.

When Shea reappeared beside me, precariously balancing two full shot glasses and a bottle of tequila, I gestured at the photos and asked, "Are your roommates gay, too?"

"Yeah. That's how we got to be friends. Leo and Cas had a crush on each other in junior high. They did their best to hide it, but it still made them targets for a lot of bullies. I was always big, so I tried to protect them. Leo and Ridley were best friends already, and we all just kind of formed this bond." That was a long speech for him, and afterwards Shea cleared his throat and shifted nervously, not meeting my gaze.

I took one of the shot glasses from his hand and studied him as he tried to fit the liquor bottle on the crowded mantel. There was an obvious sweetness to Shea. It was easy to imagine him coming to the aid of a couple smaller gay kids.

"Cheers," I said as I tapped my glass to his, then tossed back its contents. Shea squinched up his face as he did his shot. He obviously didn't care for it, but he refilled our glasses twice more and drank them down quickly. Apparently he'd decided a little liquid courage was the way to go here.

After the third shot, I took the glass from him and slid it onto the mantel along with mine, then drew him into my arms. I looked into those amazing blue eyes for a long moment before kissing him gently, and then I asked, "Was your birthday yesterday or today, since it's after midnight?"

"It's today. We went out at midnight to start celebrating."

"Well, I'm glad to be a part of it."

"I'm glad you are, too."

"Want to continue this in your room?" He nodded and took my hand. Shea was unsteady on the stairs though, and when we reached his bedroom door I paused and asked him if he was drunk.

He shook his head and swung open the door to his bedroom, and I grinned a little as we stepped inside. Apparently he was a huge Marvel fan, because comic book-style superhero posters covered every inch of the walls and ceiling. He glanced around and then looked at me. "I don't usually have guys over and I know this is all kind of—"

"Charming," I interrupted. "I like people who are passionate about things. This is obviously your passion."

"You're being so nice again. I know how this looks." He lowered his gaze, but I stepped close and raised his chin, kissing him gently.

"I'm not judging you, Shea," I said when I finally broke the kiss.

He watched me for a moment, as if he was trying to decide something, then lunged in for another kiss. He came in way too fast though, and even though I jerked my head back a bit, we still knocked our front teeth together. "Oh my God," he exclaimed, wide-eyed. "I'm *so* sorry."

I ran the tip of my tongue over my teeth, which were aching a bit. They weren't chipped though, and neither were his. "It's fine," I told him. "Just an accident."

He looked mortified. "I swear I'm not always this bad. I'm just so nervous."

"I know." I hugged him for a long moment before kissing him. As our kisses deepened and intensified, I began to undress him. The muscular body under that polo shirt was astonishingly perfect, his skin smooth, tan and flawless. If you made assumptions about him based solely on his physical appearance, you'd think he'd be really confident, maybe even cocky, instead of debilitatingly shy.

I led him to his queen-size bed and continued to undress him as he laid back against the pillows and watched me. I dropped his sneakers onto the floor, then tugged his socks off and massaged his feet before sliding my hands up his long legs to his belt. I removed his jeans but left him in his boxers for now, because he was still so anxious. After I pushed my shoes off, I climbed in bed beside him and drew him into my arms.

He looked like he was about to hyperventilate though, and after just a few moments he exclaimed, "Condoms! I have some in my sock drawer, I'll get them." Before I could point out that I had a couple in my wallet, he leapt to his feet, but immediately staggered and dropped to his knees. "Whoa," he murmured, falling forward and catching himself with his hands on the red and blue area rug.

"Shit!" I dove out of bed and helped him into a seated position, both of us leaning against the bedframe. "You okay?"

"I guess I'm drunk after all, I hadn't realized."

I put my arm around his shoulders and said, "You know we can't do this if you're drunk, Shea. It just wouldn't be right. I'd feel like I was taking advantage of you."

He pulled his knees to his chest and dropped his arms and head onto them. "I'm such an idiot. I thought it would help with my nerves, but I don't drink very often and I guess I overdid it."

"How many drinks did you have back at the bar?"

"Three and a half Long Island iced teas."

"You know those have about five shots apiece in them, right?"

He raised his head and blinked at me. "Five? They didn't really taste alcoholic."

"I'm kind of surprised you're still conscious."

Shea sighed and said, "I'm so sorry about all of this. I completely messed up tonight. I just want to curl up in a ball and die."

"Instead, get under the covers with me. You're starting to get goose bumps."

"You mean you're staying?"

"Only if you want me to. Do you?"

"God yes. But why aren't you running for your life, given all I've put you through tonight?"

I smiled at him and said, "I'm enjoying talking to you." As soon as sex was off the table, he'd relaxed a lot. I stood up and held my hand out to him, then pulled Shea to his feet.

We got under the quilt together. It was a patchwork of various plaids, all of them red, blue, or both on white backgrounds. I drew him into my arms as we settled in, and he exhaled slowly and put his head on my shoulder as I ran my hands up his broad back. My cock tried to hijack the moment, but I ignored it as I kissed the top of his head. After a while he said quietly, "I've seen you before. You're friends with a guy named Skye, aren't you?"

"Yeah, he's my best friend. You know him?"

"Only a little. I met him at my cousin's wedding, then again when he was brought in to the station where I work, after he and a crazy little old lady broke up an antigay rally in Golden Gate Park. He and I chatted for a while, he seems like a good guy."

"Does that mean you're a police officer?" I hadn't intended to sound quite that surprised.

Shea glanced up at me and very nearly smirked. "I know it's hard to believe that they let me carry a gun. Somehow though, I manage to go days and sometimes weeks at a time without accidentally shooting people."

I smiled at him. "Good job."

That made him smile, too. "So, how's Skye doing these days?"

"Great. He got engaged recently."

Shea must have heard something in my voice, because he asked, "Don't you approve?"

"Oh, I do. He and his fiancé obviously adore each other. I just...I miss him," I admitted. "They're always together now, so he and I don't hang out like we used to." I shifted a bit and murmured, "That was going to happen when the school year ended anyway, but I thought we had more time together."

"Where do you go to school?"

"Sutherlin College."

"So, you're an artist."

"I'm a wanna-be."

"What's your area of interest?"

"Murals, mostly." Since he was a cop, I really wasn't going to elaborate on the less-than-legal aspect of what I did.

"I admire people with artistic ability," he said. "I wanted to draw comic books when I was younger, more than anything. But I sucked at it."

"It's a learned skill, you could have taken classes."

"I did, but I was hopeless. My high school art teacher gave up on me. He told me that drawing wasn't my thing and I should apply myself to something else." He grinned, but I could tell that had hurt him.

"I'm sorry. No one should ever be told not to follow their dreams."

"It's okay. I'm better off where I am now."

"Do you like being a police officer?"

Shea considered the question before saying, "There are some things I like about it. I feel like I'm making a difference, and that's a good thing. I don't love the constant conflict, though. That takes its toll on me."

"How'd you decide on that career path? It seems like a huge leap from comic book artist to cop."

He shrugged and said, "It's pretty much the family business. My father, brother, uncles, and a bunch of my cousins all work in law enforcement, so I was always encouraged to take that path."

"Even though it's not what you really want."

"It wasn't, but I've learned to make the best of it."

I hated that, the resignation and disappointment he was trying to disguise. I murmured, "I wish I could teach you to draw."

That made him smile. "That's sweet, but I'm a lost cause."

"No you're not, there's no such thing. You just had a shitty teacher."

Sometime later, he fell asleep in my arms. I started to reach for the lamp on the nightstand so I could shut it off, but instead I paused and studied his handsome face as he slept, from his flawless skin to the sexy curve of his full lips. Shea was my favorite thing, an incredibly gorgeous guy that had no idea how attractive he was. I couldn't stand guys that were totally full of themselves, and he was the exact opposite. In fact, he could use more confidence.

Eventually I shut off the light and settled in. I never spent the night with anyone, let alone guys I just met. But there was something about Shea, an inherent trustworthiness that put me at ease. I knew I was safe with him.

*****

I awoke before him the next morning and slipped out of bed. After using the toilet, I rinsed my mouth with water in an attempt to fight back my morning breath and looked in the mirror. My hair was a disaster. I looked like Einstein on crack. I tried to finger comb it, but that only made it worse. Soon I gave up and slipped back into bed.

I started to drift off again, and Shea stirred beside me. A moment later, he darted off to the bathroom. When he returned five minutes later, the unmistakable smell of toothpaste accompanied him. I opened one eyelid and grinned at him as he slipped into bed beside me. "That's not fair," I murmured as I drew him into my arms. "You're all minty fresh. You even combed your hair! I'm completely disgusting by comparison."

He smiled at me sweetly. "You're really not."

I leaned in and kissed him before murmuring, "How hung over are you?"

"Surprisingly, not very."

I kissed him again, deeper this time as my cock stirred in my jeans, running my hand down his body. He was getting hard too, his cock tenting his boxers, so I pulled his underwear down to mid-thigh and began stroking him. He moaned against my lips, grasping two handfuls of my t-shirt as a little tremor went through him.

I took my time, ignoring my straining cock as I licked and kissed my way down his body. He gasped when I ran my tongue up his shaft and took his swollen cock between my lips. There was already a drop of precum waiting for me and I savored it as I began to suck him.

Not a minute later, I was startled as his cum hit the back of my throat and he stifled a yell. I swallowed reflexively as he blurted, "Oh my God, I'm *so* sorry! I was trying so hard to hold it back, and then...oh God."

"It's fine," I murmured as I sat up and pushed my hair out of my eyes.

"It's really not." Shea sat up too and pulled up his boxers before leaning against the headboard. He looked upset. "You must feel like you're back in high school, between the comic book posters and my total lack of experience." Someone pounded on the door just then and he sighed and added, "Not to mention my chaperones."

The door burst open and his three roommates started to charge into the room, but then they all stopped as if they'd hit an invisible barrier. "Oh snap, the hot guy's still here," the blond exclaimed.

"Sorry, Shea. We didn't know you still had company," another said.

"We wanted to take you out for birthday pancakes," the third chimed in.

I smiled at the trio over my shoulder and said, "Shea will be ready for birthday pancakes in about two hours, guys. I'm not done with him yet." They all beamed delightedly at that as I turned to Shea and asked, "Is that okay?" He blushed and nodded, looking surprised. I noticed he'd pulled the quilt over his lap to hide his boxers. I turned back to his friends and said, "Sorry to hog your roommate on his birthday, but you can have him back soon, I promise."

"Oh no, take all the time you need," the African American guy told me with a huge smile.

"You're Leo, right?" I asked and he nodded. "So, which one is Cas and which is Ridley?"

"I'm Cas," the brunet said. He gestured at the blond. "That's Ridley. His name's really Ronnie, but he's a huge Ridley Scott fan. Dork."

Ridley rolled his eyes at that. "As if your parents actually named you Castiel, Cory."

"Is Leo a nickname?" I asked. "Big Ninja Turtle fan, maybe?"

They all chuckled at that and Cas said, "Nah, that's actually his name."

"What about Shea? Does he have a nickname?"

"Yeah, Captain America," Leo told me.

I smiled at that and said, "You know, that was what I called him too when I first spotted him at the bar."

"Seriously?" Leo asked, and I nodded.

Ridley's eyes went wide and he blurted, "Holy hotness, Batman! If you don't marry this guy, I will!"

"Oh God," Shea murmured. When I glanced at him, he was blushing furiously.

I turned back to his roommates and said, "It was great meeting you guys. Oh, I'm Christian, by the way. Now if you'll please excuse us, I really need to have sex with your friend. We drank too much last night, so we didn't have a chance to do anything." I gave them my friendliest smile.

They backed out the door like they were one six-legged unit, grinning like maniacs. "Oh *hell* yes! You guys have fun!" Leo said.

"We'll be at the diner for a couple hours," Cas said, "so feel free to yell, moan, pound the headboard against the wall, whatever."

"I feel like a proud parent," Ridley was saying as he pulled the door shut behind them. "Well, not that most parents are probably all that proud when their son finally gets laid. I don't think mine were thrilled in the slightest."

I turned back to Shea and found he'd sort of curled up in a ball, pulling his knees to his chest and resting his head and folded arms on them. "I like your friends," I told him. "It's obvious they really care about you."

He glanced up at me. "I know they can be super embarrassing. Sorry they burst in like that."

"It's okay." I crawled around and leaned against the headboard, too.

Shea didn't look at me as he asked, "Are you really still planning to have sex with me?"

"Only if you want me to."

Now he met my gaze. "Oh, I do. But I can't figure out how my total dorkiness hasn't repelled you yet."

"You're not dorky." He shot me a look and I grinned at him. "Okay, you're a little dorky. But I happen to find it adorable."

"It's not."

I reached up and lightly finger-combed his dark hair. "I disagree."

"I still don't get it. You could have gone home with any guy in that club. Why'd you pick me?" His eyes went wide all of a sudden and he exclaimed, "Wait, is this pity sex? Are you here because you felt sorry for me after the way I humiliated myself?"

"Of course not!"

"It has to be. There's no other explanation for it, and—"

I cut him off with a kiss as I wove my fingers in his hair. When he responded, I pulled him down onto the mattress with me and rolled on top of him, straddling one of his thighs. He moaned softly, his lips parting, and I slid my tongue in his mouth.

I felt him getting hard again and I lightly brushed my stiff cock against his leg as I whispered, "I want you, Shea. Pity doesn't have a damn thing to do with it."

His voice sounded rough when he said, "Okay. I believe you."

I kissed him tenderly and then pulled back to look at him. "Are you a virgin?" He turned his head away, color rising in his cheeks. "I'm not judging. I just need to know." When he nodded, I kissed his cheek before asking, "You sure you want me to be your first?" He looked in my eyes and nodded again. "I'm going to make this so good for you, Shea," I promised.

I took my time with him, kissing him and caressing his body, and gradually he began to relax. He reached up and touched my face tentatively and I looked in his eyes and smiled, which earned me a breathtaking smile in return. Eventually I stripped off his boxers and lightly stroked his cock before reaching lower and massaging the sensitive area beneath his balls. He spread his legs for me, so much trust in his eyes.

I leaned over him and kissed him tenderly as I began to lightly trace his opening. His breath caught when I gently pushed just the tip of my finger inside him, and I withdrew and went back to massaging the outside of his little hole. After a while I asked, "Do you have something we can use as lube, Shea?"

"There's some lotion in the nightstand."

I pulled open the drawer, noting the well-worn sketch pad that was in there along with a bunch of colored pencils, and grabbed what I was looking for, then slid the drawer shut again. After dispensing a bit of the cream onto my fingertips, I went back to kissing him as my fingers explored his opening slowly, carefully, taking my cues from the little sounds he made. He held on to me as I worked a finger into him and I sat up just a little so I could watch his eyes. It was vitally important to me not to hurt him or go too fast.

When I found his sweet spot and began to rub it, he let out a moan, his eyes sliding shut as he relaxed against the pillow. "That feels amazing. What are you doing?" he managed as he began to rock his hips gently, fucking himself onto my finger.

"I'm massaging your prostate." I decided now was a good time to take him a bit further, and I slid a second finger inside his well-lubed little hole. It was a tight fit, but he took it without complaint.

"Oh. Wow. I'd read about that, but I had no idea it was so intense."

I kept up that incredibly intimate massage as I worked him open, increasing the pressure on his spot incrementally. I didn't want to make him cum yet, but I loved the way he was relaxing, spreading his legs wider, his full lips parting as his breathing sped up.

With my free hand, I unfastened my belt and jeans, then pulled my hard cock from my briefs and began stroking myself. I rotated my hand inside him and he arched his back, a soft, "Ahhh," leaving his lips. He was probably as ready as he was going to be for this next part.

I applied some more lotion to my fingers and worked it into his warm, tight opening, then wiped my hand with some tissues from the box on the nightstand. Shea propped himself up on his elbows and watched me as I pulled a condom from my wallet and tore off the wrapper. "Aren't you going to get undressed?" he asked.

"Oh. Um...no. I don't...I don't do that." I couldn't offer him more explanation just then and fortunately, he let it go.

I rolled on the condom, slicked it with a bit more lotion, and positioned myself between his legs. As I leaned over him and the tip of my cock pressed against his hole, I kissed him tenderly, then murmured, "Push back, baby. It'll help you open up."

"How?"

"Bear down, as if you're trying to push me out."

As soon as he figured out what I meant, the tip of my cock was able to slide past his tight outer ring. He gasped and I wound my arms around his shoulders, holding him as I let him get used to the feeling of me inside him. When the tension in his body gave way, I rocked my hips, slowly sliding forward until half my length was in him. Again I paused. He'd been holding his breath, and I only began moving in him when he released it.

"You're doing great, Shea," I told him. He smiled at me, one of his hands tangling in my hair, the other resting on my lower back where the t-shirt rode up. I began taking him just a little faster and harder, watching his reactions closely.

I could tell when he truly started enjoying it, when thinking and worrying gave way to pleasure. His eyes slid shut as he arched his back, his hips moving in rhythm with mine, and he murmured, "God yes," before words gave way to sexy little moans and cries of pleasure.

I ramped up my thrusts even more, to the point where my body was slapping against his with each down-stroke. I kissed him deeply, my tongue claiming his mouth as I pumped in and out of his tight little hole. He clutched me to him, his legs coming up to wrap around my waist, and I threw my head back and cried out, overwhelmed with pleasure.

I fucked him hard as he yelled and started to cum, shooting all over his belly. In the next moment I was cumming too, my body almost convulsing from the force of my orgasm. I'd let my lids slide shut, but I opened them now, staring into the depths of his impossibly blue eyes as I ground out, "Oh fuck, Shea." We clutched each other as our orgasms shook us. I came so hard that I saw spots, thrusting into him again and again, yelling incoherently.

As I started to come down from that shattering orgasm, I was grateful for his strong arms around me. It felt like they were holding me together. I buried my face between his neck and shoulder, the last few reflexive thrusts of my hips slowing until I finally stilled in him. Both of us were shaking. Shea reached over and pulled the blanket over both of us, then continued to hold me securely as I tried to come back to myself. I had no explanation for it, but that had been the most intense sex of my life.

"You okay, sweetheart?"

That had come from Shea. He was hugging me to him, nuzzling my hair. It was as if I'd been the virgin, not him. All I could do was nod for now, not trusting my voice.

It was a good minute or two before I finally began to regain my senses. That was when I realized I was laying right on top of Shea and probably crushing him. I reached down and held the base of the condom as I eased myself from his body, then rolled off him and discarded the rubber in a nearby wastepaper basket before pulling up my briefs and jeans. When I turned to face him, he drew me into his arms and kissed me gently.

When I found my voice, I looked in his eyes and whispered, "Are you okay? I didn't hurt you, did I?"

"I'm so much better than okay." His smile was glorious. I curled up against his bare chest, wondering when exactly our roles had reversed, when I'd become the one that needed comforting and reassuring. He must think I was completely nuts for acting like this, but he was too nice to say anything.

For just a few minutes, I let myself enjoy this. Being in his arms felt *so good*. It felt safe, like nothing could hurt me as long as I stayed right here.

Finally though, I sat up and pushed my hair out of my eyes. There were voices downstairs, Shea's roommates had obviously returned. "I think that's my cue to get out of here and let you get back to the plans you made with your friends," I said.

"Or don't." He looked so tranquil as he tucked a hand under his head and watched me.

"I have to. I'm expected in Oakland and you have a birthday to celebrate."

"Stay, Christian."

I was already pulling on my shoes, though. "This was just a one-time thing, remember?"

"I know you said that, but you can't tell me what just happened between us wasn't extraordinary. Even I know that."

I turned to look at him and admitted, "It was. That was absolutely amazing. But when I said it was just going to be this one time, I meant it."

As I stood up and zipped my jeans he asked, "What are you so afraid of, Christian?"

I fastened my belt and didn't look at him as I said, "Hurting you. I don't want to start something I can't finish."

I started to go, but Shea was up in a flash, gathering me in his arms and resting his head on my shoulder as I leaned my forehead against his bedroom door. "Thank you for not wanting to hurt me. I'm a full-grown man though, despite all evidence to the contrary," he gestured at the posters beside us, "and I can take care of myself."

"I know. But still."

"I have no idea what you're running from, Christian, but I want you to know something." He turned me gently to face him and picked up my chin so I was looking into his eyes. "I'll be right here. If you change your mind in an hour or a day or a month, you know where to find me. I want more from you, whatever you have to give."

I leaned in and kissed him, because I *had to*. I wanted more too, so much more. But that was such a mistake. He'd get hurt if I let him get close to me. That was an absolute, unavoidable fact.

"Thank you, Shea," I said, keeping my voice fairly steady even though I felt really emotional. "I'll never forget this. I hope you have a great birthday."

I left him there and went downstairs. His roommates were in the living room, clustered around the board game. Everyone stopped talking and looked at me with so much hope and anticipation when I appeared in the foyer.

I paused and told them, "You have an amazingly wonderful friend. Take good care of him for me, okay?" I left without waiting for their reply.

Chapter Three

I walked several blocks back to the bar, trying to recall where exactly I'd left my Jeep. It really felt like December, a strong wind cutting through my thin t-shirt and making my teeth chatter. When I finally reached my car, I pulled a black ski jacket from the backseat and put it on. I also located a little zip-top bag of pills that was in a duffle bag on the floor and washed them down with a half-empty water bottle. Then got behind the wheel and started the engine.

Instead of driving away, I just sat there for a while, trying to process what had happened. That hadn't just been great sex, it had been much more. I felt such an intense connection to Shea. If things were different, I knew for a fact I'd want to pursue something with him. I'd have loved to get to know him and spend time with him. It would have been a joy to teach him to draw, and to let him teach me who the rest of those cardboard figures were that lined his living room.

Okay, enough already. I was depressing myself, and that just wasn't helpful. I turned up the heater and put the car in gear.

Before visiting Skye, I decided to stop by the mural I'd been working on last night to see what it looked like in the light of day. I cut through town and found an almost-legal parking spot half a block away. When I rounded the corner into the alley, I was surprised to find someone was already there, studying the mural thoughtfully.

"Hey, Chance."

He turned his head to look at me and smiled. He was dressed in a black denim jacket along with a marled dark red scarf and matching fingerless gloves, one hand wrapped around a big cup of coffee, the other stuffed in the pocket of his jeans. "So, you're insane," he said by way of greeting.

"Quite possibly. What gave me away?"

He gestured at the mural with the coffee cup. "You were painting here, and yet your escape route was over there." He swung the cup to indicate the seedy hotel two doors down. "Does that mean you actually leapt from rooftop to rooftop like Spiderman in your efforts to allude the authorities?"

"Yes." Chance raised a dark eyebrow at that and I added, "It worked out. I survived."

He shook his head, turning his attention back to the mural. "You clearly have a death wish."

"I *really* don't."

"This is extraordinary, though. It's going to end up being one of the best things you've ever done."

I eyed the girl's face critically and said, "I don't know about that. Now that I see it in the light, the highlights are all wrong."

"You're just a perfectionist, this is amazing. I like the way your style's evolving. I can always tell your earlier works from your more recent stuff. You're really starting to figure out your voice."

"There isn't much of my early stuff left. It's either been painted over or the buildings have been demolished. Just goes to show the incredible futility in trying to leave a lasting mark on the world."

"You kept photos though, didn't you?" Chance asked. "I always take pictures of your murals and I'm so happy every time I come across one I haven't seen before. It's like a giant, city-wide Easter egg hunt."

"Nah, I never keep pictures of anything. It's nice that you do, though. Someday, that'll be all that's left." I turned to him and asked, "Are the pictures on your phone? I'm curious which ones you've found."

"There are a few on here, but I always go back and take photos with my real camera after I discover a new mural. They deserve better than just a snapshot." He pulled his phone from his pocket and swiped through it, being careful not to tip over the coffee in the process.

"This was one of my favorites," he said, turning the screen toward me. "It was right around the corner from my apartment. I was so sad when someone bought that old building and painted over this." On the screen was one of my earliest murals. It was of two young boys, each eight feet high, laughing, running and holding hands, a colorful fantasy city around them. "They painted that building grey," Chance continued. "From this to grey. I wanted to cry."

"Wow, you really are a fan. I kind of wondered if you'd just been bullshitting me last night."

"Oh no, I'm the real deal. I'll even admit that I've been in this alley for two hours, just hoping you'd come by." He returned the phone to his pocket.

"Okay, now that has to be bullshit. No one would do that."

"I would, and here's proof." He reached up and touched his fingertips to my cheek. They were icy. "The coffee went cold over an hour ago, too. But somehow, I just knew you'd come back here sooner rather than later."

"Based on what?"

"Based on the fact that you live for this and you got interrupted last night. I knew you'd want to come take a look and see how far you'd gotten, maybe plan ahead for tonight."

"I can't come back here tonight," I told him as I picked up his free hand and held his frigid fingertips between my palms to warm them up. "The police know to check back repeatedly with works in progress. It'll be a few days before they give up and go back to their usual patrol patterns. I'll have to start another mural somewhere else in the meantime." I looked back at the mural with more than a little longing. That was what I really wanted to be working on, but I didn't have much choice.

"That's too bad."

"I know. So what are you doing today, now that you've successfully stalked me?"

Chance shrugged. "Nothing."

"You're not working today?"

"Nope. I really needed a day off, for the sake of my mental health."

"In that case, come on a field trip with me. I'm about to head over to Oakland, my best friend's renting a warehouse over there. He's a sculptor, I think you'd love his work."

He tilted his head and looked at me curiously. "I'm a total stranger and you know what I do for a living. Are you really willing to trust me around your friend and his studio? What if I'm a druggie looking to rip him off for my next fix?"

"You're not."

"How do you know?"

"Because I trust my instincts, so I know you're a good guy, Chance. Now come on, let's get you a fresh cup of coffee and then crank the heater in my Jeep. I feel responsible for turning you into an ice cube."

"That's stupid. You didn't tell me to wait out here."

"Yeah, okay. I don't feel guilty." I started to head out of the alley the way I'd come in. When Chance started to follow me, he was limping severely. "Shit, what happened?"

He sighed and said, "It looks worse than it is."

"But what happened?"

"That trick last night was a total freak. When he tied me up, my leg was in a really bad position and I ended up straining a muscle. I would have told him, but he'd already bound my hands and put a ball gag in my mouth by that point."

I turned my head to look at him. "Do you mean the baby-faced guy that you picked up at Rounders?"

"Yup."

"Wow. He looked so vanilla."

"Never judge an ice cream by its carton," Chance said, tossing his empty cup in a trash can when we reached the street. He paused and asked, "Don't you need your painting gear? You must have stashed it somewhere, since it wasn't on you when we met last night."

"Nah, I have duplicates of everything I need. I'll leave that stuff here for when I can start working on that mural again."

At a neighborhood convenience store, I bought us both large coffees and a couple good-looking bagels that were stuffed with cream cheese and diced black olives. "A man who laughs in the face of carbs. I like it," my companion said as I pocketed my change and handed him his breakfast.

"I forget to eat half the time. So I figure, when I do eat, I can pretty much have whatever I want. It all evens out."

"Plus, running from the police is excellent cardio," he said.

"It really is."

*****

We pulled up in front of my friend's warehouse art studio about an hour later. Traffic had been heavy crossing the bridge, but Chance was good company. We'd both seen the same artists' retrospective at one of the local galleries a couple weeks ago and discussed it in depth. He really had a passion for art, though he claimed he had no discernable talent of his own.

"This place is huge," Chance murmured as he stepped onto the sidewalk and looked up at the building.

"It needs to be. Skye does really large-scale sculptures. Also, half of this space is being converted into his fiancé's dance studio and eventually a theater for the performing arts. Dare had surgery a few months ago and is still healing though, so they've been going slowly on the renovations."

We could hear Lady Gaga blaring even before we stepped into the warehouse. Skye and Dare were in the middle of the big open space, ballroom dancing to her song Applause. It was an odd mix, yet somehow they were making it work.

Chance leaned close and yelled over the music, "Okay, I'm officially in love with your friends."

"Just wait. You'll never meet anyone like Skye, not if you live to be a hundred."

A big black and white dog loped over, greeting us both with a wagging tail and slobbery licks. Benny didn't really understand the concept of strangers. "Hey pup," I said, scratching his ears. Chance held out a hand tentatively for the dog to sniff, then kept an eye on him as the boxer trotted off to jump up and down around his owners.

It took him a minute to realize we were here, but once Skye spotted me, he let out a whoop and ran at me flat out. I burst out laughing and tried to dodge him, but he caught me around the waist and swung me in a circle. He dropped me back onto my feet and dotted my cheeks with kisses, then hauled off and punched me in the arm. "I missed you!" he yelled over the music. "And that's for being allegedly too busy for your best friend. Douche!"

His fiancé turned down the music and crossed the space to us as Skye aimed his brilliant smile at my companion, introduced himself and said, "Welcome!"

"I'm Chance, and thank you. I like your blue hair."

"Thanks. It's fading out though, I need to color it again." He blew upwards, ruffling his overgrown royal blue bangs, then picked up his partner's hand as he joined us. "This is my fiancé, Dare. Dare, Chance."

"Nice to meet you," Chance said.

"Likewise. Come on in and join the dance party. Skye's supposed to be welding, but you know how that goes." He grinned at Skye affectionately.

"I was working up to it. You know the routine. First Gaga, then work. Then more Gaga," Skye said as he led the way into the space.

As soon as we stepped around a little partition, Chance exclaimed, "Holy fuck!" His blue eyes had gone wide at the sight of Skye's sculptures.

The middle piece was just about complete. It stood about fifteen feet high and depicted a male dancer leaping through the air, arms over his head, one muscular leg stretched in front of him, the other behind. Somehow the whole thing was balanced on a thin, arched beam, meeting the figure at the ankle of the backwards-facing leg. The support was made of shiny stainless steel, along with the base it was attached to, while the figure was composed of rusty scrap iron. Somehow the support suggested movement instead of grounding the dancer. The whole thing was completely brilliant.

Two huge armatures were just beginning to take shape on either side of that sculpture. They were still in the earliest stages, little more than iron cages. But I could already see how they were going to complement and even emphasize the central piece.

"I really wish I'd brought my camera," Chance murmured, approaching the dancer slowly. "This is beautiful. Skye, you're amazingly gifted, just like Christian."

"That's sweet, thanks. Feel free to come back any time if you want to take pictures." Skye was studying the piece and knitting his brows slightly. I knew that look. He was even more of a perfectionist than I was, and if he saw one little thing that seemed out of place to him, he wouldn't hesitate to pry it off and re-weld it. That was why, even though the sculpture was technically complete, it wouldn't truly be finished until the day six months from now when he turned it in for his senior project.

"Are you okay?" Dare asked as he watched Chance's pronounced limp. "Want to come sit down in the living room?"

"Oh. Yeah, I'm fine. Sitting down does sound like a good idea, though," Chance said.

The living room was actually a corner of the warehouse that they'd decorated with a futon couch, a few secondhand upholstered chairs, a big area rug and a scuffed coffee table. The couple pulled on sweatshirts over their t-shirts as we sat down. There was no way to heat this huge space, and they didn't have dancing to keep them warm now.

"So, how long have you guys known each other?" Skye asked, settling in right beside Dare on the futon and wrapping his arms around his fiancé's big bicep.

"Since last night," I told him. "The cops rolled up on me when I was working in the Tenderloin, so Chance posed as my newlywed husband and we were able to escape with only minimal harassment. Then I offered to buy him a drink and he made me go to Rounders."

"My God why?" Dare asked.

I was curious to see if Chance would out himself as a prostitute, but all he said was, "Because it's a great pick-up joint. Which reminds me, Christian, what happened with you and that hot guy in the blue shirt?"

"Oh. Um, we went back to his place," I said, shifting a bit in my chair.

"I knew he was into you. Did I not tell you?" Chance said happily.

"You actually know him, Skye," I said. "His name's Shea. He said he remembered you from his cousin's wedding and from when you and Nana got arrested."

Skye smiled at me. "Shea Nolan's a total sweetheart. I saw him checking you out that day at the police station. You didn't even notice."

"I was a little preoccupied," I told him. "My best friend had just been arrested and was plastered all over the news."

"That's why you look familiar," Chance exclaimed. "You were the blue-haired go-go boy in the limo who was dancing with the giant cock! I saw the picture in the paper of you and that old lady busting up an anti-gay rally!"

"I wasn't dancing with the giant cock," Skye clarified with a grin. "I was merely cock-adjacent."

"Either way, that was epic." Chance smiled delightedly. "It totally figures that Zane would have such interesting and awesome friends."

"Oh," Skye said. "You know about Zane?"

"I'm a huge fan of his work," Chance said. "For the last couple years, I've been trying to find and photograph all of his murals, before they're painted over or otherwise destroyed."

"And you said no one ever notices your work." Skye was beaming at me.

"They don't. Just you and Chance. You because you know me and Chance because he's kind of nuts." I grinned at my new friend affectionately.

"You have no idea how many people are aware of your paintings," Chance said. "I'm sure you have quite the cult following. You're too good not to."

"You should help him, Z," Skye said. "Take him around the city and show him your hiding places. I'd love to see the photos, by the way. I have some on my phone, but they're not all that clear."

"I have some on my phone too, but they're not as good as the ones I take with my DSLR camera." Chance pulled out his phone and pulled up the pictures, then handed it to Skye.

"Wow, these photos are incredible," Dare said as he and Skye flipped through the pictures. "Do you do other types of photography, too? We've been meaning to find someone to take our engagement photos."

"Oh! Um, yeah. I can do whatever you need," Chance said.

I watched him as he and my friends chatted about photography. He seemed so earnest and excited. I wondered what his story was, and really wanted to ask the question he'd forbidden me from asking. What the hell was a smart guy like that doing selling his body? I knew better than to bring it up, though.

We'd been hanging out for just a few minutes when someone threw open the door to the warehouse. A familiar voice yelled, "You decent, boys? I'm coming in, so if you're in the middle of some sexy gay homosexual lovemaking, you better cover up!"

Nana Dombruso came bustling around the partition. She was a tiny little fireball of about eighty with a huge handbag over her arm. I chuckled and asked Skye, "Why does she expect you to be naked?"

He colored slightly and told me, "Because she actually busted in on Dare and me in the middle of a sixty-nine last weekend. We dove for cover, but I'm pretty sure she still saw way too much."

"You might want to learn to lock the front door," I said.

"You're not wrong."

Nana had reached us by now. She was wearing a purple velour track suit and a rhinestone-studded matching baseball cap. "So, big deal," she exclaimed. "I raised three sons and four grandsons. I know what a weenie dongle looks like." She turned to me and said, "Christian! Where have you been keeping yourself? And who's your new friend? Are you two an item?" She squinted at Chance and told him, "I assume you're a gay homosexual, because now I just assume everyone is until they tell me differently."

"Why yes, I *am* a gay homosexual," he said with a smile.

She dug a pair of big round glasses out of her purse and stuck them on her face. "Oh my, you're a cute one! What's your name?"

"Chance Matthews, ma'am."

"What do you do, Chance? And more importantly, are you doing Christian? I don't like it when my boys are single. Seems like such a waste!"

Skye answered for him. "He and Christian are just friends, Nana. He's a photographer, we're going to have him take our engagement pictures. Weren't you saying something about needing a photographer the other day?"

She clapped her hands together and exclaimed, "A photographer, perfect! Now I can cross that off my to-do list. Listen, you boys are on winter break from Sutherlin beginning on the thirteenth, aren't you?" Skye nodded and she said, "If you have anything planned for the week before Christmas, cancel it! You're going to be busy."

She squeezed in next to Dare on the futon, then fished around in her handbag until she found a stack of thick, white envelopes and some glossy brochures. She flipped through the envelopes, finally handing Skye one addressed to him and Dare, then one to me that said 'Christian George and Guest (hopefully a hot boyfriend)'. Inside was an elegant wedding invitation. As she passed out the brochures she said, "We're taking a Dotsy Cruise around the Hawaiian Islands!"

"We who?" Dare asked.

"All of us, including you boys!"

"But...why?" Skye asked as I looked at the person in a grinning Dalmatian costume on the cover of the brochure.

"Because I'm throwing a surprise wedding for my grandson Vincent and your friend Trevor! I'm also hosting a wedding for my boys Hunter and Brian, only they know about it because they're not pig-headed like my grandson. Him I need to ambush."

"Oh wow!" Skye exclaimed.

"All that celebrating in one fun-filled week at sea, can't you just picture it? It's gonna be a real hum-dinger!" She looked immensely pleased with herself.

"That's amazing, Nana," Dare said. "Can we help with any of the preparations?"

"No thanks sweetie, I got it all under control. Now, I wanted to talk to you two so you don't feel left out," Nana told the couple. "I would throw a wedding for you at the same time, of course, but you two already started talking about a lovely ceremony next June, so I'm not gonna interfere with that. These other boys though, bah! They'd all just run off to the Justice of the Peace if I let them!"

"We understand, Nana. Are you sure this a good idea, though? Trevor and Vincent just wanted a small ceremony," Skye said. "And what about all the grooms' friends and families?"

"My grandson's just shy, his sweetie is, too. But they're gonna love this, just you wait and see. I'm going to make it so magical for them that they can't help but love it! As far as their friends and family members, they're all invited, of course! I was in luck because Dotsy just added one extra voyage for the holidays, so I could book a great, big block of rooms for all of us. That's why it's happening on such short notice, I had to jump on this the moment that cruise was added. Otherwise, good luck getting that many rooms together! Oh, and I'm paying for everyone's plane tickets to Honolulu too, of course. That's where we sail from, a week from tomorrow."

"Wow Nana," I said, "that's incredibly generous."

She waved her hand dismissively. "What's the point in having money if you can't enjoy it? And I plan to enjoy the hell out of this cruise, lemme tell you! Isn't this going to be exciting?" Her dark eyes sparkled with delight.

Skye smiled at her and said, "It'll be wonderful. Thank you, Nana."

I just had to ask. "Out of curiosity, why did you decide to go with Dotsy?" The cruises were geared specifically to families with young kids.

"Well, because Trevor and Vincent have Joshie now. There'll be plenty of other kids in the wedding party, too.

Besides, who doesn't love Dotsy Dog? All my boys grew up on the cartoons!" Nana leapt to her feet and said, "I got a million things to do, I better hustle on out of here! Don't worry about renting tuxes, boys, we're going cruise ship casual here. Chance, you're hired as the official wedding photographer. That right there is a load off my mind, lemme tell you! I didn't know where I'd find someone for a whole week." She paused to consider that, then asked, "You are available that week, aren't you?"

"Yes, ma'am," he said. "But you don't even know if I'm any good."

"If a great artist like Skye is hiring you to do photos of him and his sweetie, you're good." She rushed toward the door as she called, "I gotta go bikini shopping next. Hawaii, here I come! I'll call you, Christian, to make arrangements and get Chance's photographer fees paid. See you soon, boys!"

We just sat there for a few moments in dazed silence after she left. Finally I said, "So, that just happened. Are we really going on a cruise with a dog for a captain?"

Skye grinned at that. "Yup." He turned to Dare and said, "We need to take a look at our schedule. There are a few things we'll need to move around."

"Damn," I muttered. "I really like Trevor and want to attend his wedding, but a week at sea on a kiddie cruise? I

71

really might lose my mind. Think anyone would notice if I gave it a skip?"

"You're doing this!" Skye exclaimed. "Trevor's going to want you there, and I do, too. Plus, don't you think Chance might need some moral support? The poor guy was just hit by Hurricane Nana for the first time."

"You better really be a photographer," I told him.

Chance looked at me. "I am. Well, kind of."

*****

When we drove back into the city later that afternoon, Chance murmured, "This has been the weirdest, most unexpected day. I think I should bow out of that job, though. It sounds like so much fun, but I've never done anything as important as a wedding and I don't know if I'm good enough."

"Why don't you show me your photos? Maybe you're underestimating yourself. I'd like you to give it a shot, because frankly, I'd love some company. When you're not taking pictures, you can be my drinking buddy."

"Your best friend's going to be there, you don't need me."

"Yeah, along with his fiancé. The last thing I want is to be their third wheel while they're enjoying that cruise."

He hesitated before saying, "None of them know I'm a prostitute. As soon as they find out, they won't want me along."

"Nobody will care. Do you know how Nana Dombruso's family made all that money?"

"How?"

"They were old-school mafia for generations."

Chance's eyes went wide. "You're shitting me."

"I think they've pretty much gone legit by now. But still, they won't even blink when they find out you're in a less than legal line of work."

"People consider it immoral too, though. Won't Mrs. Dombruso care about that?"

"Nana's not the judgmental sort."

Chance studied his slender hands, which were folded in his lap. Finally he said, "Would you let me bunk with you?"

"Of course."

"Aren't you concerned that I'm going to steal your money and credit cards?"

"Nope."

"Aren't you worried about me turning tricks on the cruise and landing the entire wedding party in hot water?"

"Are you planning to turn tricks during the cruise?"

"No."

"So, we're fine then."

He was quiet for a while before saying softly, "Thank you for trusting me. Most people don't."

I found a parking space in his neighborhood and accompanied him to his little studio apartment. It was in the Lower Haight, above an import store. The place couldn't have been more than two hundred square feet, but it was bright, clean and inviting.

One wall was covered floor to ceiling in photographs. I recognized little details from my murals in several shots. "Did you take all of these?" I asked, and he nodded. "And you think you're not good enough to be a wedding photographer? Dude, you're actually way too good for that." Chance had an incredible eye. He found beauty in things most people would overlook, like a tiny blue violet growing through a crack in the sidewalk and a little girl's dirt-streaked hand clutching a worn out doll.

"You really think they're okay?"

"No, Chance, they're not okay. They're fucking brilliant! Do you not know this?"

He shrugged and said, "I like them, but I was always worried about showing them to other people."

"Why?"

"Well, what if they hated them? I'm self-taught, so a real photographer would probably see so many flaws. This is the only thing I'm any good at, or that I hoped I was good at. I just...I was scared that someone would come along and tear down my dream."

That reminded me of Shea and the teacher that had dashed his dreams of becoming a comic book artist. I felt a pang in my chest at the thought of that sweet, gorgeous guy, who'd given me his virginity for some reason. Had that really just been this morning? I missed him more than I cared to admit.

"Hey." Chance touched my arm lightly. "You okay?"

"Fine. Why?"

"You went away for a minute there."

"I was remembering the guy from last night. Shea." I grinned a little when I said his name.

"Oh man. That was more than a one-night stand, wasn't it?"

"No."

"Bullshit. Go sit down, I'm going get us a couple beers and then I want to hear about this guy."

I did as I was told. The only place to sit was on a neatly made narrow daybed. I sat down at one end and when Chance limped over to me and handed me a beer from his little dorm fridge, I said, "Put your leg up, you should have been resting it today."

"The bed's too small. I'd have to put my foot on your lap."

"So, go ahead."

He considered that for a moment, then tugged off his boots and sat at the other end of the little bed, leaning against the armrest. He winced when he raised his leg and I asked, "Should you maybe be thinking about a hospital? What if that guy did some real damage to you?"

"I can't afford a hospital. Besides, nothing's broken. It'd hurt a lot more if it was." He exhaled slowly as his foot came to rest on my thigh.

We opened our beers and I raised mine and said, "Cheers," before taking a long drink.

"So, tell me. What went on last night that would inspire a look of such incredible wistfulness?" Chance grinned at me as he said that.

"You don't really want to hear this."

"You're wrong. I want to know what's going on with you two."

"Why?"

"Because," he said with a sweet smile, "all my life, I wanted a guy to look at me the way that guy looked at you."

"What are you talking about? There were tons of guys checking you out last night. Every single one of them wanted to take you home."

"Exactly. Even without knowing I was a prostitute, they all looked at me like I was a piece of meat. I was nothing to any of them, just a means of getting laid. That's not how that guy looked at you."

"How did he look at me?"

"Like you were a priceless work of art in a museum."

"What?"

"That's the only way I can describe it. He looked at you with awe and reverence, like you were the most amazing thing he'd ever seen."

"You're reading an awful lot into a look."

"I'm not. I know people, Christian. Goes with the job. If I wasn't able to read people accurately, I could end up going home with a complete sociopath."

"Kind of like the guy last night."

"He wasn't a sociopath, he just didn't know what the hell he was doing."

"You really need to find a different job, Chance."

That earned me an eye roll. "Thank you for that, Captain Obvious."

"I'm just saying."

"I know."

I sighed and said, "I think you're right, though. Last night wasn't just about sex. But it was supposed to be! I told him right up front that I didn't have any more to offer him. We both knew the score going in so I shouldn't feel bad for the way I ended it this morning."

"Would breaking your own rule and seeing him again be the worst thing in the world?"

"For him it could be. I'm going away in six short months, just as soon as I see my senior year through. It would be incredibly unfair to get involved with him, knowing for a fact that anything we started had an absolute expiration date." I took off my ski jacket as I said that and draped it over the back of the daybed, then pushed up my shirt sleeves.

"Six months is actually a long time. Think of all the fun you could have!"

"And think of all the heartache when it ended." I pushed my hair back from my forehead and said, "Is it hot in here, or did I suddenly develop a raging case of dengue fever?"

"It's hot. I don't have control over the thermostat, the people in the unit next door do since this used to all be one big apartment. Apparently they're reptiles because they always keep the heat at tropical levels, but I can crack a window if you want."

"I'll do it, just rest your leg." I raised his foot carefully and slid out from under it, then opened each of the three panes of the big bay window a couple inches. "Hand me your coat and scarf, I'll put them away for you," I said, coming to stand beside him.

Chance hesitated for a long moment, some sort of emotion welling up in his blue eyes. Finally he said, "Promise me you won't overreact."

"To what?"

He unwound the scarf from around his neck, revealing dark bruises against his pale skin. I could actually make out handprints where someone had tried to strangle him.

"Oh my God, Chance!" I sat down right beside him, taking hold of his shoulders. They felt so thin and fragile under his clothes.

"Remember two seconds ago when I made you promise not to overreact?"

"Who did this to you? That guy from the bar?" He nodded and I said, "Tell me you went to the police."

"No. Why would I?"

"Because he tried to kill you!"

"No he didn't. He just choked me as he was fucking me so he could get off." Chance couldn't look me in the eye. He was trying so hard to act like it was no big deal, but he couldn't hide the fact that last night had rattled him. I drew him into my arms carefully, since I didn't know how much more damage had been done to his body, and he sank into the hug even as he told me, "Quit it. You're gonna make me cry, and that's ridiculous."

"Why is that ridiculous?"

"Because I'm stronger than this. I have to be! Yeah, last night got scary. That guy went way beyond what we'd agreed to and I couldn't do anything about it because I was tied up. But I've been turning tricks for eleven years and have dealt with far worse."

I kept holding him, gently rubbing his back as I asked, "Eleven years? How old are you, Chance?"

"Twenty-five."

"Oh God," I murmured.

He wrapped his arms around me and put his head on my shoulder. "Why do you care, about me, about any of this? You haven't even known me twenty-four hours."

"Friendship isn't measured in days, months or years, it's measured in the way someone makes you feel. I knew you'd be a friend right from the start."

"I hoped you would be, too. I don't really have a lot of friends. Thanks for giving me a chance."

I let go of him and we both grinned self-consciously. "Okay, enough of this Hallmark moment. You hungry?" When he nodded I said, "I'll order us some dinner, you get comfortable."

I had way too much Chinese food delivered, just to make sure he had plenty of leftovers for later. We hung out into the evening, talking about famous photographers and their work, a subject he knew a lot about. It was probably about eight when we made plans to meet in a couple days and I said good night.

Just go home, Christian, I told myself as I left Chance's apartment. I never took my own advice though, even when it was really good, so instead I drove across town to Shea's neighborhood. I didn't know what I hoped to accomplish. I'd meant it when I'd said we couldn't start something.

And yet.

I was undeniably drawn to him. I couldn't stop thinking about him. I kept remembering the clean scent of his skin and the feeling of his hands on me and the taste of his lips and I wanted more, so desperately, with every part of me.

Don't start something you can't finish. It might have been a cliché, but I lived by those words. It was my truth. I kept reminding myself of that as I drove across town. But I went anyway.

Shea's block was crowded, there was a party going on. I stopped in the street and looked up at his house. It was all lit up, full of life and people and laughter. His friends were celebrating his birthday. That made me happy.

I pulled into an illegal space across the street and put the car in park, then rolled down the window and rested my crossed arms on the door frame. Music was playing, but it was too faint from here to recognize the song. I watched the big front window, wanting just a glimpse of Shea. I told myself that would be enough, just one last look and then I'd go home and work on thinking of anything but him.

I was being ridiculous. I knew this. I sighed and put my chin on my crossed arms. What good would one last look do? If anything, it'd just make me want him more. Somehow, knowing that didn't make me pull away from the curb, though. Minutes passed and still I sat outside his house. I didn't want to leave, because at least I was close to him.

"Parties are a lot more fun when you actually join in."

Shea's voice was so close that it startled me. I sat up with a gasp, then stuck my head out the window and looked at him. He was leaning against the side of my Jeep, hands in his pockets, dressed in jeans and a blue and white striped button-down shirt with the sleeves rolled back. He offered me a little grin and I stammered, "Shit, sorry. I totally didn't mean to stalk you. I just...." Just what? What the hell was I doing here?

"You've been here for several minutes. Were you ever going to go up and knock on the door?"

I shut off the engine and got out of the car. "No."

"Why not?"

Instead of answering, I gestured at the house and asked, "Why are you out here and not in there?"

"My cousin and her kids left a few minutes ago. I walked them to her car. She had to park a few blocks away and I wanted to make sure they got there safely."

"Oh."

He took a couple steps toward me, stopping when we were maybe two feet apart, and asked gently, "What are you doing here, Christian?"

"I don't know."

"And if you had to guess?"

I dropped my gaze to the asphalt. "I really don't know why I came here, besides the fact that I'm an idiot. I can't start something with you, but I can't stop thinking about you, either."

He got a little closer, only a few inches separating us as he said, "I'm sure you have perfectly good reasons for not wanting to get involved with me. Do it anyway."

"You'd get hurt. It would be so unfair to you."

"I don't care about that."

"Well, I do."

Shea said, so softly, "You want this as much as I do, Christian. I know you do. That's why you couldn't stay away."

I pressed my eyes shut, trying to find the strength to get back in the car. He got a little bit closer, still not touching me, but just barely. His warm, already familiar scent filled my senses. I managed, "Please go inside and forget I was this stupid, forget I came here."

"No."

I took a deep breath and said, "I'm sorry."

In the next instant I pinned him against the Jeep, his face between my hands as I kissed him wildly, passionately. He cried out and grabbed me, his hands sliding under my ski jacket and pulling at my t-shirt until they reached bare skin. Every part of me responded, my body thrumming with need, demanding *more, more, more* as I ravaged his mouth.

I ran my fingers through his hair and kissed my way across his cheek, then nibbled his soft little earlobe. He asked, his voice rough, "Why'd you apologize?"

"Because you're going to get so fucking hurt," I whispered before licking his ear and sending a tremor through his body.

"Totally worth it." His hand slid down to cup my ass.

We both jumped at a loud cat call behind us. I looked over my shoulder and found that we had an audience, most of the party guests spilling out onto the little front porch of his house or clustering in the big front window. As the crowd erupted into cheers, whistling and applause, he muttered, "Oh man," and dropped his head onto my shoulder.

I chuckled a bit, even though I felt myself blushing. "Well, damn. I kind of forgot where we were for a minute."

"Me too." Shea straightened up and took a deep breath, then picked up my hand. "Want to come inside and meet almost everyone I know?"

"I can't."

"Why not?"

"I'm parked illegally. Besides, I haven't even been home yet. I'm completely disgusting and really don't want to meet people looking like this."

"You're not disgusting."

"I really am. I can't even take my jacket off."

"Why not?"

I whispered, "Because your jizz is dried onto my t-shirt from this morning."

An embarrassed bark of laughter escaped him. "Okay, so maybe you do need to clean up a bit. Come inside and I'll take you straight up to my bedroom. You can use my shower and borrow some clothes."

"There's a wall of about 80 people to get through. I'll end up meeting all of them while looking like a slightly warmed-over crap pile."

"I have an idea, get in the car." As I got behind the wheel, he called, "I'm going to help my friend find a parking space. Back in a few minutes!" That stirred up a bunch of comments about us running off for a quickie.

Shea got in the passenger seat. I was hyper-aware of him in that confined space and it was all I could do to keep my hands to myself. We lucked into a parking spot two blocks away, and the moment the engine was off, I climbed over the gear shift and straddled his lap, kissing him hungrily. He tried to tilt the seat but accidentally released the catch, so it fell straight back with a thud. We both laughed at that and then went back to kissing as he wove his fingers in my hair.

Both of us were completely hard and I rocked my hips a little, rubbing against him. "I need you inside me," he murmured as I kissed his neck.

"Are you sore from this morning?"

"Doesn't matter."

I sat up a little so I could look in his eyes. "Sure it does, Shea. Are you okay?" I brushed his dark hair back from his forehead.

"I'm fine, just a little tender. I still want you in me."

I kissed him softly, then opened the passenger door and slid off him. "Come on. I'm being really selfish right now and making you miss your own birthday party."

"This is so much better."

"You can have both. Your party now and me afterwards."

That made him smile. He took my hand as he stepped onto the curb and kept hold of it as we returned to his house. We didn't go up to the front door, though. Instead, Shea led me to the end of his block and then down an alley. When we got to his back gate, he opened a combination lock and told me, "We can reach my room from the back stairs."

We climbed an exterior staircase to a second floor landing. After he unlocked the door to a narrow sun porch, the two of us slipped down the hall to his room. "Made it," I said with a smile as he closed and locked the bedroom door behind us. "I won't be long, I'm going to take a quick shower. You don't happen to have a spare toothbrush, do you?"

"Sure, let me get it for you." I followed him to the bathroom and after he handed me a new toothbrush from his cabinet, he kissed me gently. "I'll find you a clean shirt and leave it on the bed for you."

"Thanks. After you do that, why don't you go downstairs? I'll meet you there in a few minutes."

"You sure?"

"Yeah. Go have fun. I won't be long."

"Alright." He kissed me and said, "Don't forget to lock the bedroom door behind me, just in case someone decides to use my bathroom."

"Okay." I wrapped my arms around his neck and kissed him again.

"I'm so glad you came back," he murmured against my lips.

"Me too." I had to force myself to let go of him after a couple minutes, and we both smiled at each other shyly before he left the room.

After brushing my teeth, showering quickly and washing my unruly hair, I wrapped a towel around my waist, then tried to finger-comb my damp curls. Why hadn't I gone home and cleaned up this morning? I'd spent the whole day looking like a total slob. Well, I actually knew the answer to that. I'd tried to stay busy to stop myself from coming back here.

I heard the bedroom door open and close, and assumed Shea had come back. But then the bathroom door was flung open and a tall guy built like a linebacker demanded, "Do you know who I am?" Absolute terror coursed through me as I shook my head no. Oh God, I'd forgotten to lock the bedroom door like Shea told me to.

The guy was really angry about something, veins standing out in his forearms from his balled-up fists. "We met once. I'm friends with a guy named Sammy Petroski. Does that name ring any bells?" Again I shook my head, sliding around the edge of the sink until my back was pressed to the wall. Panic began to narrow my vision, blackness closing in from both sides.

"Really? You don't know that name, you fuck? You should. You spent most of last summer screwing Sammy whenever it suited you, and then when he no longer amused you, you dumped him like yesterday's trash!"

I tried to think. I was almost paralyzed with fear but finally managed to stammer, "S...Sam?"

"Oh, very good, asshole, you managed to remember him. Now if you think for a minute that I'm going to stand by while you do the same thing to my kid brother, you're sorely mistaken!"

I was shaking by now, my heart racing as I cowered beside the tub. The huge guy stopped ranting for a moment to ask, "What the fuck's wrong with you?"

Shea burst into the bathroom just then and demanded, "What are you doing, Finn?"

The linebacker turned and bellowed, "No fucking way are you getting involved with this guy, Shea! This is the asshole that Sammy's still talking about. You know the one!"

"This isn't your call. Get out of my way!" As soon as Shea got around his brother he exclaimed, "What did you do to him?"

"Nothing! I just yelled at him, I don't know why he's acting like this."

Shea reached for me, but I pulled back reflexively. Even though my heart was racing and my breathing was so quick and shallow that I felt light-headed, his calming voice cut through my anxiety. "You're okay, Christian. I'm here. Sorry about Finn. My brother's a pain, but he won't hurt you." I managed a couple deep breaths and he said gently, "Can you tell me what's happening? Are you having a panic attack?" I shook my head no.

Shea looked over his shoulder and told his brother calmly, "Go downstairs, Finn."

"I didn't mean to freak him out."

"Just go, please."

"I'm going, but this conversation isn't over," Finn said as he stomped out of the room.

I slid into a seated position and Shea said, "I'll bring you your clothes, and when you're ready, you can meet me in the bedroom. Okay?" When I nodded, he picked up my jeans and briefs from the floor and put them beside me, then got the shirt he'd left on the bed and put it within reach, too. He closed the door behind him as he left the bathroom. I got dressed quickly as I struggled to calm down, putting on my own shirt and jacket again. I sighed before opening the door and stepping into the bedroom.

Shea was sitting on his bed, watching me closely. I leaned against the doorframe and said, "I owe you an explanation. That must have seemed completely nuts."

"You don't have to explain if you don't want to."

"I need you to know what happened." I took a deep breath and studied the area rug as I said, "I was raped when I was seventeen. It happened in the dorm bathroom on my fourth day at college. I never got a look at my attacker's face, but I know he was tall and built like your brother."

"Oh God," he whispered.

"All of a sudden, when Finn was confronting me, I had a really intense flashback to that night. I've tried to move past that incident, but it's not gone. It's never gone. In fact, it's actually why I stay clothed when I'm having sex. My attacker tore my clothes off before he raped me, so now being naked makes me feel way too vulnerable."

"Christian, I'm so sorry."

I couldn't make myself shut up once I'd started. "That was actually how I lost my virginity. For a few years after that, I couldn't stand the thought of anyone touching me, so I didn't have sex again until I was twenty. At that point, I'd built up a lot of anger and I took my sexuality back with a vengeance. I slept with so many men, but I made sure it was always on my terms. I'd only top, I'd always remain clothed, and I refused to get emotionally involved with my sex partners. I tried to tell Sam that last summer. I explained that it was only sex and I thought he was on the same page. I swear I never meant to hurt him."

"I believe you."

After a pause, I crossed the room and sat on the bed beside him, a couple feet separating us. "I'm really sorry," I said quietly, not looking at him. "Your birthday party's going on downstairs and I'm up here completely oversharing."

"I'm glad you're opening up to me."

I looked at him and said, "Would you do something for me?"

"Anything."

"Go back to your party and forget this happened while I let myself out the way we came in."

"Anything but that."

"I mean it, Shea. I just...I wanted you to know what was behind my freak-out, so you didn't blame your brother. I said too much though, and it wasn't the right time or place."

"It's good you told me."

I got up and said, "I'm going to get out of here. Again, I'm so sorry."

"I really don't want you to leave."

"It's for the best."

He got to his feet and started to reach for me, but he stopped himself. *I knew it.* I knew my confession would make things awkward between us. He didn't even know what to do with me now.

I tried to smile and kind of failed at it. "Take care, Shea."

"Christian—"

I didn't stick around to hear what he had to say. I left through the sun room and jogged down the back stairs. The gate to the alley was locked, but I scaled it easily.

When I finally got home, I changed into my favorite worn-out t-shirt and some sweats, shut off the lights and got under my thick blanket. I really tried, but after a while I couldn't hold it in anymore. I curled up on my side, hugging my pillow as a sob slipped from me, followed by another. And another. It took a long time, but eventually I cried myself to sleep.

Chapter Four

The next morning, I was pretty thoroughly pissed off at myself. I'd done everything wrong last night, from going back to Shea's house to freaking out when his brother confronted me to giving in to self-pity when I got home. None of that was okay.

I felt like crap, too. Crying never did a bit of good. I knew that, which was why I almost never let myself go there.

Dragging my blanket with me like a turtle shell, I went into the kitchen to make coffee. While it brewed, I opened a cabinet that was empty except for seven prescription bottles. I placed a paper towel on the counter and shook out a total of thirteen tablets. The coffee pot was half-full by now, so I executed an Indiana Jones-style maneuver, swapping out the pot with a spare cup so I could pour myself a mugful and use it to wash down the pills. Breakfast of champions.

After standing under a hot shower, I got dressed and picked up the four heavy Amazon boxes just inside my front door. This made both locking up behind myself and the long walk to my Jeep problematic. I had a crimp in my shoulder by the time I heaved the boxes into the backseat.

The grocery store was my next stop. I had a list, but there was no reason to refer to it, since it never, ever changed. Maybe thirty minutes later, I loaded five full canvas sacks beside the boxes, got behind the wheel and pointed the car north.

The drive over the Golden Gate Bridge was usually enjoyable, but today the bay and sky were gunmetal grey, a thick blanket of fog obscuring the city behind me and the Marin headlands up ahead. I clicked the heater up a couple notches and turned on some music to try to lighten my mood.

Traffic wasn't bad, so it only took about half an hour to reach the town of Larkspur and then head west on very familiar roads. The houses thinned out as I approached Baltimore Canyon. Eventually I came to a gated drive and entered a code, then offered the closed circuit camera a little salute as the gate swung open. I drove another ten minutes on a gravel road before reaching another gate and repeating the process.

My father's house, which sat by itself amid rolling hills, madrone trees and bay-laurels, was deceptively understated. It just looked like a typical ranch-style family home from the driveway. You had to go around back and see the way its three stories were built into the hillside to understand how it could be almost eighteen thousand square feet.

I used my key on the side entrance and carried the groceries down a long hallway, sidestepping two white garbage bags while barely glancing at the nineteen gold and platinum records lining the walls. In the kitchen, I set the bags on the stone countertop and paused to listen. Piano music was coming from the den. That was a good sign.

Once I'd schlepped the Amazon boxes to the kitchen, I got busy unpacking the groceries, not only from the bags but also from any extra outer packaging. The food went in the pantry and refrigerator, obviously, and the books I took from the boxes got categorized and placed in neat stacks on the breakfast bar. I'd brought up the idea of an ereader to my father a dozen times, but apparently that fell squarely under the heading, 'Things Distrusted by Alexzander Tillane'.

I quickly gathered up the boxes, shopping bags and packaging, took them back down the hall and deposited them in my car for later sorting and disposal. Then I went back for the two white garbage bags, which also got put in the Jeep's backseat. I really didn't have to worry about them leaking, since they were triple-bagged.

My dad was still playing the piano when I finished. I didn't want to interrupt him, so I sat on the reclaimed barn wood floor outside the den and leaned against the wall, arms resting on my bent knees. The whole house had a rustic, almost woodsy feel, very masculine and no-nonsense. It had been decorated by a high-end designer about twenty years ago, and I always got the impression that he hadn't consulted or even met my father when he was putting this place together.

I closed my eyes, letting the music wash over me. No matter how many times I heard him sing or play an instrument, I was always floored by my dad's talent. He'd been a child prodigy, pushed into the spotlight far too young by an overly ambitious stage mother. I often wondered how many of his issues might have been avoided if he'd just been allowed to have a normal childhood.

Right now my dad was playing a gorgeous remix of one of his biggest pop hits, adding texture and layers to the instantly recognizable melody. As I sat there taking it in, my thoughts drifted to Shea. Beautiful Shea. It was surprising how much I missed him, given the fact that I'd known him a day. But what had I just said to Chance about relationships being measured not in time, but in how someone made you feel? I'd had a point there.

Not that it had been a relationship. Not that it could ever be that. I still missed him, though. I sighed, dropped my head onto my arms and just left it there for a while.

"Hey." My father startled me. I hadn't noticed that the music had stopped. He sat cross-legged on the floor in front of me, his dark brows knit in concern as he tucked a long strand of hair behind his ear. "You okay, Christian?" He and I looked nothing alike, except for our eyes. Mine were the exact shape and shade of green that his were, and he was staring into them at that moment.

"Yeah, fine," I said, pulling up a veneer of composure. "How are you, Zan?" I'd met my father for the first time when I was ten years old. Somehow the idea of calling him Dad to his face sat funny with me, so I usually didn't do it.

"I feel good. I'm playing again, as you heard." Sometimes his music deserted him for months at a time. It didn't go in cycles with his bipolar disorder, it just seemed arbitrary. He'd made international headlines when he walked out of a sold-out concert at the L.A. Coliseum mid-song in 2002. His fans had been outraged, even though he refunded their money.

He totally withdrew from the public eye after that, spawning a media frenzy. Thirteen years later, it still hadn't completely died down. There were a million stories circulating about what had happened to him, when the simple truth was that he just wanted to be left alone.

That was the reason I never used my last name. It was unusual enough to attract attention, and the paparazzi didn't know about me because I'd been illegitimate. Zan had quite a few lovers (both male and female) while he was married to Dev Holland, one of the most famous women in Hollywood. My mother had given me his last name though, which hadn't been the smartest idea since I was supposed to be a secret. I always assumed she did that to cement my relationship with the superstar that had fathered me.

Apparently it had worked, too. He'd financially supported my mom and me all of my life, even after she got married. When I was fifteen and showed up on his doorstep because my home life had become unbearable, he took me in without question. Zan Tillane might have more than his share of flaws, but he was a good dad.

"You look like you have the weight of the world on your shoulders, boyo," he was saying. Thirty years in the States had only slightly diminished his English accent.

"I had a really weird day yesterday."

"Weird how? Alien abduction? Bad drug trip? Bad drug trip making you think you were abducted by aliens?" His green eyes sparkled. It was good to see him happy.

"Not quite. I met a great guy and then totally freaked out in front of him. His pro wrestler-sized brother got in my face, and I flashed back to that night in the dorm bathroom and went all Girl, Interrupted on him. I hadn't done anything like that in ages."

"Shite, sorry to hear that. I thought you'd gotten a pretty good handle on it."

"I had. There were just a lot of similarities to that night and it flipped a switch."

Zan got up and offered me his hand. "Come on, let's pretend it's a reasonable hour to have a drink. Sounds like you could use one."

I let him pull me to my feet, then followed him into the den. My father used exactly three hundred and sixty square feet of his huge home, plus the kitchen and one of the bathrooms. He lived his whole life in this one room, which was packed to the point of bursting with books and movies, all stacked around a grand piano, an elliptical trainer he used obsessively, and the big, brown leather couch that was the epicenter of his existence. There was a giant flat screen on the wall, nestled between two gorgeous oil paintings by obscure artists, but it wasn't for watching television, it was just for playing DVDs. Zan also didn't own a computer and the only names in the cellphone I'd forced on him for emergencies were mine and his lawyer's. He preferred to live his life completely cut off from the rest of society.

I didn't know how much of this was just his own brand of eccentricity, and how much stemmed from legitimate mental illness. He had a whole laundry list of diagnoses that had been stuck to him back when he still saw doctors: bipolar. Paranoid. Obsessive-compulsive. Agoraphobic. There was no denying that a lot of that fit. But somehow, I just couldn't see my dad as a bunch of labels.

I thought about all of that as I watched him mix up a couple drinks at the little bar in the corner. He was barefoot and dressed as always in old Levis and a wrinkled, slightly bohemian button-down shirt with the sleeves rolled up, the faded fabric covered in a tiny monotone floral pattern. Zan was pushing fifty, but the streaks of grey in his thick, dark hair and the laugh lines around his eyes somehow just enhanced his striking good looks.

I tried to imagine him up on stage in front of a crowd of eighty thousand people, but I just couldn't, not even after watching his concert tapes a million times in an effort to understand that side of him. Somehow, the man the public knew and my father were just two totally distinct people to me.

"Grab some ice, kid," he said, handing me a silver bucket and pulling me back to the present. I did as I was told.

Once we were settled on the sofa with matching whiskey sours (the only drink he made) Zan said, "So, tell me about the great guy that preceded the freak out. What's his name?"

"Shea."

He grinned at that. "Watch out for those Irish boys. They'll steal your heart every time." It always threw me off a bit when my dad said something like that. I knew he was bisexual, but I'd only ever heard about the famous women he'd been involved with. And my utterly not famous mom, of course.

Still, I grinned too and said, "You're not wrong."

"And what does the lovely Irish Shea do?"

"He's a cop."

"Ah, excellent. They always have handcuffs at the ready, you know." His grin got wider. He was trying to make me blush and it worked. He chuckled at my embarrassment and asked, "Did you two meet while he was arresting you for vandalism?"

"Did you get a call to bail me out of jail?"

"No."

"Then you already know the answer to that."

Not that he would have shown up personally. He hadn't actually left the house in a decade, but he kept a lawyer on retainer to deal with stuff that cropped up. If I ever did get in trouble, I knew he'd have my back.

My big fear though was that my last name would go public if I got arrested and someone would make the connection to Zan. I didn't want to live in the public eye if the press ever found out who I was, but far more than that, I sure as hell didn't want the paparazzi following me here. My dad was too messed up to return to life under a magnifying glass. And yes, I knew I should change my name officially, but somehow I just couldn't bring myself to do it. Truth be told, I liked having that tie to my dad.

"So, where did you meet him? If you say Craigslist, I'm locking you in here with me."

"How does your computer-shunning self even know about Craigslist?"

"You told me all about its wonders and horrors, remember?"

"Oh, that's right. And no, I didn't meet him there. I met him at a tourist bar that I'd never go to under normal circumstances."

Zan took a sip of his drink and asked, "So what were you doing there?"

"Actually, I went with a new friend. He's a prostitute and wanted to work the crowd."

That earned me a big smile. "I love it when you try to shock me."

"But it never, ever works! I tell you I was out with a prostitute and you take it in stride."

"It'd take far more than that to shock your old man, boyo." He was still smiling. "So, this Shea fellow. Was he a tourist, fresh off the boat from the Emerald Isle?"

"No, he lives here." I proceeded to tell him more or less the whole story, up to and including last night's fiasco, but glossing over the sex. I was what Zan had in place of television, so he always wanted to know all about my life. But obviously, some things were too private to share with my dad, even if he was super cool.

When I finished, he asked, "So, what are you going to do about this boy?"

"Nothing. I ruined it. You know I can't start something anyway, so it's probably for the best."

"You didn't ruin anything! The lad's a copper, he's used to seeing people in crisis. Did you ever think of that?"

"Well, no," I admitted.

"And you're wrong that you can't start something, son."

"Six months, Zan. That's when I'm going away, you know that. Before that happens, by the way, we need to get serious about finding someone we trust to come in here twice a week and take over for me."

He tossed back what was left of his drink and told me, "I'm not ready to have that discussion yet." I suppressed a sigh. He was *never* ready to have that discussion. This was going to become a real problem, I just knew it.

Zan deflected the subject back to me. "Do you know how much you could do in six months? You and this fella could travel the world. You could make love a thousand times. You could dance in the moonlight and fall asleep all wrapped up in each other on the shores of paradise." Sometimes it was really obvious that my dad used to write pop songs.

"And then I could leave him all alone and break his heart."

"He's already alone! So, you give him six months before putting him back where you found him. You give *both of you* six months. Enjoy him, Christian, and let him enjoy you."

"That really isn't much time. Plus, I have school to finish. I'm going to be busy."

There was a lot of sympathy in my dad's eyes when they met mine. "I know you set that goal for yourself to finish art school, son. But all I been hearing is how half the professors in that place are drivin' ya mad, and if I'm being honest, it doesn't sound like your heart's really in it anymore. I know you wanted to get as much out of it as you could to make yourself a great artist, but if you ask me, you got there. Your work is brilliant. And you know what? It always was. That didn't come from that fancy art college, it came from here." He rested his palm on my chest. "Maybe it's time to live a little and enjoy yourself, and maybe this Irish lad is just the way to do it." He removed his hand from my heart and tucked my hair behind my ear, just like he always did with his.

"He couldn't even touch me, Zan. After I told him I'd been raped, he reached for me and then he stopped. That's how awkward and uncomfortable I made it for him."

He shook his head. "Son, don't you see? Let me remind you yet again that the boy is a police officer. That means he's seen and heard it all. What do you think, that he was repulsed when he found out you'd been raped? That he thought less of you somehow?" I dropped my gaze to the couch as he said, "No feckin' way is that what happened. He'd just watched you break down and was giving you some space. He probably figured you didn't really feel like being handled right then, so he was respecting your boundaries."

I considered that, then looked up at my dad and offered him a half-smile. "You're pretty smart sometimes. You know, for a crazy hermit."

He laughed at that and lobbed a throw pillow at me, which I deflected. "Craziness is hereditary, son. You get it from your kids."

That made me laugh, too. "Where'd you get that? Were you up on your roof with a telescope, reading bumper stickers on the 101 freeway?"

"Nah. It was in one of those books you brought me last week. I don't think I can handle any more so-called comedies, by the way. It's time to change gears. I'm thinking about reading a few romance novels."

"You're kidding."

"Don't judge me."

"Sorry. Gay or straight?"

"Gay." He smiled at me pleasantly.

"Alright, I'll see what I find."

"Make sure they're really hot with loads of sex."

"Because that's not awkward, shopping for things that I think might turn my dad on."

"Yeah, a bit skeevy when you put it that way. Just make sure there's a cute guy on the cover and I'll take it from there."

"Will do." I pivoted around so I was facing him and said, "So, there's something else I need to tell you. I'm going to be gone for a week, beginning next Sunday. I'll still be here Wednesday as usual and I'm planning to come on Saturday before I leave, but then it'll be the Sunday before Christmas before I can make it back here."

"No worries, I can cope for a week." He really was in a good place today. There were times when information like that would have thrown him. "Doing something fun, I hope?"

"No. I'm going on a Dotsy cruise."

My father burst out laughing. "Good heavens, why? Do you have a missus and two or three little rug rats that you neglected to mention?"

"Because that's likely. No, a friend's getting married on the cruise, only he doesn't know it yet." I told him the whole story, which seemed to amuse him.

I hung out with my father well into the evening. We cooked dinner together and as we sat down to salmon and salads he asked, "How are your parents?"

I frowned at him, even though I myself was guilty of saying that occasionally. "Mom and her husband are fine.

My *dad*, however, is five years overdue for a haircut and in desperate need of some new shirts."

"Both the hair and the shirts are just how I like them."

"Reminiscent of the seventies?" His hair reached his elbows.

"Classic." He took a bite of salad, then asked, "So your stepdad's still sober then, I take it?"

"Yeah, coming up on a year. Harold's all about making amends now. He and Mom keep showing up at school events, as if it's the third grade recital or some shit, and they're always inviting me to dinner. Thanks, but no thanks."

"You're not ready to forgive him," he guessed, and I shrugged. My stepfather had been an alcoholic as far back as I could remember, certainly ever since he married my mom when I was five. I was skeptical that he was a changed man all of a sudden. I also wasn't ready to overlook the fact that he'd made my life and my mom's miserable for the better part of two decades.

Later on, Zan and I somehow decided to watch Jurassic Park, joking and laughing throughout it. I loved it when he was like this, so carefree and upbeat. It was all going so well and he was so exceptionally happy that I didn't bring up the subject of finding someone to replace me again. I didn't want to throw off his good mood.

That conversation had to happen, though. My dad couldn't function on his own, and June was going to be here before we knew it. I worried about what was going to happen to him, more than I worried about what was going to happen to me.

Chapter Five

My dad had a point about the faculty of Sutherlin College. Some were great, but the rest were pretentious douche monkeys. It was all I could do to sit through a lecture on themes and symbolism in post-modern eastern European sculpture without banging my head on the desk repeatedly.

At least Skye was waiting for me with a big smile on his face when the class *finally* ended. "That's a really subtle t-shirt," he said before giving me a hug.

"I know, but I couldn't fit any more words on it." I'd used a thick, black Sharpie to completely cover the white shirt with every swear word I could think of. I wasn't a fan of that last uptight professor and enjoyed rattling his cage.

To complete the look, I'd even slapped on a little black guyliner. Until recently, I'd been cultivating a bit of a rock and roll persona to go with Art School Christian, but aside from today, I'd sort of lapsed into Boring T-shirt and Jeans Christian. I just couldn't muster the enthusiasm to go full-on rock star somehow.

"You going to wear that on the cruise?"

"I wish, but I'll bet there are all kinds of rules for acceptable conduct on those things."

"Probably. We sail in four days, aren't you excited?" he asked.

"Excited isn't exactly the word I'd go for here."

"Come on, it'll be great!"

I asked him, "What are you basing that statement on?"

"Well, I've never been to Hawaii, for one thing. That'll be fun. And Trevor's getting married! I'm so happy for him and Vincent."

"I just hope the surprise wedding doesn't freak them out."

"It won't," Skye said. "I've been to a wedding planned by Nana before and it was magical. She's going to make it amazing for Trevor and her grandson, they're both going to love it." I wished I had his optimism.

We went to the student union for lunch. Skye got a sandwich and I got the biggest coffee they sold. I almost got two of them. Once we'd found a table, my friend said, "Dare and I are considering getting married here next summer." He gestured at the campus sculpture garden outside the windows. Two huge pieces dominated the landscape, a pair of men reaching desperately for each other. Skye had completed them during our junior year. "I'm just worried that it's too much about me and not about *us*. What do you think?"

"I think Romeo and Julian might be a bit too distraught to RSVP to the wedding." That was our nickname for that particular pair of sculptures, which looked like unseen forces were pulling them apart. "The Three Lords A-leaping would be livelier party guests. If you found a nice outdoor setting for them, you could get married there. Those sculptures are definitely about both you and your fiancé." He hadn't actually named his trio of ballet dancers that, I was just being goofy.

"You have a point." Skye leaned forward and said, "Speaking of the wedding, I have something to ask you. I want you and my brother to be my best men. I'd been assuming you would be, but then it occurred to me that I never actually went through the formalities. So I'm asking you officially, will you?"

"Of course! I'd be honored."

He hesitated, then said, "Even if the wedding's in July?"

"I thought you two were looking at early June, right after we graduate."

"We were, but I just found out yesterday that my mom's pregnant and the baby is due at the end of June."

"She...wow."

"I know. She's forty-five and this wasn't exactly planned, but her doctor says the baby's healthy. Mom's having trouble with her blood pressure though and is on bed rest for the duration of her pregnancy. It should all be fine as long as she takes it easy."

I looked down at my hands, which were wrapped around the coffee cup, as Skye continued, "I know you're planning to move away when we graduate, but I hope you can come back for the ceremony. I really want you at my wedding, Christian."

I whispered, "It's just...it's not possible, Skye. Not if it's in July."

"Where will you be then?" When I didn't answer, he said, "Come on, Christian. *Talk to me.* I've always tried to respect your privacy, but I really don't understand why you keep so many secrets."

"I have my reasons."

He reached across the table and cupped my hands, the coffee still sandwiched between them. I looked up at him as he said, "I love you, Christian, so I'm not going to push, even though it's obvious that something's tearing you up inside and that just kills me. I'm just going to say this: if there's any way I can help with whatever you're going through, I really hope you'll let me."

"You *do* help, every single day. Your friendship has been the most amazing gift and I'm so grateful for it, Skye."

"I feel the same way about you."

He let the subject drop after that, even though it was far from resolved. The idea of missing my best friend's wedding was heartbreaking, but July was impossible. I was glad I hadn't gotten anything to eat for lunch, because I felt sick to my stomach at the thought of hurting him like that.

When he finished his sandwich, I walked him to his on-campus studio, where he was working on a painting for the cross-disciplinary requirement we needed in order to graduate. I didn't have a clue what I was going to do for mine. I didn't care, either.

*****

I ended up blowing off the rest of my classes and went home and took a nap instead. It seemed like a better use of my time. The ringing of my phone startled me awake after a few hours. It was dark in my apartment and I knocked it off my nightstand, then tumbled out of bed after it. Chance's name was on the screen and I answered it with, "Hey."

He was crying softly and after a few moments he managed, "I'm sorry, Christian. I didn't have anyone else to call."

I leapt to my feet and turned on the lights, immediately going into high alert. "What's wrong? Where are you?"

"I'm at the Roosevelt. Oh God, there's so much blood."

A prickle of fear ran down my spine. "What room are you in?"

"Four-twelve."

"Do you need an ambulance?"

"Please don't call one."

Shit. "I'll be there as fast as I can."

"Thank you." The line went dead.

I stuffed my feet into my boots as I shoved the phone in my pocket, then pulled on my coat as I ran out of my apartment. *There's so much blood*...he didn't say it was his, though. What was I about to walk into?

I broke every traffic law on the way to the hotel where Chance and I had met, then ditched the car in a loading zone and ran to the fourth floor. I was winded as I knocked on the door to room four-twelve. It took Chance a while to answer. Finally the door opened a crack and a blue eye peered out, just a couple feet above ground-level. When he saw it was me, he dragged himself out of the way and laid down on the filthy rug to catch his breath as I pushed the door open.

"Oh shit," I whispered, crouching down beside him. His thin, naked body was battered, and his face was so bloody. "Is it okay if I lift you?"

When he nodded, I scooped him into my arms. He was really light. After I gingerly moved him to the mattress and covered him with the blanket, I got a damp towel from the bathroom, climbed up on the bed and carefully tried to wipe away some of the blood.

"I'm so sorry," he whispered.

"For what?"

"For bringing all this drama into your life."

"It's not your fault."

After a pause he told me, "I'm not infected."

"What?"

"You're getting my blood all over you, so you might have been worried. I don't have any diseases." Talking seemed to take a lot out of him and his eyes slid shut.

"I wasn't worried. Do you know where all this blood is coming from?"

"I hit my head." He raised a shaking hand to lightly touch a spot right above his forehead. "That's when the bleeding started."

I pushed his hair aside and found the spot, then put pressure on the wound with the towel. "As soon as I stop the bleeding, I'm taking you to the hospital, Chance. I'll pay for it. You might be seriously injured."

"No. No hospitals."

"Please don't argue."

"I mean it. No hospitals."

I sighed quietly as I pulled the blanket up a bit higher. "What happened here?" I asked after a while.

Chance's voice sounded hollow as he recited, "My trick told me to strip and once I was naked he just started punching me. After I fell and hit my head on the nightstand, he kicked the hell out of me before he got on top of me and fucked me. Then threw some money at me and left." There was a used condom on the rug along with a few crumpled bills. A lump formed in my throat.

Eventually the bleeding stopped and I carried him to the bathroom to clean him up a bit. "Is my face bruised?" he asked as I sat on the edge of the tub with him on my lap and ran a damp wash cloth over his cheeks. He looked up at me with so much sadness in his eyes. "I tried to shield it. I want to go on that cruise so bad, but everyone will stare at me if I'm all beat up."

That made me feel like an asshole. I'd been rolling my eyes at the idea of going on a cruise geared toward kids, but this poor guy was really looking forward to it. "It's okay, Chance," I told him. "Your face isn't bruised." He seemed relieved.

I carried him back to the bed and helped him get dressed. I hadn't cleaned him up all that well, but the bathroom in this place was completely disgusting so I decided to finish up at my apartment. The sooner we got out of this hell hole, the better.

His movements were slow, it was obvious he was in pain. When we'd gotten his boots and jacket on, I helped him up and started to lift him but he told me he'd walk. I began to guide him to the door with an arm around his shoulders, but then he said, "Wait." He limped around the bed and stooped to pick up the crumpled bills, which he stuffed in his pocket. That just broke my heart all over again.

It took us a while to get downstairs. Fortunately, the Jeep hadn't been towed. We drove to my apartment and I dropped Chance off with a key so he could let himself in. But when I returned from parking the car, he was sitting on the steps in front of the building, waiting for me.

Once we got upstairs, I drew him a bath and brought him some ibuprofen. While he was soaking, I washed up in the kitchen sink and changed into clean sweats, then found some for him. When all of that was done, I led him to my bedroom and curled up with him under the covers, cradling him gently. He hadn't said anything for the last hour. I could tell he was trying so hard to keep himself from crying.

When he finally spoke, what he said was, "Do you want to fuck me, Christian?" His voice was small and almost child-like. I said no softly as I held him a little closer. He asked, "Why not?"

"Because friends don't do that."

"But I don't have anything else to give you."

"Who says you need to give me anything?"

"You've done so much for me," he said. "I'd still be on the floor in that hotel room if you hadn't helped me, and I don't have any other way to repay you."

"I don't expect repayment, Chance. This is just what friends do, we help each other."

He was quiet for another minute before whispering, "Thank you."

I kept holding him after he fell asleep. I'd already wanted to do all I could for Chance before today, but now I was absolutely determined to help him turn his life around. There was so much I needed to do, both for my dad and this sweet, fragile person that had let me be his friend, and there was so little time. I pressed my eyes shut and held him tighter.

Chapter Six

Chance stayed with me for the next few days, until it was time to make our way to the airport. We'd gone to his apartment and he'd packed all his camera equipment and a small suitcase of clothes, fretting that he didn't own anything nice enough for a cruise. I packed more than enough for both of us and told him he could use whatever he needed.

He'd never been on a plane before and was a bundle of nerves at SFO, so I decided to get us both drunk while we waited for our flight. After we'd been in the airport bar about half an hour, a pair of handsome Italian guys came up to us. "You look familiar," the one in a white polo shirt said. "Are you here because a crazy little old lady is making you go on a Dotsy cruise?"

"Yup." I extended my hand and introduced myself and Chance.

"I'm Gianni Dombruso and this is my cousin Nico. My brother Vincent is getting hitched on the cruise, though apparently this is news to him."

They joined us for drinks, and we found out we were on the same flight. "Nana went on ahead yesterday," Nico said. "I'm pretty sure she did that in order to stage a mutiny and take over the cruise ship before we could stop her." He was a conservatively dressed guy of about twenty-six with glasses and tidy dark hair. His cousin Gianni looked slightly younger and came across as a wealthy playboy. His slightly long hair was cut to perfection, his clothes were flawless, and his watch cost as much as a car.

"We're both living with Nana temporarily," Gianni told us. "Which means we spend half our time talking her down from one crazy scheme after another."

"And yet you didn't talk her out of the Dotsy cruise," I said with a smile.

Nico grinned at that. "There was no talking her out of this one. She locked on to it like a shark with a friggin' laser beam."

"And Vincent and Trevor seriously have no idea she's throwing them a surprise wedding?"

"Oh, I think they know something's up," Gianni told us. "My brother's not stupid."

"You must be talking about Vincent," A deep voice behind us said. "You always call me a dumbshit."

"Only as a term of endearment, bro. Christian and Chance, do you know my brother Dante and his husband Charlie?" Gianni asked as he got up and gave the newcomers back-slapping hugs. Greetings and introductions were exchanged as we made room at our little table and ordered another round.

I studied the brothers as we enjoyed a couple drinks. Dante was tall, dark, and ruggedly handsome, about six-four and totally ripped. He actually looked a lot like his brother Vincent. Gianni was also movie star gorgeous but in a different way than his brothers. He was beautiful as opposed to rugged with a paler complexion, lighter eyes, and a leaner build. I wondered what Nana had fed those boys when they were growing up, because they'd all turned out pretty extraordinary.

Chance wasn't saying much and I gave his shoulder an affectionate squeeze. "Are you two a couple?" Charlie asked. He and his husband seemed to never actually stop touching. Right now their joined hands were resting on Charlie's thigh.

"Oh no," Chance answered. "We're just friends. Christian here is pining for a sexy hottie he met last week."

"I wouldn't say pining, exactly." Liar. I'd forced myself to stay away from Shea the last few days, but I couldn't stop my thoughts from straying to him again and again and again.

"Oh, there's pining! Any more pine and we could build a freaking log cabin." Chance flashed me a tipsy smile. "Not that you're willing to do anything about this guy."

"Why not?" Charlie asked.

"He thinks he has reasons," Chance answered for me. "But he's wrong. He should be all over that guy like orange on a Cheeto."

I grinned at that, then changed the subject by saying, "Our flight's boarding soon. We should move this party to the gate."

Chance tossed back the last of his fourth Jack and Coke, then clapped his hands together and leapt to his feet. "Okay, I'm drunk and ready. Let's do this thing!"

"He's never flown before," I explained as we gathered our belongings.

"Nope, but I can do this! So we'll be hurtling through the sky, tens of thousands of feet in the air, in an aging metal tube that might possibly have been repaired by drunken lunatics. It's all good!" Chance flashed me a big smile and headed toward the gate.

"Super comforting," I called after him.

When we boarded, I gave him the window seat. He bounced up and down a little with nervous energy once we started taxiing and as we sped down the runway he began a steady chant of, "Oh shit, oh shit, oh shit," finally culminating in a scream and then a whoop of delight when the plane left the ground. That got him plenty of looks from the passengers around us and smiles from the nearby Dombruso contingent.

Chance turned to me and said, "I don't know why I was scared. This is awesome!"

"I could really take a lesson from you," I said. "And you know what? I will. Lead the way while we're on this cruise, we'll do whatever you want. I'm going to let your enthusiasm rub off on me." That could actually be just what I needed, total distraction from my troubles.

He beamed at me and said, "You're in for it. I was reading online about all the shipboard activities. There's twenty-four-hour-a-day costumed karaoke, and game shows where you can win prizes, and a family talent show. Let's enter! There are classes all day long, too. I want to take one on how to draw Dotsy Dog, and a cooking class, and dance lessons! Take dance lessons with me, Christian!"

I smiled at him. "Anything you want. We're going to do the hell out of this cruise. When it's all over, I want us to be so worn out that we sleep for a week."

He threw his arms around me and kissed my cheek. "I've never been so excited about anything in my entire life!"

*****

I'd expected the interior of the Imagination to look like a circus clown's acid trip, but the ship was surprisingly tasteful. Sure, a guy dressed like a huge speckled dog in a captain's hat greeted us when we came onboard, and okay, maybe the ship's designers could have cut down on the gilding by about three hundred percent, but the huge lobby was actually pretty, with a big curved staircase, glass elevators, and elegant ironwork framing the three stories of balconies that opened onto the grand foyer.

Chance took my hand and dragged me over to the guy in the dog suit, insisting that we get our picture taken. My smile for the camera was genuine. This was going to be fun.

There was some kind of commotion at the ship's entrance and we turned to watch Nana sweep onboard with her entourage. She was dressed in a crisp blue and white suit and a captain's hat (probably because she had every intention of piloting the ship). Five tiny little white-haired women flanked her, all with giant handbags over their arms and all dressed in navy and white nautically-inspired outfits, not quite identical but pretty close. Behind them were at least thirty members of Nana's family, Trevor and Vincent among them. They smiled and waved when they saw us.

Nana was positively beaming. She made us join her family for a group photo with the ship's mascot, then grabbed Chance and me in a hug. After a million introductions, Chance and I finally went off to find our cabin.

Nana had reserved a significant portion of deck nine for her party. Surprisingly, Chance and I had a room with a balcony. It seemed like those cabins would have gone to her relatives. I was grateful for that feature, because it might have felt a bit claustrophobic without it.

The cabin was set up like a tiny apartment. A tied-back curtain could separate the bedroom from a seating area with a compact couch, coffee table, desk and television. The bathroom was split into two tiny rooms, one with a shower, the other with a toilet, and each with a sink. "Our home for a week. It's so cute!" Chance exclaimed, then snatched up a schedule that was on the bed and began studying it.

"Think the pool's open yet?" I asked.

"It is."

I unzipped my backpack, tossed him a pair of swim trunks and grabbed a pair for myself. Our luggage was going to be brought to our cabin later, so it was lucky these had made it into the carry-on (just because I'd almost forgotten them and packed them at the last minute). "Last one down the giant waterslide has to wear a pair of Dotsy Dog ears the rest of the day," I told him with a smile.

"You're on, even though I was totally going to get a pair of those ears anyway." He unbuttoned his shirt, but then he hesitated and looked at me. The hand prints around his neck had faded out, but he had the remnants of a huge bruise on his rib cage from where he'd been kicked.

"Two choices," I told him. "Decide you don't care what people think about that, or keep a t-shirt on. Either solution works."

"Do you have a t-shirt I can borrow?" I handed him one from the backpack and we both got changed.

We went up on deck and rode the waterslide six times in a row, then splashed around in the pool for a while. Finally we toweled off, and on the way to finding a place to sit, I bought us each a pair of big, floppy Dalmatian ears from a souvenir stand. They were fastened together by a furry black headband and reached past our shoulders. Chance chuckled delightedly.

Gianni and Nico were sitting at a table in the shade and waved us over. "Well, you two are certainly getting in the swing of things," Gianni said with a grin.

"When in Rome," I told him.

A cute, blond waiter with an Australian accent came to take our drink order. He flirted shamelessly with Chance, and the two made eyes at each other before he went back to the bar. When he returned with our neon blue cocktails, he slipped Chance a note and told him, "I could get sacked for this, but it's totally worth it." He winked at my companion before moving on to the other tables.

Chance read the note and grinned before slipping it in the soggy pocket of his swim trunks. "What's it say?" Gianni wanted to know.

"He gets off work at ten and wants me to meet him." Chance looked pleased. "I shouldn't, though."

"Why not?" I asked before taking a sip of my big blue drink.

"Well, because I don't want to ditch you during our first night on the ship. That wouldn't be very nice of me."

"Go get laid, I insist," I told him.

"We can keep Christian occupied," Nico said. "I believe Nana has us scheduled to play Family Feud in the Starlight Lounge at eleven. There are already about fifty people on her team, so Christian can be number fifty-one." He smiled at me cheerfully.

I grinned at that. "Awesome."

"Alright. In that case, I'll go." Chance looked happy.

A kid in a green Army surplus jacket and Harry Potter-style glasses snatched a chair from another table and plunked it down between Gianni and me. "Greetings, menfolk," he said as he took a seat. "I'm currently AWOL from the kids' club, so if you see anyone dressed like a total spaz in a lime green Hawaiian shirt, alert me. That'll be one of the kids' club henchmen, coming to drag me back to hell." He was holding a coffee cup and took a drink before settling back in the chair.

"Hi Joshie," I said. "Where are your dads?" Trevor and Vincent had adopted the boy a few months ago. He was eleven going on thirty-five and incredibly smart. I adored the kid.

"Off doing some romantic shit," he said. "A couples massage, I think. I'm trying to give them some space, so I said I'd go to the kids' club. Problem is, when Nana registered me, she accidentally checked the box that said I could only leave if a parent signs me out. That's why I chose to go AWOL instead of bugging my dads."

"That bad, huh?" I asked.

He looked at me over the top of his glasses. "They were decorating cookies shaped like dog biscuits. Let's think about all that's wrong with that for a moment. Next up they were going to do a canine version of the hokey pokey and wanted us to put on ears and tails. You two are halfway there." He gestured at our dog ears with his chin before taking another sip of coffee. I chuckled at that.

Joshie turned to Gianni and said, "Uncle Gi, who are you bunking with, Nico?" When he nodded, the kid asked, "Do you have room for one more? Nana put me in with my cousins, Petey and Patty, and I'm going to go mental if I'm confined in an enclosed space with those two."

"Sure. There's a pull-down bunk above the fold-out sofa, so we have plenty of room," Gianni said.

"Awesome." All of a sudden, Joshie slid down in his chair and said, "Aw crap. There's one of the kids' club goons." A guy in a lime green Hawaiian shirt was crossing the deck, headed in our general direction. "I think I've been made. I'll catch you guys later." Joshie slid out of his seat and disappeared into the crowd.

"God I love that kid," Gianni said with a smile. "He spends most afternoons at Nana's house while his dads are at work, so we've been bonding."

"Why are you staying there?" I asked. "Is your house being renovated or something?" I'd heard all about his palatial mansion on the coast, because Skye had gone to a wedding there and kept raving about it. Apparently the house had been left to Gianni by an older sugar mama when she passed.

"The house is no more," Gianni said.

"What happened to it?"

"Basically, my lawyers weren't as good as Glenda's nephew's lawyers. Even though the will should have been iron-clad, they figured out a way to take everything from me. Oh, and not only did my lawyers lose, they cost me all of my savings in the process. So, long story short, it kind of sucks to be me right now."

"I'm sorry to hear that," I said.

Gianni sighed and looked at the drink in his hand. "At least the court proceedings are over. It got so ugly. The nephew made me out to be a gold-digging slut who was only using Glenda for her money. I really did love her, but it didn't matter. Everyone who looked at our age difference, including the judge, totally assumed I'd manipulated her to get that house. I swear I didn't."

His cousin leaned over and put his arm around Gianni's shoulders. "Your family knows the truth, that's all that matters."

"Even my own family doubts me. Not all of them, but some. I see it in their eyes when they look at me."

"Well, fuck them," Nico said. "I for one totally get it. You've just always preferred men and women who are older than you. That's hardly a crime."

Gianni smiled embarrassedly at Chance and me. "Sorry for the personal drama. This all just finally came to a conclusion last week, although I'd been forced to leave the house with a temporary court order before that. I'm still kind of picking up the pieces."

"No need to apologize," I said. "We all have stuff we're dealing with. My recommendation? Lots of booze, waterslides, and silly dog ears. That's my recipe for coping this week."

Gianni raised his glass. "I'm down with the booze. If I have enough of it, the rest of that might not sound so batshit crazy."

We hung out with the two Dombrusos, chatting and drinking until sunset, which was when the ship's deep baritone horn sounded. A crew member came around and gave each of us a petite, silver pompom, and we shook them and sang the Dotsy Dog theme song along with the rest of the ship's three thousand passengers as the Imagination pulled away from the dock. Maybe it was the booze, but I found it exhilarating.

Gianni and Nico left their pompoms behind when they went to get changed for dinner. Chance and I picked them up and I began working out a cheerleading routine as we made our way back to our cabin. Both of us were drunk enough to be giggly.

"Ready? Okay!" I yelled, putting my hands on my hips. We were in a public space with plenty of people around, but I didn't care. I raised the pompoms and swung them around as I cheered, "You fell down and missed that pass, get up now, brush off your ass! The other team thinks we are beat, but our tight ends look oh-so-sweet!" To accompany that line, I twirled around, bent over and shook my butt at Chance. Then I spun to face him again and circled my hands around each other as I chanted, "Time's almost up but that's not all, come on team and grab those balls! Gooooo Team Gay!" I quickly spelled Y-M-C-A with my outstretched arms, then whooped and clapped as I bounced up and down.

Chance doubled over with laughter. Publicly humiliating myself was totally worth it, just to see him laughing that hard. "Oh my God, you're so drunk," he said as he gasped for air. "And that's the worst cheer ever."

"It is not! It even rhymes!" I cracked up too and Chance and I leaned on each other, brushing tears from our eyes.

I looked up after a few moments and my breath caught. At first, I thought it was a drunken mirage. But no.

Shea stood at the ship's railing maybe ten yards away, on the other side of some shuffleboard courts. Our eyes locked and my heart jumped. He started to take a step toward me, just as a little girl playing shuffleboard sent the puck sailing in his direction. He slipped on it and lost his footing, staggering for a moment before flipping backwards over the railing and disappearing from sight.

"Oh shit," I yelled, "man overboard!"

Chapter Seven

I ran to the spot where he'd been standing and looked down. It turned out the deck below us was much wider than this one, and Shea had landed on it instead of plunging into the Pacific. He was flat on his back though, so I leapt over the railing and rushed to his side. "Are you okay?" I asked.

"Super embarrassed, but otherwise fine." He sat up and rubbed his shoulder. "What are you doing on a Dotsy cruise?"

"My friend Trevor is getting married and Nana, his fiancé's grandmother, is hosting a wedding ceremony for the couple. What are you doing here?"

He grinned at me. "My cousin Brian's getting married. His fiancé Hunter doesn't have a family, so Nana pretty much adopted him and is throwing them a shipboard wedding, too."

"Ah." I helped him to his feet and asked, "You sure you're okay?"

"Yeah."

A few crew members pushed through the crowd around us and started asking a lot of questions, then insisted that Shea get checked out by the ship's doctor. "Well, um...good to see you," he called as they led him away.

"You too."

"Next time don't jump over the railing, sir," one of the crew members told me flatly.

Next time? As if people were going to be falling over railings left and right and they expected me to keep leaping after them? "Yeah, sorry. Wasn't thinking."

Chance had joined me by way of the stairs. He held an armload of pompoms, mine and his. "So, that just happened," he said as we headed to our cabin.

"Yup."

"Quite a coincidence, the object of your desire ending up on the same cruise."

"If I'd stopped and thought about it, I could have predicted that. I knew he and one of the grooms were cousins."

"So what are you going to do about this?"

"Do about it? Nothing."

"Oh, come on! This is totally meant to be. The universe is trying to push the two of you together!"

"No it isn't. Shea and I just know some of the same people, including my friend Skye. Speaking of which, I hope he and Dare made it onboard. I haven't seen them yet."

"Stop it."

"What?"

"That blatantly obvious attempt at changing the subject. We were talking about you and Shea."

"Shea Nolan?" Nana appeared at my elbow, wearing so many floral leis that I couldn't see her mouth. "Hi boys. I couldn't help but overhear, because I was eavesdropping. What's this about you and Shea, Christian?"

"It's nothing."

"It's not nothing," Chance said. "Christian's crushing on this guy, but he says they can't get involved because he's moving away in a few months. That's nuts though, because think of all the fun they could have between now and then!"

"Shea...oh, the cop! Brian's cousin. Is he a gay homosexual? I didn't know that. He's a fox, that I did know. I don't even mind all that much that he's a cop," she said. "That seems to run in his family. His cousin Kieran's a cop too, and he's perfectly lovely, so good for my boy Christopher. They're both around here someplace. I tell you, it's hard to keep track of a hundred and seventy-eight people!"

"Wow! That's how many people you invited?"

"No, I invited a lot more than that. It was short notice though, so not everyone could get the time off." Nana looked disappointed. She stopped at a cabin door and said, "This is me. You boys coming down to dinner?"

"Yes ma'am," Chance said, "as soon as we get changed."

Nana nodded and said, "You just leave this thing with Shea to me. It'll work out fine, you'll see." She dug into her handbag and fished out a plastic card, which she tapped on the keypad to her cabin. As she pushed open the heavy door she said, "By the way, I'm proud of you boys for getting into the Dotsy spirit! I saw you on the waterslide earlier, and the ears are very cute." She flashed us a thumbs up before disappearing through the door.

"Oh hell, I forgot I was wearing the ears," I said, knocking my forehead against the wall. "I'll bet Shea saw that cheerleader routine, too. That's just all kinds of awesome."

"Dude, how could you forget you're wearing the ears?"

"I don't know, I just did."

"But I'm wearing them, too. All you have to do is look at me and you're reminded."

"Still."

Chance grinned and started heading toward our cabin again, and so did I. "You're so into that guy," he said.

"Who says?"

"You. Just look how bummed you are about making a fool of yourself in front of him. Then again, he's pretty much the clumsiest guy ever, so your respective embarrassments kind of cancel each other out. I mean, he fell over the railing! I was waiting for a splash! Would you have jumped in and saved him if he'd landed in the ocean?" I just shrugged. "You would have, wouldn't you? Come on, admit it."

"Well yeah, especially since it was pretty much my fault he fell. I distracted him by being such a dork and doing that cheer."

"He didn't fall because he got distracted by the cheer, he fell because he got distracted by *you*. Did you not see the look on his face right before he went boots over britches? It was the same look from back at the bar, like a starving man staring at a great, big club sandwich."

"I used to be a priceless artwork in your analogy. Now I've been downgraded to cold cuts."

"I realized my earlier analogy was missing a key component. Yes, he looks at you with reverence, but he also looks at you with intense longing," he said. "Hence the sandwich."

When we reached our cabin, I turned to Chance and raised an eyebrow. "What do you think Nana meant when she said we should leave the thing with Shea to her?"

"No idea," he said with a big grin, "but I can't wait to find out."

*****

At dinner that night, I kept finding myself scanning the crowd. Skye and Dare had turned up and shared a table with Chance and me. Apparently they'd been 'relaxing in their cabin' all afternoon, which obviously meant they were having loads of sex.

My best friend noticed what I was doing as my gaze once again swept the restaurant. "Who exactly are we looking for?" he wanted to know.

Chance eagerly filled him in on what had happened with Shea and me earlier that evening, and when he finished, Skye beamed at me. "Remember, I was the first person who knew he was into you."

I never did see Shea during dinner, but then there were five huge restaurants aboard the ship. He could be in any one of them. Even if I did spot him, then what?

When we finished our meal, Gianni and Nico came over to our table along with Trevor and Vincent. Trevor hugged Skye and me as he said, "Hey guys! Sorry we've barely had a chance to say hello. We've been sucked up into the Dombruso vortex. Did you know that my fiancé has thirty-three cousins on board this ship and that they're all crazy?" He flashed a smile at Vincent. "No offense."

"Oh believe me," Vincent said, adjusting his silver-framed glasses with a smile, "I'm well aware of that. It was like growing up in an insane asylum with my grandmother as warden. Which is pretty ironic, since she's the craziest of the bunch."

"Guess what else?" Trevor said with a big grin. "We're getting married tomorrow. Thanks for the heads-up, guys!"

"We were sworn to secrecy by order of Nana," Skye said.

"So, are you okay with having it sprung on you like that?" I asked.

"Sure," Trevor said. "Nana's so happy, and that makes us happy. Besides, we never would have been able to get away with a small wedding anyway. The Dombrusos are a package deal."

"What about your family?" Chance asked him. "Were they able to make it?"

"Yup, my entire family's onboard," Trevor said. "My dad is parked in the sports lounge because some game's on, and my cousin Melody and her husband and baby are at a toddler play group. As for our son, he went AWOL from the kids' club earlier and they put out an APB on him, but now he's tucked away in his uncle's cabin with room service and a paperback, so all are present and accounted for."

"After that huge meal, we're going dancing to burn off some calories," Gianni told us. "It's Lady Gaga night in the over-twenty-one lounge. You guys want to come?"

Skye was out of his seat like a shot. "Um, hell yes!"
Dare grinned and got up too, putting his arm around Skye's
waist.

Chance and I both said we'd pass, and then I asked,
"Wait, what about Family Feud?"

"Oh crap, that's right," Gianni said. "If Nana asks, tell
her Nico and I went out to find boyfriends. She'll accept
that excuse."

Once they left, and as Chance and I lingered over
coffee, he said, "I've met so many new people today. Run
me through how everyone's related again."

"Dante, Vincent, Gianni and Mikey are brothers. You
haven't met Mikey yet, but he's probably around here
somewhere. They were all raised by Nana, their
grandmother, after their parents were killed. Nico is one of
their many cousins. Vincent's marrying my friend Trevor,
and Joshie, the kid from earlier in the Army surplus jacket,
is their adopted son."

"Okay, got it."

"So, the wedding tomorrow is the Dombruso side of
things. The wedding later in the week is for two guys that
aren't related to Nana, but don't tell her that. They're
family as far as she's concerned."

"Do they have actual families?"

"One of the grooms has a huge family, but his fiancé Hunter doesn't because they disowned him when he came out. That's why Nana's taken him under her wing."

"I see."

"Don't be surprised when you meet Hunter, by the way. He used to be a famous porn star, so you'll probably recognize him."

"Really? What's his last name?"

"His stage name was Hunter Storm, but he doesn't go by that anymore."

Chance's eyes went wide. "Hunter Storm, holy shit! He was *huge*, and then he just up and quit the business. I always wondered what happened to him."

"Love happened."

"And now he's marrying Shea's cousin?"

"Yup, Brian Nolan. Funnily enough, the Nolans are a family of police officers, the Dombrusos are former mafia, and they're all on this boat together. Go figure."

Chance said, "Why didn't Nana just let the Nolans handle Brian and Hunter's wedding? It must have cost her a fortune to bring them all onboard."

"Because she's incredibly generous and I'm sure she just wanted to do that for her boys."

"Wow."

"Yup."

Chance asked me for the time, and when I told him it was almost ten, he pushed back his chair and said, "I'd better go meet my date. I'm actually a little nervous! Isn't that silly?"

"Not at all. I hope you have fun. What's this guy's name, anyway?"

"Kip. In case you're wondering, I'm planning to totally lie to him and tell him I'm a college student who works in a library. Reality has no place on a cruise ship." He stood up and looked at me. "What are you going to do while I'm out with the Aussie?"

"I'll probably go back to our stateroom, unless you think you might want to use it."

"Maybe. I bet the crew doesn't have private quarters. I'd feel bad kicking you out, though."

I got up from the table and said, "I can easily go find something to do. Just text me when the coast is clear."

He gave me a hug and said, "Will do."

After he took off, I explored the ship for a while, then found a quiet nook on the top deck and settled onto a cushioned lounge chair. I could feel the motion of the ship, just a little. It was soothing, actually. We were somewhere between Oahu and Molokai, surrounded by inky black ocean with a clear, starry sky overhead. I really hadn't expected to find any peace on a cruise ship full of kids, but this was nice.

I'd closed my eyes and was letting the gentle rocking of the ship lull me when the lounge chair beside mine creaked. My heart leapt when I opened my eyes. Shea sat facing me, hands on his knees. "I probably shouldn't be disturbing you," he said. "You looked so peaceful."

"It's okay," I murmured, pushing myself into more of an upright position. "How are you feeling after that fall?"

"Still embarrassed, but otherwise fine. My shoulder was a bit sore but some ibuprofen took care of it."

"Glad it wasn't worse."

"Me too."

The conversation faltered at that point, so I just sat there staring at him. God he looked good. He was dressed in a button-down shirt and khakis, his dark hair neatly combed. I really wanted to mess it up.

Shea hesitated before moving over and perching on the edge of my chair. Slowly, deliberately, he reached out and rested his hand on mine. My heart started beating in double time at his touch. With my free hand, I held on to the frame of the lounger, trying to physically restrain myself from reaching for him.

"I'm not the only one who's feeling this," he said softly, "am I? This attraction, it's not just me, right?"

"It's not just you." My voice was barely a whisper.

"I think about you all the time," he said. "You think about me too, don't you?" I nodded.

Shea pulled something from his shirt pocket. Then he turned my hand over, put it in my palm, and curled my fingers around it. As he held my hand in both of his, he told me, "I'm yours for the taking, Christian, even if all you can give me is just one more night." He kissed my cheek and whispered, "Nine forty-eight," before he got up and walked away.

I stared at the key card in my hand as I weighed my options. It was one of those pivotal moments with the power to change everything. If I didn't go to him, that would be the end of it. I was sure he wouldn't keep trying to pursue something with me.

If I went, that would mean the start of something, because I knew I wouldn't be satisfied with just tonight. Not a long term relationship, it couldn't be that. But still, even if we just took it day by day, I knew we'd both get attached and it would be incredibly painful to walk away when it was all over.

I had to ask myself which would hurt more: ending this in a few months, or missing out on Shea. The second option meant never again getting to touch him, to hold him and make love to him. Never getting to know him and spend time with him. Never again caressing his skin or hearing his voice or experiencing the incredible security of his arms around me.

I stood up, turning the little white key card over in my hand. I took a deep breath. Then I didn't walk to Shea's cabin.

I ran.

Chapter Eight

I was winded when I finally reached cabin number
nine forty-eight. It was right next door to mine. For a solid
minute, I leaned against the wall, trying to catch my breath.
Then I swept my hair back from my face and brushed the
white card over the keypad. It unlocked with a click. It was
fairly dark inside. I passed the closet and the split
bathrooms and stepped into the main part of the cabin.

Shea was naked on the bed. He wasn't in some sexy
pose though, like in the movies. Instead, he knelt in the
center of the mattress, sitting back on his heels, a throw
pillow on his lap to cover himself. His nervousness showed
in his eyes.

I had to pause and just stare at him for a moment. His
smooth skin was luminous in the soft light of the two little
sconces that flanked the bed, his handsome face upturned to
me. "You're the most beautiful thing I've ever seen," I said
softly. He ducked his head shyly, but I reached out and
cupped his chin, lifting it until he met my gaze again. "I
mean it," I murmured before leaning down and brushing
my lips to his.

Shea set the throw pillow aside and laid back against
the bedding, offering himself to me. He still looked
nervous, as if it was his first time all over again. I pushed
my shoes off and climbed onto the bed, drawing him into a

hug. Shea slid his arms around me and held on tight. A sigh slipped from me. I realized it was a sigh of relief, as if I'd been waiting and waiting for this moment. And really, I had been.

We kissed softly, for a long time. It made my heart ache. I needed this, I needed *him* so desperately. I knew I'd never have my fill of Shea. Even if we spent every moment together between now and June, it wouldn't be nearly enough.

After a while, he pulled back and looked at me, concern in his eyes. "Are you okay, Christian?" His voice was so tender.

"Yeah. Why?"

"Because you're shaking, sweetheart."

"I know," I murmured. "I'm sorry. I'm such a mess when I'm around you."

"Don't apologize." He held me for a while before tilting my chin up and kissing me. Eventually he deepened the kiss. I melted into it.

I ran my hands down his broad back as my cock stirred, then slid my thigh between both of his. We worked each other up slowly with soft caresses, until he crawled between my legs. After he unbuttoned my pants and slid down the zipper, he stroked my erection through the fabric before pulling my briefs down to just beneath my balls.

When his warm, wet lips wrapped around the head of my cock, I moaned with pleasure.

Shea sucked me carefully at first, ramping up his efforts as I responded to him. It felt incredibly good, but I whispered, "I need to be inside you." He slid his mouth off me, rolled onto his back and parted his legs for me, running his palm down my arm.

I worked him open carefully using a little tube of lotion from the bedside table, then wiped my hands on some tissues and fumbled for my wallet. There was one condom in it. I was achingly hard by now, my hands shaking a bit as I tore off the foil wrapper. When I tried to put it on, I accidentally drove my thumb right through the thin sheath and swore under my breath. I held it up to show Shea what I'd done and said, "Did you pack any condoms?"

He grinned at me. "No. I had no idea you'd be on this cruise." I grinned at that, then stretched out beside him and settled into the crook of his arm.

"Didn't you think there'd be any other single guys on the ship?"

"I didn't care."

"I'm really sorry I broke the condom."

He looked in my eyes and asked, "Have you been checked?"

"Yeah. I get checked twice a year, even though I never have unprotected sex. Well, except for that first time." I broke eye contact. "I got checked over and over after I was raped. I was so worried. The results always came back negative, though."

"This has to be your call," he said, "but I'd be willing to go without." I looked up at him and he said, "I get tested yearly as part of my routine physical, and I've had sex with exactly one guy. He used a condom." He grinned at me.

"Why did you get tested before you had sex?"

"Because I come in contact with drug paraphernalia on the job. I'm always extremely careful, but it doesn't hurt to get the test and gain that extra peace of mind."

"Why would you believe me, Shea? You barely know me. What if I'm lying to you?"

"You're not."

"You're right, but how do you know that for sure?"

"Because I trust you, Christian." He gave me the sweetest smile.

"I trust you, too. Please though, after me? Don't ever believe a guy who tells you he's been tested. People lie."

His smile widened. "I know I come across as pretty naive, but I am actually a police officer, Christian. People lie to me every single day and it's my job to see through it."

I grinned at that, then kissed his cheek. "You have a point there."

"So. You want to?"

I paused to consider it. I had a lot of trust issues when it came to sex, but I knew, just absolutely knew for a fact, that Shea would never lie to me or intentionally hurt me. If he said this was okay, then it was. I nodded and leaned in to kiss him.

Shea stroked me as we kissed and soon I was hard again. I slicked my cock, then worked a little more lotion into him and quickly wiped my hands on another wad of tissues before grasping his hips. I positioned my tip at his opening, took a deep breath and pushed. He pushed back, just like I'd taught him, and I slid inside.

With one long, slow thrust I bottomed out in him, then held still until I felt him relax under me. I looked in his eyes as I began moving in him. When he smiled, it flooded me with happiness.

We made love slowly, watching each other in the soft light. I'd always disliked that expression, 'making love', but it was so apt right now. This wasn't just fucking. It was sweet and tender and if I wasn't careful, I was going to get so overcome with emotion that Shea would think I was a total mental patient.

That thought was enough to make me pick up the pace, thrusting into him harder and faster. I sat up just a little so I could stroke him and he moaned and arched his back, grasping the sheets with both hands. After a while, he cried out and shot all over his stomach and chest, rocking up to meet my thrusts.

I came too, deep inside him, staring in his eyes as my body shook and convulsed. I never thought I'd experience this. Never. It was so incredibly intimate, more than I could have imagined. It felt like he was giving me an incredible gift, a sacred part of himself.

When the aftershocks died down and I found my voice again, I whispered, "Thank you." I was still inside him and laying on top of him, supporting my weight on my knees and elbows. His cum soaked into my shirt. I didn't care.

He put his arms around me and kissed the side of my head. "That was so intense," he murmured.

I raised myself up to look at him. "Too much?"

"No, not at all. I'm so glad I got to share that with you."

"Me too." I eased out of his body and settled in right beside him, my head on his shoulder, lightly tracing his chest with my fingertip. After a while I asked, "Is your cabin mate going to come bursting in here any minute?"

"No, I ended up with a bachelor cabin. I was supposed to bunk with my brother, but he works at the same station and we both couldn't take the time off. It would have left the department short-handed. We flipped a coin to see who'd get to go."

"I'm so glad you won that coin toss."

"I lost actually, but Finn decided I should be the one to go since I'm closer to Brian. You must think he's a grade-A jerk, but he has his moments. That said, I'm still sick about what he did to you."

"He really didn't do anything. It's not his fault that I went PTSD all of a sudden." Shea hugged me a little tighter and kissed my hair.

We relaxed in each other's arms, just enjoying each other for a while, and I asked, "Are you attending the wedding tomorrow?"

"I don't know if I should. My whole family was invited, but I don't actually know either of the grooms."

"Will you be my date?"

"Do you want me to?"

I grinned and said, "That's why I asked."

"You said when we first met that this was only going to be about sex."

"I also said it would be a one-time thing."

"What changed your mind?"

"I'm so drawn to you, Shea, and I don't want to fight it anymore. I can't make you promises or tell you this is going to be a long-term thing. It won't be. But if you're willing to just take this day by day, I'd love to spend time with you."

"I can do that."

His eyelids were getting heavy, so I leaned down and kissed him before saying, "Get some sleep. I'll see you tomorrow."

He gave me the most radiant smile. "Looking forward to it."

*****

Chance was sitting on the bed perusing the next day's itinerary, dressed in a t-shirt and pajama pants when I returned to my cabin. "Don't tell me, let me guess," he said when he saw me. "You tracked down Shea."

"He tracked me down. His cabin's right next door, by the way." I tossed my shoes on the floor, dropped onto the mattress and touched the headboard. Shea's room was a mirror image of this one, so his bed and mine lined up. I glanced at my companion and said, "How did you know?"

"You have sex hair. Also, your shirt's totally rumpled and quite possibly covered in cum. Were you so eager to do him that you didn't bother to get undressed first?"

"Something like that. How was your rendezvous with the Aussie?"

Chance grinned happily. "So good. Why don't guys like that exist in real life?"

"This *is* real life."

"No it isn't. It's a magical dream world where Chance Wayne is a photography major at a prestigious university by day, and by night catalogues books in the basement of a regal, hundred-year-old library."

I raised an eyebrow at him. "Did you name yourself after Bruce Wayne?"

"I panicked. I even almost started giving him Batman's backstory, but fortunately I was able to head off that train wreck."

"Why'd you decide to go with a fake name?" I asked.

He gave me a look that said *well duh*, and answered, "So I could be somebody else."

"You don't feel bad lying to him?"

"Not in this case. He doesn't really care about me. I'm just the Twink of the Week, something cute for him to play with until we return to port. I know for a fact that at the end of the week, he won't even ask for my phone number."

That all struck me as a bit depressing, even though Chance seemed fine with it. "So what's this guy's story?"

"He graduated from some university last June and set out to see the world. Must be nice. He landed this cruise ship gig and thought he'd give it a go for a couple months. He didn't say this outright, but I got the impression he finds himself a cruise boyfriend on every voyage. I'm not judging, obviously."

"Did you sleep with him?"

"Of course. What kind of cruise boyfriend would I be if I didn't put out?" Chance grinned at me as I stretched out on my side. One of my palms was still pressed to the headboard. "You look tired," he said as he started to get up. "I'm going to fold out the couch."

"Don't bother. This bed is plenty big."

He glanced over his shoulder at me. "Really? You don't mind sharing?"

"Of course not. We already shared when you were staying in my apartment and you proved to be neither a snorer nor a blanket hog."

He dropped back onto the bed and flashed me a smile. "You're sweet, Christian."

"Shhhh," I said, reaching up and pressing a finger to his lips. "You're totally going to ruin my rep as a hardcore badass."

He grinned at that and pretended to nip my finger. "Where exactly do you have this reputation?"

"In my own mind. Don't shatter the fantasy!"

"Wouldn't dream of it." He stretched out on his side facing me and asked, "Are you planning to sleep in the cum shirt?"

"Apparently, since I'm too relaxed to move."

He grinned at that. "You're kind of a slob."

"I know, but I hide it well."

"Except when you sleep in cum shirts."

"Except then."

He tucked a hand under his head and asked, "Are you planning to have a torrid shipboard romance with Shea this week?"

"I have no idea what I'm planning. I did ask him to be my date to tomorrow's wedding, though. You'll be busy taking pictures, so it seemed like an idea."

"Plus you're dying to see him again."

I smiled at Chance. "Plus that."

He reached behind him and shut off the light. "I'm glad you've moved beyond the pining phase. That was silly."

"I know."

"Get some sleep, Christian. You're going to need it."

"Am I?"

"Oh yeah. We have a full schedule tomorrow before the wedding, beginning with the Upper Deck Ducky Derby right after breakfast."

"What is that?"

Chance smiled at me in the darkness. "I have absolutely no idea, but we're going to find out."

Chapter Nine

Chance really was determined to experience everything the cruise had to offer. *Everything.* So after breakfast the next morning, we found out what exactly the Ducky Derby entailed. Normally, I would have gone running in terror, but he was so excited that I sighed and said, "Sure. Why the hell not?"

A race course had been marked off on the top deck of the ship. Each of the racers, including Chance and me, had to put on huge orange swim fins and an oversized duck bill, then rush around the course while balancing three plastic eggs, one on each flipper and one on the bill (which had shallow oval indentations on them, like that would help). As if that wasn't quite enough, we were also wrapped in what basically amounted to tiny straightjackets with stubby wings protruding from both sides, so we couldn't use our hands.

Skye and Dare were in the crowd. As soon as the whistle blew and I started waddling down the track on my heels to keep the eggs from rolling off my flippers, Skye doubled over with laughter. When he pulled out his phone and started filming, I yelled over the cheering crowd, "Don't make me hurt you, Skye!" He just laughed harder and went right on recording.

Chance won the race, and I came in second-to-last out of a dozen. He was so damn happy when they gave him his prize, a little yellow stuffed duck in a sailor hat. Seeing him so overjoyed made it all worthwhile. I waddled up beside him and an extremely perky crew member helped me with the eggs. Surprisingly, none had rolled away. She unfastened the straightjacket next and I plucked off the beak and flippers.

Skye was still chuckling when he reached us. "That was the best thing I've ever seen in my entire life! Chance, you must be some kind of miracle worker. Before he met you, Christian wouldn't have done that in a million years."

"What happens on a kiddie cruise stays on a kiddie cruise. Well, unless your best friend films it and uploads it to the internet," I said. "That's grounds for justifiable homicide, incidentally."

"I haven't uploaded it. Yet," Skye told me gleefully as we stepped aside and made room for the next group of racers. They were going by age groups, adults first, teens next, then different age brackets for the kids.

Shea appeared at my side with a huge smile on his face and held up his phone to show off the picture he'd snapped of me mid-race. In it, my brow was knit in concentration behind the huge orange bill and my hair was flying everywhere. It was so absurd that I had to smile. "Would you kill me if I use this for your caller ID?" he asked.

"Oh man. Of course you saw that."

"Yup. Chance slipped a note under my door with your schedule, so I knew right where to find you."

I shot a look at Chance and he smiled and said, "You can thank me later." He was cuddling the little duck, holding it to his chest with both hands.

I took Shea's phone, but instead of deleting the photo, I typed in my number and set the picture to come up whenever I called. As I handed it back to him I said, "Whatever Chance is making us do next, you have to do it, too. That goes for all of you. Oh and Skye, you remember Shea Nolan. Shea, that's Skye's fiancé, Dare Evans. Also, did I ever actually introduce you to Chance?"

As they exchanged greetings, Nana came bustling up to us. She was wearing a bright orange track suit and was accompanied by her five little girlfriend clones, also dressed in track suits in every color of the rainbow. "Did I miss the duck races?"

"Just the adults' race, Nana. Chance won," I told her.

"Atta boy, Chance!" She gave him two thumbs up, then noticed that Shea was standing beside me and exclaimed, "Oh! You two managed to get together on your own! I guess I'd better cancel Operation Lifeboat."

"Operation what now?" I asked.

Nana was already rushing off with her friends in tow. "We gotta go, we got twerking lessons in the Starlight Lounge in five minutes! Carry on boys, carry on!"

I turned to my friends and asked, "What do you suppose Operation Lifeboat would have involved?"

"Tossing you and Shea in a dinghy and dropping it in the middle of the ocean with some champagne and a boom box playing Sinatra," Skye said with a huge smile. "No getting rescued until you'd declared your undying love for each other."

"That sounds romantic, actually," Chance said.

"Oh sure, it starts out romantic, but then it ends up as a special feature during Shark Week." I started walking and gestured at my companions to follow. "Hurry up. Whatever was next on the agenda can't be as good as twerking with Nana."

It was totally the right call. By the time we got there, she was already up on the stage with the instructor, trying to tell the young woman she was doing it wrong. Because the other people in the class were laughing and applauding, the crew finally decided it was easier to just let Nana do what she wanted. Skye and Dare jumped up on stage and started twerking with her while Chance and I teamed up with the flock of her tiny girlfriends.

Shea looked slightly terrified at first, but finally he bent his legs and tried to do the dance move. I had to chuckle. Apparently he'd never actually tried to do that before and was missing some of the finer points.

When Nana saw this, she hurried off the stage and came to his aid. "No, Shea, like this." She grabbed his ass with both hands and tried to move it for him. When that didn't work she said, "Crouch down!" He bent his knees. "Lower, and spread your feet wider!"

He did as she said and Nana grabbed his hips, then thrust her pelvis against his butt and started twerking wildly. I doubled over, laughing so hard I was crying. Shea just smiled at me and shook his head, and let her keep right on humping him until he finally got it right.

*****

The ship had been circumnavigating the island of Molokai all day. While we sailed, Chance had us take part in one crazy activity after another. I laughed so much that my sides hurt by the end of the afternoon. When we finally went back to our cabin to get ready for Trevor and Vincent's wedding, I kissed Chance on the forehead and said, "Thank you."

"For what?" He set his little duck on a nightstand and draped it in some Mardi Gras beads that he'd won, then angled the sconce to hit the duck like a spotlight.

"For being you. I had a great time today."

"I can't believe you went along with all of that," he said with a smile. "I kept waiting for you to draw the line somewhere, but you never did."

"Nope. I told you I was going to follow your lead, even if it meant doing karaoke dressed like a mackerel." That had actually happened today. It made an odd kind of sense at the time.

The ship finally docked in the early afternoon. Nana had three tour buses lined up in a row for the wedding party when we disembarked. A white, vintage Rolls Royce was waiting for Trevor and Vincent and it led the procession.

We headed toward the heart of the island, climbing steadily into the lush, green mountains. Shea sat beside me, holding my hand. Skye and Dare were in the seat in front of me, kissing each other about every six seconds. Chance took up the whole seat across the aisle, checking and rechecking his camera equipment, which he'd spread out beside him. He was more nervous than the grooms.

After about forty-five minutes, the buses pulled up to a charming white plantation house with red shutters. To the right were sprawling pineapple fields, the spiky crops almost alien-looking, except for the familiar little fruits at their center. To the left was a wide lawn, set up with an airy, white canopy over a lot of round tables. Beyond the lawn rose a rocky cliff face where two tall waterfalls came together, then tumbled into a sparkling lagoon. Trevor and Vincent looked awestruck.

The ceremony began soon after we arrived. We were all given leis of fragrant white flowers as we stepped off the buses, and then we gathered beside the lagoon as a group of women in Hawaiian print dresses sang a cappella and danced the hula. The lagoon was bracketed by tropical flowers that appeared to be growing wild and the waterfalls served as the backdrop to a little stage that had been set up. I got the symbolism of this setting all of a sudden and grinned. The two waterfalls came together to form a bigger, mightier waterfall. Two shall become one. Nana was good.

Trevor walked hand-in-hand down the aisle with his dad, TJ, who had tears of happiness streaming down his face. Vincent linked arms with Nana and she walked him down the aisle next, beaming from ear to ear. TJ and Nana started to take their seats, but the grooms asked them to stay on the stage with them for the ceremony. Nana looked misty-eyed as she hugged her grandson and the man he was about to marry.

Three groomsmen stood to the right, Vincent's brothers Dante, Mikey and Gianni. The best man was their adopted son Joshie, who stood beside the wedding official. The eleven-year-old tried to remain stoic as his dads came down the aisle, but lost the battle and started to cry as he stammered, "I love you both so much. Thank you for being my dads." Trevor and Vincent both hugged and kissed him and told him they loved him, before he finally wiped his eyes and said embarrassedly, "Okay, okay, enough of the mushy stuff! Get married already." The crowd chuckled appreciatively.

After Nana and TJ took their places beside Joshie, the couple held each other in a loving embrace and stayed that way throughout the entire ceremony. The wedding official was a round little man with a friendly face, dressed in a loud, floral print shirt. The ceremony was short and sweet and was capped off with a blessing in Hawaiian. When the official said, "I now pronounce you husbands," Trevor and Vincent didn't just kiss. They made out passionately while the entire audience cheered and applauded. Apparently they'd forgotten all about being shy in the moment.

I felt myself getting choked up and reached for Shea's hand. He gave mine a reassuring squeeze and smiled at me when I looked at him. He was a bit teary-eyed.

When the couple left the stage they were inundated with hugs and congratulations. I kissed Trevor on the cheek and hugged them both when it was my turn and told them how happy I was for them. The pure joy on both grooms' faces was incredibly heartwarming.

Chance had been snapping pictures throughout the ceremony. Once everyone had congratulated the couple, Nana herded all the family members over to the edge of the lagoon to pose for photos. It looked like Chance had calmed down a bit, his brow knit with concentration as he did his job like a seasoned pro.

I picked up Shea's hand and winked at him, then snuck off with him in the opposite direction from where the family photos were happening. A little dirt path cut through the thick tropical foliage. After a couple minutes, we came to a little clearing and I took him in my arms, gingerly so I didn't ruin the leis around our necks. "Have I told you today how gorgeous you are?"

"Twice." He grinned shyly.

"Good. You should always be reminded." I kissed him softly, then said, "Thanks for being my date."

"Thanks for inviting me."

I stepped back just a little, running my hands down his arms and my eyes down his body. He was wearing a short-sleeved white button-down shirt, which brought out his tan, and khakis. The grooms had been wearing almost the same thing, since Nana had instructed everyone to dress casually, even them. I, on the other hand, was dressed in a black shirt and pants. I pointed out my failure to blend and Shea said, "I think it's cute. Very art student of you."

I grinned at that. "Skye and Christopher are art students too, but they managed not to look broody." We'd finally run into our friend Christopher and his husband Kieran when we were boarding the busses for the wedding.

Clearly they were another couple whose idea of a romantic cruise meant many uninterrupted hours in bed. I couldn't argue with that logic.

"You say broody, I say sexy."

I smiled at that, then took off his lei and mine and draped them on a nearby tree. "These would have gotten crushed," I told him.

"Why?"

"Because I'm about to do this." I pulled Shea to me and kissed him hungrily as he grabbed me in a tight embrace. I felt him go hard at the same time I did so I crouched down in front of him and unzipped his khakis, then freed his cock from his pants and boxers. As I deep-throated him, he stifled a cry and grabbed onto a branch to steady himself.

"Oh God," he whispered, biting his bottom lip and fighting back a moan. We were blocked from view, but we could hear the wedding party when they were loud, so obviously they could hear us, too.

He whimpered, thrusting his hips just a bit but then stopping himself. I grabbed his ass and rocked him forward to show him it was okay, so he began fucking my mouth with short, contained movements as I sucked him. He came just a few minutes later, fighting back a yell, his jizz slightly sweet on my tongue. I swallowed it eagerly and kept sucking until he was spent. Then I eased off him, tucked him away, and zipped him up. I kissed the front of his khakis before I stood up and grinned at him.

Shea was still clinging to the tree branch, looking flushed and even more beautiful than usual. He burst out laughing and said, "I can't believe you just did that."

"Did you like it?"

"Do you really have to ask?"

"Just checking."

"I can't believe we did that out here. What a rush! I kept waiting for us to get caught."

I smiled at him and drew him into my arms. "I have a new goal for the remainder of our cruise."

"Public sex?" When I nodded, he chuckled and said, "We can't do that on a cruise ship. We'll get caught and they'll kick us off!"

"Totally worth it. We can put on disguises and sneak back aboard for your cousin's wedding."

"You're a bad influence, Christian." He said that with a big smile.

"Or a very, very good one, depending on your perspective. We'll limit ourselves to the adults-only parts of the ship, I do have some decorum. It's going to be fun."

Shea kissed me and said, "Are you going to let me reciprocate? I want to make you cum, too."

"Oh, you will, baby, but later. We should get back. Try not to look like you just had an orgasm."

He laughed at that. "I'll work on it."

*****

The reception went on well into the night. A sumptuous meal was served and I had to almost physically restrain Chance to get him to sit down for a couple bites of food. He'd been taking pictures nonstop. Christopher and Kieran sat with us, along with Skye and Dare.

"So when did this happen?" Shea's cousin Kieran asked, smiling at us as I fed Shea a bit of diced fruit with my fingertips. I almost didn't hear what was said as I watched my date's full lips suck the juice from my fingers. Lust spiked in me instantly and I drew in my breath. I had the most overwhelming urge to lay Shea on the tabletop and take him right there in the middle of the reception.

As if he knew what I was thinking, Shea blushed and grinned at me. God, I wanted him. Finally I remembered a question had been asked and murmured, "Oh. Um, recently."

Dinner was followed by lots of dancing. I tried to claim I didn't dance, but Shea just rolled his eyes and pulled me out onto the dance floor, then gathered me in his arms and swayed with me to the music. I held on tight, resting my head on his shoulder as the entire party around us disappeared, leaving just Shea and me and this perfect moment. I was sure I'd never felt this good, this safe and happy and content, all at the same time.

When it was time to cut the cake, a grand, multi-tiered number covered in fresh local flowers, Trevor and Vincent brought Joshie to the cake table with them, and all three of them held the knife and made the first slice together. They then cut a huge piece for Joshie, which made him whoop with delight. He tucked into the cake with a big serving spoon as the grooms fed each other with their fingertips and capped it off with a tender kiss.

"Time for dessert," I whispered to Shea. My big grin made it clear I wasn't talking about cake. He chuckled at that and put his arm around my shoulders as we headed away from the crowd.

The plantation house was all lit up, the large kitchen at the back of the building bustling. We slipped through the door as Shea whispered, "I don't think we're supposed to be in here."

"I know." I pushed open the first door we came to, which turned out to be a small pantry. We went inside and I turned to him and smiled. "That's what makes it exciting."

In the next instant we were all over each other, kissing and groping wildly. Somehow we got each other's pants and underwear down, and Shea wrapped his hand around my hard cock as I looked around desperately. It was fairly dark in the pantry, but I was able to spot a tub of vegetable shortening. That would work.

I spun Shea around and he bent over for me as he whispered, "I need you in me so bad." He slid his feet as far apart as possible within the confines of his khakis and I quickly worked some of the shortening into him, then slicked my throbbing cock. I fumbled for a roll of paper towels and wiped my slippery hands before grasping his hips and pushing into him with one long thrust. I actually found myself sighing with relief, odd as that was.

Shea started to moan, so I put my hand over his mouth and kissed his shoulder as I began fucking him. When it seemed like he was going to keep it down, I wrapped my arms around him as I drove myself into him again and again. It was really difficult to be quiet when I was overcome with lust. I even had to be careful of the sound of my body slapping against his.

A steady stream of waiters and kitchen staff passed right by the pantry door, which made my heart race. The adrenaline junkie in me loved every minute of it. The threat of getting caught any second amplified my senses. I wondered if Shea was worried though, and slid a hand around his hips. That answered the question pretty definitively. He was rock hard, his cock leaking precum, and I began to stroke him. Clearly, he was loving this as much as I was.

When I was close to cumming, I pulled out of him and began stroking my cock. As much as I wanted to cum in him, cleaning him up afterwards would have been problematic. To my surprise, Shea dropped to his knees and looked up at me as he opened his mouth. "Oh shit," I whispered as my cum shot onto his tongue. I filled his mouth, burst after burst, and when I finished he swallowed and smiled at me as he whispered, "You taste surprisingly sweet."

I grinned at that. "So do you. It's all the pineapple we keep eating on this trip." The moment he stood up, I dropped to my knees and swallowed him to the root, then sucked him until I was once again rewarded with a mouthful of cum. When his orgasm ebbed, I stood up and kissed him deeply, sliding my tongue in his mouth.

We broke apart and dressed quickly as I whispered, "And you thought I was kidding when I said we were sneaking off for some dessert." He tried to stifle a laugh.

When we were dressed, I quickly straightened up the pantry, putting the lid back on the shortening and disposing of the paper towels in a plastic shopping bag. Just as we turned to leave, the door swung open, narrowly missing us. Light spilled into the little space and Skye and Dare stopped in their tracks as my best friend exclaimed, "Oh shit, sorry! What are you guys doing in here?"

I chuckled and said as we slipped past them, "Same thing you are. Second shelf on the left. Blue container. Just FYI," I said with a wink, directing him to the shortening.

*****

The ship was docked at Molokai overnight, so it didn't matter that the wedding party got back in the wee hours. Trevor and Vincent looked so happy and so in love, arms around each other as they headed to the luxurious honeymoon suite that Nana had booked them for the duration of the cruise. Gianni carried their sleeping son in his arms, Nico following with the little boy's shoes in one hand and Joshie's to-go box of cake in the other. We said goodnight to them as we continued down the hall.

Chance was clicking through the photos on his view screen and murmured, "I think I got some good shots. I'm going to download them to my laptop as soon as we get to our stateroom. I hope I don't keep you up, Christian, but I really want to take a look at these right away."

"Well, Christian, you could always bunk with me," Shea said casually, "so Chance can get some work done."

"Love to," I said with a smile.

Kieran was at the front of the little pack we were traveling in, holding his husband's hand, and he looked over his shoulder and flashed Shea a leering grin. "You shut up," Shea told his cousin, but he was chuckling.

We reached Skye and Dare's room next, and I hugged them both. "See you tomorrow, with any luck. Chance booked an adventure sports shore excursion. He's making me zip line, bungee jump, and parasail. He's obviously trying to kill me. In case he doesn't succeed, I'll text you when we get back to the ship."

"Have fun. Try not to die," Skye said cheerfully.

When we reached our cabin, Chance looked up from his camera long enough to smile and say, "Night, all," before going inside.

At the next door, we said goodnight to the rest of our little group and Shea used his card to let us into his stateroom. I slipped off my shoes, then put my belt, phone and wallet beside them and crawled under the covers. Shea used the restroom, then came to bed in a t-shirt and boxers. He drew me into his arms and I snuggled against his chest, sighing contentedly. "Thanks for letting me bunk with you," I murmured.

"My pleasure." He kissed the top of my head and settled in comfortably against the pillows.

"Tell me something, Shea," I murmured.

"Like what?"

"Anything. It can be totally random. I know so little about you."

"You know a lot, actually. You've been to my house, met my best friends, saw the dork den that I call a bedroom. You know I wanted to draw, and you know I'm a police officer. That kind of sums me up."

"What were you like in high school?"

"Shy. Quiet. Nerdy. Exactly like I am now."

I tilted my head to look up at him. "Did you date back then?"

"Nope."

"Why not?"

He grinned at me. "Besides the braces, the fifty extra pounds, the zits and the fact that I was too awkward and shy to talk to anyone I liked? No reason."

"You've really come a long way."

"No I haven't. I'm still exactly that guy. I may look better on the outside, but inside I haven't changed at all."

"Do you like me, Shea?"

"Of course!"

"Oh look, you're talking to me! Proof you've changed."

"Well okay, I'm not *exactly* the same. But I still feel like that guy."

I said, "I wish I'd met you back then."

He chuckled, his chest rumbling beneath me. "Thank God you didn't."

I laced my fingers with his, then brought his hand to my lips and kissed it. I'd really meant that. It would have been incredibly wonderful to have all those extra years with him.

Chapter Ten

I was awakened the next morning in the nicest possible way, by soft kisses along my jaw. I reached for Shea and pulled him into my arms, murmuring, "You're so incredibly warm when you sleep. You're like my own personal tauntaun."

He chuckled at that. "You geeked up that reference just for me, didn't you?"

"Oh yeah. Big time." I flashed him a smile before kissing him, then exclaimed, "Shit, you did it again!"

"What?"

"Snuck off and brushed your teeth, so I'm all gross by comparison. I need to go even things up." I rolled out of bed despite his protests and headed to the bathroom, where I used the facilities and rubbed some of his toothpaste around my mouth with a finger, then rinsed it out.

When I returned to the bedroom, I pounced on Shea and kissed him deeply before asking, "What are you doing today? Want to risk life and limb by bungee jumping with Chance and me?"

He chuckled at that. "Me and extreme sports, what could go wrong?" He brushed my hair from my eyes as he said, "I'd still be tempted to join you, but I promised my cousins I'd go on a hike to a waterfall with them."

"Ah. Well, that sounds considerably safer." I kissed him again and said, "I'm supposed to meet Chance at ten, what time is it?"

He picked up his phone from the tiny nightstand and pushed a button to light up the screen. "It's not even nine yet."

"Oh my God," I exclaimed, turning the phone to face me. "You did not make that duck picture your wallpaper!"

"It's so cute! I couldn't help myself." I moaned and fell onto the pillows, and he chuckled as he slid my shirt up, exposing my belly. "Let me make it up to you," he said between kisses down my happy trail, one hand working on my button and zipper. "I'll bet I can make you forget all about that photo."

He slid my pants and briefs down a few inches and as he licked my cock I murmured, "What photo?"

That earned me a sweet smile before he took my cock in his mouth and began sucking me. I let myself enjoy the attention for a few moments before flipping around and taking him in a sixty-nine. I moaned around his thick cock as he sucked harder. Within a few minutes I was swallowing his cum as he cried out around my cock. The feeling of him pulsing and shooting between my lips was so erotic that I came too, unloading in his wet mouth as I wove my fingers in his hair.

Afterwards, I swung back around and he gathered me in his arms. "Can we just send stunt doubles in our place and spend the day right here instead?" I murmured. My hand was up underneath his t-shirt, caressing his smooth, broad chest.

"If only."

"Hey, do you have plans this evening?" I asked.

"I'm having dinner with my cousins."

"Want to meet me in the Lido Lounge before that? There's something I've been meaning to do with you."

He grinned at that. "And you want to do it in the lounge?"

I smiled at him. "I'm not talking about sex, though I still have every intention of messing around with you all over this ship. It's something else."

"I'm down for whatever you want."

"Great, let's shoot for four-thirty since we all have to be back onboard by four." I kissed him and started to get up, but then went back for another long, deep kiss. Eventually I made myself let go of him and said, "Have fun today."

"You, too. I'm looking forward to four-thirty."

*****

Chance had left a note in our stateroom saying he'd gone to breakfast. I showered and got dressed, then washed down a bunch of pills with some flat soda. Caffeine was most definitely called for, so I went to join my friend and almost collided with someone who'd been just about to knock on my door.

Nana was decked out in a big blonde wig, even bigger fake boobs, and round, white sunglasses, along with a camouflage track suit. She peeked at me over the top of the glasses and said, "Psst, Christian, it's me. Nana! I'm in disguise!"

"So I see. Why is that?"

"I'm coming bungee jumping with you and Chance! My family's trying to stop me, bunch of stiffs! They think I'm too old for that stuff, but fuck that! Come on, let's take the back stairs so we can make a break for it. Hurry!"

"There are back stairs?" I asked as I followed her.

"Technically they're for the staff, but so what?"

"Ah."

When we reached the crew member passageway, she whirled on me and stuck a bony finger in my face. "You're not going to try to stop me too, are you? You always struck me as a fun guy. Was I wrong about you?"

"Oh, I'm not going to stop you. If you want to bungee jump, more power to you."

"I knew I liked you, Christian," she said, linking arms with me.

*****

"Wait, this is bungee jumping?" Nana asked, hands on her narrow hips. We were standing on a bridge above a deep ravine, wearing crash helmets, and Nana had just been fitted with a harness and cord.

"Yeah. What did you think it was?"

"That thing where you go sliding down a long clothesline with your ass in a sling."

"That's zip lining. We're doing that later," Chance told her. "If you don't want to do this, you don't have to."

"Did I say that?" Nana asked. "I'm doing this shit!" She stepped forward to the edge of the bridge and turned to the buff instructor. "You sure you got the ropes right, Slick? If I splatter at the bottom of this canyon, I swear to sweet baby Jesus I'm coming back to haunt you!"

"Your equipment is all in place. Now let me show you how to do it," he said.

Nana stared at him and said flatly, "We're jumping off a fucking bridge. I think I got it." She plucked off her blonde wig and thrust it at me. "Here, Christian, hold my hair." She handed her sunglasses to me. "And these." She then reached into her t-shirt and pulled out two stuffed

Dalmatians. "And my boobs." She tossed them to me, then zipped up her jacket, climbed up onto the little platform and jumped off without a moment's hesitation, cursing like a sailor the whole way down. Chance and I leaned over the railing and watched Nana as she reached the end of the cord and bounced, then swung around in a wide arc. All three of us whooped and cheered, along with the rest of the people that were waiting their turn to jump.

Chance said, "Well, she made it look easy. I have to admit that I'm scared shitless, though."

"You don't have to go through with it if you don't want to," I told him, setting Nana's disguise with his backpack, which was leaning against the railing.

"Oh, I do. I want to prove to myself I can do this."

Nana was hoisted up to a round of applause. "See? Old people can do anything young people can do! We're not all breaking hips every five minutes, either," she told the crowd.

A couple other people had their turns before Chance was up. He looked terrified, his blue eyes the size of saucers, but he climbed up on the little platform, breathing rapidly like a woman in labor. He looked at me over his shoulder and I smiled and flashed him a thumbs-up before he stuck his arms out and took a flying leap. He shrieked all the way down, but he did it.

When it was over and he was back on the bridge, he ran to me the moment the harness was off and grabbed me in a hug. His whole body was shaking, but he laughed and exclaimed, "I did it! Did you see me? I actually did it!" It was such a cute and child-like thing to say that it made me smile.

"I knew you could do it," I said. "I never had a single doubt."

"You've always believed in me. Not just with this, but with everything. Thank you for that, Christian."

"That's what friends do."

Eventually it was my turn. The harnesses were snug around my calves, and they connected to a larger safety harness around my hips. I got up on the platform, turned around so I was facing Chance and Nana, and gave them a salute. Then I executed a fairly slick backwards swan dive off the bridge.

The air rushed past me as my heart pounded. All too soon, I reached the end of the line and bounced back, then swung wide, the view swirling around me. It was a great rush, but very short-lived. As soon as I stopped swinging, the jump crew lowered a rope to me which I snapped onto my harness, and they used that to hoist me up.

"Well, damn," Chance said once I was back on the bridge. "You're completely fearless!" I grinned at him, even though that wasn't true at all. I fully understood that some things in life were absolutely terrifying, but an extreme sport just wasn't one of them. It was all a matter of perspective.

*****

Bungee jumping was followed by zip lining and then parasailing, all of which Nana tried with whole-hearted enthusiasm. We ran into a few of her family members when we got back to the ship and she yelled, waving the DVD of her day's adventures over her head, "I just jumped off a bridge, slid down a clothesline, and flew in a parachute over the ocean! Too old? Everybody who said I was too old can kiss my ass!"

She grabbed Chance and me in a big hug and kissed our cheeks before saying, "You're good boys. I can't wait to see what you come up with for Maui!" She then flipped off her family and held her head high as she marched away.

"That's who I want to be when I'm eighty," Chance said as we headed to our cabin. "Nana's got it all figured out."

"She really does."

The ship's horn blew, announcing all-aboard as we made our way down the corridor. In our stateroom, Chance fished in his backpack and found his copy of the DVD (produced on the spot by the adventure company that had organized the excursion, for an extra fee, of course). He popped it into his laptop and we chuckled as we watched Nana's and then his leaps off the bridge, fast-forwarding through the people in between. When my jump was on the screen, Chance exclaimed, "Look at you! Cool as ice."

"I figured it was a lot like jumping off a high dive."

"Backwards."

I gestured at his laptop and said, "This reminds me. How did the wedding photos come out?"

He smiled shyly. "I think they're pretty good. Want to take a look?" When I nodded, he played a slide show he'd put together. He'd not only gotten many gorgeous shots of Trevor and Vincent, both as a couple and as a family with their son, he'd also captured wonderful details, from the waterfalls to the cake to close-ups of the flowers in the leis we'd worn.

The last segment of the slide show consisted of candid portraits of many of the wedding guests, including some great pictures of Nana, laughing and dancing. When a shot of Shea and me in profile came up, Chance hit pause and said, "Says a lot, don't you think?"

I remembered that moment, but hadn't seen Chance snap the picture. I'd been just about to kiss Shea, our faces inches apart, the fingertips of my left hand resting on his cheek as I looked into his eyes. We both had the same expression, one of pure wonder.

I cleared my throat, pushing down my emotions and trying to pull myself out of the moment on the screen, and told him, "Your pictures are incredible. You should be so proud."

"Really? You think they're okay?"

"They're brilliant. *You're* brilliant. I love the way you look at the world, you find so much beauty in it."

"It's not always easy," he said softly. "But I try to do exactly that. Even when everything's grey, I try to find something beautiful to remind me why I got up that morning. The wedding made it easy because it was all incredibly gorgeous. The couple was so in love, and everyone was happy. I'd never been to a wedding before. I actually did research online beforehand so I'd know what I was expected to get pictures of and then it all just unfolded around me. It was such a great experience."

"And you have another one in just a few days."

He smiled happily. "I can't wait."

I got up and stretched my arms over my head as I said, "Trevor and Vincent are going to be thrilled with those photos. Nana, too."

"I hope you're right."

"Oh, I'm right." I picked up my phone to look at the time. I'd accidentally left it behind and saw that Shea had texted me a couple hours ago. He'd taken a selfie while holding two big, oval leaves between his lips, one curling upward, the other curling down, forming a bill. He'd written: *A duck picture for you. We're even now. By the way, my cousins and I hiked two and a half hours each way to get to the waterfall, and the one yesterday was far more impressive. Also, I keep checking my watch and wondering why it's not 4:30 yet.*

I grinned at that and pocketed my phone, then said, "I need to stop by the gift shop and then I'm meeting Shea. Want to join us?"

"No thanks, I still have a lot of photos to edit."

"Alright. Text me when you're ready to head down to dinner."

"Will do."

*****

I spotted Shea before he saw me. I was a few minutes early and apparently he'd been even earlier. He sat at a table in a sunny public space that was equal parts game room, lounge, and bar. His cousin Brian was with him, along with Brian's fiancé Hunter.

When Shea looked up and saw me crossing the room to him, his face lit up and a flood of warmth filled my chest. He stood up and when I reached him, I put down the bag I was carrying and gathered him in an embrace. The moment he was in my arms, I did that odd sigh of relief again. I realized that all day I'd been waiting for this, the moment when I could hold him again.

I couldn't just stand there clinging to him though, so I made myself let go after a few moments and greeted Hunter and Brian. "How's it going, guys?"

"It's going great! We hear you've really been embracing the Dotsy spirit," Hunter said with a big smile as he swept a strand of shoulder-length blond hair out of his blue eyes. It was easy to see why he'd been one of the most famous porn stars in the industry for a while. He was strikingly attractive, lithe and delicate. His fiancé was also a good-looking guy and Hunter's physical opposite, big and muscular with dark hair. A former Marine, Brian had lost both legs below the knee in Afghanistan, and got around on a pair of prostheses.

I shot a look at Shea. "You showed them the duck picture, didn't you?"

"Inadvertently." I raised an eyebrow at him and he said, "Well, it is the wallpaper on my phone." I grinned and asked the couple, "What does Nana have planned for your wedding ceremony?"

"No idea," Brian said. "All we know is when we're supposed to meet her on the last night of the cruise. We're looking forward to seeing what she cooked up."

"Always best to just go with it where Nana's concerned," I said.

Hunter pushed his chair back and said, "So true. Well, we'll leave you to your date. Have fun, guys."

"You can stay if you want," I told them. "I'm going to teach Shea how to draw and you're welcome to be a part of the lesson."

Shea smiled at me. "Really? That's what you have planned?"

"Yup. I even bought us supplies. All they had in the gift shop was stuff for kids, but it'll do." I reached for the shopping bag and unpacked a set of Dotsy Dog pencils and a little plastic pencil sharpener, along with two spiral-bound sketch pads with several Dotsy cartoon characters on the cover.

"Thanks," Brian said, "but I can't draw to save my life."

After the couple took off, Shea told me, "I can't draw either. You're just going to wind up frustrated if you try to teach me."

"Like I said before, it's a learned skill. I had a great teacher in high school who really broke it down for me. She taught me that drawing is ninety percent observation. Let me show you what I mean." I pulled a pencil from its little plastic sleeve and sharpened it, then gave it to Shea. "Draw your hand for me, the one not holding the pencil."

"I'm telling you, this is going to be bad."

"Good. Then you'll gain lots of confidence as you watch yourself grow."

He looked skeptical, but folded back the cover of his sketch pad and quickly drew a hand the way most people would, a simple representation with straight fingers. Then he sighed and said, "Told you it'd be bad."

I smiled at him and said, "You did exactly what I expected you to do. Now let me show you the magic." I slid my chair around so I was sitting right beside him. "You drew without really looking, because your brain already has a symbol to go with the word 'hand' and you drew that. Now I want you to look at your subject. Really look at it. Start here," I said, running a fingertip up the back of his left hand, which rested on the tabletop. "Draw this line, paying attention to the angle it forms." I traced a path over his knuckle. "Follow it, really look at the way your hand arches, right here."

His pencil followed along as he took in what I was saying. "Keep following the line over your finger. The back of your hand is fairly straight, but look at the way it subtly curves at this part." I caressed the lower half of his index finger. "Just keep really looking. Don't let yourself use your mental shorthand for what you think something looks like. Really see it."

We proceeded like that for several minutes. Shea absently chewed his lower lip as he followed along. He looked so adorable that I wanted to lean in and chew it for him, but I concentrated on the lesson instead.

After we'd gone over his whole hand like that, slowly, meticulously, I sat back and smiled at him. "Look at what you just did, Shea."

He lifted his pencil and blinked at the page. The drawing he'd made was light years ahead of his first attempt. "Oh wow." He looked up at me. "Why doesn't everyone teach drawing like this?"

"I don't know."

He studied his drawing and his face lit up with a smile. "This is kind of okay, right?"

"It's much better than okay, Shea, it's terrific. And, it's proof that you really can draw."

He shook his head in disbelief. "I can't believe how much you taught me in only half an hour. You made it seem so simple, too."

"It *is* simple," I told him. "Art, like life, is really just a matter of how you choose to look at things."

That earned me another smile. "Well said."

"Thank you. Ready for the next lesson? This is just the basic foundation, there are so many places to go from here. And of course you'll keep practicing and practicing until it all becomes second-nature."

"Let's do it later."

"Good idea, you should rest a bit. That was a major break-through, best to let it sink in."

"That's not why I want to wait," he told me, a devilish sparkle in his eyes as a sexy little half-smile curved his lips. My libido stirred immediately. He lowered his voice and said, "You had some devious ideas about misusing the public spaces on this ship. Care to put them into practice?"

I smiled at him as I began packing everything back into the shopping bag. "Absolutely. I know right where I want to start, too."

Deck ten contained an extensive adults-only area, for people who wanted a break from the hectic kid-packed parts of the ship. It included a swimming pool, coffee house, lounge and restaurant. I led Shea around the pool, then ducked into a little alcove with him. At night, this space housed the rolling cabinets that held towels for the guests. During the day, the cabinets were out on the deck. There was no door to the alcove, but it formed an L-shape, so once we ducked around the corner, we were out of sight of the pool area.

I dropped the shopping bag, pushed Shea against the wall and kissed him hungrily as he grabbed me and pulled me against him, sliding his tongue in my mouth. He was already hard, which made me grin. I spun him to face the wall, then quickly got his pants and boxers down. I'd had the foresight to put a little tube of lotion in my pocket (thank you Dotsy for leaving a lube substitute in our staterooms) along with a travel pack of wet wipes. After unzipping my pants and slicking my hard cock, I worked some lotion into him, then reached around and stroked his thick cock as I pushed into him.

I fucked him almost frantically, trying so hard not to moan or slap against his ass. With my free arm, I clung to him, hugging him across his chest. He turned his head and kissed me, and I whispered against his lips, "Oh God, Shea." He kissed me again, his hands splayed out on the wall, rocking his hips in rhythm with my thrusts.

In just a few minutes, a little mewl slipped from him as he came. His ass tightened around my cock, milking it as he orgasmed, which made me shoot deep inside him, fighting the urge to yell. I thrust into him again and again, wildly, desperately, until I'd completely emptied myself into him.

As we caught our breath, I kissed him again. Shea reached around and caressed my cheek, and I kissed his hand before carefully easing out of him. He pulled his pants up and whispered, "Let's clean up in my cabin."

I zipped up and straightened my clothes, then cleaned my hands and the wall he'd splattered, using the wipes I'd brought. Once he was dressed, I grabbed the shopping bag and led the way back to the pool deck, tossing the wipes in a trashcan. We drew a few looks from people. They probably hadn't heard anything, but it was a little weird to be coming from a storage nook. A woman in her forties sunning herself asked as we walked past, "Did you two just, you know?"

"Absolutely," I told her and Shea blushed. The woman smiled at us and raised her hand, which I high-fived. It was awesome when people surprised you in a good way.

When we reached Shea's cabin, I went straight to the bed and pulled him down on top of me. We made out for a long time before I undressed him and fucked him again, slowly this time. When we'd both cum again, he drew me into his arms and held me, caressing my hair as I nestled against his chest. He said softly, "I think you're a pretty remarkable guy, Christian."

"But then, you don't know me very well," I joked.

"I know plenty. This moment right now, for example, speaks volumes."

"What does it tell you, besides the fact that I'm clingy after sex?"

"You try so hard to be strong. I have no idea what you're struggling with, but I know it's big. I see it in your eyes sometimes when you think no one's looking. You pretend you're okay. But at times like this you let your guard down and show how much you need other people, and I think that's really kind of beautiful."

It served me right for getting involved with a cop. They were remarkably observant. I sat up and trying to brush off his eerily accurate assessment by saying lightly, "Or, like I said, cumming makes me clingy." He smiled at me sympathetically as I added, "It's probably close to dinnertime, I'd better get going. If you want, we can do another drawing lesson tomorrow."

"I'd like that." When I'd gathered my things, Shea followed me to the door and said, "Sorry. I didn't mean to make you uncomfortable."

"You didn't."

He reached up and brushed my hair back as he said gently, "I'm just going to say one more thing and then I'll let it drop. If you ever feel like talking about whatever's going on with you, I'm here. I've been told I'm a good listener."

I reached out and touched his chest, forcing myself not to draw him into my arms again. Even though the longing was intense, I made myself step back from him. It didn't help that he was completely naked and so stunningly gorgeous that it made my heart ache.

I kept my voice steady as I said, "Thanks, Shea. So, I'll text you tomorrow and we'll find a time for another art lesson if you want."

"I'd like that."

"Great. Well, have a good evening with your family."

"Will do. Thanks for teaching me to draw today."

"My pleasure."

I turned to go, and he said, "Any time you feel like using the spare key card to my cabin, tonight for example, feel free."

I glanced at him and he offered me a shy, lopsided grin. All I could do was smile before retreating. If I'd stayed even five more seconds, I would have pulled him back to the bed and quite possibly never left.

Once I was out in the long passageway and his door had closed behind me, I leaned against the wall and pressed my eyes shut. My desire for Shea was overwhelming. I'd never been that attracted to someone, but I had to pull back a bit. If it was already this intense after just a handful of dates, what the hell would be left of me a few months down the road when I said goodbye to him?

"Hey. You okay?"

I opened my eyes to find Chance staring at me. "Yeah, fine," I said automatically. "What're you up to?"

"I was with Skye and Dare, we decided to shoot a few engagement photos in that pretty atrium on the top deck," Chance said, gesturing upwards with his camera. "What's going on with you?"

"Nothing."

"Bullshit," he said. "You're standing out here in the hallway with an agonized expression, hugging your shoes like a teddy bear. That's not nothing."

"I'm out here because I thought you were in our room and I just needed a minute to myself."

"You must have come from Shea's cabin, right?" I nodded and he asked, "Did you two break up or something?"

"We're not together, so it would be impossible to break up," I told him.

He sighed and swiped his key card. "I don't get it. I can't even look directly at the two of you when you're together, because the heat could melt my eyeballs. Why would you hold yourself back from something like that?"

"I'm not going to talk about this," I said. "But I am going to clean up and then I'm going to go downstairs and get really fucking drunk. I'll be ready in ten minutes and you can join me, as long as you promise to drop the subject."

He rolled his eyes. "Fine. But you have issues, dude."

As if I didn't know that.

Chapter Eleven

The ship docked on Maui for two nights, first on one side of the island, then the other, before sailing on for a day at the big island of Hawaii. After that it swung around and started back up the chain of islands, stopping in Lanai. The final day and night of the cruise would be spent in Kauai before looping back down to Oahu.

Chance's adventure sports frenzy had continued throughout the cruise. Skye and Dare took part in a few of our outings and Nana joined us for absolutely everything, from kayaking to mountain biking to pub crawls. Her grandsons Gianni and Nico participated primarily in the drinking. We also saw Trevor and Vincent occasionally, usually as they were headed to or from some sort of family adventure with their son. They'd taken Joshie to see the active volcano on the big island, and he was still raving about it.

And then there was Shea. I met him daily for drawing lessons, but then we'd go our separate ways. I was trying so hard not to get too attached. I had to. It was a question of self-preservation.

But every night, I'd completely fail.

I'd go to bed, telling myself to stay put. Sometimes I'd last as long as an hour, listening to Chance's steady breathing in the darkness. But I was acutely aware that

Shea was right on the other side of the wall, and every night, at some point the pull would become too great.

I'd slip out of bed and sneak out as quietly as possible so I didn't disturb my roommate. Shea was always awake when I'd let myself into his darkened cabin, maybe because the clicking of his door woke him. He'd pull me into his arms and we'd make love wildly, desperately, until both of us were spent.

After that, we'd hold each other and talk quietly late into the night. He'd started carrying a sketchpad on his shore excursions, and would show me the drawings he'd made each day. Gradually, he was gaining confidence in his ability. I really hoped he'd take the little boost I'd given him and run with it.

Eventually lust would distract us again, and we'd join hands and head out into the ship, which was very still at three or four a.m. That made it easier to find out-of-the-way little nooks and alcoves where I could fuck him hard and fast, both of us so incredibly turned on by the risk of getting caught. We had a couple close calls, but we got away with it.

On the second-to-last night of the cruise, after I'd walked him back to his cabin and was kissing him goodnight, Shea asked, "Will you please be my date for my cousin's wedding tomorrow?"

"Sure." I'd pressed him against the wall right beside his door, my fingers laced with his.

"Really?" I kissed his neck before nodding. When I released his hands, he hugged me tightly and asked, "What's going to happen when we get home, Christian?"

"What do you mean?" I buried my face in the groove between his neck and shoulder, trying to muster the will to say goodnight and go to bed.

"I know we said this was just going to be a casual thing and that we'd take it day by day, but this really doesn't feel casual. It feels like we both want a lot more," Shea said softly. I couldn't even reply to that with the sudden lump in my throat.

He hugged me and added, "I know you've been trying to stay away from me, but it never works. You come to me every night, and when we're together, it feels like you can't get enough of me. You know what? I can't get enough of you, either. So what's going to happen when the cruise ends and I'm not a next door booty call?"

I pulled back to look at him. "That's not what you are to me, Shea. You're so much more."

"So what do we do when we get back to San Francisco? Do we date? This already feels like more than dating, even though I know you're trying not to get attached."

"I'm trying so hard. I'm going away in June, you know that. I always knew it'd be difficult to walk away from you, but it's actually going to be so much worse than I realized. You're going to get hurt so bad." I rested my forehead against his and closed my eyes, adding silently, *I am, too.*

"Bring it on."

"Damn it, Shea. This wasn't supposed to happen."

"But it *is* happening." His hands caressing my back were as gentle as his voice.

*****

Several hours later, after a final day of island adventures, I went upstairs to the cocktail party that was happening before Hunter and Brian's wedding. I could always spot Shea the moment I entered a room, as if he put out a homing beacon. He sat at the bar with his cousin Jamie and Jamie's husband Dmitri, who I'd seen very little of on this cruise.

Shea was dressed in another pair of crisp khakis and a royal blue button-down shirt that hugged his body perfectly. He must understand what that color did for him, the way it brought out his eyes and complemented his flawless skin. Not that he needed any help to look stunning, but still.

Once again, his face lit up when he saw me. He got up and gave me a hug, then remained standing with his arm around my shoulders since there was only one empty barstool. "Hey guys," I said to Jamie and Dmitri. "Have you been enjoying your cruise?"

"We totally have," said Jamie, a cute surfer with sun-streaked hair and an engaging smile. "It's the first time we've managed to take a vacation since we started running the bar and grill."

"We almost forgot what it's like to have down-time," Dmitri added. He was an interesting contrast to his laid-back husband, an elegant and sophisticated Russian-American with black hair and blue eyes. I always liked seeing these two together. Despite seeming so different, they actually were two halves of a whole.

"Goes to show that we really could get away more often," Jamie said. "Our staff has everything under control."

"You two should sneak off for a month, while you still can," Shea told them. To me he said, "They're expecting their first child. The baby is due at the end of summer, and after that, forget about romantic getaways."

"Wow, congratulations," I said. They both looked so happy.

We ordered drinks, and soon the couple was whisked away by another cousin. I sat down on one of the vacated barstools and picked up Shea's hand. "Are they using a surrogate?" I asked, and Shea nodded. "Which one's the father?"

"They don't know, it could be either one. They both, um, contributed to the sample."

"Ah."

"Do you ever think about having kids, Christian?"

I was surprised at the sharp pang of regret that shot through me at that question. It was something I hadn't really thought about, but my reaction told me a lot. I kept my expression neutral as I said, "That, um...that's not in the cards for me." I finished my drink and signaled to the bartender for another before deflecting the question back to Shea. "What about you? Do you want kids someday?"

"I don't know. I mean, I love kids, but I can't quite imagine having one of my own."

I nodded at that and focused my attention on my drink. Damn, I was kind of a mess tonight. All my emotions were right at the surface. It probably didn't help that I'd been averaging three or four hours of sleep a night for the last few days.

Soon Nana arrived on the scene, bursting into the lounge and exclaiming, "Look alive, people! We're going to be heading out in groups of twenty-five or so. Hunter and Brian are already there, so let's get a move on! This group over here, follow me." She gestured to some people near the door, then spun around, her sparkly pink party dress rustling as she departed.

"I thought the wedding was going to take place on the ship," Shea said.

"Me too."

Bit by bit, the entire wedding party was ushered downstairs. When our turn came, we went out onto the dock and boarded a big motorboat, which ferried us into the harbor. "Holy crap, is that our destination?" Shea asked, pointing at an enormous yacht up ahead.

"I guess so. Wow. Nana really doesn't know how to do anything halfway."

"No kidding."

The motorboat came up alongside the much larger vessel and a few crew members tied it off. Our group then climbed one by one up a wide ladder onto the deck. The yacht was dazzling, all burnished wood and shiny brass, opulent and elegant.

I spotted Chance and the grooms near the front of the boat, taking photos with the island in the background. Their surroundings were breathtaking, but Hunter and Brian seemed oblivious to everything but each other. As they embraced, the thin blond reached up to gently caress his fiancé's cheek and Brian bent to kiss him sweetly. They'd both had rough lives before they found each other, but they seemed so strong together, ready to face whatever the future held as a team. I thought there was really something special about those two.

Their wedding ceremony was held on the top deck of the yacht at sunset. Skye and Dare were in the last group to board, and they sat with us. Brian's brother Kieran and Hunter's friend Christopher were the best men. Nana sat in the front row, beaming at the couple, and Chance circled at a distance, snapping photos. The grooms were dressed casually, Hunter all in black, his fiancé in a white button-down shirt and black pants. Brian was standing without a cane, so I assumed he'd finally become comfortable with his prostheses. From what I'd heard, he'd been working hard in physical therapy to get to that point.

The couple pledged their love and their commitment to one another, their vows simple and heartfelt. Toward the end of the ceremony, the wedding official, an elegant woman of about fifty with short grey hair, had everyone stand. I was already holding Shea's hand to my right, and I picked up Skye's hand to my left. The official said, "Hunter and Brian consider all of you family, regardless of whether you're related by blood. Offer them your support and encouragement. Stand by them. Celebrate with them and always remind them of the love and friendship that surrounds them. Will you do this?"

As one, the audience said, "We will."

"Hunter Jacobs and Brian Nolan, you are now married. You may kiss your husband."

Their kiss was so tender. Then they just stared at each other in absolute wonder as the crowd cheered and applauded. I saw Brian mouth the words, "Thank you," to his husband, and Hunter grabbed him in a tight embrace. I'd already been emotional throughout the ceremony, and I really had to fight back tears at that one.

Shea slipped his arms around my shoulders and drew me to him, my back against his chest. Even without seeing my face, he somehow just knew when I needed a hug. I kissed his hand, then held on to it as the couple joined hands and walked back down the aisle together and music filled the air.

*****

The ceremony was followed by a lavish sit-down dinner and cake, then a wild party. Wedding guests with young kids left around nine, the motorboat piloting them back to the cruise ship, but everyone else stayed and partied. Nana had hired a local rock band, and the interior of the yacht was transformed into a night club. We were supposed to return to the cruise ship by midnight, but that never happened. Instead, the yacht just sailed alongside the ship as it left the dock and headed for its final port. The party went on until morning.

After celebrating most of the night with his family and the happy couple, Shea and I found a quiet little nook on the main deck and curled up together on a lounge chair. There was a wool blanket on the back of it, and Shea covered both of us as I nestled in his arms.

"Will you come to dinner at my house tomorrow night?" he asked after a while.

"I can't. I have to go see my dad."

"Does he live in San Francisco?"

"Marin. He's a shut-in. I made sure he had everything he needed before I left, but I still want to check on him. I called him a few times over the past week and he kept insisting he was fine, but he sounded a bit down."

"I hope he's okay."

"Me too." I brushed his hair back from his forehead as I asked, "What are your parents like?"

Shea sighed and told me, "They're two extremely unhappy people. They make each other miserable but won't get a divorce because they're devout Catholics."

"Have you come out to them?"

"I came out to the rest of my family last year, so my parents know. I didn't discuss it with them directly though, because I knew exactly how it'd go. Three of my cousins have come out in the last couple years and my parents went ballistic. They shunned not only Jamie, Kieran and Brian, but also everyone in the family who didn't immediately condemn them for being gay. For the most part, I've been pleasantly surprised by my extended family. A lot of people like my Uncle Ray, Jamie's dad, really rose to the occasion. But my parents have made no effort to contact me since I came out, and that pretty much tells me all I need to know."

"I'm sorry."

"I came to terms with it a long time ago. I always knew I wasn't going to live my life in the closet, and I also knew for a fact they'd disown me when I came out." There was both sadness and resignation in his eyes as he said that. Then he steered the subject away from himself by asking, "What about your mom, what's she like?"

I considered the question, then told him, "Beautiful. Sadly, that's almost all I can say about her."

"How come?"

"She seemed to think her looks would be enough to carry her through life, so she never tried for anything more. She was a model when she was younger and when that dried up, she latched on to guy after guy because she never learned how to make it on her own. Somehow she ended up with my stepdad, a recovering alcoholic who can't hold a job. Between the two of them, they have fewer life skills than the average high school freshman."

"Ah."

"My stepdad's not my favorite person," I said. "Before he got sober a year ago, he was a mean drunk. And yet, my mom stayed with him. She let me grow up in that environment, until I finally got old enough to realize I had alternatives and went to live with my dad at fifteen."

"Wow, I'm so sorry."

I tried to shrug it off. "It's okay, it was a long time ago. I don't have a lot to do with them now, even though he's on a mission to make amends and they keep trying to involve themselves in my life. I guess that's part of his recovery program or something, but to me it's just too little, too late. I needed him to sober up when I was five, not twenty-two." I sighed and said, "Maybe I'm being a dick. I know that when someone holds out an olive branch, you're not supposed to slap it away."

"I can see why you'd be upset with both of them, though."

"I really am trying to get past all this anger. It's such a pointless emotion. But every time I see him, I just want to yell in his face."

"So, maybe you just need to give it some time."

"That's the one thing I don't have," I murmured.

"Where are you going, Christian?" I closed my eyes and held onto Shea a little tighter. He'd asked me before, more than once, but I never answered. I didn't this time, either. He added, "Wherever it is, we can still see each other. Long distance relationships are difficult, but not impossible. I'll do whatever it takes to make this work."

"That's not an option."

"I don't understand," he said quietly. "I think you want this as much as I do, so it's really confusing."

I did. I wanted this so much. For the first time in my life, I could imagine building a real relationship. After I was raped, that felt impossible because my trust had been shattered. I thought it would always be like that. But Shea was amazing. He was everything I could want and I trusted him completely. When this ended, it was going to break me. I said quietly, "I don't have a choice, Shea."

He tilted my chin up and kissed me tenderly. "If you say you don't have a choice, I believe you. And if all you can give me is the next six months, I'm not going to turn that down. I won't lie, it's going to break my heart when you walk away from me. But I'd also be heartbroken to miss out on that time with you."

"I'm so sorry, Shea."

"Don't apologize. Let's just make the most of the time we have, okay?"

I nodded and held on tight. So did he. I wished we could freeze the moment and stay like that forever.

Chapter Twelve

Chance was quiet on the return flight, staring out the window. I put my hand on his arm and said, "Hey. You okay?"

There was so much sadness in his eyes when he turned to me. "Yeah. I'm fine."

"No you're not. What's wrong?"

He sighed quietly and said, "It's just hard to get back to reality after the best week of my life. I got to be someone else for a change. I got paid to take pictures, which was a dream come true, and go to fascinating places and do so much fun stuff. I actually bungee jumped! And I went out with a cute guy who believed I was a college student. He didn't ask for my phone number, by the way. I knew he wouldn't. It was fun while it lasted, though. All of it was amazing, the whole week. So how the fuck am I supposed to go back to being Chance Matthews after all of that?"

I chose my words carefully, "Maybe this could be a turning point. Maybe you don't have to go back to your old life. I don't know what Nana paid you to photograph the weddings, but maybe there's a way to use that money to make some changes."

"Nana was incredibly generous. The cruise itself would have been payment enough. I'm not going to use that money for myself though, as much as I'd love to invest in a new camera and some equipment. My mom and kid brother are really struggling. I help them out as much as I can, but they're barely keeping a roof over their heads. This money is going to make a real difference in their lives."

I wondered if his mother had any idea of the sacrifices he was making for her, or what he had to do to help her out. I raised the armrest between us and put my arm around Chance's shoulders, and he hugged me around my waist. We stayed like that most of the way back to San Francisco.

*****

My father was in a dark place, both literally and figuratively, when I went to see him that evening. I found him sitting in the den with the lights off, staring out the windows at absolutely nothing. It looked like he hadn't showered or changed his clothes in a few days.

My heart sank. He'd been so upbeat the last couple times I'd seen him, but this was the nature of his bipolar disorder. Those euphoric highs would always eventually swing back to this state of apathy.

It took a lot of coaxing, but eventually I convinced him to go take a shower. While he was in the bathroom, I confiscated his dirty clothes and laid out clean ones for him, because he was liable to put the old ones on again.

Then I went in the kitchen and unpacked the books and groceries I'd brought for him.

I'd left him plenty of food, more than enough for the week I was gone, but it looked like most of it had gone untouched. He hadn't let himself starve, he'd just eaten his comfort foods, the crackers and other zero-prep items that filled his pantry. I swapped out the spoiled produce for the fresh things I'd brought, then set about making dinner.

I went to find him when the meal was ready. Zan was back on his couch, dressed in the button-down shirt and jeans I'd left out for him, his tangled hair dripping down his back. He hadn't bothered to shave, but that was okay. "Come have some dinner," I said.

"I don't feel like eating."

"Want me to bring it here instead of eating in the kitchen?"

"I don't want it at all." I took his meal to him anyway, placing it on a little folding table. "I told you I didn't want it," he said, his tone harsh.

"Please Zan, just a few bites. I made your favorite." I'd try to feed him if he let me, but that would only piss him off.

He turned his head away from me. I thought he was sulking at first, but then I noticed his shoulders were shaking almost imperceptibly. I put the tray aside and circled around to the front of him. He tried to turn his head away to hide his tears, but I grabbed him in a hug and held on tight. It was very unusual for him to start crying, so I assumed this must be a particularly bad episode.

He sobbed into my shoulder for a while before putting his arms around me and saying, "What the fuck am I going to do without you, Christian? I missed you so much this past week. I just don't know what I'm gonna do."

"You're going to let me find you a caregiver," I said softly. "I'm going to find you someone terrific, someone kind and fun and dependable. It's going to be okay," I promised, trying to hold back my own tears.

"But it won't be you."

"I know. I wish it could be."

"I'm going to miss you so fucking much," he told me, his voice gravelly. "I love you, son."

"I love you too, Dad," I whispered as my heart shattered.

*****

Eventually, I got my father to eat a little as I stood behind him and worked a comb through his tangled hair. This was a difficult task at the best of times, let alone when he'd gone a few days without brushing it. Truth be told though, I liked doing this. It made me feel connected to him, and I always longed for more of that. After I finally got his hair combed out, I managed to do a bit of cleaning before he told me he wanted to go to sleep. I covered him up on his couch and kissed his forehead. "See you soon, Dad," I promised before heading back into the city.

My emotions were raw as I headed back into the city. It was always upsetting when my father went into one of his blue periods, especially because I never knew how long they'd last. Sometimes it was just a few days. Once, it had lasted four miserable months.

On top of that, I missed Shea, even though I'd just seen him this morning as we said goodbye on the dock beside the cruise ship. It was so incredibly tempting to go to his house. The thought of spending the night in his bed and in his arms sounded like the most perfect thing I could possibly imagine.

But I *had to* put at least a little distance between us. We'd grown incredibly close on the cruise, and even though we'd both agreed to see each other over the next six months, that was supposed to be half a year of dating, not being together twenty-four/seven. The reason for that was simply one of self-preservation. I knew we'd both be devastated in June, but there was still a chance we could go our separate ways without it destroying me completely.

I really didn't need what happened next. The thought of going home to my empty apartment was so depressing that I decided to put it off, and drove past my work-in-progress instead. When I got to the alley where I was painting the girl in the field of daisies, I threw the Jeep in park and leapt from the car.

I wanted to yell and cry and hit something, all at the same time. Some malicious little fuckers had climbed up onto my makeshift scaffold and destroyed my work by scribbling and tagging right over it. The back of the building was a vast expanse of open space, so if all they'd wanted to do was express themselves they could have done that easily, just a few feet to the right. But what they'd chosen to do instead was destroy. I never understood that malicious tendency in some people, the need to tear down what others worked so hard to create.

I shoved the tower of pallets and boxes over with a yell of frustration. They landed with a huge clatter. I was mad at myself for giving those assholes such easy access to my painting. I should have thought to take down the structure before I left on my trip, but I'd thought people were better than this.

I was shaking as I got behind the wheel and started the engine. Why that one, of all my murals around the city? I'd been really attached to that painting. Too attached, frankly, because I knew that half the stuff I did would get destroyed eventually. Usually though, I got to finish them first.

I still didn't want to go home, now more than ever. In the past when I was feeling like this, I would have gone to a bar and picked up some random guy, distracting myself with sex and taking comfort in at least a little human contact. But now that Shea was in the picture, I really wasn't about to do that. I hadn't told him, but I planned to be monogamous for the duration of our time together, not only because he was trusting me to keep him safe, but because he was all I wanted. Since we'd only been together a matter of days though, I wasn't going to make this into a big announcement. He'd probably think I was nuts, committing to him that fast.

I pulled out my phone and sent Skye a text, asking if he and Dare had made it home okay. They'd been on a later flight. It had been nice to spend a little time with him on the cruise, but it had been exactly that: a little. I knew I needed to make more of an effort where my best friend was concerned. There had to be a middle ground between becoming a third wheel and distancing myself.

He texted back a minute later: *Hey! We're back safe and sound. Benny was so excited to see us, although he clearly enjoyed getting spoiled rotten by our landlady while we were gone. The cat is acting indifferent, but I think he's secretly pleased we're home. The Royal Rodent could care less.*

That was the name of his pink pet rodent, who'd started off wild. He still was, frankly. Another text from Skye popped up: *What are you doing right now? Have you had dinner yet? We're about to order pizza, you should join us.*

I'd intended to eat at my dad's, but never actually got around to it. I wrote: *Love to. I'll bring cocktails, because why not?*

For the next couple hours, I tried to force myself out of my funk. I stopped by a liquor store and got the ingredients to make Blue Hawaiians, because Skye had loved them on vacation. At the little garden apartment he shared with his fiancé, I joked and laughed as the three of us hung out. Their cat Draco decided he liked me, and spent the evening sitting on my feet.

I could only tolerate one fruity day-glow cocktail. After that, I switched to straight tequila, which it turned out that wasn't actually an ingredient in Blue Hawaiians, but I'd bought it anyway. Dare switched to the hard stuff too, but Skye stuck with the neon blue drinks.

I drank so much that things got messy. The messiness crescendoed with me sneaking off to the bathroom and drunk-dialing Shea. Twice. I was heavily buzzed by that point, so I pretty much made a total fool of myself with my rambling, telling him he was 'awesome' about eighteen times and saying I missed him over and over until voice mail cut me off.

Later on, I started crying and hugging Skye and apologizing for being a terrible friend and not making more of an effort to see him after he became part of a couple. He was pretty drunk too, so this turned into a mutual hugfest. Dare laughed at us until I pulled him into a group hug and slurred, "I'm sorry I was such a douche, and I'm sorry I kissed Skye. I was so jealous of you. I didn't want you to take my best friend away. But you two, you're so good together! *So good!* It's like you were made for each other. Promise me you'll always, always, always take care of Skye for me, 'kay?"

Dare patted my back and said, "I promise."

"I've never actually seen you this drunk before," Skye said with a grin. "How much tequila did you have?"

"All of it." I picked up the empty bottle and shook it. "Well, Dare had some, too. But I had the rest."

"You can sleep on the couch tonight," Skye said. "No way are you driving home like this."

"No," I said, shaking my head. That made me a bit dizzy, so I stretched out on the area rug. "Drunk driving is *bad*. Really bad. Just say no to drunk driving, kids." I considered that and added, "Wait, why are kids drunk? That's so wrong."

Skye got up and smiled at me. "You just stay right there and continue your public service announcement. I'll find you a blanket and pillow." His phone buzzed and he pulled it out of his pocket. When he looked at the screen, his smile got even wider and he sent off a quick text.

"Okay," I mumbled. "I love you, Skye. I love you too, Dare. I didn't at first. I thought you were a douche. Well, you *were* a douche when we first met you. But after that I was the douche. There was much doucheyness. But now, we've put all that douche behind us. Wait, that sounds gross. Kind of crossed over into enema territory." I paused for a moment, then asked, "What was I talking about?"

Someone knocked on the door just then, and Skye laughed at me as he went to answer it. Dare held out his hand to me and said cheerfully, "Let's get you off the floor, Christian."

When he pulled me to my feet, I said, "Damn. Everything's all spinny. Did I really drink that much?"

"Yup."

I held on to Dare's arm to steady myself. "I have a really high tolerance to alcohol, though."

"Well, we all have our limits," he said.

Just then Skye returned to the living room, which was at the back of their apartment. Shea was with him, in full police uniform. "Oh my God, you look hot!" I exclaimed. The dark blue short-sleeved shirt emphasized his big arms and looked like it'd been painted onto his muscular body. "I didn't think I had a thing for men in uniform. Maybe I still don't. I just have a thing for Shea in uniform." He grinned at me and took over the job of keeping me upright. I gave him a big smile. "Hi, baby."

"Hi, sweetheart."

"Whatcha doing here?"

"Making sure you get home safely. I listened to your voicemails when I got off work. You sounded really drunk."

"Oh, I am." I put my arms around him and held on tight. "How'd you know where to find me?"

"You told me that you were in Skye's apartment in the Western Addition, so I headed that way and texted Skye for the address."

"I forgot I did that. You had Skye's number?"

"You told me that in your voice mail, too," he said.

"I did? Why?"

"Something about nearly dropping your phone in the toilet, so you wanted me to have that number in case your phone got flushed out to sea." He looked amused.

"Oh, right."

"Come on, Christian, let's get you home."

I hugged my friends goodbye and promised to call them soon, then held on to Shea as we left the apartment. It was cold and windy outside, which helped sober me up a bit. "Don't you have a coat?" I asked him.

"I forgot it in my locker."

Shea asked where my car was and I directed him to it before asking, "How'd you get here?"

"One of my coworkers dropped me off."

"How come you're working today? You just flew home from Hawaii a few hours ago."

"I wasn't supposed to work until tomorrow, but the flu's taken out nearly half my station. Since they're desperately short-handed, I agreed to go in."

"Because you're awesome," I told him with a big smile.

*****

When we reached my apartment, Shea looked around curiously as I took off my jacket and dropped it on the floor. I'd never bothered to personalize this space, so it was little more than white walls and functional furniture. It was always meant to be temporary, so I hadn't wanted to get too attached to it.

I pulled off my boots as I headed to the bedroom, hopping on one foot, then the other. My socks followed. Shea had to keep me from tipping over a couple times as I did that. I took off my shirt next, throwing it away from me, then my jeans. I dropped onto my bed in just my briefs and said, "I want you to fuck me, Shea. You're the only person I'd ever trust enough."

He sat down beside me on the mattress and gently brushed my hair back from my face. "You're way too drunk, Christian. We're not going to have sex tonight."

"I want it, though. I want you in me. I'm not sure if I'll be brave enough to go through with it when I'm sober. Please, Shea?"

"No, sweetheart."

I felt disappointed as I picked up his hand and held it with both of mine. "I hate how much my rapist took from me. It's because of him that I can't bottom and can't even be naked during sex."

"I know." Shea was still tenderly stroking my hair. My eyelids were growing heavy, and he said softly, "Get under the covers, I'll tuck you in."

I scrambled around and did as he said. "Please spend the night with me, Shea. I want you with me."

"I'll only spend the night if you agree that sex isn't an option." When I nodded, he stripped down to just his boxers, putting his uniform on a chair in the corner before climbing under the blanket.

As soon as he took me in his arms, I sighed and relaxed. He chuckled a little and I asked, "What?"

"It's really cute that you do that. I always feel the same way, that it's a relief to be in your arms again, but you actually vocalize it." He kissed the top of my head and rubbed my back soothingly as I drifted off to sleep, his heartbeat strong and steady under my hand.

Chapter Thirteen

Something was definitely wrong.

I awoke in the middle of the night feeling far too hot. At first I thought I had a fever, but then I realized it was coming from Shea. His skin glistened with sweat in the light from the living room as his body twitched. A quiet moan slipped from him as he became more agitated.

He woke himself up a few moments later and was temporarily disoriented, but then calmed when he saw my face. I put my hand on his forehead, which was surprisingly hot. "I'll be right back, Shea. I'm going to find a thermometer."

I was rooting around in one of the drawers in my bathroom when Shea burst in and dropped to his knees, then emptied the contents of his stomach into the toilet. His retching went on and on until he was just dry-heaving. Finally he fell back onto the tile floor, panting and shaking. "Oh God, I'm so sick," he mumbled.

I wet a washcloth with one hand as I flushed the toilet with my other, then knelt beside him and cradled his head as I gently washed his face. "Want to try to get back in bed, baby?" I asked him.

He shook his head no. "I feel like I could throw up again at any moment."

I pulled a clean towel off the rack and folded it into a little square, then put it under his head as a makeshift pillow before getting up to look for the thermometer. When I found it, I slid it under his tongue and caressed his damp forehead until it beeped. "One-oh-two," I told him. "How'd you get sick so fast? You were only at your workplace a few hours ago."

"This is something different," he murmured. "The flu going around the station is all respiratory. Bad cough, not vomiting. Oh God!" He lurched back up and threw up in the toilet again.

He was trembling when he laid back down on the cold tile floor and curled up in a fetal position, arms wrapped around his stomach. His body was covered in goose bumps. I retrieved a pillow and the comforter from my bed, along with a spare blanket from my closet and made him a little nest on the bathroom floor. Then I knelt beside him and said, "Some people want to be left alone when they're sick. What about you?"

Shea reached out to me feebly and I carefully drew him into my arms as I stretched out beside him. He curled up against my chest, shaking with chills, and I pulled the blanket up over his shoulders. After a while he whispered through chattering teeth, "You should go back to bed. You must be so uncomfortable."

"I'm not going to leave you here on the floor, baby, I'm going to stay and make sure you're okay. If you get tired of being held, just say the word and I'll scoot over and sit by the tub." He hugged me tighter.

*****

Shea was violently ill all the next day and called in to work, apologizing profusely for not being able to come in (all while being so sick he could barely talk). When the vomiting had leveled out a bit, I'd moved him to the bed with a trash can close by. He couldn't even hold down water at first, so I brought him ice chips to suck on, just so he wouldn't become completely dehydrated.

That evening, he still had a fever and was incredibly weak. I even had to help him to the bathroom. But he'd begun holding down water at least, and managed to nap on and off. I sat beside him, propped up against the headboard, and read to him from my Kindle between naps because he found it soothing. I'd selected a short story collection by Ray Bradbury, something I'd loved in high school.

I held Shea's hand and his other one snaked out from under the covers and absently stroked my bare knee. I'd pulled on a pair of gym shorts and an old sweatshirt at some point, and had helped Shea into a pair of sweats, some socks and an oversized t-shirt of mine to try to make him comfortable. He was so pale, his eyes underscored with dark circles, his hair spiky with sweat. It hurt to see him this way.

When I finished one of the stories, I asked him, "Do you want to try to eat something, baby? Some crackers, maybe? Or I could make some soup if you feel up to it."

He shook his head, his voice weak when he said, "I can't. Not yet. My stomach seizes up when I even think about food."

"Okay. Tell me when you think you want to give it a shot. Do you want another story?"

"Yes please," he murmured. I flipped a page with the tip of my index finger and started reading aloud again.

A few minutes later a chime went off, so I set aside my ereader and retrieved Shea's phone from the pocket of his uniform. His hands were shaking as he looked at the screen. "It's Cas, could you let him know what's going on?"

"Of course." I sent a text telling them where he was and started to put the phone on the nightstand, but picked it up again to read the almost immediate reply. Cas had written: *Oh noooooo! Feel better soon, Shea! Let us know if you want us to bring you anything. Hugs!*

"Do you want anything from home?" I asked him, but he shook his head.

"I have everything I need right here." He gave me a weak smile.

"You look tired, baby. Why don't you take another nap?" He nodded and shut his eyes, and I turned off the lamp on the nightstand, then stroked his hair until he fell asleep.

A while later, I was startled by loud knocking on the front door. I glanced at Shea, but he was still out. I was surprised to find his brother Finn in the hallway. I also wondered how he'd gotten into the building, since guests were supposed to enter a security code at the main door. "Where's my brother?" he snapped in lieu of a greeting.

"He's napping," I said. "Keep your voice down."

"I want to see him."

"How'd you know where he was?"

"His roommate texted me," Finn said. "Now are you going to let me in, or what?"

"No. I just said he's sleeping."

"Doesn't matter. He's coming home with me."

"Like hell he is! He's really sick!"

"Well he sure as hell isn't staying here with you!"

I squared my shoulders and glared at him. "Look, asshole, I know I'm not your favorite person, but don't take that shit out on your brother. He spent all last night throwing up, and his fever keeps coming and going. Dragging him out of bed just to spite me isn't going to do him any favors."

He narrowed his eyes. "I don't trust you to take care of my brother. I don't trust you at all, because you're a liar and a user."

"I'm neither of those things. Your friend Sam knew the score this summer, I never lied to him or led him on. I know you're not going to believe me, but it's still the truth."

"What's your name?"

I knit my brows. "Christian George."

He smirked at me. "Bullshit! I looked you up, there's no record of anyone with that name. You're a total fraud."

"You looked me up? What the fuck!"

"Let me see some ID."

"Hell no!"

"That's what I thought, a fraud and a liar. I'm getting my brother out of here." He made a move to step around me and I jumped in front of him. "Get out of my way, Christian. Or whatever your name is."

"You're not dragging Shea out of bed and into the cold night air. I won't let you!"

"How do you think you're going to stop me?" he sneered.

I hit him with a level glare. "I'd be happy to show you."

"You get that I'm a police officer, right? You lay one finger on me and I'll arrest you so fucking fast it'll make your head spin!"

"And you get that you're trying to enter my apartment illegally, right? I'll have your ass thrown in jail for that."

"Good fucking luck," he growled.

A shaky voice behind me said, "Knock it off, Finn."

I rushed to Shea's side as he leaned on the bedroom's doorframe and put an arm around him. "Sorry we woke you, baby. Come on, let's get you back to bed."

"He's coming with me," his brother insisted, marching up to us and obviously trying to intimidate me with his size as he puffed up his chest.

I stared at him and said, "What the hell are you going to do, tug on him like a wishbone? Go home, Nolan. Your brother needs to rest."

"I'm staying with Christian," Shea said, and we turned our backs on Finn as I helped him back to bed.

"Don't trust that guy, Shea! Have you forgotten what he did to Sammy?"

"Nothing," Shea said. "He did nothing to Sam. He told him not to get attached, and Sam did anyway. He never lied to him."

"But he *is* a liar, Shea. Christian George isn't even his real name!" Finn exclaimed. "I don't know what angle he's working, but I know he's not who he says he is!"

Shea dropped wearily onto the mattress and shot his brother a look. "You're being such a tool right now."

Finn changed his approach. "Come on, Shea." His tone was imploring. "Come home with me. If you're this sick you need to be with family, not with some sleazebag you picked up in a bar." I rolled my eyes at that.

Shea laid down and said as I pulled the blanket over him, "I need to be with my *boyfriend*. Thanks for your concern, Finn, but you're completely off base. Now please go home. This has all been exhausting."

Finn hesitated for a long moment, then told his brother, "I'm going to check on you in the morning. Be sure you answer your phone, or else I'm coming back here." To me he said, "This isn't over, asshole." Then he turned and stormed out of the apartment.

I got under the covers with Shea and took him in my arms as I asked, "Was your brother adopted? Raised by a pack of wild boar, maybe, before being poorly integrated into society?"

He grinned at that, his eyelids heavy. "He's overcompensating."

"Tiny penis?"

That got a hoarse chuckle from him. "I mean he wants to make up for the fact that my parents have passive-aggressively disowned me. He's trying to be my whole family now, but he doesn't know how to go about it."

"He really doesn't."

As I rubbed Shea's back gently he murmured, "You're totally going to catch this virus. I feel so bad for exposing you to all these germs."

"I don't care. All that matters is taking care of you."

He snuggled against my chest and murmured, "You're so sweet. Just the kindest person. My brother's so wrong about you."

"Not about everything," I said. "George is my middle name, I don't use my last name."

"Why not?" His eyes were closed, and he rubbed his forehead against me.

"Because my dad's a famous singer and I don't want people to make the connection." I wanted to be truthful, but figured that was vague enough.

Shea opened his eyes and looked up at me with a lopsided smile. The poor thing still looked so pale. "How famous? Are we talking Bowie? Hendrix? Tillane?"

I tried to play it off, even though that had startled the hell out of me, and joked, "I do bear an uncanny resemblance to Jimi Hendrix."

Even while virus-riddled, he was still observant as hell. "Wait. Did I guess it? Is your dad Zan Tillane?" There really was no such thing as a poker face around him.

"Please don't say anything, okay? I'm sure you can imagine the media frenzy that would erupt if people found out I was Zan's son. I've always been afraid that the paparazzi would track him down through me somehow, and that's the last thing he needs."

"There are all those stories, from him committing suicide to getting in debt to the mob and being buried next to Hoffa. I can think of at least a dozen different urban legends about his disappearance."

"The truth is, he's a recluse with a lot of problems." I sighed and added, "He was in pretty bad shape Sunday. Sometimes he's great, other times, he's just a wreck. I never know what I'm going to walk into."

"That must be hard."

"He's just so stubborn. Medication would help with his bipolar disorder, but he refuses to take it."

"Why?"

"Because he says he doesn't feel like himself when he's medicated. He hates the lows, but I think he hates missing out on the highs even more."

"That's so unfair to you and his other caregivers."

"There are no other caregivers, just me."

"Oh wow," he murmured.

"I mean, I get it, though. Yeah, it's hard on me, but I remember what it was like when he was drugged up. He was just sort of...there. It was like he didn't really feel anything. I don't know, maybe he didn't give the meds enough of a chance. Maybe he would have learned to adapt to them or the doctors could have worked on finding the right dosage for him or something. But now, well, he and I just sort of deal with it."

Shea reached up and touched my cheek, sympathy in his eyes. "Your secret's safe with me. I promise."

"I know. I really do trust you, Shea." I kissed his forehead, which felt warm. "Shit, I think your fever's coming back again."

He nodded and said, "This thing isn't done with me yet."

*****

It turned out that brief reprieve was just the eye of the storm. Shea spent the next night and day either throwing up, burning up, or both. He told his brother he was fine though, so at least Finn left us alone. I caught the bug too but wasn't nearly as sick as Shea, so I was able to keep taking care of him.

Chance checked in at one point, and when he found out we were ill, he brought us groceries, stuff like tea and crackers and soup, the few things we could tolerate. I had him leave them outside the door so he wouldn't catch what we had. I called and checked on my dad too, and was pleasantly surprised when he actually answered the phone. He seemed down, but not as bad as he'd been on Sunday and said he was fine with me missing our mid-week visit. "But I'll be there Saturday," I told him.

"Don't push it, not if you're sick," Zan said.

"I won't come if I think I'm still contagious, but I really hope I can make it."

"Why?"

"Because it's Christmas."

"Oh." He sounded surprised. "I forgot that it's December."

*****

By Thursday, Shea and I both turned a corner. I still felt shaky, but I could entertain the idea of eating without instantly feeling nauseous, so that was progress. I got up and showered and put on clean clothes, then went to help Shea. He was still really weak, but his stomach had settled and his fever had been gone for a while now. Some color was even returning to his complexion, which had gone almost grey for a while there.

I filled the tub and bathed him gently, then helped him put on some clean sweats and a t-shirt. After I combed his hair for him and he brushed his teeth, I guided him to the living room and tucked him in on the couch, then stripped the bed and washed the sweat-soaked linens in the little laundry closet off the kitchen.

I returned to the living room and knelt beside him, stroking his damp hair as I asked, "Can I bring you anything, baby?"

"No thanks. Just come here." He slid back and made room for me on the couch, and I stretched out on my side beside him as he pulled the blanket over me.

"You look so tired. You've barely slept the last few days," he said softly.

"It's okay."

He put his arms around me. "You've been amazing, Christian. Even when you got sick too, you took such good care of me. I can't even begin to tell you how much I appreciate all you did."

"It's no big deal. That's just what you do for people you care about."

"Not everyone would do what you did. You could have sent me home with Finn right at the beginning and saved yourself days of grief."

"No chance. I wanted to take care of you."

Shea smiled at me. "That's because you're sweet."

"Shhh."

I kissed him and he chuckled. "You can't silence me that easily. I know you hate taking compliments, but tough. You're a sweet, kind, wonderful guy, Christian. Deal with it."

"Right back at you."

"Now that I'm back among the lucid and showered, I'm embarrassed that you had to see me that sick. Talk about being at my worst."

"I don't care about that at all, Shea. The only thing that matters is that you're feeling better now."

"That virus was something else. I don't recall ever being quite that ill."

"But hey, at least you're over it in time for Christmas. You can still do whatever you had planned."

"I was supposed to go to my cousin Jamie's Christmas Eve party tomorrow night after I got off work, but I doubt I'll feel up for it. I was going to ask you to be my date, by the way. Saturday I'm working a double shift and I don't plan to miss that."

"You're working a double shift on Christmas? How come?"

"A lot of the men and women I work with have kids. They need the day off a lot more than I do."

"What about your roommates, what are they up to?"

"They're probably already on the road. They go down to Leo's parents' house in Orange County every year. On Christmas Eve, they have a giant lasagna feast with about thirty relatives. Then on Christmas after they open presents, the whole family goes to Disneyland."

I raised an eyebrow at that. "Disneyland is open on Christmas?"

"Yeah, and it's packed. They love it, though."

"Do you ever go along?"

"I went one year, but usually I'm working."

"You know, it's really not fair that you always end up working on the holiday, just because other people have kids."

"I don't mind it that much, especially now. I'm not welcome at my parents' house anyway. It would have been nice to see my relatives on Christmas Eve, but that's okay, too. I did just spend a week at sea with an awful lot of them," he said.

"Well, maybe by tomorrow night you'll feel well enough to go."

He grinned at that. "Brushing my teeth almost wiped me out, so it's pretty doubtful."

Chapter Fourteen

After sleeping most of Thursday, I was pretty much back to normal by Friday. Shea was really weak, but he still wanted to go to work. "I just sit behind a desk. It's not that strenuous," he told me when I tried to talk him out of it.

"There's no way," I said. "You're just not well enough yet." My point was made for me when he got tired halfway through trying to put on his pants and needed to lay down for a couple minutes.

"Maybe you're right," he finally conceded. I handed him his phone and some sweats, then sent a couple messages of my own. I texted Skye, Dare, and Chance, asking if they wanted to drop by in the evening for a little Christmas Eve get-together. We were past the point of being contagious and I figured Shea should still have some fun, even if he couldn't really go anywhere.

Nana dropped by in the afternoon, wearing a Santa hat and a red dress with white trim that made her look like a tiny Mrs. Claus. She gave me a highly flammable rum-inundated fruitcake and made a fuss over us when I told her we'd been sick. I had to assure her we were fine repeatedly before she finally believed me and stopped trying to dial 911. "Merry Christmas, boys," she said before continuing on her rounds. "You make sure you eat up all that fruitcake now. It'll cure whatever ails you."

Around six, Skye and Dare arrived along with Skye's brother River and his boyfriend Cole. All of them were bearing shopping bags. "You two just relax," River told us. "We know you've both been little sickies, so let us handle the food and libations."

"And decorations," Skye added, unpacking some twinkle lights and sparkly garland. Cole and Dare helped him quickly festoon my apartment while River made some appetizers.

Chance got there a few minutes later. "Thank you for inviting me," he said as he gave me a hug. "I'm so glad you're feeling better."

"The question now," Skye said, "is whether you're feeling well enough for cocktails."

Shea and I declined, opting for gingerale instead, but we encouraged them to go drink up. Skye mixed up a big batch of something really pink, then poured drinks for everyone else and added an elaborate pineapple-and-plastic-palm-tree garnish to each glass. When he handed one of the drinks to Chance, my friend asked. "Thanks. What is it?"

"A Big Fucking Cock," Skye told him.

Chance laughed at that. "Well hell, who doesn't want one of those?" he said before taking a sip. Apparently he liked it, because he then drank down half of it.

Skye said, "Whoa there, bud. I know. People always get excited when they get their first taste of Big Fucking Cock. But trust me, you want to take it nice and slow." They both grinned delightedly and Dare chuckled.

"So, you decided not to go up to your mom's?" I asked Skye as he squeezed in beside me on the couch.

"We were all set to," he told me. "River and Cole were going to go with us. Mom caught some kind of respiratory thing from her boyfriend's kid though, and since the doctor already has her on bed rest, we all decided a visit might be a bit much right now."

"Sorry your plans fell through."

"It's alright," Skye said. "No one's without family as long as Nana's around. She invited us to the Dombruso Christmas Extravaganza at a restaurant owned by one of her relatives. Are you going?"

"She invited me, but I already had plans."

"Well, when you get done with whatever you're doing, you should come by," Skye said. "There's always room for more at a Nana Extravaganza. You too, Shea and Chance, if you don't have family stuff all day."

"Thanks, but I'm working tomorrow," Shea said.

"No you're not. You're resting," I told him.

"I'll rest at my desk at work." I rolled my eyes at that and he added, "How about if we just see how I am in the morning?"

"Fine." I turned to Chance and said, "What about you? What are you doing for Christmas?"

"I'm spending the day with friends," he said. "We do a special celebration every year."

"Cheers to that," I said, raising my gingerale.

About two hours into our impromptu shindig, Shea fell asleep on the couch. He looked so cute curled up in a little ball against the armrest. I pulled the blanket up and tucked it around him, then lightly brushed back his soft hair before turning to my friends.

Skye was beaming at me. "Wow," he said.

"What?"

"I've never seen you like this."

"Like what?"

"You know," he said. "You're so...what's the word, Dare?"

"Nurturing? Doting? Madly in love? The last one is more of a phrase," Dare said with a grin, "but it still seems to apply."

"He just needed someone to take care of him this week. I liked doing it."

My friends took off soon after so Shea and I could get some rest. They left behind the garlands and twinkle lights. Chance was the last to leave. He said as he lingered in the doorway, "Talk to you soon, okay?"

"For sure. I'm off from school until well after New Year's. Maybe you can come with me and help scout a location for a new mural."

"I saw what happened to the girl in the field of daisies," he said. "It broke my heart."

"Mine too actually, even though I know better than to get too attached."

"Are you going to repaint her?"

"No. Seeing what was done to her just kind of killed it for me."

When he hugged me goodbye, I was once again struck by how fragile his thin body felt. I planted a kiss on the side of his head and said, "You take care of yourself, Chance. I hope you have a great Christmas with your friends. I have a present for you, by the way, but since I got sick I haven't had a chance to pull it all together."

"I have one for you too, but I'm still finishing it up. I don't have a good excuse like being sick, it's just taking longer than I expected."

After Chance left, I curled up on the couch with my boyfriend and watched him as he slept. Dare was absolutely right. I couldn't pinpoint the exact moment I'd fallen in love with Shea Nolan. I'd been wildly attracted to him right from the start, but somewhere along the line, that had deepened, strengthened. I loved him so much. He was exactly the right guy, at exactly the wrong time.

Well, then again, our timing could have been even worse. What if I'd met him in June, right before I took off? Hell, what if I'd never met him at all? I was trying to look on the bright side. At least we had six months together. I should be so grateful for that.

Shea stirred, then opened his eyes and sat up, blinking at his surroundings. "Oh," he murmured, "the party's over."

I got up and took his hand, helping him to his feet. "Yup. It was fun while it lasted, though. Come on, baby. Let's go to bed."

Chapter Fifteen

Shea felt quite a bit better on Christmas morning, so he showered and put on his uniform. I thought he should still be resting, but he was adamant about going to work so no one would have to cover his shifts. We held each other for a long time, standing at the front door to my apartment. Then I said, "Oh, wait." I jogged to my bedroom closet and came back with a coat that I thought might fit him. "It's cold out and you forgot yours at work."

"Thanks," he said with a smile as he pulled it on. "Taking care of me right to the end."

I kissed him and said, "Please try to take it easy today."

"I'll do my best, and I'll call you when I get off work. Maybe we can do a late holiday celebration."

"You'll probably be way too tired after working a double shift," I said, caressing his cheek.

"No I won't. I'll see you later."

"Okay. Merry Christmas, baby."

He kissed and hugged me again, holding me for another long moment. "Merry Christmas, sweetheart. I'll talk to you in a few hours." I nodded and made myself let go of him. He looked back at me as he left the apartment, and I offered him a little wave.

After I closed the door behind him, I sighed and trudged to the shower. In the spirit of Christmas, I'd decided to accept the olive branch and was going to have brunch with my mom and stepdad. I wasn't looking forward to it, but I knew it was time to let go of that anger.

Once I was cleaned up and dressed, I picked up a stack of boxes that was just inside my front door and carried them to my dining table. I tore them open and sorted the presents into groups based on recipient. I'd managed to do some online shopping early in the week, right before I got sick, and thought I'd done pretty well, all things considered. I pulled out the fancy Belgian chocolates for my mom and some snobby imported cigars for my stepdad and set them aside.

Next I checked out the present I'd gotten Shea on eBay. It was a vintage Captain America comic book. I knew nothing about comics, but this one had come with an insane sticker price, so I assumed it was probably a good one.

My Dad's gifts had come in two boxes from Amazon, so I combined them into one. Not exactly festive holiday wrapping, but he wouldn't care. Skye and Dare's present was in a thin envelope among the boxes. It was a gift certificate for a romantic night on the bay in a private, chartered sailboat, complete with catered dinner and an onboard couples massage. I'd been so stupid about their relationship at first, so now I was trying to make amends.

Lastly, I sorted out Chance's gift and packed it into its new, cushioned case. I knew he'd balk at the extravagance of this gift, but I didn't care because I really wanted him to have it. I'd bought him a new camera and equipment from an online specialty shop. I didn't know if I'd selected the right things, even though the shop owner had been really helpful in advising me, but I was assured Chance could exchange it if he needed to. I'd gotten him a top-of-the-line DSLR camera and several lenses, along with the aforementioned case, extra rechargeable batteries, and a few miscellaneous odds and ends that the shop owner recommended.

Yeah, it was a bit much. But the fact was, I could afford it. I was uniquely lucky as the kid of a pop star in that I'd never had to worry about money. I didn't feel right about abusing my father's generosity, so I usually kept my spending in check. But I did have a healthy bank account that was automatically replenished every month regardless of whether or not I spent any of it, so this gift was well within my means.

Knowing Chance, he was probably going to try to turn it down and say it was too much, but I was determined that he have this. I hoped it would help him transition to a better life. I also just hoped it made him happy, because he needed that.

*****

I didn't stay long at my mom and stepdad's. They tried too hard and were way too nice to me, and it really freaked me out. I picked at my breakfast, then snuck a look at them over my glass of orange juice. Whenever they noticed me looking at them, I got these huge, ridiculous smiles, so it was kind of like a solar eclipse. You could watch it as long as you didn't look directly at it.

My mom was carefully made up and nicely dressed, just like always, her long blonde hair framing her face. She was still a beautiful woman. If anything, she'd become even more attractive as she aged, not that she felt that way. My stepdad wasn't aging nearly as well. His boyish good looks, the thing that had probably drawn my mother to him in the first place, were now an odd fit on a man of fifty.

They'd both color-coordinated to their surroundings. I wondered if that had been intentional. We were in the formal dining room of the upper-middle-class home they'd purchased a couple years ago in Burlingame, just a few minutes south of the city. It was professionally decorated in shades of pale blue, white, and yellow, and both of them were dressed accordingly. The house, like everything else they owned, was paid for by Zan. He'd given my mom a huge child support check every month when I was growing up, and hadn't cut her off to this day.

"So, Christian," my stepfather said, making yet another attempt at conversation. I looked up at him and was blinded by a way too enthusiastic smile. "How's your spray painting going?"

"Now Hal," my mother chimed in. "He doesn't do *spray painting*. He's a graffiti artist, just like that handsome black man in that movie we watched, remember?" I fought back an eye roll. They'd rented the film 'Basquiat' at some point and were forever trying to draw on it to show they were 'hip' to my lifestyle.

"It's going like it always does. I paint, the police chase me away, and other people come along and fuck up what I've done." Okay, that had come out a bit surly. I needed to try harder. I flailed around for something to say to him, but all I came up with was, "So, how's that whole sobriety thing working out?"

That had sounded pretty insincere, despite my best efforts at playing nice. They didn't seem to notice. They both went on for about fifteen minutes, enthusiastically praising Harold's sponsor and the program, and my mom gushed about how well her husband was doing.

Finally, the meal was over and I pushed back from the table. "Thanks for brunch. I'd better get going, Zan is expecting me."

"How's he doing?" My mom tried to keep her tone light as we headed for the front door, but I suspected she'd never really gotten over Zan Tillane. I glanced at Harold. His expression was the same every time my father's name came up: slightly pained. It had to be a bit hard on him, forever living in the shadow of a man as handsome, rich and successful as Zan, not to mention emasculating to realize everything he had was paid for by his wife's former, famous lover. Then again, Harold had certainly never made the slightest effort to earn his own income and turn down the fat checks that appeared in his mailbox each month.

"He's doing fine. Same as ever," I said. They knew what had been happening with Zan these past few years and kept his secret, even though they probably could have made a mint selling my dad out to the paparazzi, or hell, publishing a pretty scandalous tell-all biography. They might be freeloaders, but these two did have some scruples.

"Oh," my mom exclaimed, "your gift!" She rushed off, then returned a few moments later and handed me a slim, beautifully wrapped package. I'd given them their gifts as soon as I'd arrived.

Under the thick, embossed wrapping paper was a copy of what had been my favorite book as a kid, A Wrinkle in

Time. "It's a first edition, signed by the author," she told me. "I remembered how much you loved that book."

The prickle of tears behind my eyes startled me. "It's really great, mom. Thanks." I gave her a quick hug. "Merry Christmas, both of you."

As I opened the heavy front door, she said, "Merry Christmas sweetie, thanks for coming by. We'd really love to see more of you. Maybe we can get together in the new year."

I turned to look at her. There was so much hope in her eyes, and I felt bad for the way I'd been keeping her at a distance. "Sure. Maybe we can all go out to dinner. I'll bring my boyfriend."

"Oh, you have a boyfriend! Well, we'd love to meet him!" My sexual orientation had never been an issue with my mom. My stepdad had been a little uncomfortable with it when I first came out to them, but I didn't really care.

"Alright. Well, see you soon," I said as I stepped outside.

As I left Burlingame and made the drive to Marin, I decided that the visit had gone pretty well, all things considered. It was awkward being around my stepdad, but I hadn't felt as much anger as I usually did. Maybe he really had changed and this sobriety thing was going to stick. I really hoped so, for my mom's sake.

I glanced at the book on my passenger seat and ran a fingertip over the cover. That had been quite thoughtful. The gift said a lot, too. My mom and I hadn't been close these last few years so she had little concept of who I was now. The book was for the Christian she remembered, the boy I used to be. That made me sad somehow, but I pushed it down and tried to concentrate on the road.

Zan was kind of middling when I got to his house, not real happy, but not particularly depressed, either. He did seem pleased to see me though, and greeted me with a hug. "How are you feeling?" he asked.

"Better, and so is Shea. Mostly. He went to work today, which I didn't approve of. He's going to get so tired. But the guy's a saint, he didn't want his coworkers to miss Christmas with their families."

"So, things are going well with the irresistible Irishman, I take it." My dad grinned at me as we settled onto the couch.

"Yeah, they really are." I'd already told him about running into Shea on the cruise, followed by a week of nursing him back to health in my apartment.

"I'm glad you took my advice and decided to give yourself and him those six months," he said.

"I wonder if there's enough alcohol in all the world to deaden the pain of leaving him in June, though." I ran my thumbnail along the edge of the cardboard box in my lap, studying the crease it made.

"Shite. You've fallen hard for him, haven't you? I expected you to just keep it light, have some fun. But that's not what's happening here, is it?"

"I love him, Zan. I had every intention of just keeping this casual, but that fell apart so damn fast."

"Aw, boyo," he said, giving my shoulders a squeeze. "I suppose we don't get to choose when that happens, ay?"

A thought occurred to me, and I asked, "Have you ever been in love?"

He considered the question for a few moments, then said, "I thought I was, many a time. Looking back now though, maybe that wasn't love at all. Maybe it was all these other things, like lust, or attraction, or infatuation. The only person I've ever really, truly loved is you, but have I ever been in love? Nah, I don't think so. I came close with your mother. That was so passionate and intense, but it burned out like a meteor entering the atmosphere. I don't think love just burns out like that." My dad glanced at me with a wry smile. "A bit ironic, isn't it? I got famous singing songs about love, but I guess your old man's a bit of a fraud. It was stuff I knew nothing about."

"Well, you faked it really well," I told him with a grin.

He chuckled at that. "I suppose I did. Had 'em all fooled pretty good." Zan changed the subject by knocking on the box I was holding. "So, what did you bring for your old dad?"

"Well, I'd been thinking about what to get you for months. What does one get an internationally renowned superstar recluse, who also happens to be your father?" He smiled at me and I said, "You know what? I still have no clue. But it did occur to me that you missed out on something pretty special over the last few years, so I'm helping you catch up on it." I pried open the flaps of the box and handed him one of the seven books it contained.

"Ah, Harry Potter," he said, flipping the book over to read the back. "You mentioned this. It was quite the phenomenon, yes?"

"Still is."

"Isn't it meant for children?"

"Don't question, just enjoy it. And once you finish reading the books, I'll join you for the movie marathon." I handed him the 8-DVD box set I'd bought him.

"I look forward to this. Thanks, Christian."

"I really hope you like it."

"I'm sure I will." He turned to the first page of the book he was holding and started reading, but I plucked it out of his hand.

"That's number six. You have to read them in order, it's important."

"Alright, if you insist."

"I do." I swapped out the book with the first in the series. Then I ventured as I put the box on the floor and he read the back cover, "So, when we do our movie marathon, how would you feel about Shea joining us?"

That earned me a huge smile. He put the book on the top of his to-be-read pile beside the couch and said, "Really? You want your boyfriend to meet your old man? Even if I am a daft bugger? I'd love the opportunity to meet him, of course."

"I'd like him to meet you, too. I wasn't going to tell him about you, at least not right away. I don't exactly talk about you, for obvious reasons. But I trust him to keep this quiet."

"I know you've always been really concerned about my privacy, and I thank you for that, son. But you don't think anyone still cares about old Zan Tillane, do you?"

I shook my head at that as I pulled out my phone, then searched his name and showed him the screen. Google claimed there were over sixty-five million entries, not that that was accurate, but still. The top three listed a recent TV special about his disappearance, yet another best-of album being released by his former label, and an article about casting a big-screen film of his life. "They've been talking about making that movie for a few years now," I told him. "I assume your lawyer mentioned it to you."

"Yeah. I don't care about it one way or another, though. Whether or not I tried to have any say in it, they'd just go ahead and make the movie they wanted. Whatever salacious drivel sells the most tickets, no doubt."

I put the phone away and said, "So, no. No one's forgotten you, Zan, not by a long shot. In fact, the longer you stay hidden, the more myths and rumors spring up."

"Well, then it's a damn good thing I'm completely cracked," he said lightly. "Sounds like I couldn't venture back out into the world even if I wanted to, not with a media circus out there waiting for me."

"Do you ever think about that? Leaving here, I mean? I guess I've never really been clear on how much staying here is a conscious decision."

"Honestly? I don't know anymore, either. It was definitely intentional at first. I was done with the world and everything in it, present company being the one and only exception. But then a year went by, and another, and another...and now, I don't know. I can't imagine a life other than this, honestly. I like it here. I have my books and my movies and my piano. And you, of course." The unspoken part of that was, *for now*. Before we both became melancholy, Zan exclaimed, "Let's have you open your present!"

"You got me a present? How? Did you make it out of stuff you found in the backyard?"

He grinned at that. "Wish I'd thought of that! I could have fashioned you a bunch of little Blair Witch dolls from the twigs that blow up onto the deck." He'd seen that movie for the first time last month. "That would have been a lot easier to complete by Christmas. But instead, I got you this." He reached under the couch and pulled out a thick manila envelope, which he handed to me.

I flashed him a big smile. "You got me paperwork! Bless your heart!"

"Just open it, smartass." He looked at me with the same eager expression that my mom had when she'd given me the book.

I unwound the little string holding the envelope shut and pulled out a thick legal document. "What am I looking at here?"

"A deed to a building."

"Wait, you're giving me a building?" I asked as I scanned the form in my hand.

"I am."

"Why?"

"Because I'm bloody well sick of people painting over your artwork, so I bought you a canvas. It's been in the works for nearly a year. My lawyer hired people, they got the place all renovated and up to code so apparently it's quite spiffy now. What you want to do with the interior is up to you. I have a couple ideas, but it's your call, of

course. The main thing is that it's one great, big canvas!"
He took the envelope from me and tilted it into his hand.
Three photos slid out, along with a set of keys on an ornate
metal fob. "See?"

I put the deed on my lap and took the keys and
pictures. The building looked enormous. I realized it
seemed a bit familiar, too. "Where is this?"

"In the city, in the South of Market district or whatever
you call it."

"SOMA."

"Yeah, that."

"This is unbelievable, Zan. You didn't have to do this
for me. It must have been incredibly expensive," I
murmured.

"Well, I can bloody well afford it, now can't I?"

I studied each of the photos carefully. The grey
concrete building was basically one huge, four story cube,
the second and third floors rimmed by glass balconies. It
was, in fact, a perfect blank canvas.

"I know you're a big fan of the clandestine nature of
your art," he was saying. "Sneaking around at night,
evading the coppers, I get that that's part of the appeal. I
figure you can still sneak around at night though as you
paint this building, even though no one can arrest you for it.
Not with you being the owner and all. You may be losing
the thrill, but in return you're gaining a canvas that's all

yours, one that no one's going to knock down or paint over. I even had my lawyer file all the permits with the city to clear the way for the whole thing to become one huge mural. But like I said, you can still turn it into a covert operation if you want to."

"I don't know what to say."

"Do you like it? I really hope that you do."

I grabbed him in a hug as I stammered, "I love it. I'm overwhelmed. This is absolutely amazing, thank you."

"Oh good. I had my doubts about how this would go over."

"So, what were your ideas about the inside of the building?" I said as I let go of him and looked at the photos again.

"Well, I thought maybe if you wanted to, you could call it the Christian George Tillane Center for the Arts, and bring in people to run an art-based community center. I've always seen your artwork as a form of activism. You slip in all these messages of hope and community, so I thought you might like it if there was a place to teach kids to paint and express themselves the way you do. If you happened to want to include a music curriculum in honor of your old man, I'd donate the instruments. But of course, this is all just a thought. You can do whatever you want with it."

"I love that idea. I don't know about putting my full name on the building though, for obvious reasons." I pulled my keys from the pocket of my jeans so I could add the new ones to my key ring, and that was when I took a good look at the fob in my hand. "Oh my God," I murmured.

Throughout Zan's career, he'd always worn the same pendant on a leather cord around his neck. It appeared in every single photo of him back then. He'd called it his good luck charm. It was an antique, brass symbol a little more than an inch square, which he'd picked up in Tibet. He stopped wearing it when he quit performing. I always wondered what had happened to it but had never thought to ask.

I grabbed him in another hug and whispered as my voice broke, "Thanks, Dad."

"Aw, hell." I could feel his chuckle more than I heard it. "So all I had to do was give you a trinket. You're more into that than you are the entire sodding building!"

"Not true," I said, sitting back and dabbing my eyes with the sleeve of my grey cotton sweater. "I'm really into the sodding building, too." I smiled at him as I held up the charm. "This though, this is a piece of you, so I love it."

"Ah shite," my father said, his green eyes going a bit bright. "Quit that, you're going to make me start blubbering."

"Hey, do what you have to do. I'm not judging."

He pulled me close with a hand on the back on my neck and planted a kiss on my forehead. "You're a good kid, Christian. I don't say it enough, but you've always made me proud. Without a doubt, you're the best thing I ever did."

I felt myself getting misty-eyed again and exclaimed, "Oh come on! It's like you're trying to make me cry!"

"Apologies. I'm turning into a sentimental fool in my old age."

"Please. You're not even sort of old. As for the rest of it...." I shot him a big smile. Then I said, "We should name it the Alexzander Tillane Center for the Arts. An art and music-themed community center would be a wonderful use of that building."

"Oh no, absolutely not. We're not naming it after me."

"Why not? Everyone thinks you're dead anyway, so we could just claim it was named in memoriam."

"We could, but we're not going to. That building isn't about me, it's about you: your art, your vision, your message. I've had more than my share of the spotlight, I don't need more. This is your time to shine like the star you were always meant to be."

"Wow," I said with a grin. "Last Christmas we drank whiskey, talked about the weather, and watched all the Indiana Jones movies. What the hell is up with us this year?"

As soon as I said that, I knew the answer. I wouldn't be here next Christmas, so Zan was pulling out all the stops. "You know, we were onto something with the whiskey," I said as I got up and headed to the bar in the corner.

*****

I had lunch and cocktails with my dad as we sat in front of the TV and watched his favorite holiday movies, Die Hard and Die Hard 2. Yeah, Zan wasn't the most traditional guy. It was early evening by the time I headed back into the city. I stopped off at one of my favorite Chinese restaurants, which was always open on Christmas because the family was Buddhist, and placed a huge order.

While the food was cooking, I popped into the liquor store next door (run by a nice Hindu gentleman so it was also open). He did sell a little selection of decorated live Christmas trees in little plastic pots though, and they were now half off. Only three remained and they were a bit on the Charlie Brown side, but I bought them all anyway, along with several bottles of nonalcoholic cider and a package of plastic wine glasses. I then loaded my car with my purchases and the food, which they'd packaged into an empty produce box because there was so much of it, and drove to the station where Shea worked.

I saw him sitting alone behind the front counter as I walked up to the glass doors. His head was bent, his brow knit in concentration. When I got closer, I saw that he was drawing something in a bound sketch book.

He looked up when I pushed the door open with my hip, quickly closed the sketchbook and slipped it under the counter. "Hey! What are you doing here?"

"I brought dinner for you and everyone else that's working today. I also have some fake wine and this." I'd brought in the nicest of the little Christmas trees and placed it beside him on the counter. "Are you going to get in trouble for that?"

He smiled at me as he fished around in a drawer. "No one who'd complain about it is on duty right now." He produced an extension cord and ran it from a wall outlet to the little tree. When it lit up, it turned out all the little round bulbs were orange instead of red.

"Well, that's festive," I said.

"It's cute. They look like tiny, glowing tangerines."

I laughed at that. "Sure. Why not."

There were eight officers and dispatchers on duty, but I'd brought enough food for twenty. We carried the box back to the break room and his coworkers descended on it like a pack of hungry piranhas. Shea filled the glasses with sparkling cider and everyone drank a toast to Christmas before he and I carried a couple of the white takeout containers and our drinks back to the front counter.

"How are you feeling?" I asked as I grabbed a stool and sat across from him. I was out in the empty public reception area so he wouldn't get in trouble if a supervisor showed up.

"Tired, but coping. How about you?"

"Not bad at all." I smiled at him.

We ate our dinner from the takeout boxes as we talked. Shea had his own approach to using the chopsticks, which basically involved spearing the food, then using the second chopstick as a lever to get it to his mouth. It was incredibly cute.

He asked between mouthfuls, "How did the parental visits go?"

"Better than expected." I told him about brunch and the book, then about my visit with my dad and the building. I also showed him the charm on my keychain. "I'm actually as excited about the charm as I am about the huge piece of property I suddenly own in SOMA," I admitted.

"Holy crap," he said, blinking at the little brass square. "Your dad is," he lowered his voice to a whisper, "*Zan Tillane*."

"Yeah, like I said."

"I mean, I heard you when you told me earlier, but it didn't really sink in until just now. He always wore that, I remember it from the cover of one of his albums."

"It *is* a lot to process."

"No kidding." He cantilevered a water chestnut to his mouth and mulled it all over for a few moments before saying, "I used to sit in my room when I was in high school playing his song 'Never to Have You' over and over, whenever I was pining for some guy who didn't know I was alive." Shea looked a bit stricken all of a sudden. "Oh, ew."

"What?"

"I just remembered that I used to have a crush on him when I was about twelve or thirteen. Now he turns out to be your dad! Talk about awkward."

I laughed at that and said, "It doesn't have to be. You got over it, right?"

"Yeah. I became infatuated with Kurt Cobain instead."

"Zan would approve of that. He loved Kurt and was so sad when he died."

"So was I."

"Before I forget," I told him, "I want to take you to my dad's house for a Harry Potter movie marathon sometime next week. He just started the series, but he'll probably be through all seven books in just a few days."

Shea's eyes went wide. "Yikes. I've never met a celebrity in person, talk about starting at the top!"

"There's nothing to worry about. Once you meet him, you'll realize he's just this dorky guy with outdated hair and weird taste in floral-patterned shirts."

"Is it really okay with him that I come visit?"

"Yup. He's looking forward to meeting you."

He chewed on his lower lip for a moment, then said, "I really hope I don't embarrass myself."

"You won't."

"There's at least a fifty-fifty chance of me doing something incredibly clumsy out of sheer nervousness."

"Eh, you'll be fine." I tossed a vegetable in my mouth, then asked as I looked around the station, "Out of curiosity, is the fabulous Finn working tonight?"

"Yeah. He's a patrolman though so he only comes in when he's made an arrest."

"Did he work a double shift, too?"

"No, he spent the day at our parents' house. He came on at five." That made me smile, and he said, "What?"

"You're so totally the better brother."

He chuckled at that. "He's not as bad as he's led you to believe."

"He really is." I popped a shrimp in my mouth before asking, "Is it always this quiet, or do the bad guys take time off at Christmas?"

"It comes and goes in waves. We were really busy earlier, and sadly, we'll be extremely busy tonight."

"How do you know?"

"It happens every year. Domestic violence always increases on holidays."

"Wow, that's terrible. Why is that, do you suppose?"

"A lot of reasons. The holidays are emotionally draining, for one thing. There's a lot of drinking and plenty of stress, which just adds to the mix. Plus, people are home at the holidays, so there's simply more opportunity for an incident to occur."

"Wow, Christmas through the eyes of a police officer. Not terribly cheery, is it?"

"Cheery isn't a word I'd usually use to describe my job."

A huge cop with a crew cut came up to us just then and put down a paper plate with homemade sugar cookies. "I didn't catch your name," he said in a deep voice.

"Christian."

"I'm Duke. Thanks for bringing in that feast, it beat the hell out of the sandwich I'd packed for myself. Thought you guys might like some cookies, I made 'em myself."

"Thanks," I said. "They look really good."

"I called my mom for her recipe, but somehow they don't taste as good as hers. Anyway, Merry Christmas and thanks again."

"You're welcome."

When Duke left, Shea smiled at me. "That's the most I've ever heard him say willingly. Normally, you can barely get more than a one-word answer out of him."

"You should have plied him with Chinese food a lot sooner."

"Apparently. Oh, and that's one of the good aspects of my job, by the way."

"Getting to work with giant men who bake cookies in the shape of tiny Christmas trees?"

Shea smiled at me. "The sense of camaraderie. Granted, everyone's a bit cranky today because they'd rather be home, but still."

We each sampled a cookie. They were surprisingly good. Then I exclaimed, "Oh! I left your Christmas present in the car. Hang on, let me get it."

I dashed out to the Jeep and was back a minute later. His gift was still in the mailing envelope, which I handed to him. "I'm sorry I didn't have time to wrap it."

Shea looked distraught. "I'm so sorry. Your gift isn't done yet."

"You didn't have to get me anything."

"I tried to make you something, actually, but I didn't count on getting completely ill the week before Christmas."

"It's fine, Shea. Honest."

"I'm still planning to finish it, but it looks like it'll be more of an Easter present at the rate I'm going." He dropped his gaze. "It's kind of childish anyway. I should have just bought you something."

"Baby, if it's from you, I'll love it."

"Can I show you a little of it? Then if you don't like it, I can do something else." He reached under the counter and pulled out the sketchbook he'd been working on when I'd first arrived. "I'm trying to draw you a comic book. I figured, since you'd been teaching me to draw, this made sense, but now I'm just worried that it's dumb and amateurish and something a seventh grader would do for his boyfriend." He opened to a page randomly and turned the book to face me. "It's all of those things, isn't it?"

I picked up the book and stared in wonder at the carefully rendered scene. He'd drawn both of us as superheroes and in the page he'd turned to, we were holding each other in a passionate embrace high up in the night sky, San Francisco sprawled out below us. "Oh my God, Shea," I murmured.

"That bad?"

I looked up at him. "This is absolutely wonderful. Not only is it incredibly well done, I'm so touched that you'd do this for me. Thank you. It's the best gift I've ever received."

"Oh come on. Just today, someone gave you a *building*."

"The building was a thoughtful gesture, but this is even more so, because you're making it with your own hands and I can see how hard you're working on it."

He blushed slightly and looked down, then glanced at me through his dark lashes. "Do you really think it's okay?"

"It's so much better than okay. It's spectacular. Can I please look at a bit more of it?"

Shea came around the counter and turned to the beginning of the book. "There are only a few pages. It's taking so much longer than I anticipated, because I'm really trying to do a good job."

He walked me through the start of the comic book. It was the story of two gay men that didn't realize they were extraordinary until they found each other. When they teamed up, they both became much more together than they'd been separately, and that was when their superpowers were revealed. "It's corny, I know," he said.

"Baby, it's *so good*. I'm not just saying that. You need to publish it so other people can enjoy it, too."

"I don't think I'd ever have the courage to do that. Besides, this is just the beginning. When you read the rest of the story, you might decide it's really dumb."

I leaned over and kissed him, since none of his coworkers were in sight. "I know the ending will be just as amazing as the beginning. Thank you so much for doing this."

"You really like it? You're not just being nice?"

"I really love it." He smiled me and closed the sketchbook, then went back behind the counter and put it away. I told him, "Take your time with that. I don't want you to feel pressured to finish by a certain date. I want you to have a good time with it." He was still smiling when I indicated the envelope on the desk. "Open mine. It seems so impersonal after seeing the incredible thing you're doing for me. I hope you like it, though."

"I'm sure I'll love it," he said, and tilted the envelope so its contents slid into his hand. It was upside down, and when he flipped it around, his mouth fell open. "No freaking way," he murmured.

"Is it okay? I have to admit I really don't know the first thing about comic books. I just knew you liked them, and I figured Captain America was one of your favorites since you had three of his posters on your bedroom wall."

"It's...oh my God." He raised a hand and covered his mouth.

"Is it really, really good, or really, really bad? I can't quite tell."

He looked at me with huge eyes as he gingerly placed the comic on the counter. "It's Captain America number one, from 1941. I've wanted this my whole life, ever since I was five years old and discovered comic books. It's my own, personal Holy Grail. But Christian, this is way too expensive. I can't possibly accept it."

"Please don't say that. I really want you to have this, especially now that I know what it means to you."

"Seriously, it must have cost a fortune."

"It wasn't as expensive as you might be assuming. It was listed in very good to fine condition, because there's some wear on the cover. I'm sure you know what that means, but I had to educate myself. I read up on the grading system and found out it's about a five on a scale of point-five to ten. I thought you'd still like it though, even if it isn't perfect."

He grinned at me. "I do know how the grading system works. I've also been following the price of this comic book for the last several years, so I know exactly what you would have paid for it in this condition, assuming you didn't get ripped off."

I shrugged and said, "The seller had excellent ratings on eBay, I doubt he ripped me off."

Shea looked at the comic book and ran a fingertip over the protective plastic cover. "This was so nice of you, Christian. I mean, it really was incredibly thoughtful. But I just wouldn't feel right about accepting it."

"I really want you to have it, though. Please? I hate sounding like a spoiled brat, but honestly, I can afford it. I rarely do anything extravagant with the money my dad gives me, but I just really wanted to do this for you. And why not? I mean, I might as well spend some of my money. It's not like I can take it with me."

That should have been an innocuous statement. It was just a cliché, something people said all the time. But as soon as the words were out of my mouth, I knew I'd slipped up. I tried to cover my reaction, but it was too late. Shea spotted it immediately.

He stared at me as I tried to fix a neutral expression on my face. "What do you mean?" he asked quietly.

"Nothing," I said quickly, trying to backpedal. "It's just, you know, what people say about money."

His voice was low as he pinned me with his gaze. "Christian, what aren't you telling me?"

I felt like everything was falling apart around me and there was nothing I could do to stop it. He was so good at reading my reactions, he'd probably already guessed what I was hiding. I wished I could wind back time just a few seconds and correct my slip-up, but there was no fixing this. There was already pain in his eyes. It was too late. "Oh God, I'm so sorry," I blurted. "I didn't mean to tell you like this, especially on Christmas."

His voice was almost a whisper as he asked, "Tell me what?"

I took a deep breath, hating myself for having made that mistake and for how much I was about to hurt him. But he had to know, I couldn't take it back. Besides, I owed him the truth. I'd owed it to him all along.

"I'm dying, Shea."

Chapter Sixteen

The look on his face was one of sheer devastation. Shea was just frozen there, staring at me, his hands splayed out on the counter. His eyes brimmed over and then tears spilled down his cheeks, while the rest of him remained completely immobile.

Finally he whispered, "You can't be. Please tell me it's not true."

"I wish more than anything that it wasn't."

"Oh God." It came out as a sob.

"I'm so sorry. God, I'm sorry. I didn't mean to do this to you on Christmas," I stammered. He stared at me as he raised a shaking hand to brush away his tears. I added softly, "This is why I told you when we met that we couldn't get involved. I didn't mean to let you get attached to me, but I just couldn't stay away from you." My chest was so tight that it was hard to breathe. "I never, ever wanted to cause you this kind of pain. I'm so incredibly sorry, Shea."

It hurt so much to see the look in his eyes that I turned and fled from the police station. The night had grown cold and windy, my hair whipping in my face. The Jeep was parked in the small visitor lot and I ran to it, then dropped my keys when I took them out of my pocket. I bent to retrieve them and when I stood up, Shea spun me by the shoulders and grabbed me in a fierce embrace. I hadn't heard him follow me.

I burst into tears as he held me. "I'm sorry," I said again, clutching him to me. The words seemed so feeble.

"Please stop apologizing."

That just made me want to apologize again. I buried my face in his shoulder and we held each other for a long time. But after a while I felt him shiver and pulled back to look at him. "You need to go back inside. It's cold out here and you've barely gotten over being sick."

"I don't care."

"Please, Shea? You're also in the middle of your shift."

"Come back inside with me."

"I know you must have a million questions and we need to talk about this, but not in there."

"I need to know what's going on with you."

"I'll tell you everything. But please, not here," I said, pushing my wind-blown hair out of my face. Just then, a police cruiser pulled up at the side of the building and two big cops got out. One of them was Finn. He shot us a look as he went to get someone out of the back of the car.

Shea frowned as he watched his brother and muttered, "I need to go process that arrest." He turned back to me and said, "I'm coming over tonight, the minute my shift is over." I nodded and he hugged me again. When he let go, he paused for a long moment and looked at me, reaching up to touch my hair. There was raw heartbreak in his eyes as he turned and headed back into the building.

I was so miserable as I drove away. Why did I have to let that slip on Christmas, of all days? That was just such incredibly bad timing. Not that there'd ever have been a great time to tell him, but still.

Once I was a couple blocks from the station, I pulled over and just sat there for a while, trying to calm down. I was sick about the hurt I'd caused Shea. I needed to get a grip, though. By the time he came to see me tonight, I needed to be able to talk about this calmly. The last thing I wanted was to upset him more.

Eventually, I put the car in gear and kept driving. The police station was in a dicey part of town, and I had to cut through an even dicier section on the way home. Prostitutes regularly worked this neighborhood, but not many were out this cold Christmas night. A few were though, hunching their shoulders against the sharp wind. I recognized one of them and muttered, "Shit."

As soon as I pulled to the curb, two boys approached me. I rolled my window down and Chance glanced over as they propositioned me. When he recognized me, he hung his head in embarrassment, then walked slowly to the Jeep. I delivered a thanks-but-no-thanks to the boys, both of which were probably barely eighteen, and when Chance reached me I said softly, "Get in the car, Chance." He did as I asked.

He was quiet for a while as I pulled away from the curb and continued down the street. Finally he said, "I like to pretend I'm someone else when I'm with you. I mean, you know what I am, but...I don't know. I feel like you don't just think of me as some rent boy. Maybe that's why it's embarrassing to have you find me like that."

"What happened to the plans you'd made with friends?"

"I lied, I didn't have any plans. It sounded too pathetic to tell you I was going to spend Christmas selling myself. I actually only have two friends, you and Zachary. He's a prostitute too and was booked with a client for the whole weekend."

"What about your mom and brother, didn't you want to spend the holiday with them?"

"They're in Wyoming. Rather than spending money to go see them, I just sent them the cash. They need it more than they need to see me."

"You should have told me, Chance. No one should be alone on Christmas."

"It's just another day," he said, shrugging his slender shoulders. "It's not like we ever really celebrated when I was growing up, so I'm used to it not mattering much."

"Why didn't you celebrate?"

"My mom...I mean, I don't want to totally put her down, but she has a lot of problems. She could never really get it together to celebrate holidays or birthdays or anything like that. Part of it was because money was so tight. You're not going to spend money on a tree when you can barely afford to keep the heat on through the winter. Beyond that though, she was always just too wrapped up in some kind of personal drama to ever really think about doing anything for my brother and me." Chance sighed and looked out the passenger window as I drove us across town. "Whatever, though. It's not the end of the world if you don't celebrate or get any Christmas presents." He was trying so hard to hide the sadness in his voice, but wasn't quite succeeding.

I stopped at a red light and pulled the camera case out from behind his seat. "This year, you did get a present. Merry Christmas, Chance," I said as I put it on his lap.

"What's this?"

"A gift. I was going to come by your apartment tonight and give it to you, but now here you are. I bought it online, so if I got the wrong thing the retailer said you can exchange it. You're not allowed to return it and send the money to your family, though. Sorry, but this one's just for you."

He opened the latch and folded back the cover on the padded case. Then he whispered, "No fucking way."

"Please don't tell me I spent too much," I said as the light changed and I rolled through the intersection. "I just really wanted to do something special this Christmas for both you and Shea." A fresh pang of regret echoed through me as I recalled my earlier slip-up.

"How could you afford this?" he murmured, staring into the case.

"My dad has a lot of money and he gives me an allowance. Basically, your assessment of me when we first met was dead-on, just another over-privileged white boy."

"This is astonishingly generous. Too generous. I can't accept it."

"Oh no. I just had this discussion with Shea and I'm not having it again. Please just indulge me, Chance. I know it's a lot, but I really wanted to do this for you."

"Why?"

"Because you're a good friend, and because I really believe in your talent. You're a gifted photographer and I want you to have the right tools for the job."

He turned his head to look at my profile. "Plus, you want me to stop working as a prostitute."

"I'm not judging, Chance. But in the few weeks I've known you, you've gotten severely injured twice on the job. I know you said that was a fluke and it's not usually that bad, but what kind of a friend would I be if I didn't try to offer you an alternative after witnessing something like that?"

"I really hate being a charity case."

"How are you a charity case?" I asked. "You're an awesome photographer and I believe in supporting the arts. That is *not* charity."

"Damn it," he mumbled.

"What?"

"I feel like crying. I'm such a wuss when I'm around you."

"Whatever. I've lost count of the number of times I teared up today. I always tried to live behind this mask before, pretending everything's fine when it so totally isn't. But you know what? Fuck it. Sometimes we just need to let that shit out."

"What's wrong?"

"Oh no," I said. "We're not talking about my shitty life on Christmas. I accidentally just dropped a huge bomb on Shea when I went to see him at work. No freaking way am I going to do that to you, too."

"That bad?"

"Yeah, it's that bad, but we're not talking about it today. For now, tell me how far off I was with the camera I selected. There were so many choices and I didn't know what the hell I was doing."

He gingerly picked up the box the camera body was in and turned it over in his hands. "It's perfect. Man, I'm afraid to touch it. I've never owned anything even remotely this expensive. If I drop it, I'll pretty much have to kill myself." I smiled, and that brought out a little grin at the corner of his mouth. "My imminent suicide is funny somehow?"

I rolled my eyes at that. "No. But you're accepting the gift! You're thinking of it as yours, so that must mean you're done arguing about trying to get me to take it back. That makes me happy."

"It really was way too much. Also, it's weird to find out you're insanely rich."

"I'm not rich, my dad is."

"Well, I know what this cost, so you're insane either way." He picked up a box containing one of the lenses and said, "This was so nice of you, though. But still insane. It makes the gift I have for you seem like a joke."

"You didn't have to get me anything."

"Oh no. Don't even try to go there after this grand prize lottery winner of a Christmas present!"

"Fine. Not going there."

When we reached his apartment, I selected the nicer of the two remaining trees in my backseat and brought it upstairs for him while he carried the camera case carefully, as if the whole thing was made of glass. I put the tree on his tiny kitchen counter and plugged it in, then gave it a little water using a tea cup that had been in the sink.

Chance said he approved of the little tangerine lights. "Appropriately offbeat for my first Christmas tree," he said with a grin. When he saw me looking at him sympathetically he added, "Oh, put your pity away."

He offered me a beer and we carried the cans over to the little daybed, where we raised a toast to Christmas. After we took a sip, he said, "This seems so anticlimactic now." He set the can on the floor and wiped his hand on his jeans, then reached under the daybed and pulled out a twelve-inch-square cardboard box, which he handed to me.

Inside was a dark blue album, its black cardstock pages lined with copies of the photos Chance had taken of my murals. "There are blank pages at the end, and it comes apart to add even more," he told me. "I know I haven't discovered all of your murals, and I also know you'll be producing lots more in the years to come, so now you'll have a record."

That made me feel more than a little choked up, for a number of reasons. I put the album in my lap, then grabbed him in a hug and kissed the side of his head. "Thank you so much, Chance. What a great gift. I really appreciate that you took the time to make this for me."

"Damn it! If I make it through the day without you driving me to tears, it'll be a Christmas miracle."

I grinned at that and let go of him. "I promised you a guided tour around the city to show you my hidden murals. We still need to do that."

"We totally do! I can bring my new camera and document them, although it's kind of too nice to actually use." When I shot him a look, he said, "Okay, okay, I'll use it anyway."

He unpacked the camera and all its components, and as the battery charged I told him about the features that the retailer had mentioned. Chance then pointed out a million more features as he looked the camera over and flipped through the thick instruction book. He was so happy, his eyes bright, a big smile on his face. It felt wonderful to see him like that.

As soon as the battery was charged a bit, he selected one of the lenses and made me pose for him. I hammed it up and struck some ludicrous poses, which made him laugh. We hung out for a couple hours, until he started to get tired. He walked me to the door and grabbed me in a hug. "Thank you so much, Christian, not just for the insanely wonderful gift, but also for being such a good friend."

"Right back at you on both counts." I carefully cradled the album in my arms.

On the way home, I drove past Skye and Dare's apartment. The lights were still on, so I knocked lightly.

When Skye answered, he exclaimed, "Hey! Merry Christmas!" We hugged each other and I gave him the envelope with the gift certificate. "Come on in," he said.

"Nah, I'm not going to disrupt your Christmas with your fiancé. I just wanted to give you that and tell you I love you. Sorry for dropping by so late, the day kind of got away from me."

"I love you too. Your present's at my studio, I'm still putting the finishing touches on it," he said with a smile. "It would have been done on time, except a crazy little old lady made me go on a Dotsy cruise for a week."

I grinned at that and turned to go. "Next week. You and me. Major art supply dumpster diving with bonus criminal trespassing! I've missed doing illegal and disgusting things with you," I called over my shoulder. The sound of his laughter followed me as I returned to my double-parked car.

All in all, this would have been an absolutely perfect Christmas. In fact, it would have been the best one I could ever remember. If only I hadn't slipped up and said what I did to Shea.

I was dreading the conversation we were going to have tonight. I'd attempted to shove it to the back of my mind while I tried to make Christmas merry for my friends, but it had been hanging over me all night. I remembered the pain in his eyes and knew it was only going to get worse. With a sigh, I swung the Jeep around in an illegal U-turn in the empty street and headed for home.

Chapter Seventeen

I still had a couple hours before Shea got off work, so as I waited, I read the book my mother had given me. The album from Chance and the envelope from my dad sat beside me on the coffee table. As I read, I idly played with the pendant around my neck. I'd taken it off the key chain and had put my dad's lucky charm on a long black cord, the way he used to wear it.

Shea must have driven like a maniac to get across town, because he knocked on my door only five minutes after his shift ended. He was still in uniform, again with no jacket, and was cold to the touch when he grabbed me in an embrace. "There's something I need to say to you," he told me. He pulled back to look at me and blurted, "I'm in love with you, Christian. I didn't tell you because I was worried you'd think it was too soon, and you'd said we were supposed to be taking this day by day. But I love you so much, and whatever you're going through, I want you to know I'm going to be right there with you."

Opposite emotions slammed into me, joy and heartbreak. I couldn't say anything for a long moment, and then all I managed was, "See, the thing is...you're not."

"What do you mean?"

I led him into the apartment, his hand in mine, then sat on the couch with him. I took a deep breath and said, "I'm moving away on June fifteenth. There's something I need to do. And after I do it, I'm not coming back."

"Why not?"

"Let me start at the beginning." I didn't look at him as I recited the facts that had been presented to me almost three years ago. "I have a brain tumor. It's big, it's malignant, and it's spreading steadily. Eventually, it's going to kill me. My doctor doesn't know if that's going to happen in the next twelve months or the next twenty-four, but it *is* going to happen."

I swallowed hard and forced myself to continue. "Before it kills me though, it's going to take everything from me. It's already begun to invade the part of my brain that controls motor function. I'm on a lot of medicine to try to slow it down, but slowing it is the best case scenario. There's no stopping it. The tumor is spreading at a consistent rate even with the drugs I'm taking and my doctor is sure that by summer, I'll lose the ability to do even the simplest things as my motor skills break down."

"Oh God," Shea whispered.

"In June, I'm going to be participating in an intensive eight week drug trial. There's almost no chance that the drug will help me, but my hope is that it'll help others with this type of tumor down the road."

I paused and cleared my throat. Shea was gripping my hand tightly. I still couldn't look at him as I continued,

"I'm going to be living on-site while I participate in the study. Afterwards, I'm going to move to an assisted living facility, because my doctor is sure that by then I'm going to need help with even the most basic things, like feeding and dressing myself. So far, I've only noticed minor changes, like my handwriting becoming illegible, but...it's going to get bad."

"You don't need a care facility," Shea said. "I'll take care of you, Christian."

"No, baby," I finally turned to look at him. "That's exactly what I don't want. I refuse to become a burden to you, or to any of my friends or family. That's why I'm going away. I didn't choose to get a brain tumor, but I sure as hell can choose how many more lives it ruins besides just mine."

He stared at me for a long moment, then asked, "Who knows you're sick?"

"Just my dad, mom and stepdad."

"Skye doesn't know?" When I shook my head no, he asked, "Why not?"

"Skye was going through a really hard time when we met. No way was I going to compound his troubles with my own." He'd actually tried to kill himself just days after we met, but that wasn't my secret to tell. "After we grew close, I knew this would hurt him, so I never told him. He just thinks I'm moving away this summer, he doesn't know where I'm going or why."

"Your best friend loves you. He deserves to know the truth." I nodded and Shea asked, "What about your other friends?"

"I don't have a lot of friends anymore. There's Trevor, who I mostly know through Skye, and Skye's brother River, and Zandra, who moved to L.A. with her boyfriend so I barely hear from her these days, and Chance. That's about it. I withdrew from a lot of people when I found out I was dying."

Shea was quiet for a long moment before asking, "When, if ever, were you going to tell me?"

"I really don't know."

"There's no way I'd let you go off and live out the last part of your life in some assisted living facility. I'm going to take care of you." His jaw was set in a line of grim determination.

"Shea, you've known me a few weeks. It's incredibly sweet that you want to take care of me. That just goes to show what a great guy you are. But there's absolutely no way I'd even consider this. Caring for me would be a full-time job."

"Fine."

"No, it's not fine! No way would I want you to give up your life and burden yourself with a complete invalid."

He asked, his voice low, "Did you hear what I said when I first came into your apartment?"

"Yes. You think you love me. But—"

Shea cut me off. "No. I don't *think* I love you. I *know* I do, with every part of me."

I jumped up from the couch and took a step back from him. "I love you too, Shea, and I won't let you sacrifice your life like that!"

"You love me?"

"Shit. I didn't mean to just blurt it out."

His voice rose a little. "So, you weren't going to tell me that, either? You're dying, you love me—didn't it seem like maybe I should know this stuff?"

"No, absolutely not and this is why! I didn't want you to get some crazy, heroic notion in your head about stepping in and becoming my Florence Nightingale, at the cost of every other aspect of your life!"

Shea knit his brows as he rose to his feet. "So, you'd rather go off and be a martyr."

"I'm not going off to be a martyr! I'm just going. I won't become a burden to the people I love. I absolutely refuse!"

"Well, that's just great!"

"Why are you so angry?"

"Because you're fucking dying, Christian!" He covered his mouth as a sob tore from him.

I grabbed him and held him tight. His voice was pure anguish as he said, "How can this be happening? I just found you. I'm in love for the first time in my life and you actually love me, too. We're supposed to have a future together, not a few months!"

"I'm sorry."

He put his arms around me and held on tight. "There's no reason to apologize. You didn't choose any of this."

"But I let you get close. I started something I knew for a fact I couldn't finish."

He pulled back and took my face in his hands. "If the alternative was never getting to know you and never sharing what we've already had just in this short time together, no thanks. I'll take the pain. I'll take all of it if that's the price for getting to be with you."

"It's too high a price."

"Not to me it isn't."

We sat back down on the couch, holding each other tightly. After a while he asked quietly, "Are you in pain?"

"Not really. I had terrible headaches at first, that's how the doctors discovered the tumor. Now I always have a low-grade headache, but I'm used to it. I take pills to keep it in check. They won't keep working as it spreads, but they work well enough for now."

He whispered, "You can't go off and die alone, Christian. You just can't."

"We all die alone though, Shea. Even if we're surrounded by others, it's still a solo journey. And it's so much harder on those left behind. It's bad enough that the people who care about me have to say goodbye to me. They shouldn't have to watch it happen, too, especially the way I'll go out. It won't be quick and painless, it'll be this slow spiral as my body fails and the pain intensifies. I'll probably be so drugged up at the end that I won't even know what's happening. I might not even really be me by that point. As more and more of my brain is affected, it'll start to alter my personality. I'd much rather have you remember me the way I am now, instead of remembering whatever I might become."

"How can you talk about this so calmly?" He was still whispering.

"I don't know. Sometimes I think it's because I've come to terms with it, and sometimes I think it's because I'm in some weird form of denial. Like maybe it's all just too much, too big, too horrible, and I've just sort of boxed it up so I can look at it from a distance."

"Are you scared?"

I felt tears welling up at that question, but I held them back. My voice was quiet as I answered him honestly. "Yeah. I'm really fucking terrified. I don't want to die. And I'm going to hate being so helpless and dependent on others when my motor skills fail. You know what else I'm dreading? The day my hand-eye coordination degenerates to the point where I can't paint anymore. It won't be long. My handwriting's already going. One day soon, I'm going to try to paint and my hand won't do what I tell it to."

"Oh God, Christian." His voice was rough with emotion as he held on to me.

After a few moments I said, "My poor dad. He feels so helpless with all of this. I know that's why he gave me that extravagant present. He can't make me well, so instead he's trying so hard to make me happy. I doubt I'll get the whole building completed before my ability to paint is taken away, though."

"It's kind of like what you did with the comic book," Shea said. "You wanted to give me something big to make me happy. It's almost a consolation prize. You can't give me a future with you, but you wanted to give me something at least."

"I didn't think about it that way. I just really wanted to do something nice for you, and why not spend some of my money? Hell, why not spend all of it? I'm going to use a lot of my savings to set up an art center in that building and my dad will help with long-term funding. He wants a piece of me to live on, so he suggested naming it after myself and turning it into a place where kids can learn art and music."

"I think that's a great idea." Shea sounded so tired and he probably was, both mentally and physically.

I stood up and took his hand. "Come on baby, let's go to bed. This has been such a long day for you."

He let me lead him to the bedroom and we both stripped down to our underwear before climbing under the covers. Immediately, we gravitated into each other's arms. We lay there in the dark for a long time, sleep eluding us even though we were exhausted.

After a while, Shea told me, "There's something you should know." His voice was resolute. "I'm dead serious about what I told you. There's no way in heaven and earth I'm letting you go off alone to some facility. I absolutely refuse. You may have these noble ideas about not burdening your loved ones, but you need to get over it. I'm really, truly in love with you, Christian, and if you think for even a second I'd consider letting the man I love meet his end like that, you're completely high."

"This isn't something I'm willing to discuss."

"Me neither. I'm just telling you how it is."

"No," I said. "Absolutely no way am I going to put you through that."

"You aren't doing this alone."

"You're not going to out-stubborn me on this one," I told him.

"I really am."

I sighed and put my head on his shoulder, and he kissed my forehead. I was never going to agree to this, and

I had a feeling he wouldn't back down easily. There were going to be some major arguments in the days to come. But not tonight. He'd been through enough for one day.

Chapter Eighteen

I awoke before Shea the next morning and slipped out of bed. After I got the coffee pot going, I washed down my morning pill pile with tap water, then tucked away all the prescription bottles in the back of a drawer. When he'd been sick in my apartment all week, I'd hidden the bottles and snuck the pills because I didn't want to have to tell him what they were for. I'd done the same thing when Chance had been my cabin mate on the cruise ship. Now, even though Shea knew the truth, I really didn't want him to be constantly reminded of what was happening so I kept the pills stashed away.

After using the facilities and brushing my teeth, I slipped back in bed as quietly as possible. Still half-asleep, Shea grinned a little and murmured, "I smell toothpaste. You snuck off and groomed."

He raised his lids and for just a moment there was nothing but love in his eyes. But then, as he woke up a bit more, yesterday's conversation crashed into him and something that looked an awful lot like pity took over. He reached up and touched my face carefully, like I was a little porcelain doll or something. Damn it. I rolled out of bed, muttering, "Fuck, Shea. I'm still *me*."

"What does that mean?"

"Nothing." I went to the kitchen, where I poured myself a cup of coffee.

He followed and asked, "Did I do something wrong?"

"Not intentionally." My back was to him and I blew on the surface of the coffee, then took a cautious sip.

"So, what did I do unintentionally?"

I turned to face him. "Can you try not to look at me like I'm completely pitiful? That's part of the reason I never tell anyone what's happening with me. It isn't just because I don't want to hurt them. I also don't want *this*. I want people to treat me like I'm a regular person, not like some poor pathetic thing that's dying."

He frowned and said, "What about sympathy? That's what I was actually feeling, not pity. Am I allowed to show that?"

"Shit." I put down my coffee cup and pushed my hair back. "You're entitled to your feelings, Shea. I just—"

"Don't want to be pitied. I get that."

I sighed and leaned against the counter. "That, and I don't want to be constantly reminded of what's about to happen to me. I have so little time left to get to pretend I'm just like everyone else. Sometimes, I manage to go hours at a time without thinking about the thing that's growing inside my skull, like when I'm with you, or when I'm painting. Maybe that means I'm living in denial, but I don't care. I don't want to think about it all the time. I also don't want people to just see the tumor when they look at me. It's not the only thing that defines me, although someday it will be. I want them to see *me* and I don't want them to treat me differently."

Shea considered that for a long moment before saying, "Makes perfect sense to me." He then scooped me up and tossed me over his shoulder in a fireman's carry.

A little burst of laughter escaped me. "What are you doing?" I asked as he carried me to the bedroom.

"You're right that my first impulse was to handle you with kid gloves, like you're made of glass or something. But I can see why you'd hate that. I'd hate it too, if the situation were reversed." We'd reached our destination now and he tossed me onto the bed, where I landed with a bounce. "If we'd never had that discussion last night, I'd have been all over you the moment I woke up this morning." He stripped off his boxers and tossed them aside.

As I ran my gaze down his naked body he added, "Let's face it, a few sympathetic looks are going to slip out occasionally, because I *am* sympathetic to what you're going through. I'm going to try like hell not to treat you differently though, starting right now."

We hadn't had sex in a week thanks to that virus, and I was desperate for him. We worked each other up rapidly and fucked frantically until I came in him and he shot all over the sheets. Afterwards, I eased out of him and said,

"Be right back," then kissed his shoulder and stood on shaky legs. I stepped out of my briefs, then went to the bathroom to clean up a little.

When I returned, Shea was spreading a towel over the wet spot on the bed. He grinned at me and said, "My turn."

I smiled at him and dropped onto the mattress as he went to clean up. When he returned a few minutes later, he climbed in bed with me and pulled up the covers. "I have to be to work at six. Can we keep doing this until five fifty-five?" he murmured as he rubbed his cheek on my shoulder.

"Absolutely."

After a moment he asked, "Is this making you uncomfortable?"

"No. Why would it?"

"Because you don't like to be naked during sex. Granted, we've finished for now, but I'm planning to start up again just as soon as we've both recovered."

"I didn't even think about it. Just goes to show how much I trust you." I ran my hand over his smooth chest and added, "I've been giving some thought lately to that other thing I've never been comfortable with." I glanced at him self-consciously and asked, "Does the idea of topping me hold any interest for you?"

He looked surprised and stammered, "Oh! I mean, it's not something I have to do, so if you never wanted me to

I'd be fine with that. But, um, if you felt you wanted to give it a try, we could do that."

I grinned at him. "That doesn't tell me how you feel about it, though. Say for a moment you were dating a totally versatile guy with no hang-ups when it comes to sex. Would you want to trade off with him?"

He considered the question and finally said, "All else being equal, I'd want to try it. Bottoming feels completely natural, but I'm curious about the other aspect of it, too. It's not like this need or anything, though. If you never wanted to go there, I'd be fine with that."

"Okay. So, I'm still kind of working up to being able to do that, but, you know, maybe at some point we could try it. Like, somewhere down the road or something." I shook my head at myself. If it was that hard to talk about, how did I think I'd actually be able to go through with it?

*****

We ended up spending half the day in bed, kissing and talking, emerging just long enough to grab some coffee before getting back under the covers. We'd both set aside the topic of my tumor for now, probably because we'd had all we could take earlier. I knew we'd revisit it all too soon, but this brief reprieve felt good.

Somehow, we got on the subject of Christmases past. I told him, "When I was growing up, holidays were wildly inconsistent. Some years, my mom would try to go all out, maybe to overcompensate for the way things were for us living with an alcoholic. My stepdad would pretty much always wreck it, regardless of how nice she tried to make it. He'd pick fights and there'd be a lot of yelling. He loved to break stuff. One year, he grabbed the Christmas tree and threw it right out the front door, ornaments and all."

Shea brushed my hair back from my eyes. "I'm sorry. That must have been hard."

"It was, but I guess I kind of got used to it. He didn't reserve those moments for holidays, my stepdad would blow up randomly a couple times a week."

"Where was your real dad during all of this?"

"Touring and recording. I'd get these extravagant gifts in the mail. My dad was bad about hitting my birthday and Christmas dead-on, but he'd usually get something there within a few weeks. The weird thing is, until I was ten, my mom didn't tell me who my dad was. She didn't want us to live under the scrutiny of the paparazzi and when I was little, she didn't trust me to keep the secret. I had all these ideas about my dad. I knew he had to be rich, based on the gifts he'd send me, so I concocted all these crazy theories, like maybe he was a prince, or the president, or a rock star. I remember watching a Zan Tillane concert special on TV when I was about eight and thinking, 'Could that be my dad?' But then I dismissed the idea because we look nothing alike."

"That must have been really strange for you," Shea said.

"Looking back, I see that it was. At the time though, it was just my reality. When I was ten, Mom decided I was old enough to keep the secret and finally took me to meet him. He was on a world tour and had a stop in San Francisco. I remember it was late at night and he was staying in this fancy hotel. We went up to the penthouse suite, and there was Zan Tillane. It was a weird moment for both of us. I remember he and I just stood there awkwardly, staring at each other, and then I blurted, 'Shit. I thought maybe you'd be a prince.' My mom shrieked at me for cursing, but Zan burst out laughing. We had a good talk after that. He got us hot fudge sundaes from room service at one a.m. That's the kind of memory that sticks with you when you're ten. Anyway, he was only in town that one night but after that, we started writing letters back and forth. They dropped off a bit when he disappeared from the public eye, which happened the year after we met, but a few months later they picked up again. We kept corresponding until I moved in with him when I was fifteen."

"And you kept the secret of who your dad was."

"Oh hell no," I said with a grin. "Come on, I was ten. I blabbed to everyone at school on Monday morning, but of course no one believed me." Shea grinned at that and I said, "How did we go off on this Zan tangent? We were talking about Christmases growing up."

"This is way more interesting."

"I want to hear about your childhood traditions, though. What was Christmas like for the Nolan boys?"

"Typical. We'd go see relatives on Christmas Eve, then Christmas morning my brother and I would open presents in our pajamas and spend the rest of the day playing with our new toys."

"Sounds perfect."

"I guess it would have been if my parents could stand each other. Holidays were tense because they were forced to spend extra time together."

"Did they always hate each other?"

"Except for about ten minutes in their senior year of high school. They went to the prom together and my dad got my mom pregnant. Apparently they were both virgins. A shotgun wedding followed."

"Damn."

"I'm kidding about them only liking each other for ten minutes. They had me four years later, so I'm evidence of a time when things weren't all bad. I don't remember those days, though. All I remember is this quiet, life-long cold war, just because their religion told them they weren't allowed to get a divorce."

"I'm sorry you had to grow up with that."

He shrugged and kissed my forehead. "It could have been worse."

"Could have been better, too. I wish they'd managed to get their shit together for your sake."

"They just weren't capable of that. But, what're you going to do? All parents make mistakes. They're only human, so all of us grow up with at least a few invisible scars. But maybe that's okay, because the hard times are what make us strong enough to survive all the crap life throws at us down the road."

"I guess so."

"You asked me once if I wanted kids, and this is pretty much why I said no. I wouldn't make the same mistakes my parents did, but I'd still make plenty, guaranteed. I might have screwed up so badly that my kids would have turned out really messed up."

"You wouldn't do that. You'd have been the world's coolest dad," I told him, caressing his arm. "You've retained such a youthful outlook. I could just see you and your kids going to superhero movies and comic book conventions together."

He gave me a wry smile. "That's a really nice way of saying it, 'retained a youthful outlook'. Sounds so much better than 'incredibly immature'." He kissed my cheek and changed the subject as he sat up. "I don't know about you, but I'm starving. Do we have anything in this apartment besides incredibly bland food meant for people with stomach viruses?"

It turned out we didn't, so we decided to go out for lunch. After we showered, he once again borrowed some clothes, since all he had was his uniform. We then walked the three blocks to one of my favorite Thai restaurants. It was totally dead the day after Christmas for some reason, so the middle-aged couple that ran it were thrilled to see us and ended up visiting with us throughout most of the meal.

The city seemed quieter than usual, too. Not many people were out on the sidewalks as we walked home after our meal, even though the sun was shining. It was still fairly brisk, but a gorgeous day nonetheless.

I surprised Shea by grabbing his hand and pulling him into a little vestibule at the side entrance of a closed business. He burst out laughing and said, "Are you doing what I think you're doing? In broad daylight?"

As he was talking, I ran my hands down his back and kissed his neck. "It's up to you," I said before licking his earlobe. "We won't do it if it doesn't excite you." When I rocked my hips forward and my cock grazed his, I found he was already getting hard.

He moaned quietly and rocked forward too, rubbing against me. I dropped into a crouch and pulled down the front of his jogging pants, then freed his cock from his underwear and sucked it for a couple minutes as it swelled between my lips. As I sucked him, I lowered my zipper, pulled out my cock, and slicked myself with a little tube of lotion I'd brought along. Then I got to my feet and kissed him deeply as I pushed a lubed finger inside him. He gasped against my lips.

Shea turned around for me and bent over slightly, bracing himself against the wall. I tried to hold back a moan as I pushed into him, his little hole tight and warm around my hard shaft. We fucked urgently as people passed on the sidewalk just a few feet away. We were pretty exposed, but blocked from sight as long as no one chose to come into the little space between buildings and peer into the alcove.

It was so exhilarating that we both came fairly quickly. I grasped his hips as I emptied into him, and he drew in a sharp breath as he shot all over the wall. As soon as we were finished, I pulled up his pants, then quickly put myself back together. He took a look at the mess he'd made and raised his foot to the wall, using the sole of his sneaker to wipe down the trail of cum. "Good as new," I said, and when he turned to me and grinned, I pulled him into a kiss.

After we returned to my apartment we went back to bed and cuddled, snug and warm under the blankets. When I looked up at Shea sometime later, his blue eyes were somber. I knew it was just a matter of time. We'd been distracting each other for the last few hours, but of course the bombshell I'd dropped on him was hardly forgotten. He said softly, "Can I ask you a question?"

"Go ahead."

"I know you don't want to keep talking about this, but I was pretty overwhelmed earlier so I didn't think to ask about the clinical trial you'll be participating in. You said there's almost no chance it'll help you. But 'almost no' isn't the same as zero. Is there a possibility of it making a difference?"

I sat up and pushed my hair out of my eyes. "We don't really know. This will be the first time this drug has been tested on people with brain tumors. But mine is already so advanced that my doctor isn't optimistic. Besides, this is a research study. I could end up with a placebo. It's not about trying to cure me, it's about testing a drug that might end up helping others down the road."

Shea sat up, too. "What does the clinical trial involve?"

"A new drug has made it through several years of testing, both in labs and on healthy human subjects. In June they'll conduct tests on subjects with various types of tumors. They'll try to isolate the effects of the new drug by administering it in a controlled setting."

Shea knit his brows. "Could the drug actually worsen your condition, maybe accelerate the growth of the tumor?"

"There's no way of knowing."

"But with so little time—" He cut himself off abruptly as his emotions overwhelmed him. After a moment he continued quietly, "The tumor is going to begin affecting your quality of life soon as it is, and I'm worried that this is going to rob you of some of the good days you have left."

"It might or might not. I want to do it either way, though. If I play even a small part in getting a beneficial drug to the people who need it, then...well, I guess it's a way of having my life mean something."

"Your life does mean something!"

"But what am I leaving behind? A few murals that no one notices anyway? We only have one shot at life and maybe this is my chance to make it count."

He was quiet for a while before saying, "I think what you're doing is noble. I do. I just wish it didn't have to be you. Couldn't someone else volunteer to test the drug?"

"There are several participants in this study group, actually, gathered from all over the country. It also already went through a round of testing on healthy subjects to check for possible side effects and to determine dosages. According to my doctor, I'm the only one in the Phase Two group with a tumor this advanced, so the data I provide could be really valuable."

Shea sighed quietly and gathered me into his arms. "This is your choice, of course, and I do understand your reasons for doing it. You get why it's hard for me, though."

"I do."

We laid down again, cocooned by the blankets and each other's arms. He was quiet for a long time before he said softly, "My natural instinct is to protect you. I can't though, not from anything that's happening to you, and that makes me feel incredibly helpless."

"I know."

After another pause he asked, "Why can't they operate and remove the tumor?"

"It was already too widespread by the time I was diagnosed."

"Did you get a second opinion?"

"I got a *seventh* opinion. I've been to the best doctors in the U.S. and Europe. They all said the same thing."

Shea buried his face in my shoulder. After a while, his body began to shake as he sobbed silently. I rubbed his back as I held him and told him, not for the first or last time, "God I'm sorry. I never wanted to hurt you like this."

Chapter Nineteen

Throughout the week between Christmas and New Year's, Shea was at my apartment every minute that he wasn't at his job. The intensity that had always existed between the two of us was amplified somehow. There was an urgency when we kissed and when we made love. We both felt the need to be together as much as possible, as if we could somehow fit an entire relationship into the space of a few months.

Once all Shea's questions were answered, we stopped talking about my condition. It was always the elephant in the room, though. He tried so hard not to let his sadness and worry show, but it was there in his eyes whenever he thought I wasn't looking. He treated me just a little differently, too, even though I knew he didn't mean to. He kept doing little things for me, like opening doors, and cooking, and cleaning up around the apartment. Yes, he was just being nice, but I didn't want to feel helpless before that actually became my reality.

Three nights that week, once Shea left to work the swing shift, I got in my Jeep, picked up Chance, and drove to Skye's studio in Oakland. I'd been a shitty friend lately and was trying to make up for lost time. Plus, it just felt really good to spend time with my friends.

Dare had started teaching dance classes at one end of the big warehouse and they were usually just finishing up by the time we arrived. We'd stay until well past midnight, either hanging out or helping Skye with his sculptures by dismantling some of the weird odds and ends he had stacked around the edges of his workspace. Chance alternately helped out or took pictures of Skye's work, which he found endlessly fascinating.

River and his boyfriend Cole joined us one night, along with Trevor, Vincent and their son Joshie. The kid spent a lot of time running around and playing tag with Benny the dog. After that, we all settled in to eat pizza and play a makeshift PG-13 game of charades while trying not to add colorful new words to Joshie's already colorful vocabulary.

I hadn't told any of them what I'd told Shea yet. That was part of the reason it felt so good to hang out with my friends, aside from simply enjoying their company. I could just be Christian, instead of The Boy Who Was Dying. I'd have to tell my friends soon, especially now that Shea knew, but not during the holiday season. In the meantime though, I was going to enjoy the hell out of just being one of the guys.

*****

On New Year's Eve, I took Shea to meet Zan and have our movie marathon. He was incredibly nervous, even though I told him he had no reason to be. "My dad already likes you," I pointed out.

"It's bad enough that I'm meeting my boyfriend's dad for the first time," he said, wiping his sweaty palms on his jeans. "That alone is enough to freak me out. But on top of that, he also has to be incredibly famous."

"He's not *that* famous," I hedged. "He's not like, Elvis famous."

"He's pretty freaking famous, actually."

"Okay, but so what? He's just a guy that used to sing in front of people."

Shea rolled his eyes. "He's a just guy that used to sing in front of people *by selling out the world's biggest concert venues*. Not like he was working the corner coffee house."

"Famous people are no different than the rest of us. We act like they are, but they have their flaws and insecurities just like everyone else. And hell, as far as that goes, Zan has way more than his share."

He mulled that over before asking, "Is your father alright? I mean, you said he never leaves the house."

I focused on the traffic around us on the Golden Gate Bridge as I considered the question. Finally I said, "I don't know. I mean, physically, he's in perfect health. Mentally...I have no idea. I was just thinking about this a few weeks ago, actually. I don't know if he's just eccentric or if the things he does can be attributed to mental illness. He's definitely bipolar, I know that for a fact. But I'm really not sure why he isolated himself like that. The doctors he used to see were quick to call him agoraphobic, paranoid, a whole laundry list of things, but all of that felt off to me. The isolation always struck me as a conscious decision."

"It's hard to imagine someone cutting themselves off from everything on purpose," Shea said.

"When I asked him about it recently, it sounded like it just started as a break from the pressure of being in the public eye, but then it grew into something else. Maybe he only intended to step back for a little while, but now that he's been gone so long, he might be afraid to face the world again. And who can blame him? Can you imagine the media frenzy if Zan Tillane simply showed up at a Starbucks one day? He basically has zero chance of a normal life if he ever leaves his house."

"That's sad," Shea said. "It's like he's imprisoned by his own success."

"Pretty much."

By the time we reached my dad's house, Shea had built up such a case of nerves that he was on the verge of hyperventilating. A sheen of sweat had appeared on his forehead, and he was wiping his palms on his jeans every few seconds. He asked me as I shut off the engine, "What if, hypothetically, I wasn't able to do this? Would you be willing to tell him I had to stay home while I hid out in the Jeep?"

"You can do this, Shea. It really is going to be fine, you'll see."

I went around to the passenger side and opened his door for him, and he looked up at me with wide eyes. "What if he doesn't like me?"

"That's impossible."

"It's not."

"It is. What's not to like about you?"

"Well, there's the fact that I'll most likely throw up on your dad the moment I meet him. Nobody likes a barfer."

I grinned at that and reached across him to unfasten his seatbelt. "My advice? If you feel you need to throw up, aim away."

"Please don't let me make a fool of myself. I mean, doing that to some extent is totally inevitable, but if I start rambling aimlessly about something stupid, please shut me up."

I put an arm around him after he slid out of the Jeep. "Shut you up how, exactly?"

"I don't know. Think of something."

"This is going to be fine, baby. I promise." I drew him into a hug. He nodded against my shoulder and then let go of me to wipe his sweaty palms on his jeans yet again.

I retrieved a couple bottles of champagne and a canvas grocery sack from the backseat, then let us in through the side door. "Hey Zan, we're here," I called as we made our way down the long hallway. My dad knew that, of course, since he had the whole place hooked up to a closed circuit surveillance system that fed to two little screens in the den, but I liked to announce my arrival anyway.

"Holy crap," Shea muttered and I glanced at him as I picked up his hand. He was staring at all the gold and platinum records we were passing. The awards didn't mean much to my dad, which was why they'd been relegated to a back hallway, but my boyfriend was clearly awestruck.

When we reached the kitchen, I let go of Shea long enough to deposit the champagne in the refrigerator and put the bag on the counter. I then put an arm around his shoulders. As we rounded the large kitchen island and headed for the den, Zan appeared in the doorway. Both he and Shea froze in their tracks when they spotted each other.

My dad looked...odd. It took me a moment to pinpoint what was weird about him, then I realized it was a combination of things. His shirt, which he always wore just a little too open, was buttoned almost to his neck, his hair was parted in the middle and awkwardly slicked down, and he was wearing shoes. I wasn't aware that he actually owned any.

Zan and Shea both started moving again at the same moment, blurting greetings and heading toward each other with their hands extended. Right before they were about to shake hands, my dad tripped over absolutely nothing and lunged forward, accidentally tackling Shea, who hit the floor with an, "Ooomph," as my dad landed on top of him.

"Bloody hell," Zan exclaimed, scrambling gracelessly off my boyfriend. As he hauled Shea to his feet he rambled, "Terribly sorry, lad. I reckon I'm a bit nervous. My son's never brought a boyfriend home before. Plus, you know, I'm a bit out of practice with the whole company thing. You alright? I didn't dent you, did I?"

Shea just stared at him for a long moment. I started to wonder if I should intervene. But then, my boyfriend burst out laughing. "Oh wow," Shea managed. "I'm so glad you did that before I had a chance to."

My dad chuckled at that and pulled off his shoes, then held them up as he told Shea, "It's the fault of these damned things. Christian always teases me about looking like an old hippie, so I thought I should try to make a decent impression."

I laughed at that, too. "So you put on espadrilles? Really?"

"That was all I could find," Zan said with a smile, tossing the fabric shoes over his shoulder. "I figured they were better than going barefoot." He turned toward Shea and said, "Let me try this again. Zan Tillane. Nice to meet you."

They shook hands as Shea introduced himself and added, "It's completely surreal to meet you. I used to sing 'Loved You Forever' to myself when I was little and trying to go to sleep, it was my favorite song." He colored slightly. "Maybe that's a weird thing to admit. Sorry. I'm pretty nervous."

A huge smile erupted on Zan's face. "That song was actually meant to be a lullaby. I never told anyone that. Come, let me show you how I first intended it."

The two went into the den and sat down at the grand piano, and my father started to play a much slower, simplified version of one of his biggest hits. "Christian doesn't know this," Zan said as his long, slender fingers glided effortlessly over the keys, "but I wrote this song for him. I was shite as a parent when my boy was little, totally consumed by the fame monster. But part of me longed for a simpler life, the kind where I'd be home every night to tuck my kiddo in and sing him a lullaby. I came up with this song one night in some anonymous hotel room in New York, while I was missing a son I'd yet to meet."

"I always thought it was a love song," Shea said.

"Oh, it is. Just not the kind everyone assumed." When Zan started to sing, I felt like I was hearing the words for the first time, instead of the thousandth.

Emotions welled up in me and I mumbled, "We've been here three minutes and already you're trying to make me cry. I'm getting a drink."

As I went to the little bar in the corner and poured myself a whiskey, my dad's voice washed over me and gave me goose bumps. It was still absolutely gorgeous, clear and resonant, totally undiminished by time. As he performed for Shea, I could suddenly picture that other Zan, the superstar known to millions, up on stage.

I moved to the couch and watched the two of them as they bonded. Shea was awestruck, watching Zan with rapt attention. "If you know the words," my dad told him, "sing along with me."

Shea joined in shyly, quietly. His voice was surprisingly good. They harmonized perfectly on the chorus: *loved you before I met you/never could forget you/wouldn't ever try.*

When they reached the end of the song, Shea asked gently, "Why'd you stay away from Christian for such a long time?"

"It was his mother's idea. Partly, she didn't want him to grow up with the paparazzi always breathing down his neck. She saw what the fame thing was doing to me and she didn't want any part of that for her son. Also though, she didn't think I could commit to him. I was never able to maintain a relationship for very long, so she took that to mean I was flighty and untrustworthy. She was afraid Christian would get attached to me and then I'd just blow him off. Like I did with her," Zan admitted, looking down at his hands, which hand stilled on the keys.

"I'm sorry you had to miss out on his childhood," Shea said. "I'll bet Christian was a really special kid."

"Special," I repeated with a smirk. "Like, short bus special?"

"He was the cutest little bugger to ever walk on two legs," my dad said, ignoring my efforts to offset some of the sentimentality that had taken hold of the room. "I have pictures around here somewhere, let me find them." Zan got up and rummaged around on his cluttered bookshelves until he produced a white, leather-bound album. He sat down beside Shea again and said, "His mum would send me photos several times a year. Have you ever seen any of Christian's baby pictures?"

Shea grinned delightedly as my dad flipped back the cover. "Oh, come on!" I exclaimed, crossing the room to stand behind them and look over their shoulders. "You're showing my boyfriend baby pictures? Really? I'm so totally withdrawing your membership in the Cool Dad Club. Your new place is over there with the Dork Dads

Contingent. You already had a charter membership just based on whatever it is that you did to your hair today."

My Dad chuckled at that and ran the fingers of his left hand through his slicked-down locks, creating a messy, off-center part and flipping his hair over to the right. "Just trying to make a good impression, boyo. Wouldn't want you embarrassed by the old man."

"But embarrassing me with baby pictures, that's fine." I peered over his shoulder. "Mom sent you a photo of me dressed like Shirley Temple? What the hell?"

Shea chuckled at that and my dad said, "Oh no, not Shirley Temple. You just happened to have curly hair. You were actually dressed like one of the Olsen twins from Full House."

"My God why?" I asked, horrified.

"It was a phase," Zan explained.

Shea burst out laughing, so hard I thought he might hurt himself. "Oh my God, that's awesome," he managed as he wiped away tears with the back of his hand. "Most embarrassing kid picture ever."

I chuckled at that and told him, "This is so unfair. When do I get to see your baby pictures? I'm sure there are plenty of embarrassing shots of you, too."

"Yeah, but come on. How could anything top a cross-dressing four-year-old Olsen twin wanna-be?"

"I'm definitely having another drink." I left the two of them to the ridiculousness of young Christian, boy of a thousand bad ideas all captured on film, and refilled my glass. I then settled on the couch and watched the two of them. They had an easy rapport that I wouldn't have predicted. Zan and Shea were very different people, after all. But then I realized something: the fact that they both loved me gave them a lot of common ground.

I used my toes to push my black Chucks off my feet, then curled up in a corner of the big couch and sipped my drink. After they made it through the album, Zan started playing the piano again and he and Shea sang several of my dad's biggest hits. Shea knew all the words, which was surprising. "You would have made a fine performer, lad," Zan told him at one point. "That's quite the set of pipes."

"Thanks, that means a lot coming from you," Shea said as my eyelids got heavy. "I could never get up on stage in front of people, though. I'm way too shy for that."

*****

Apparently I drifted off, because sometime later I awoke to find myself covered in a blanket, the lights in the room turned down low and a soft breeze stirring the air. My ever-present headache was thrumming a bit more persistently tonight for some reason. I waited to see if it would ease off.

I heard voices and looked out the wall of windows to my right. The back door was open and my dad and boyfriend were sitting on the small deck right off the den, illuminated by the soft glow of a lantern on the iron table before them. They had their backs to me and my dad was patting Shea's shoulder.

My boyfriend sounded emotional, his words drifting to me on the breeze. "How can you stand it, Mr. Tillane? How can you stand knowing he's dying? The pain just wants to swallow me whole. It hurts so bad that I don't even know how to cope with it."

"Now laddie, I told you to call me Zan. As for the rest of it, I'll tell you how I cope: by believing in miracles with all my heart and soul. I never was what you'd call the religious sort, but I do believe in a higher power. And every day since I found out my baby boy was sick, I've been praying to the powers that be and begging for divine intervention. I just have to believe something's going to happen before it's too late. The doctors will find a treatment, or some new cure will be discovered. There's no rhyme or reason why an otherwise healthy boy in his twenties should be struck down in the prime of life like that! Not with all the advancements in modern medicine.

Every single day they're making new discoveries. One of them is bound to help my son."

I sighed quietly. No wonder my dad never wanted to talk about finding a caregiver to replace me. He was living so deep in denial that as far as he was concerned, I wasn't going anywhere. And since when did he have any faith whatsoever in the medical profession? He refused to see doctors and flat-out rejected everything they'd tried to do to help him with his bipolar disorder.

"I hope you're right," Shea said softly.

"I am. You just have to believe, it's simple as that."

After a pause, Shea said, "I keep messing up around him. I'm trying so hard not to treat him differently, but I keep catching myself doing it anyway. The other day I actually took a jar out of his hands and opened the stuck lid for him before I realized what I was doing. Christian hates stuff like that so much. He doesn't want people to treat him like he's helpless. I'm getting so frustrated with myself."

"It's understandable to behave that way," Zan told him. "I was the same way when I first found out. My every impulse was to coddle him. You're right though, he can't stand that and it'll just make him withdraw from us. Let's face it, you and I are the people he needs most, so we just need to figure out ways of being supportive without babying him."

"Thanks for talking to me about all of this. Since he wants to keep it a secret, I haven't told any of my friends or family what's happening to Christian. It's been a lot to hold inside."

"Give me your phone, son," my father said. I could hear a faint rustling and then he said, "I'm putting my number in here for you. I'm not the best at answering my phone when I go into one of my dark periods. But you can always leave a message and I'll call you back. This is too much to bear on your own."

"Thank you so much, Zan. I really appreciate that."

"I want to say one thing to you, Shea, before Christian wakes up and jumps on me for being a sentimental old fool. You're exactly what I've always wanted for my son. You're kind and decent and easy on the eyes, and it's obvious that you love him with all your heart. I know you didn't exactly come into each other's lives at an ideal time, but I'm so happy you found each other all the same. He needs you. Not because he's sick, but because he deserves to be happy. He told you what happened when he was seventeen and went away to that other college, yeah?"

"Yes."

"I honestly don't know why that boy should have to endure so much suffering in his life. I really don't. But the point I'm trying to make is that it was hard for him for a long time after that. I thought he might never learn to trust again or open himself up to another person. But then he found you, and you changed him, Shea. You brought love into his life and I'm so incredibly grateful to you for turning the light back on in his eyes."

"Thank you for saying that. You're a wonderful dad, by the way. My own parents would rather pretend I don't exist than accept the fact that I'm gay. And here you are, giving your son and me so much support."

"It's the least any parent could do for the child they love. Now come on, son," my dad said as he got to his feet. "It's getting a bit nippy out here. Let's go back inside and rouse sleeping beauty. We don't have long before midnight and Christian won't want to miss it. He likes to pretend that holidays and celebrations are no big deal, but deep down, he loves them. He's just a kid at heart. I tend to think it's because his childhood was less than ideal, so he makes up for it wherever he can."

"Did you know his stepdad was an alcoholic?"

"Not until the day Christian showed up at my door when he was fifteen and told me all about it, then asked to live with me. His mother certainly didn't discuss her home life with me, and you know how my boy is. He keeps stuff bottled up inside, he never wants to tell anyone how bad things really are. I would have gotten him out of there years sooner if I'd had any idea of the shite he was forced to endure."

When they stepped inside, Shea exclaimed, "Oh, you're awake."

I got to my feet, pulled my boyfriend into an embrace and planted a big kiss on his lips. Then I told him, "I love you, Shea."

When I let go of him, I gave my father a hug and kissed his cheek. "I love you too, Dad. I'm really lucky to have you both in my life."

Zan smirked at me when I let go of him. "In other words, you overheard our entire conversation. Thought you knew better than to eavesdrop, boyo."

"I only heard the last couple minutes, through no fault of my own. You're both cold to the touch, by the way. What were you thinking, sitting outside at this time of year?"

"It's really peaceful out there," Shea said, pulling the sleeves of his dark blue sweater over his cold hands and then rubbing his pink nose with his knuckle.

"Why don't the two of you clear away the hoarder-like pileup of books and DVDs around the fireplace and get a fire going while I make some coffee?" I said as I headed to the kitchen.

"He completely changed the subject away from his eavesdropping," Shea said to my dad, and I grinned and kept walking.

While the two of them did as I suggested, I pulled the coffee maker out of a cabinet and placed it on the counter, then located my stash. Zan wasn't a coffee drinker. I always found it baffling that any adult human on this planet could live without coffee, but whatever. I tossed a bag of ground beans on the counter, then went to open a drawer to find the little measuring scoop I'd left there. I missed the wide drawer pull on the first try, which was weird. Apparently I wasn't quite awake yet. Good thing I was making coffee.

The little plastic measuring scoop was right where I left it. I went to pick it up by its slender handle, but I missed and ended up pushing it across the drawer bottom with my fingertips. I whispered, "What the hell?" and tried again. The results were the same. Suddenly I realized what was happening and murmured, "Oh God." Panic rose up in me, constricting my chest.

When Zan and Shea found me in the kitchen sometime later, I was rooted to the same spot, my hands splayed out on the stone countertop, tears streaming down my face. "Christian, what's wrong?" Shea asked, rushing to my side.

"It's starting to happen," I told him, looking into his big, worried eyes. "My doctor had been so good about predicting the progression of my tumor. He was confident it'd be another six months."

"What wasn't supposed to happen?" Zan asked, coming around the counter to stand beside us.

"My motor skills are breaking down," I whispered. "It's the beginning of the end."

Chapter Twenty

My revelation ruined New Year's pretty thoroughly. Shea and I went home soon after that, since all of us were too upset to celebrate. I called and left a message for my doctor as soon as I got home and found out from his service that he was on vacation through the following week. It took me four tries and two misdials before I was able to place that call. My fingers just wouldn't do what I told them to.

On January second, I picked up Chance and took him to Skye and Dare's apartment, and then I ruined everyone's day. I came clean about everything that was happening to me. Now that my condition had been made visible, I knew it was just a matter of time before they noticed, so I couldn't keep it to myself any longer. All three of them had identical expressions of devastation as I quietly recited the facts.

When I stopped talking, they all grabbed me in an embrace. Skye started sobbing, his face buried against my neck. Chance held on to me tightly, his slender body trembling. Dare asked, his arms around me, "Is there anything we can do to help?"

"There's nothing to be done," I told him. "Thanks, though."

"We knew you must have had a good excuse for missing your best friend's wedding," he said, "but Skye and I never expected it to be something like this."

"I shouldn't have kept it a secret so long. I'm sorry, Skye." I kissed his forehead and he sat up and looked at me, wiping his wet cheeks with the back of his hand.

"Oh God, Christian. How can this be happening? It feels like a bad dream and I just want to wake up."

"I know," I told him, stroking his overgrown blue hair. "I've felt that way for the last three years."

"So you've always known, the whole time we've been friends. Yet you never said anything," his eyes searched my face, looking for answers that weren't there.

"I thought if I just went away before it got bad it'd make it easier on you. It wasn't supposed to affect me so soon."

Chance straightened up and looked at me. It made my heart ache to see the pain in his big, blue eyes. "Does Shea know?" he asked me.

"Yeah. I accidentally let it slip on Christmas. Worst timing imaginable. Other than him and my parents, no one else knows." I looked at Dare and asked, "Would it be really awful of me to ask you to spread the word? I want Trevor, River and Zandra to know, along with their partners. Nana too, of course. But every time I talk about this, it just destroys me."

"Of course. We'll take care of it," Dare said, and Skye sniffed and nodded his head.

I stayed a few more minutes and answered their questions. There would be a million questions later, once the initial shock wore off. But for now, they really just needed time to process it.

When Chance and I stepped onto the sidewalk, he turned to me and said softly, "I think I'm going to go for a walk. I'll talk to you soon, okay?" I nodded and hugged him, then kissed the side of his head before I let go of him. He looked so vulnerable as he walked away from me, his hands stuffed in his pockets and his shoulders slumped.

I went back to my apartment, which was way too still without Shea in it. He was working a split shift today. To try to cheer myself up, I plugged in the little tangerine tree and the strands of lights Skye had left behind on Christmas Eve. That felt like a long time ago.

Aside from the holiday decor, the apartment was blank and cheerless. I'd moved in shortly after my diagnosis and had always treated this place as nothing more than a temporary living arrangement, even though I'd been here three years. I sat on a chair at my dining table and looked at the drawings spread out before me.

Before New Year's I'd begun sketching some ideas for a mural to paint on the future art center. It was pretty daunting trying to come up with a concept for an entire building. I'd gone to see the place a couple days after Christmas and ended up just standing on the sidewalk staring at it for about half an hour before finally turning and heading home.

My sketches were a bit rough, since my drawing skills had already declined just like my handwriting by that point, but I'd still been able to get ideas down on paper. I was afraid to find out where they were now. I needed to know, though.

It felt awkward when I picked up a pencil and even worse when I tried to draw. No matter how hard I concentrated, I just couldn't get my hand to do what I wanted it to. Tears of frustration welled in my eyes and I cleared the tabletop with a sweep of my arm, sending paper and pencils and sketchbooks cascading onto the floor.

I launched myself from my chair and strode to the kitchen, then stopped and rested my forehead against the refrigerator. The headache that used to remain just below my pain threshold was now right above it, all the time, a constant *thrum thrum thrum*, refusing to be ignored. I yanked open a door and rummaged among my prescription bottles until I found my strongest pain pills. At least I could still remove the big, white lid, although I knew it was just a matter of time before I wouldn't even be able to do that. I dumped a few pills into my palm and tossed them in my mouth, then made a cup with my hand and caught some water from the tap to wash them down.

Again I rested my forehead on the refrigerator, the metal slightly cool and therefore a bit soothing. Not enough, though. My head went right on throbbing to the beat of my heart. I was acutely aware of it right now. I needed the pain pills to hurry up and work, but I knew it would take at least half an hour.

I couldn't wait that long though, not today. Not when my emotions were so raw, not when it felt like everything was unraveling around me. I opened the liquor cabinet and grabbed the bottle closest to the front. I didn't even look to see what it was. I didn't care. I pulled off the lid and tossed it aside, then drank right from the bottle, several deep, burning gulps. I knew it was wrong to mix booze and pills, but I didn't care. I hadn't taken enough painkiller to OD. Hopefully I'd taken enough to *stop fucking feeling* though.

It was just too much. Too much pain, too much emotion. I kept seeing Shea's eyes on Christmas and a hundred times since then, Skye's and Chance's and even Dare's today, so much sadness. Exactly what I'd never wanted was happening. Everyone who cared about me was hurting. It was my fault. I'd let them all get close to me, selfishly. Each of those relationships had been formed after my diagnosis, even though I'd predicted exactly this outcome.

I took another long drink from the bottle, then slid down until I was laying on the kitchen floor. What the hell was I going to do? I thought I had more time. Time with Shea, with my dad, with my friends. I had to find someone to take over for me with Zan, even if my dad was in total denial. I had planned to finish school, but that seemed irrelevant right now. I'd wanted to paint more. A lot more. I wondered if my motor skills had already deteriorated to the point where I couldn't direct a spray can. I wanted to set up the art center and create something lasting, both inside and on the outside of that building.

I wanted more time with Shea most of all. I wanted *years*. I wanted him like I'd never wanted anything in all my life. Sweet, beautiful Shea. He loved me. That gorgeous, amazing, kind man loved me. But all that meant for him was so much heartache. It had already started for him and it was only going to get worse.

I curled up in a little ball, hugging my knees to my chest. I was so scared. How fast would my body fail? How much time did I have before I couldn't even pick up a fork or work a doorknob or tie my shoes? I feared that more than I feared death, the utter helplessness that was so totally inevitable. I'd planned to check myself in to that assisted living facility as soon as things started to turn, but this was too soon. I wasn't ready. I needed more time. I couldn't leave Shea yet. I just couldn't.

*****

I awoke in darkness, my body stiff on the cold, hard kitchen floor. Something had awakened me, but I wasn't sure what it had been. I sat up, pushing my hair back from my face. A moment later, someone knocked on the door, loudly.

Shea looked distraught when I opened the door. "Are you alright?" he asked, stepping into the apartment and taking hold of my shoulders as he looked me over. He was still in his uniform, this time with an SFPD windbreaker over it.

"Yeah. What time is it?"

"I don't know. Ten p.m., maybe. I was out there knocking for a while."

"I fell asleep," I mumbled. The booze and pills were making everything fuzzy.

Shea noticed the fuzziness, of course. "Are you drunk?"

"Not entirely. I'm going to work on that." I leaned in and kissed his lips, then spun and headed to the kitchen.

He trailed after me. "You seem more than drunk. You seem...altered."

"Altered. Good word. I am indeed altered. With any luck, I'm about to become far more altered." The headache was still there, but the edge was off of it. Yay to that. I really had no interest in sobering up, though.

I retrieved the bottle from the kitchen floor, the one I'd been drinking from earlier. Turned out it was bourbon. Usually not my first choice, but it had done the trick. I took a long drink, then offered the bottle to Shea. He frowned and took the bottle from me, but instead of taking a drink as I'd intended, he put it on the counter. "Really?" he said. "Is this your plan? Getting drunk instead of dealing with the situation?"

"Better living through alcohol," I quipped.

"Come on, Christian. You can do better than this."

"I can, but I don't want to."

"Are you mixing bourbon with pills? Is that why you seem so out of it?"

"What if I am?"

Shea's frown deepened. "Do I have to tell you how incredibly dangerous that is?"

"No, you really don't. I had a headache. I *always* have a headache, but this one was worse. It needed to stop, so I took a few pain killers. But I'm not stupid, Shea. I didn't take enough to overdose."

His voice rose. "Maybe not intentionally, but accidents can happen! How many pills did you take?"

"I don't know. A few."

He stared at me for a long moment. When he spoke again, his voice was low and angry. "Where's the bottle, Christian?"

"Why?"

"I want to see what you took."

"I don't need you checking up on me. I'm not a child."

He narrowed his eyes. "The phrase 'I'm not a child' might carry a bit more weight if you hadn't made the incredibly immature decision to mix drugs and alcohol."

"I really don't need this right now, Shea! My day sucked, my head hurts, my whole world is falling apart, and *yes*, I acted immaturely. So the fuck what? I don't need you to judge me for it!"

"I'm not judging you, Christian, I'm scared for you. What if you'd accidentally ODed?"

"I didn't!" I stepped back from him and took a deep breath. Then I said, more calmly, "I'm going to go to bed and put this shitty day out of its misery. I'll talk to you in a couple days, okay?"

"A couple days?"

"I need to sort this shit out. Don't worry, I'm not going to mix any more pills and booze. I swear. I just need some time to myself."

He hesitated, looking like he wanted to argue. But after a while he said, "You sure you're going to be alright?" When I nodded, he murmured, "Well...okay. I'll call you in a couple days. Remember, you swore. No more pills and alcohol."

"I won't do that again. I promise." He kissed my forehead and paused for another moment, then stroked my hair before leaving the apartment.

I felt terrible pushing him away like that, but I just couldn't take any more pain right now, mine or anyone else's. I picked up the bourbon from the counter, drank the rest of it, and put the empty bottle in the sink before laying back down on the kitchen floor. The cool tile felt good against my cheek.

I knew I was being self-destructive and that ultimately, hiding out at the bottom of a bottle was no solution. But right now, I didn't care. I needed oblivion. And I loved Shea way too much to let him watch.

Chapter Twenty-One

"Oh, *hell* no."

I pried an eyelid open and looked up to see who'd spoken. Skye and Shea were standing over me. They looked pissed. I was in the bathtub for some reason, fully dressed.

My best friend said, "You've got to be kidding me. You, of all people! You grew up with an alcoholic and know for a fact how damaging booze can be. Yet this is your solution? Getting drunk off your ass for days?" He bent over and plucked something from my hand. It turned out to be a bottle of scotch. "What the fuck, Tillane?"

I mumbled, "You know my last name."

"Yeah. Thanks for not telling me who your dad is. What, did you think I was going to blab to the media?"

"No, I didn't think that."

"I went to Skye for help when you wouldn't answer your phone or your door," Shea explained. "He was with me when I called Zan for advice and your dad asked to speak to him. I wouldn't have given away your secret under normal circumstances."

"It's okay. Skye can know. I love Skye, he's a good egg. He's not gonna tell anybody." Wow, I was still really drunk.

Skye spun the dial on the shower and a jet of cold water jolted me fully awake. I yelped, pushing back to get out of the stream, and said, "Do you really have to be this pissed off?"

"Yes."

"So I got drunk," I slurred. "We've all gotten drunk at one point or another. Don't you think I'm entitled to do that once in a while? I kept my promise to Shea, too. I didn't take any more pain killers. So what's the big deal?"

"What's the big deal? Shea and I have been worried sick about you!"

"Why?"

"Because you went missing!"

"I didn't go missing," I said, pushing my wet hair out of my face. "I just spent the night getting drunk. You two are acting like that's some huge catastrophe."

Skye stared at me for a long moment, then said, "You've been holed up in here for four days, Christian. Do you not know that?"

"No I haven't. I just saw Shea last night."

"You saw him on January second. It's now the sixth," Skye told me. "At first, he gave you a couple days like you asked. He was worried because he knew you'd been drinking, but stupid me told him that was nothing to worry about because you always drank a lot and you knew your limits. Little did I know you were in here steeping yourself like one of Nana's fruitcakes." When I grinned a little he said, "Oh no. Don't you dare try to laugh this off!"

"That's funny, though. Did you try the fruitcake she gave you? I tried mine. I'm pretty sure Nana poured an entire bottle of rum over it. It was tasty, though. Fruitcake gets a bad rap but this one had some things going for it, as long as you kept it away from open flames." Skye frowned at me. When I glanced guiltily at Shea, he was staring at me with a stony expression, his arms crossed over his chest. I told them, "I'm really sorry. I didn't know it had been four days."

"I'm going to call his dad and tell him he's alright," Shea muttered to Skye, then left the bathroom.

Standing was a lot of effort, so I kept sitting in the tub with the now-warm water hitting my knees and looked up at Skye. "How'd you guys get in? Did Shea have some kind of special cop way of busting into my apartment?"

"What, like a battering ram?"

"Is that what you used? I wish I could have seen that!"

Skye stared at me and said flatly, "A friend of mine lent me a lock pick kit."

"Oh." I looked down at my wet jeans. After a moment I said quietly, "I really am sorry about worrying you."

His expression finally softened and he sat down on the edge of the tub, even though spray from the shower was hitting his arm. "I'm just glad you managed to avoid liver poisoning."

"How mad is Shea?" I asked.

"Do you have any idea how much that guy loves you? I kept trying to tell him you were probably just sulking, but he was worried sick. I don't think he's eaten in days."

"Will you help him, Skye? When I die, I mean. It's going to be so hard on him. I know it'll be hard on you too, so maybe, I don't know. Maybe you could help each other."

Skye swore under his breath and looked away.

"I'm sorry. I know I'm not supposed to just blurt out the 'd' word. I'm still not thinking clearly." When he didn't say anything, I added, "Do you see now why I didn't tell you for so long? I never wanted to tell you at all. I was just going to go away and let you think I was some asshole who couldn't bother to keep in touch. That way you would have been angry, but not hurt. Hurt is worse."

Skye turned to face me again, his blue eyes bright with tears. "You're such an idiot," he said. Then he climbed in the tub with me and pulled me into a hug. "Yeah, it hurts like hell. But you know what's worse? The thought of you going off and dying alone!"

"You were never supposed to find out about that, though."

"You've always been like this," he said, holding me tightly. "You keep everything in. Everything! How am I supposed to help you if you never tell me what's wrong?"

"You don't have to help me."

"But I want to! That's what best friends do! Hell, look at all you've done for me in the two years we've been friends. You barely knew me when I overdosed, but for those first few months after I got out of the hospital, you were there for me every single day, just like my brother was. You didn't have to stick around, but you did. You made sure I ate, and brought me groceries, and helped me in a million little ways. You've been a true friend to me, Christian. Why on earth wouldn't you let me return the favor?"

I sat back and looked at him. "But this isn't the same thing. You were depressed in those early months, but you were still able to care for yourself. I just provided a little assistance. What's happening to me isn't going to require an occasional bag of groceries. I'm going to get to the point where I can't do anything for myself."

"I know, and I want to help. No, scratch that. I'm *going to* help."

"Do you get what I'm saying, though? I won't be able to get a spoon to my mouth, or comb my hair, or shave, or bathe myself, or do *anything*. That's why I'm going to a care facility."

"That's a terrible idea. You'd be so unhappy there!"

"That's where I'll belong, it's exactly what places like that are for."

"But you have friends and family who can provide the care you'll need. You have so many people that love you, and we're going to be there for you."

"But I don't want you to be!" I shut off the shower with a hard twist, then climbed out of the tub, forming a puddle on the floor. "Don't you get it, Skye? I don't want you or Shea or my dad or anyone I know to see me like that! Do you think I want you to watch me drooling on myself when I've lost the ability to control my facial muscles, or changing a fucking diaper for me because I can't get to the bathroom? The thought of you seeing me reduced to that makes me physically ill! That why I don't even want anyone to visit me in the nursing home, because it's too fucking humiliating!"

He stood up too, his blue hair dripping onto his shoulders as he stepped out of the tub. "So that's it. This all comes down to pride."

"That's not the only reason. Caring for me will become a full-time job, and I refuse to become a huge burden to the people I love!"

"Get over it." That was from Shea, who stood in the doorway. I turned to face him and he said, "Dying alone in some anonymous facility is *not* an option."

"Neither is giving up your life to be my nursemaid, Shea."

"That's my choice."

"And moving to a facility is mine," I told him.

"But it's not the right call!" he exclaimed. "You'd be so lonely and miserable. You need to be surrounded by the people who love you. And that's what love is, Christian. It's holding on tight while the worst storms that life can hit us with try to tear everything apart." He came up to me and cupped my face between his palms. "There's a reason the terms 'for better or for worse' are included in marriage vows. That's the essence of true love, not just being there for the good times, but also facing the storms together."

"It's too much, though," I told him as I took his hands. "No one should have to sacrifice everything for their partner. And you would have to sacrifice *everything*: your job, your time, your whole life."

"But it's not a sacrifice, Christian, because I love you."

"It won't all just be on Shea's shoulders, either," Skye said. "I'm going to help too, and so is your dad."

"My dad can't help anybody," I said.

"Sure he can," Skye insisted. "He just has certain limitations. I had a long conversation with him over the phone. Zan's willing to do whatever he can to help you. He loves you so much, Christian. Granted, he's pretty heavily in denial. But he said until a cure's found, which he totally

346

believes in, you and Shea can move in with him and he'll help take care of you. He also suggested hiring nurses to come in several hours a day for the stuff that you might be too embarrassed to have one of us deal with. I thought that was a good idea."

"We can't bring a bunch of strangers into Zan's home," I said. "What if one of the nurses went to the paparazzi? They'd make a fortune by ratting him out."

"There are plenty of agencies that screen their employees thoroughly and ensure privacy," Skye said.

I stared at him for a long moment before saying, "So basically, I go off on a drunken bender and meanwhile you two, along with my slightly unhinged father, plan my entire life for me."

"Yup, and we're totally right while you're totally wrong. Now get that shower, Z. You reek. Use lots of soap. Probably want to lather, rinse, repeat." Skye spun around and vacated the bathroom.

I sighed as I watched him walk away, then turned to Shea and asked, "Are you still mad at me?"

"Not really, but you did scare the crap out of me, Christian."

"I'm so sorry. I know I'm not dealing with things very well."

"You think?" He kissed my forehead, then said, "I'll go get us some dinner, I bet you're starving. I am, too.

Don't forget what Skye said about the soap." He closed the door behind him as he left.

I stripped off my wet clothes, turned the shower back on, and stood under the warm water for a long time. My head was absolutely pounding, but I figured most of that was a hangover. My mouth felt like cotton, too. Ugh. That was the problem with drinking. Sooner or later, you had to sober up and then you had all of that waiting for you.

I shampooed my hair and washed myself thoroughly, then toweled off and brushed my teeth. As I combed out my overgrown hair, I stared at myself in the mirror. My green eyes were bloodshot and my complexion had a slightly grey tinge to it, putting me somewhere in the zombie-to-vampire range. Awesome.

A visit to my closet reminded me I hadn't done laundry in quite a while. I pulled on a pair of black low-slung jeans and a grey t-shirt consisting of more holes than fabric and went out into the living room. "Wow," Shea said with a smile, turning his attention away from the takeout containers he was unpacking onto my table. "That's quite a look."

"You missed Christian's rock star phase," Skye told him. "It's a shame too, because it was really something to behold. He'd show up in nothing but those jeans and a couple silver necklaces and call that dressed. Why'd you outgrow your rocker phase, Z?" he asked me. "I miss it."

I shrugged and said, "Just not feeling all that rock and roll lately."

"What's the Z stand for?" Shea wanted to know.

"Zane, the name Christian uses for his art," Skye said. "Has he ever shown you his work?"

"Just the scrapbook his friend Chance made for him."

"I want to see that," Skye exclaimed, and after I pointed it out to him he vaulted over the back of the couch, took it from the coffee table and started leafing through it.

"Why Zane?" Shea asked as he folded the brown paper bag the take-out had come in.

"It's the names 'Zan Tillane' merged together," I explained. "I was always worried about using my last name because it's fairly uncommon, so I guess I started using Zane as a way of...I don't know, honoring my relationship with my dad, I guess. It's kind of weird. I'm proud to be his son, yet I could never tell anyone, in case the media found out about me and my entire life got dragged into the spotlight."

"I never knew the story behind that name," Skye said, looking up at me from the scrapbook. "I'm glad I do now."

"Speaking of Zan, how was he when you spoke to him?" I asked. "I was supposed to go see him yesterday. I really fucked up."

"He was relieved when I called him a few minutes ago," Shea told me. "He also said, 'Remind my son that once he gets his shite together, he still owes me a Harry Potter movie marathon.' You've now been reminded."

"He's right, I do."

Shea followed me into the kitchen and took some plates from the cabinet as I sighed quietly and pulled all my prescription bottles from the back of the drawer, then lined them up on the counter. I slid one bottle toward him. "This is what I took the day you came by and wanted to know what I'd combined with alcohol. It's my strongest pain killer. I don't take it every day, just when needed." I separated out seven bottles and said, "This is what I take every day. These four," I pulled some bottles forward, "are taken in combination to slow the growth of the tumor. The remaining three help with the headaches I always have. They started getting worse recently, right around the time my motor skills took a downturn."

"Did you call your doctor?"

"Yeah. He's on vacation until next week."

"Couldn't you speak to someone else?"

"There's no point," I said as I grabbed a paper towel and started shaking pills onto it, some in multiples. "He's the only one that understands my history and the million different drug combinations we've tried over the last three years. No other doctor can step in blindly and do anything for me."

"Why have I never seen these pill bottles before? Were you intentionally hiding them from me?"

"Pretty much. You don't need to be continually reminded of what's happening to me."

"Skye's right. You do keep a lot to yourself."

"I guess so."

He took a glass from the cupboard and filled it with water. "I'm not giving you this because I think you're too frail to do it yourself," he said. "I just have good manners and like to help out." He grinned a little as he handed me the glass.

"Thank you." I scooped up the tablets in three batches because I'd learned the hard way that it was impossible to swallow over a dozen pills at one time. After I washed them down, I told him, "I know I have a major chip on my shoulder about people treating me like I'm infirmed and I know I really need to get over that. I also realized, once I stopped and thought about it, that you were always the type of man to open doors and do thoughtful things for me, long before you knew I was sick. That's just who you are. It wasn't fair of me to resent your natural helpfulness after I told you about my condition."

His grin got a little wider and he slipped his hands around my waist. "Where'd that come from all of a sudden?"

"I don't know. It's the truth though." I leaned in and kissed his cheek, then said, "Disappearing for days was a really shitty thing to do to you and I feel terrible about it. I promise I'll never do anything like that again."

"You're dealing with a lot and the pressure got to you."

"Still. That was such a stupid thing to do."

"I'm just relieved you're alright. When you disappeared I imagined the worst, but Skye kept talking me down and assuring me it was going to be alright. He's such a good guy."

"I really am," he called from the other room, and Shea and I both chuckled. "Now would you wrap up the not-at-all-private conversation and come back in here so we can eat this Chinese food? I'm hungry enough to gnaw on the couch!"

I went to put the glass in the sink and that was when I noticed it was completely full of empty liquor bottles. "Well shit," I murmured. "I see where those four days went."

Shea knit his brows as he looked at the bottles. "I didn't think it was possible for one person to drink that much and live to tell about it."

"None of those started out full, but still."

"Well, that's good at least. Now come on, let's go pry Skye off the furniture."

We joined my friend at the dining table. He'd picked up the sketches I'd scattered all over the floor and asked about them, so I explained about my father's extravagant present as I scooped fried rice onto my plate and passed the container. "I love the idea of an art and music center," Skye exclaimed. "Can I volunteer to teach the kids to sculpt?"

"Absolutely. No giving the ten-and-under set welding torches, though. I'm going to guess there are laws against that sort of thing. Also, you may not be allowed to give them rusty hunks of metal that you find in dumpsters."

"Well, despite your efforts to immediately suck all the joy out of it, I can work around your totally oppressive rules." Skye grinned at me and added, "Seriously, this sounds like so much fun! I'll help you get it up and running too, if you want."

"Thanks. The whole thing's pretty overwhelming. My dad's having his lawyer look into zoning ordinances, setting up nonprofit status, insurance, and so on. At least I don't have to worry about that stuff. Meanwhile, I've gotten hung up on the outside of the building. My dad intended it to be a great big canvas for my artwork, but I guess I'm kind of daunted. The thing's huge and I don't have a clear idea of what I want to do, but I feel like I need to hurry up and think of something right now, before I lose the ability to paint. Actually, for all I know, I might have already lost it. I've been in a bit of a slump and haven't painted in weeks. I'm afraid of what I'll find when I give it a try."

Skye considered what I'd said for a few moments as he chewed an eggroll, then pushed his chair back and crossed the room to a canvas bag in the corner. He plucked three cans of paint from it, stuck them under his arm, then slid both my living room windows open before coming back to the table and lining up the cans in front of me. "So, go find out."

"You want me to paint something now?"

"Yup."

"Where?"

Skye waved his hand. "Pick any one of your painfully dull white walls and go to town. Normally I wouldn't advocate doing something like that to a rental, but it turns out you're filthy freaking rich. So, screw the security deposit!" He smiled at me before tossing the end of the egg roll in the air and catching it in his mouth.

I considered that for a beat, then said, "Yeah, okay." I got up and tucked two cans in the crook of my left arm. I shook the third as I walked over to the biggest empty wall in the living room. After thinking for just a moment while chewing on my lower lip, I popped the lid off the can of black paint with my thumb and started to paint. I was used to working quickly (usually under the threat of imminent arrest) and this was really small-scale compared to what I was used to, so in just minutes I'd completed my picture. I used the hot pink and blue paints to add some accents, and then I crossed to my front door and threw it open, because the apartment now reeked of spray paint. That immediately created a strong cross-breeze with the open windows, so the apartment began to air out quickly. It also made me break out in goose bumps, but it was worth it.

Skye let out a whoop and leapt to his feet, applauding, while Shea mumbled, "Oh wow."

It was just a picture of the three of us sitting around the table, but it had turned out pretty good. I'd managed to capture Skye's and Shea's personalities in their expressions and their body language, which had been my main objective. Since I worked in fairly broad stokes I'd barely noticed the changes in my fine motor skills, which was a relief.

"I've never seen you work before," Shea said as he got up and crossed the room to me. "That was amazing."

"It was?"

"You're incredibly gifted. Not only that, but between watching you produce this work of art out of nowhere and this, um, thought-provoking outfit, that was pretty much the sexiest thing ever." He grinned at me before leaning over and kissing my shoulder, which was exposed through a big rip in the t-shirt.

Skye came over to us, eating directly from one of the white take-out boxes with a pair of chopsticks. "You need to start dressing like this again, Z, because you *are* a freaking rock star. This is so awesome! You just need to go down to that big, giant building, quit overthinking it, and paint the hell out of it. You totally got this."

"You're right," I told him.

He flashed me a brilliant smile. "I know! I usually am. My brother disagrees, but it really is the truth. Now let's put on some parkas and finish our dinner. This food's going to be stone cold in about two minutes now that we've turned it into the arctic tundra in here."

*****

Skye hung out with us for a couple hours. He acted no different than usual. Maybe he was great at keeping up illusions, or maybe he really was coping well with my revelation. Either way, he treated me the same as he always had. The three of us laughed and joked, and Skye regaled my boyfriend with every embarrassing Christian anecdote he could come up with, of which there were many. I was surprised how happy I felt, given the incredibly dark place I'd been in just a few days ago.

When my best friend went home to his fiancé, Shea gently pushed me back on the couch, then climbed on top of me and kissed me for a long time. He rested his forehead against mine and said softly, "I missed you so much. I didn't know what was going on, but I knew it had to be bad. Part of me thought you might have packed up and moved to that care facility already, even though your Jeep was still out front."

"I wouldn't do that without telling you."

"Please don't do it ever. You have to admit the idea your dad, Skye and I came up with is a good one. We'll all help take care of you along with a team of home health care nurses."

"Let's not talk about this now. Please?"

He looked in my eyes and sighed quietly. But apparently he was willing to let the subject drop for now, because he ran his tongue up my neck, then licked my earlobe. Desire shot through me, and I slid my hands down his broad back and cupped his ass. Shea ground his hips against me and I could feel his erection already straining in his jeans as mine swelled beneath him. He reached between us and began massaging my cock through my clothes as he kissed me again, his tongue claiming my mouth.

I really liked the way he was taking the lead. His confidence had grown so much in the time we'd been together, and that was really sexy. It actually felt incredibly good to let him take control. I realized what I needed and wanted all of a sudden, and whispered, "Fuck me, Shea."

My heart started racing as he sat up a little and looked at me, a question in his eyes. I just nodded, pushing down my nervousness.

Shea swung off me and picked me up, then carried me to the bedroom as he kissed me tenderly. He stripped us both, then took his time exploring my body with his lips and tongue and fingertips. I knew I was ready for this, even though I gasped and flinched instinctively when he lightly ran a fingertip over my opening. He looked up at me and I told him, my voice rough, "Please don't stop. I really want you inside me."

"You sure?" When I nodded, he kissed my stomach and began lightly massaging my thighs as he took my cock between his lips and sucked me. It was a good instinct, relaxing me and giving me something else to focus on. I moaned, parting my legs for him, and he began lightly tracing soft little circles around my opening.

I pulled open the drawer on my nightstand and retrieved the lube with a shaking hand. I didn't say anything. I just laid it on my belly, signaling I was ready for the next step.

Shea was incredibly tender and patient with me. I whimpered when his lubed fingertip first penetrated me and he stopped what he was doing and looked up at me. "I'm okay," I told him. "Please keep going."

It was the first time anything had been inside me since the night of my rape so many years ago and panic had welled up in me. But I wasn't that boy anymore, scared and helpless and forced. I was a man in love with a partner I trusted completely, and I wanted my man inside me. That faceless rapist had taken a lot from me, but he wasn't going to take this, too. I breathed deeply and parted my legs wider, gently stroking Shea's soft hair as he kissed my inner thigh.

He worked me open slowly, carefully. For all I knew, it might have taken hours before he got one finger in me, then a second. I lost all sense of time. He kept alternately kissing me or sucking my cock, his free hand lovingly caressing my body.

Eventually I told him I was ready, and he eased his cock into me slowly, a fraction of an inch at a time. It really hurt at first and I gasped at the pain. He eased off and said, "You gave me good advice when it was my first time. You told me to push back as if I was trying to push you out of me. That really helped, so maybe you should try it, sweetheart."

Once he reminded me of that trick, it got a little easier. It was still an incredibly tight fit, and pretty uncomfortable, but my body was able to open up enough to accommodate him. He kissed me and stroked my cock, his other arm around me, sliding in slowly until finally he bottomed out in me. He looked in my eyes to gauge my reaction and I smiled up at him. "You okay, Christian?" he asked, and when I nodded he began moving in me.

As his cock started rubbing that spot deep inside me, pleasure took over. My body relaxed and I exhaled slowly. I began to stroke my cock, rocking my hips in time with his thrusts, and begged, "Harder, baby. Please."

Shea got up on his knees, his hands grasping my waist, and watched as his cock slid in and out of me. He moaned and began thrusting harder and faster, his orgasm building. When we were both close I sat up and hugged him to me, bouncing on his thick shaft as I cried out. As soon as I felt his cock twitch and the first blast of cum fill me, I began cumming, too, my cock pressed between us. He held on to me, thrusting wildly, yelling as he came.

Both of us were shaking by the time he eased out of me and dropped onto his side, still clutching me to him. He kissed me before whispering, "Thank you."

I reached up to brush his hair back from his damp forehead. "Thank you, too."

"Are you alright?" he asked as he caught his breath.

"Definitely. Did you like it?"

He grinned shyly and nodded. "It felt so good to be inside you." I smiled at that and curled up in his arms as he asked, "What made you want to do that today?"

"It was time. I'd been carrying around all that fear and hurt for too many years. I love you so much, Shea, and I trust you completely so there was no reason not to."

"It was a big step, though. I thought it would take longer before you were willing to give it a try."

"Everything that's been happening lately has been a wakeup call. I'd been acting like I had plenty of time to deal with all these things in my life, but that's not really true." Shea pressed his eyes shut and I hugged him as I continued softly, "I really wanted to get past my fear, because I wanted to give that to you. To both of us."

"It's surprising that you can talk about what's been happening so calmly."

"Well, my first response was to totally freak out, as you saw. I scared myself with that drinking binge, I've never gotten drunk enough to lose time before," I said. "But here's the thing. My back may be against the wall, but I now realize I do have a choice. I can either get really angry about what's happening to me, do stupid things and ruin the time I have left, or I can look at each day as the gift that it is. I hate the fact that I missed four days with you and I'm not going to miss any more because I can't cope."

The trick would be to hold on to that positive outlook as everything kept unraveling.

Chapter Twenty-Two

Over the rest of January, I really tried to focus on the positive. That would have been a little easier if my motor skills hadn't taken another downturn just three weeks after New Year's. I was seeing my doctor weekly now. He'd upped all my meds as soon as he returned from vacation and immediately sent me for an MRI. I'd had so many of these over the last few years that they seemed perfectly routine.

Doctor Halpern could offer no explanation for the sudden acceleration in the growth of my tumor. He consulted with a colleague in the UK, pored over the latest medical research and did every test on me he could think of, but in the end all he said was, "We'll just keep watching you closely and fine-tune your meds. That's about all we can do." He was never one to sugarcoat it.

During that same time, Shea and I kept ourselves busy by working on converting the big building my dad had given me into an art center. I'd decided this was a better use of my time than school, so I'd taken a leave of absence from Sutherlin. I wasn't sure if going back would ever be an option.

It turned out that a lot of our friends were willing to help with the art center. Skye in particular was incredibly excited about it. He was working on an enormous kinetic sculpture to hang from the lobby's high ceiling, a whimsical mobile that would spin and sway at the slightest breeze. Dare usually accompanied him and helped out where needed. Skye was using scrap aluminum and cutting out wings of all sizes and shapes, which he embossed or painted or both, then hung from crisscrossed aluminum rods over twenty feet in length, suspended with steel cable. It was going to be phenomenal.

River, Cole, Trevor and Vincent were around a lot, too. River, who was a caterer, and Trevor, a chef's apprentice, decided the art center needed a good cafeteria. The building had come with a pretty basic kitchen, and the guys made plans to upgrade it. I gave them my credit card and told them to go nuts, and River's eyes lit up as he went on about cooktops and various gadgets. Cole just chuckled and kissed his boyfriend's cheek, then promised to reel River in before he spent the art center's entire budget.

Meanwhile, Vincent brought in a crew and wired the whole place with a state-of-the-art security system. I tried to pay him for it but he refused, saying that was his contribution to the art center. He also proved to be a skilled handyman, so he helped out in a lot of other ways, too.

Christopher was also really enthusiastic about the art center and would show up at odd hours around his other obligations, usually with his husband Kieran. He'd volunteered to paint the walls of the huge room on the ground floor that would become the music center, and he really went to town. His style was a lot different than mine, his paintings incredibly detailed and photorealistic. Bit by bit, he was covering the walls with a fantasy trompe l'oeil landscape and it was going to be spectacular.

My friend Zandra, who'd been MIA since moving to L.A. with her boyfriend, began driving up every weekend and helping out as well. Skye had told her about my medical condition and when she first came up, she burst into tears and hugged on me for a good two hours. But after that, she got it together and went to work on what would become one of the main studios, a big, sunny space on the second floor. She decided to go with fanciful illustrations on the walls, working in tandem with her boyfriend Scott.

Meanwhile, Chance had been dealing with my news in his own way. He'd become really quiet, but spent a lot of time around me, haunting the building from behind the lens of his camera. He was documenting the transformation from generic warehouse and offices to a bright, vibrant art space. Whenever I asked him how he was doing, he insisted he was fine and changed the subject.

And then, of course, there was Nana. She took the news of my brain tumor by going into full-on denial, then busied herself with the art center like the rest of us. Nana was a woman who *loved* projects. She'd show up every morning with her new chauffeur in tow, the two of them bearing bagels or doughnuts or some other treat, and would immediately get the big, industrial coffee pot going, which she'd brought on her first visit. After that, she'd bustle around, supervising and making suggestions.

The old chauffeur had apparently resigned in a huff over some random antic that Nana had perpetrated. He'd been replaced with Jessie. At first glance, Jessie seemed like just another party boy, especially because the petite blond had selected a pretty sexy chauffeur's uniform for himself. He wore form-fitting shorts and a tight, short-sleeved shirt with a chauffeur's cap and combat boots, all black. To that he'd added a pink bowtie. My first thought when I saw him was, *really*? He looked like a strippergram. But Jessie was a lot more than met the eye and actually turned out to be a smart twenty-four-year-old with a quick sense of humor. I didn't know where Nana had found him or what his story was, but the two of them clearly enjoyed each other's company.

"Isn't he just the cutest little thing?" Nana gushed one day as Jessie left through the big front door to fetch some shopping bags for her. "I tried to set him up with Gianni, but my grandson claims Jessie's not his type. Have you ever heard anything more ridiculous? What part is not his type, the fact that Jessie's adorable, smart, funny, or a gay homosexual? Because from where I'm sitting, all of those things add up to a catch!"

Gianni often accompanied Nana or came on his own to help out where needed. His cousin Nico was in law school and since his classes had resumed, Gianni seemed a bit aimless. One evening after everyone else had cleared out, he stood on the roof with Shea and me, looking out over the city as we drank beer, and said, "My life sucks. Here I am in my mid-twenties. I'm single, I can't find a job, and I'm living with my grandmother. This was so not the plan." His eyes went wide all of a sudden and he turned to me. "I'm sorry, Christian. I just realized how that sounded. Here I am, complaining about my petty shit when you're—" Gianni cut himself off abruptly and I squeezed his arm.

"It's fine, really. I want to know what's going on with you, Gi."

"What kind of job would you want?" Shea asked him. "I could keep an eye out for you."

"I don't even know," Gianni said. "I used to think I wanted to be a nurse when I was younger because I had this romantic notion of helping people, but I was such a failure. I did fine in nursing school right up until we had to do an internship at a hospital. That was when I learned that I'm incredibly squeamish. If there's blood or vomit involved, forget it. Turns out it's pretty hard to assist patients while losing your lunch."

Shea grinned and said, "I can see why that'd be problematic."

Gianni grinned, too. "Nursing would be a great job if it wasn't for all the sick people."

A thought occurred to me and I asked, "Do you have a car?"

"Yeah. Why?"

"I actually need to hire someone to look after my dad," I told him. "He's in good health, but he doesn't leave the house. Right now, I visit him in Marin a couple times a week to bring him groceries, books, whatever he needs. I also just keep him company, since he's so isolated. A few months from now, I won't be in a position to do that anymore and I need someone to take my place. Do you think you'd be interested in a job like that?"

"Absolutely! But why's he housebound if he's in good health?"

I filled him in on my dad's issues and added, "There's one problem. He refuses to accept the fact that I'm going anywhere, so I'm guessing he's going to be pretty stubborn at first."

That made him smile. "Given my family, I've learned to deal with everything from somewhat stubborn to utterly pig-headed."

"I'll arrange a meeting sometime soon," I told him. "It's a relief to finally be moving forward on this."

He left for a date a short time later, and Shea put his arms around my shoulders, leaning against my back. We kept watching the city lights, the breeze stirring our hair as I rested my elbows on the wall around the rooftop. After a while he asked, "Did you give some thought to the idea of moving in with your dad? If you did that, Skye and I would be able to bring Zan the things he needed while being there for you."

"I thought about it, but there's just no way. Even if I decided against moving into that care facility, I would need health care workers around the clock. I just can't see allowing all kinds of strangers into my dad's home, no matter how much their agencies promised discretion."

"So, scratch the idea of living with Zan. You could move in with me, or I could move in to your apartment and the nurses could assist you there. Either option is light years ahead of a nursing home."

"Can we please not talk about this now?" Shea sighed quietly and rested his head against mine. I turned and kissed him, then said, "You must be tired, baby. You're always either at work or here helping with the building. Why don't you go home and get some sleep?"

"Are you coming, too?"

"Not yet, I need to fix the mural." By 'fix' I meant paint over it and start again, for the fourth time. I was starting to feel a bit panicked, because I knew it was just a matter of time before I lost the ability to paint and I really wanted to get this done. That was probably why I was having such a hard time. I was putting a lot of pressure on myself, but I couldn't help it. This mural was incredibly important to me.

"If you're staying, I am too," Shea told me. "I'll get us some coffee and meet you on the balcony."

I headed to the second story, which was spanned by a five-foot-wide glass-fronted walkway that ran the length of the building. After I emptied some white paint into a tray, I grabbed a paint roller with a long handle, then began covering over my latest failure. I'd painted a stylized San Francisco skyline with musical notes weaving among the buildings. It was total crap.

"Again?" a loud voice called from the street. "That one was pretty!" I walked to the edge of the balcony, a plastic tarp crinkling under my feet, and peered over the railing. Nana's white stretch limo was double-parked in the street and she was sticking out the sunroof. Jessie was out of the car too, resting his forearms on the roof of the limo and smiling up at me.

"It sucked, Nana. I just can't get this right. What are you doing out so late?"

She rolled her eyes so dramatically that I could see it even in the dim light. "It's barely midnight. What, you think old people turn into pumpkins when the clock strikes twelve?"

"Okay, what are you doing out so early?"

369

"Come down here so I can talk to you," she yelled. "All this screaming isn't very lady-like!"

I grinned at that and dropped the roller, then went downstairs and out the front of the building. When I was standing beside the limo, she said, "Jessie took me to a nightclub in the Castro. We got the whole place twerking! You shoulda been there, only you never have fun anymore. What happened to the Christian I used to know, the one that would run around shirtless and barefoot with his little silver flask? He was fun."

I shrugged and said, "I guess he grew up."

"Fuck that!" Nana exclaimed. "I mean, I get that you got some heavy issues you're dealing with, but now's not the time to go all serious on me. Just the opposite! Look at me, for example. I'm eighty fucking years old! I could be dead tomorrow! You think I'm going to squander even one day by sitting around fretting over how much time I got left? Hell no!"

"You're right, Nana."

"Of course I'm right! You shone so brightly when I first met you, Christian. You're a star, through and through. Now you just gotta find your sparkle again. It's still there. You just let all this shit pile up on you and dim your light a bit. But I guarantee you can shine again. Isn't that right, Shea?"

"Absolutely." I hadn't heard him come out of the building. He wrapped his hands around my waist and kissed my neck.

"Come on, boys," Nana said. "None of us are getting any younger. Let's go out and have some fun."

"Why the hell not?" I said. Shea locked up the building before following me into the limo. "I'm going to text Chance and tell him to join us. He really needs to have some fun, too."

Chance sounded happy to hear from me and told us where to pick him up. He was nowhere near his apartment, so I wondered if he was working. He hadn't had anymore incidents after the two right after I met him, but I still worried about him. I'd tried talking to him about a job change a couple times, but he always got extremely defensive. I'd even suggested hiring him to work at the art center but he'd given me a look and told me flatly, "Come on. You can't hire someone with a criminal record to work around children. If anyone found out, it'd ruin the art center's reputation." That was when I found out he'd been arrested twice for prostitution. I thought he was wrong and that no one would hold that against him, but he refused to discuss it further.

Once Chance was with us, I said, "You know, I've been promising my friend here a tour of all my hidden murals around the city. Would you guys mind if we did that before heading off for whatever sort of debauchery Nana has in mind?" Everyone seemed enthusiastic about that idea, and Chance asked us to drive him by his apartment so he could grab his camera.

We ended up stopping at a liquor store too, then making a mini party of it as Jessie drove us around the city. Chance got out and photographed every mural, even ones I knew he'd seen before, and gushed over the ones he was seeing for the first time. He also kept taking pictures of Nana, Shea and me, and finally I borrowed his camera and took a few shots of him as well, despite his protests. "You're not just an observer," I told him as I leaned in close and snapped a selfie of the two of us. "You have a ticket on this crazy train just like everyone else." He smiled happily.

I was careful about how much I drank. Ever since my four-day bender, I'd been leery of alcohol. Shea and Nana decided to cut loose though, and after the first hour they were both drunk and singing along to the Elton John CD that she played over and over. I was glad that they were so jolly, because it counteracted the depressing fact that only eleven murals remained out of almost thirty that I'd scattered around the city over the years.

Nana fell asleep after a while, her head back and mouth open, snoring loudly. Jessie took Chance back to his apartment, then drove to Shea's house and dropped us off.

When I thanked him, he gave me a smile and a little salute. "Just doing my job," he told me. "Have I mentioned it's the best one in the entire world?"

"Hey, roomies," my boyfriend bellowed when he swung open the front door and found the three of them in the living room playing a board game.

"Greetings, clearly drunken long-lost roommate!" Cas exclaimed. He was wearing a hat shaped like a wedge of cheese.

"What're you guys playing?" Shea asked as he wove his way over to them. "Can we play, too?"

Leo glanced at me from beneath the brim of his orange baseball cap. It was adorned with two stuffed, yellow lightning bolts, one above each ear. "We're playing Firefly, The Game. I'm not sure if it's your hot boyfriend's idea of a good time."

"Firefly as in *Firefly*? The most awesome, unfairly cancelled TV show of all time? Are you telling me someone made a game based on Joss Whedon's masterpiece?" I asked.

Ridley raised an eyebrow at me. He was wearing a top hat for some reason. "Are you just pretending to suddenly have some geek cred, or did you actually watch this show?"

"I *loved* Firefly. Doesn't mean I know how to play this game, though."

"Well, maybe you and Shea can team up and he can show you what to do. We've only been playing for a few minutes, so we can begin again," Leo said.

"Excellent," I said as Shea and I settled on one of the oversized chairs together. "Quick, someone bring us some hats."

Shea explained the game to me, then fell asleep after about half an hour. He'd slid down to the floor, his head resting on my thigh. He was wearing Captain America's leather cap and mask and looked impossibly cute. "I'm out without my pilot," I said, leaning back in the chair and adjusting the R2-D2 mouse ears that Cas had acquired on a recent trip to Disneyland.

"You've got the hang of it now," Leo said. "Why not continue while Shea sleeps it off?"

"I can't, actually," I admitted. "Shea was acting as my hands. The ships are too small for me to move around the board and I don't have the dexterity to turn those cards over."

Leo asked, "Do you like playing?"

"Yeah."

"So I'll flip your cards and move your piece for you. No biggie."

"Alright. Thanks," I said.

We proceeded like this for the next hour, until Ridley and Cas decided they really needed to run to the corner convenience store for some Doritos. After they left, Leo got up and stretched, but I stayed where I was so I wouldn't disturb Shea. He was snoring softly, his full lips slightly parted, and I was lightly caressing the silky hair at the back of his neck, beneath the edge of the cap.

Leo watched me for a moment as he perched on the arm of his chair, then said, his voice quieter and lower than usual, "Let me ask you something. When Shea got so sick before Christmas and you looked after him in your apartment, did that feel like a burden?"

"Of course not."

"Why not?"

"Because I love Shea. It wasn't a burden at all."

"From what I hear, he was pretty sick, though. He said he was so weak he couldn't even get to the bathroom by himself. He also said he was puking his guts out. That must have been disgusting. Why didn't you call his brother to come get him?"

I knit my brows at him. "Why would I? Like I said, I love him and didn't want to hand off the responsibility of caring for him."

"Why not?"

"As long as he was with me, I knew he was getting cared for properly. I wanted to be able to keep an eye on him and make sure he had everything he needed. No one would have taken better care of him than I did."

"And yet you expect Shea to just step back and let you go off to some nursing home."

I grinned a little and said, "Ah. I was wondering why we were talking about this, but now I see. You were setting me up."

"No, not setting you up. I'm just trying to get you to look at this from a different perspective. Shea's really upset at the thought of you putting yourself in the hands of strangers. He knows that absolutely no one will care for you as well as he will, because no one loves you the way he does. That guy right there would do absolutely anything for you."

"I know, but—"

"But nothing. Think about who you're dealing with for a minute. Shea's always been the kind of guy that would take a bullet for the people he cares about, no questions asked. And now that he's in love, can you even imagine how loyal and devoted he is to you? That's who he is, right down to his core. He was born to help others and you're trying to deny him that."

"I'm not. I just don't want—"

"I know what you're going to say. You don't want to be a burden to him and also, you don't want him to see you when you're all Stephen Hawking-ed out. Right?"

A little bark of laughter escaped me. "That's incredibly politically incorrect."

"Whatever. I know that has to be a part of it. You think Shea's shallow enough to think any differently of you when you're no longer this pretty boy?"

"*I'll* care. If it was you, wouldn't you want your boyfriend to remember you while you were still relatively healthy and not a shell of your former self? The way I am now is what I want him to remember."

Leo rolled his eyes at that. "That's more than a little shallow."

"Thanks."

"Well, it's true. You'd rather leave him with the memory of your choosing rather than have all those extra months with him."

"But think about what those months would be like for him! He'd get to watch me break down, slowly, painfully. He'd watch as my personality eroded and as everything I once was fell away. That's what I'm trying to spare him, Leo."

"That's what you're trying to spare both of you."

"Okay, yes. That would be as hard on me as it was on him. I'd much rather disintegrate in front of total strangers than the man I love. Call it being shallow if you want. But all of that is going to be hard enough to live through without also seeing the agony in my sweet boyfriend's eyes as he watches me die."

Leo scratched his chin and mulled that over for a few moments. Finally he said, "I can see your perspective. But put yourself in his shoes. Imagine, *really imagine*, what it would feel like if the situation were reversed. What if Shea was the one that insisted on going off to die alone? Is there any part of you that would be okay with that?"

I looked away, staring at the cluttered fireplace mantel without really seeing it. "No," I admitted.

"Exactly."

I muttered, "Shit," just as Cas and Ridley returned. They burst in the front door laughing loudly, their arms full of paper grocery sacks. Shea woke with a little snort and sat up, blinking at his surroundings. He turned and looked at me, and the moment his eyes focused on me, the most beautiful smile lit up his face. "I love you so much," I said quietly.

"I love you, too." He squeezed in with me on the chair again and kissed my cheek. "You're so cute in those mouse ears that I can barely stand it."

I reached up and straightened the hat as I offered him a little grin. "I forgot I was wearing them."

That just made him smile even more. His friends passed around beers and snacks, and we resumed the game, Shea once again working in tandem with me. I tried to concentrate, but I was distracted. For the first time, I was actually considering the possibility of not checking myself in to that nursing home. Leo was right, I would never let Shea go off alone to some impersonal facility. Given that, how could I expect him to let me go?

Eventually, I tried to get my head back in the game. "I forgot to ask," I said. "Why are we wearing silly hats?"

Ridley flashed me a big smile. "Because we can."

That made me smile, too. I loved the fact that all of these guys, my boyfriend included, had managed to stay in touch with their inner child. In fact, when I tried to imagine them as kids, I decided they wouldn't really be much different than they were now. I could just see them all ten or fifteen years ago, sitting around a different board game, wearing a different set of silly hats, just having fun. Ten or fifteen years from now, they'd probably be doing the same thing.

"Hey," I said to Shea as Leo took his turn, "I know this is random, but do you have any pictures of yourself as a kid?"

He looked embarrassed and said with a shy smile, "My brother actually found some old photos of us the other day and snapped pictures of them for me." He pulled his phone from his pocket and flipped through a few screens. "Promise not to laugh." He turned the screen toward me to reveal a posed school portrait of an adorable little blond kid with braces.

"Oh man, look how cute you were," I said sincerely as I took the phone from him.

"I was a dork."

"No you weren't, you were so sweet! And blond! I just assumed you'd always been a brunet."

"Nope. I was a blond, chubby, brace face."

I beamed at him and handed the phone back. "You were cute then and you're absolutely stunning now."

"And this makes you very happy for some reason," he said with a smile as he returned the phone to his pocket.

"I just figured out what I'm going to paint on the front of that huge building, so yes, I'm ecstatic. Having that hanging over me was really stressing me out."

"You're going to paint a bunch of dorky kids with braces?" he joked.

I smiled and told him, "Absolutely."

Chapter Twenty-Three

What I actually ended up painting on the front of the building over the next couple weeks was all of us, larger than life, Shea and Skye and Chance and Zandra and Nana and all the rest of our friends, every single person that came to help out with the art center. Only, I painted us the way we looked when we were children and put us all together on a big, colorful playground. Some of us were running or playing, the rest drawing with chalk on the blacktop. The playground was backed by a wall with a big mural, a painting within a painting. On that wall I'd painted my father playing the piano, his hair hanging down so you couldn't see his face clearly, and I'd surrounded him with lines of swirling music against a deep blue starry sky, the stars representing the crowds of people he'd once performed for. Behind that wall were trees and a bright, sunny sky. The mural covered the entire face of the building from roofline to sidewalk. It was not only the biggest thing I'd ever done, it was also the best. I felt really satisfied when I looked at it.

Even though my fine motor skills were giving me a lot of problems, I was still able to paint, and that felt like such a tremendous gift. My doctor explained it by telling me I was using a different part of my brain when I painted. Whatever the reason, I was incredibly grateful for it.

A deep voice close by startled me. "That's supposed to be your dad, right?" I turned to look at Finn Nolan. He was dressed in his police uniform, his big arms crossed over his chest. "In the painting, I mean, the one playing the piano." When I didn't respond, he said, "I did some digging, found out who you are. Found out who your dad is, too."

A cold feeling settled in the pit of my stomach. "So, what are you going to do with that information?"

"Nothing. I did tell Shea, but he knew all about it. He told me he'd even met the man, and that Tillane had made him sit through all the Harry Potter movies back-to-back, three times." Finn grinned a little, but I just stared at him. He fidgeted and said, "I was on patrol and saw you standing out here." He tilted his head toward a police car double-parked in front of the building. "So I just...I don't know."

"Thought you'd pull over and threaten to reveal my identity?"

"No! That's not it at all. I did consider going public with this information when I first uncovered it, because I figured it'd fuck you over pretty good. But it'd fuck my brother over too, and your dad, who according to Shea is a really nice guy."

"It would."

"Look...I don't like you and I don't know if I'll ever trust you."

"Awesome."

"The thing is," Finn said, "I don't think I'd like or trust any guy that my baby brother got involved with. He's a really great guy, and I just want the best for him, you know?"

"Yeah."

"Anyway, he told me what's happening to you and, shit man," he fidgeted again, looking at the ground. "I wouldn't wish that on my worst enemy. Sorry you're going through that."

"Thanks."

Apparently he had more to say to me, but it took him a few moments to work it out. Finally he blurted, "My friend Sammy. The one I thought you screwed over? He's been through four more guys since you and he were involved, and I watched him get way too attached to every single one of them, then act like it was the end of the world when they moved on. He also made each of those guys out to be total ogres after the fact and played it like he was this innocent victim when they broke up with him. But, see, I met some of these guys and that's not really what happened. I never realized Sammy was like that until recently. So, you know. Maybe what happened between you two last summer wasn't totally your fault."

I grinned at him. "Is that an apology?"

He shrugged his broad shoulders. "I guess it is. I was a real dick to you. Maybe you deserved it, maybe you didn't. Either way, I shouldn't have acted like that."

"Water under the bridge."

"Alright, well, I'm gonna get back to work. You did a nice job on this painting. That's exactly what Shea looked like when he was a little kid, only I don't recall him ever being that happy. He is now though, so you got that right." I watched as he returned to his patrol car and drove off. Sometimes people could be surprising in the best possible way.

"Who was that?" Skye asked as he came out the door of the art center, a coffee in each hand, then used two fingertips to tug on the door handle and make sure it had locked behind him.

"Shea's brother."

"Oh! The douche?"

"Maybe not so much of a douche after all."

We both turned to look at the mural. I'd put the finishing touches on it just that morning. He said with a smile, "You completely nailed it. I like how you gave eight-year-old me blue hair. A sign of things to come."

"I'm glad you like it." I glanced up at my favorite part, Shea and me at about age ten, over in the upper right-hand corner. Shea was smiling and pushing me on a swing, and I was clutching a little bouquet of daisies in my hand as I looked over my shoulder at him and laughed.

"I love it, especially all the little details. Is that Nana?" he pointed to a tiny little girl near the center of the scene and I nodded. "It's great that you made her the youngest one in the group."

"Nana's the youngest person I know, in spirit."

"And you made her drawing two little male stick figures getting married. Classic."

"She does love her gay homosexual weddings," I said with a grin.

"That reminds me, you ready for that surprise I promised you?" Skye turned to me with a sparkle in his blue eyes.

My grin got wider. "Does it involve gay homosexuals?"

"Absolutely."

"Then bring it on."

"I'm bringing it on as we speak. In fact, the surprise should be along any—oh, here we go." He was looking past me down the street, and I turned to watch Nana's stretch limo approaching.

When the car reached us, Jessie hopped out and opened the door for us with a flourish. "Gentlemen," he said cheerfully, "welcome aboard the Portland express."

"The what now?" I asked as I climbed into the limo.

Shea, Nana, River, Cole, Trevor, Vincent, Joshie and Dare were already inside. "Looks like a party," I said as I squeezed in beside Shea and picked up his hand. He was smiling happily.

"Oh it is," Skye said as he climbed onto his fiancé's lap. "A wedding party. Dare and I are eloping to Portland and you, my best man, are coming with us!"

"Co-best man," River chimed in. "Sorry dude, but you're sharing the honors with yours truly. I earned that title after putting up with the blue menace all these years. It's really appropriate that in the mural Skye's bugging me, by the way."

I laughed at that. "He's not bugging you, exactly." I'd painted a little seven- or eight-year-old Skye running after his big brother while holding hands with the kid version of Dare. "So, wait. Are we about to take a road trip to Oregon so your mom can attend your wedding?"

"Yup. She's not allowed to travel, so we're going to her. It's all arranged, the wedding's tomorrow. We're just keeping it simple and getting married at her house."

"On Valentine's Day," I pointed out.

"I know, it's kind of corny, but so are we." Skye flashed Dare a big smile before kissing him.

"I need to swing by my apartment. I have to pack a bag," I said as the limo made a left turn.

"Don't worry," Shea said. "I packed one for you. I got everything you need." I'd given him a key to my apartment a few weeks ago.

I returned his smile and said, "Thanks, baby," before kissing him.

We made one more stop and picked up Chance. The limo was pretty crowded by now, so he sat on the floor right beside me and smiled up at us over his shoulder. "Hi everyone," he said. "Thanks for including me. I'll take pictures of the wedding if you guys want me to."

"You can if you want, but we really just wanted you to be our guest," Skye said.

"I want to. It'll be my wedding present to you both."

"A wedding present, damn," I murmured. "I didn't get to buy you guys anything."

"We don't need stuff," Skye said. "We just need you by our side." Suddenly, I got why they were eloping. They'd bumped their wedding up from summer so I could attend. I blinked a couple times to head off the tears prickling at the back of my eyes. When I turned to look at Shea, he read my emotions in an instant and smiled as he put his arm around me and rested his forehead against mine.

"I'm the luckiest guy in the world," I murmured. Shea looked a little surprised at that, and I added, "I am. I have the sweetest boyfriend and the greatest friends." I turned to look at my best friend and his fiancé, who were seated right beside me. "Thank you for moving your wedding up. I'm honored to be a part of it."

"That's it," River said. "I'm busting out the booze. It's a long drive to Portland and we're already getting sappy!" Cole chuckled and popped open the mini fridge, then handed his boyfriend a bottle of champagne. He also pulled out a bottle of sparkling cider and poured some for Josh and Jessie. The eleven-year-old crawled through the open divider to sit beside the driver and the two of them clicked their plastic cups together. A black and white furry head popped up beside Joshie. Benny the dog panted and wagged all of himself excitedly as the kid scratched him behind the ears.

Skye meanwhile started talking animatedly about some new piece of crap he'd just found in a junkyard. I watched the total adoration on Dare's face as his fiancé was talking. I was so happy for Skye. He was marrying the man he loved, who in turn loved him with all his heart. It was exactly what I wanted for my best friend.

I looked at the faces of everyone around me and my heart felt so full. I really was lucky. I may not have been dealt a lot of years in the great, random lottery of life, but I'd been given so much. All that love and friendship and these remarkable people were such an incredible gift.

The feeling of peace that settled over me was surprising. I'd spent the last few weeks trying so hard to take Nana's advice and cherish each day as the gift that it was, but fear and anger still crept in occasionally. I'd busied myself with that mural, working on it seven days a week while also taking care of the million details that went into getting the art center operational. But it was all under control. The mural was done and the art center was coming together. It would be ready for a big grand opening in April.

I was doing what I'd always wanted to do. I was leaving a legacy. My life was going to mean something. I just knew the art center was going to make a difference for a lot of people, and if it gave even one kid hope and awakened a love of art, then it was all worthwhile.

I leaned against Shea and his arms encircled me securely. I felt the warmth of his body and the steady beat of his heart against my back. He felt so solid and reassuring.

I'd decided once and for all to forget about the nursing home, but I hadn't told him yet. I was going to stay with the love of my life right to the end. My pride still struggled with the embarrassment of him seeing what I was going to become, and I hated the fact that I was going to be such a burden, but his friend Leo had been right. If the situation were reversed, I would never, ever let Shea go off by himself. So how could I expect him to be okay with doing the same thing?

*****

As we left the Bay Area behind and began to cut through the agricultural center of the state on Highway Five, Nana started all of us on a sing-along. That made Joshie shoot us a look over his shoulder and raise the sound-proof barrier between the back of the limo and the front seat. Nana loved Elton John and would have gone through his entire song book, but eventually we managed to branch out to some other stuff as well, taking turns calling out songs. When it was Chance's turn he suggested shyly, "How about 'Evermore' by Zan Tillane?"

I smiled at that, then said, "Not all of you know this, but Zan is my father and he was always proud of that song. It wasn't a huge hit, but it's one of his favorites." It was time to let the rest of my friends in on that secret. There was no reason not to. I trusted everyone here.

Nana in particular had a million questions, but I just said, "He's in good health and choosing to live his life out of the public eye. Needless to say, we all need to keep this quiet so the paparazzi don't hunt him down and make his life miserable." Nana pantomimed locking her lips and throwing away the key.

I pulled out my phone and called Zan. When he answered, I said, "I have something for you, Dad. I'm on my way to Skye's wedding in Oregon and we're singing our favorite songs in the back of Nana's limo. This next song was suggested by my friend Chance." I put my dad on speaker and began singing 'Evermore'. My voice wasn't nearly as good as my father's, but when everyone joined in, we did it justice.

When we finished, my dad sounded a little choked up. "Ah, boyo, you remembered all the words," he said.

"Of course I did. I know every word to every song you've ever written. I don't know if I've ever actually said this to you, but I'm so proud that you're my dad."

Zan chuckled and said as his voice broke a little, "So basically, you thought you'd call your old man and make him start blubbering."

I smiled and said, "Yup, that was my plan. I love you, Dad. I'll be gone a couple days, but call my cell if you need anything and I'll make sure it gets taken care of."

"Love you too, son. Congratulations to Skye. I haven't met his fiancé, but he's bound to be a pretty remarkable man, given the fact that he won that boy's heart." I'd taken my best friend to meet my dad a couple weeks ago, and they totally hit it off.

"He is."

"Give Shea a hug for me, I could hear him singing in the background. Such a lovely voice. Say hello to the rest of your friends as well."

"Will do. Talk to you soon, Dad."

After we disconnected and I returned the phone to my pocket, River grinned at me and quipped, "And the award for most unexpected newsflash goes to Christian."

I smiled and changed the subject by saying, "I think it's Nana's turn to pick the next song. Let me guess: Elton John?"

*****

Everything was going along swimmingly until an hour or so later when Nana exclaimed, "What the fuck!" She then scrambled over Shea and me and knocked on the divider.

When Jessie lowered the glass panel, all he said was, "On it!" He then took the next exit.

"On what?" Cole asked, pushing his glasses further up the bridge of his nose.

The limo made a sharp right, so we were now on an access road running parallel to the freeway. "I need to swing around," Jessie said, sliding his cap back on his head. "I can't get it from this angle." He then brought the long car around in a wide U-turn, kicking up dust in a fallow field. I was surprised we didn't get stuck.

Once we were pointed the other way, I saw what had upset Nana. Someone had erected a home-made billboard beside the freeway that said 'God hates fags.'

"Battle stations everyone!" Nana exclaimed. "Joshie, come back here, sweetie." The boy climbed over the seat, Benny scrambling over with him, and Nana put a seatbelt on the kid while Skye scooped up the dog and held on to him. "Careful, Jessie," she called. "We don't want the airbags going off again!"

"Yes ma'am!" he called, and then he gunned the engine. The limo hopped the embankment and then flattened the big sign with a satisfying crunch. For good measure, Jessie rolled back and forth over it a few times, then threw the car in reverse and swung us around so we were back on the access road. Dust kicked up behind us as we sped out of there.

Everyone burst out laughing and applauding. "We're definitely going to jail," Skye exclaimed. He looked delighted, his eyes sparkling.

"Totally worth it," Shea said.

I chuckled at that. "And you used to be such a nice, law-abiding boy."

Surprisingly, we made it across the Oregon border a couple hours later without a police chase. Portland was still five hours away at the northern end of the state, so we decided to take a break in Ashland, a cute little theater town. Shea and I grabbed a couple slices of pizza while Nana led a shopping and dining expedition around the Plaza. We headed into a gorgeous park that was located right behind the shops and restaurants, and Shea took my hand as we walked along the creek. It was really cold, but he'd thought to pack my warmest jacket.

We went halfway across an ornate pedestrian bridge and stopped to watch the creek churning beneath us, our breath forming clouds in the air. That was when I told him I'd changed my mind about the nursing home. "I guess I'll keep my apartment because I still don't like the idea of going to live with my dad. It should prove to be fairly wheelchair accessible when I get to that point. And we're definitely going to hire nurses, lots of them. I really want to make sure you and Skye don't get stressed out."

I'd been watching the creek, but I turned to look at Shea then. His eyes were bright with tears as he grabbed me in a hug and whispered, "Thank you."

"Oh no, I'm the one that should be thanking you. I know I haven't been acting like it, but I really am incredibly grateful that you're willing to help me."

"What finally made you change your mind?"

"It was a conversation I had with your friend Leo. He told me the same things everyone else had, but I guess he did it at the right time, and in a way that finally got through to me. He asked me if I could let you go if you were the one who was sick, and I knew I couldn't. There'd be absolutely no way. I realized then that I couldn't expect you to do what I wouldn't be able to."

Shea smiled at me and said, "I'll have to remember to thank him. Speaking of Leo, it's so great that you included him and Cas and Ridley in the mural. That's exactly what they used to do when we were in junior high, too, they'd sit off in a corner and play board games during our lunch break." The trio had contributed to the art center by helping set up a rec room for the kids to use before and after classes. They'd brought in stacks of board games and had helped paint a bunch of wooden tables and chairs in bright colors.

"They were definitely a part of it."

Shea said, "I love the fact that the art center is turning out so great, and that it's the result of your friends, my friends and our friends, all coming together. With you as our fearless leader, of course."

"And you as my trusty co-captain."

"Care to act out our scene in the mural?" He tilted his head to indicate an empty playground right behind us on the banks of the creek.

We both laughed as he pushed me on the swings. After a while, the rest of our group caught up with us. They not only were accompanied by the dog on a leash, they also brought along a medium-sized kennel containing Skye's cat and a tiny pet carrier holding his pink pet mouse. I hadn't realized the whole family had been Jessie's copilots up front.

Jessie climbed to the very top of a big play structure and announced that he was king of the world while Chance got on the swing to my left. Vincent sat on the swing to my right with Trevor on his lap, and the two swayed slowly as they kissed. Meanwhile Skye, Dare, River and Cole tried to make each other puke on the little spinning merry-go-round while the dog bounced up and down and yipped excitedly. Nana followed Jessie onto the jungle gym and went down the slide over and over, whooping excitedly each time. Joshie, the actual kid in the group, was the only one who refrained, sighing and shaking his head before sitting on a bench beside the cat and mouse and pulling out a paperback. Funnily enough, that was exactly what I'd painted him doing in the mural.

The cold finally drove us back to the limo, still chuckling, our cheeks pink and our noses running. Skye, who'd spent part of his childhood in Oregon and knew his way around, directed Jessie to a drive-through coffee kiosk called Dutch Brothers, and we all got piping hot drinks before we returned to the highway. "This is a perfect day," I whispered to Shea as I snuggled with him, a big coffee warming my hands and my boyfriend's arms warming the rest of me.

He smiled and said, "Couldn't agree more."

*****

Skye's mom Tina, her boyfriend Hawk, the boyfriend's sister and a whole mess of kids lived outside Portland in what had once been a small vineyard. A charming, faded farmhouse was nestled amid rolling hills and overgrown, dormant grapevines. Apparently it had once belonged to the boyfriend's father. The current occupants didn't seem terribly interested in maintaining the place and I could just picture the vines engulfing the house in a few years.

They were all awake and waiting for us when we rolled in a little before midnight. Tina was an aging hippie with more grey than blonde in her curly hair, and Hawk was tall and lanky with two skinny blond braids hanging past his shoulders. Even though Tina was confined to bed, she was clearly running the entire operation. She gave each of us a bone-crushing hug, including the people she was meeting for the first time. The smell of rosemary enveloped me when it was my turn.

"Hi Mom," River said when she released him from her grasp. "Nice to see that being knocked up hasn't weakened your Kung Fu grip."

"I'm perfectly fine," she said with a wave of her hand, which made a row of bangles on her wrist jingle, "except for this stupid blood pressure thing. Did I tell you it's a boy, by the way? You and Skye are going to have a baby brother!"

"Have you picked out a name yet?" Skye asked. "Maybe Pond? Or Hillock? How about Moss? That goes well with River and Skye."

"Moss," Tina mused. "I like that."

"Mom!" Skye exclaimed. "I was kidding! Don't you dare name that baby Moss! At least give him a shot at not getting teased every day of his life."

She shrugged and said, "Kids would tease even if I named the baby something perfectly normal. And how boring would that be?" Tina spotted Joshie then, lingering toward the back of the group, and greeted him warmly. He'd lived with her for a while before Trevor and Vincent adopted him. Apparently he wasn't a fan of any of Tina's boyfriend's kids, so once the hellos were out of the way, he said he was going to read in the limo and took off.

"I'll go with him and make sure he doesn't freeze," Jessie said, zipping up. He'd paired a black leather jacket and black wool tights with his shorts and the rest of his uniform, the winter version of 'chauffer strippergram' apparently.

"Thanks," Trevor said before asking, "Where will we be sleeping? I'll bring in Joshie's stuff and try to shift him someplace warmer."

Hawk's sister Enid pointed the way. The farmhouse was pretty maxed out with seven or eight people already living there, but it turned out there was a bunk house back in the orchard that they'd kind of fixed up for us. Nana took one look at it and said, "I'm going to find a Marriot and I'm taking Joshie and Jessie with me. I'll be back first thing in the morning. Do you want me to bring anything back from town?"

"No thanks, Nana," Skye told her, shoving one of the bunks across the floor until it rested against the one Dare was going to use. "We're just going to keep this simple. The wedding official will be here at one and I guess we'll have the ceremony in the living room, in front of the fireplace."

Nana stared at him for a moment, then spun on her heel. "I'm going to have that herd of kids clean up in there, they're plenty old enough to pitch in. We can't have you getting married surrounded by old newspapers and dirty dishes. For that matter, what are they doing letting your knocked up mother live in squalor like that? Someone needs to take charge of this situation!"

Skye chuckled at that as we watched her march back through the orchard. "She's not wrong," he said. Meanwhile, Dare let the dog off his leash and filled a bowl for him from a water bottle. Benny began patrolling and sniffing the bunkhouse. Draco, the blond cat, was let out of his kennel, which revealed that he was wearing a little blue sweater along with a harness and leash. He settled down on a bunk, tucked his feet under him, and shut his eyes. The mouse didn't get to leave his carrier and just stared at us.

Throughout all of that, Shea had been starting fires in the three potbelly stoves that were positioned between the two rows of bunks. I glanced at the space we were in and asked, "Why would a vineyard need a couple dozen workers?"

"This was a logging camp long before someone thought to grow grapes here," Skye said as he shook out one of the blankets that had been left for us. "I know it's a bit rustic. Sorry about that."

"It's awesome," I told him cheerfully. "I never got to go to summer camp. Now I feel like I have."

"We're kind of missing the summer part of that," Shea said as he rubbed his hands together, "but these should warm us up pretty soon."

"If not, I can figure out how to stay warm," River said, slipping his arms around his boyfriend and pulling him close as Cole grinned shyly.

Vincent, on the other hand, looked skeptical. "Want to go with my grandmother?" he asked his husband. "The Marriot's sounding pretty appealing."

Trevor smiled at him. "Where's your spirit of adventure? After this you'll be able to say you slept in a real logging camp bunkhouse!"

Vincent grinned a little. "And that'll do what, exactly? Make my brothers jealous? Gianni won't stay anyplace with less than five stars."

In response to that, Trevor went over to the dirty window and drew five stars in the grime. "There you go. Also, Gi's kind of a princess. You can tell him I said that." Trevor glanced at something to his left. "I forget, are you afraid of spiders?"

"I'm definitely not a fan," Vincent told him. "Why do you ask?"

Trevor stomped his foot, then dragged it out of sight. "No reason."

"Yeah, I'm going to the Marriot." Vincent fled with his chuckling husband right on his heels.

"See you in the morning, guys," Trevor called on the way out the door.

I turned to look at Chance. He was doing that quiet haunting thing again, remaining near me but not saying anything. "What about you?" I asked him. "Do you want to retreat to a hotel?"

He shook his head. "I've never seen anything like this. I can't wait to take pictures when it's light out."

"That's the spirit," I said as I put an arm around his shoulders. "As for you," I said, gesturing at Shea, "I don't even need to ask. Look at you! You're completely in your element. I'll bet you used to be a Boy Scout, am I right?"

"Right."

"You probably even go camping on purpose, don't you?"

He smiled at me. "Yup, on purpose and everything. Do you?"

"Oh no. I'm what you call a city boy. I've never been camping, but I'm going to go ahead and say this is primitive enough to qualify."

"Not even close," Shea said as he shook out his bedding and mine, then pushed our bunks together.

"No? Then what does?"

"You and me snug in a tent, a campfire, and s'mores. Definitely s'mores."

"You've done the impossible, you've actually made camping sound appealing. Let's go as soon as the weather warms up. In the meantime, that's pretty close to a campfire," I said, indicating the flames glowing inside the potbelly stove. "Think there might be ingredients for s'mores in the farmhouse?"

Skye picked up his fiancé's hand. "We'll go find out and say goodnight to my mom."

Later on, as we took turns toasting marshmallows through the open door of the stove and drinking hot chocolate spiked with rum and cinnamon, Dare flashed Skye a huge smile. "This is the oddest bachelor party ever. It's absolutely perfect."

"Like my little brother was going to have a normal one," River said cheerfully.

"Hey, I was just thinking. Do you guys want to take a stroll down the aisle after us tomorrow?" Skye asked his brother. "The wedding official can do a two-fer so you can finally make an honest man of Cole."

"You go right ahead and be conventional," River teased. "Cole and I are just fine with living in sin. Aren't we, hon?"

Cole kissed his boyfriend's cheek and said, "This couldn't be more perfect. I say we keep doing exactly what we're doing."

"But by all means," River told Skye, "proceed with your wedded bliss. And for God's sake, move your marshmallow. It's about to burst into flames." As if on cue, Skye's marshmallow did exactly that and River said, "See? I'm always right."

*****

When we got up the next morning and wandered to the farmhouse looking for coffee, we found the place had been set to Maximum Nana. She'd completely taken over. Skye's mom seemed amused by the whole thing as she lounged on the couch sipping herb tea. Her boyfriend, his sister and the kids had apparently vacated the premises.

The living room was completely spotless and overflowing with flowers and plants. It looked like Nana had gone to a florist and bought out their entire inventory. Since today was Valentine's Day, most of it was red and pink.

Apparently she'd also gone to a bakery and had decided to record an episode of her cable TV cooking show for whatever reason. Jessie was acting as her on-air assistant, while Trevor worked a movie camera on a tripod and Vincent stood off to the side, shaking his head. A boom hung from a makeshift rig and portable lights to each side completed her set. Nana came prepared.

"Ah, there are our grooms!" she exclaimed when she spotted Skye and Dare. "Come join us, boys, we're about to make your wedding cake! We didn't know what flavor you wanted, so we went with all of them! Jessie, you ready?" He smiled and nodded. "Alright kiddo, start stacking!"

Jessie and Nana worked as a team, using two spatulas apiece to lift a series of twelve-inch-round Valentine's

Day-pink cakes and stack them on top of each other as Nana explained, "Bakers charge a premium for wedding cakes, but it's just a question of stacking, people! It's so easy, anyone can do it! Now, I didn't have a chance to custom order anything, so I just went with what they had at the bakery. Normally, you maybe want to use cakes of different sizes, but this'll work. Once you finish building your cake tower, pipe on some frosting, slap on some fresh flowers and you got yourself a wedding cake!"

"How big are we going, Nana?" Jessie asked as they piled on cake after cake.

"Big as you want!"

"This is pretty big," Jessie said, looking up at the cake tower.

"We should cap it off with this fancy princess cake as a nice finishing touch." Nana said, climbing up on a stepstool and hoisting up a rounded dome cake covered with pink marzipan. It was slightly wider than the cakes below it, and as soon as it was in place, Jessie stepped back, blinked at what they'd made, and said, "Oops." Then he started laughing. Chance had his camera around his neck and started snapping photos as he chuckled delightedly.

"Oh shit," Nana exclaimed as I doubled over with laughter, "we accidentally made a giant weenie dongle." Shea was laughing so hard that tears were streaming down his face.

The huge cake dong started listing to the right and Nana grabbed hold of it with both hands. "Fuck a duck, Jessie, we forgot a key step! We needed to keep it stiff!" He was laughing so hard by this point that he had to lean against the kitchen counter to remain upright.

"It is really important to keep it stiff," he managed.

"You were supposed to insert your wood! How could we forget that?" Nana told him. The fact that she was gesturing with her chin toward some thin wooden dowels was lost on her assistant, who was struggling to breathe.

The cake was leaning even further by now and she ended up hugging it and trying to heave it upright. Jessie collapsed on the kitchen floor, howling with laughter, and a chuckling Skye and Dare jumped in to try to lend a hand. They both hesitated though, unsure where exactly to grab the frosting-covered phallus.

"This is awesome," Trevor said as he panned the camera across the scene before him, a huge smile on his face. Joshie wandered in just then, paperback in hand. He took one look at the chaos, shook his head, and left the room again.

Meanwhile, Nana teetered on the stepstool, trying to wrestle the cock cake into an upright position with both arms wrapped around it. "It looks like she's trying to jerk it off," Chance murmured as he chuckled and kept snapping photos.

"Quick Skye, hand me that thing on the counter," Nana exclaimed.

She probably meant the dowel, but Skye grabbed a pastry bag filled with white icing and said, "This?" as he held the bag up to her.

Nana grabbed it without looking and reached for the top of the cake. She squeezed the bag too hard though as she lost her footing, sending a jet of white icing shooting toward the ceiling. It arced up and over, splattering the grooms. I laughed so hard that my sides hurt. Dare caught her easily as Nana fell off the stool.

"Well, that was a satisfying climax," Shea quipped, still chuckling as he wiped tears from his eyes.

"Does Nana really have a cooking show?" Chance asked as we watched the cock cake lean over like the tower of Pisa and just remain there, looking spent.

"She does," I said. "It's on cable TV and pretty much always goes exactly like this."

"The things I miss by not having a television." Chance shook his head.

Nana walked up to Trevor as he shut off the camera. She was totally covered in pink frosting and daintily patting her hair in place. She said, "There's probably some useable footage there, right? We can just edit it a bit, maybe blur it out once it turns into a big weenie dongle."

"Sure," Trevor told her with a huge smile. "It'll be fine."

"I bought plenty of extra cake," she said. "We can try again and make something nice for my boys."

"Out of curiosity," Trevor said as he removed the camera from the tripod, "Why'd you want to film today?"

"I decided to branch out and become one of them, you know, lifestyle experts," she told him. "I already have my cooking program, but I figure I can also show people how to throw real nice gay homosexual weddings on all kinds of budgets. Even if you're cutting costs though, you can probably do better than a big, pink peepee."

Nana went off to change and Jessie pulled out his phone and snapped a picture of the droopy dessert. "This really is the best job ever," he said happily.

While Chance went over to Jessie and showed him the photos he'd taken, I crossed the room to the coffee pot but then I hesitated. I'd gotten a new machine at home, one that dispensed directly into a cup to save myself the step of pouring, since that had become surprisingly problematic. I'd learned to adapt as my fine motor skills deteriorated, figuring out fixes like wrapping my silverware with duct tape to create thick handles that were easier for my clumsy fingers to grab onto. All in all, I felt I was adapting pretty well, at least so far. But being someplace new put me at a disadvantage.

I looked to Shea a bit embarrassedly and he stepped right up, pouring my coffee and doctoring it the way I liked it. "Come on," he said, tilting his head. "Let's sit out on the porch."

That was the first time I'd ever asked for help, even though I'd done it wordlessly. I'd been dreading getting to that point, but Shea made it a nonissue. He was just there for me. It was that simple.

We settled onto a creaky porch swing with a view of the rolling hills that surrounded us. The sky was impossibly blue, the sun shining brightly, though there was still a chill in the air. I thanked Shea as he handed me my coffee. I couldn't manage the handle, so I grasped the cup between my palms instead. "Have you started pouring milk in your coffee because it cools it down and makes the mug easier to hold like that?" he asked quietly.

"Exactly. Your observation skills never cease to amaze me."

"Is the reason you've lost weight because you're having trouble feeding yourself?"

I was only down three of four pounds and hadn't thought it was noticeable. "I'm figuring it out. Some foods are easy and others are impossible. For example, I can't get soup or cereal to my mouth without spilling it. Large, solid things like slices of pizza or bagels are perfectly manageable." I'd been making a point of not eating with silverware in front of him because I didn't like to broadcast how bad it had gotten. But if I was going to accept Shea's help, it was time to let him see the whole picture.

"What do you think about the idea of me moving in with you?" he asked. "I mean, I'm there all the time anyway and you gave me a key, but it seems like maybe we should make it official."

"I really want to live with you, and that has nothing to do with my failing motor skills. I love you, Shea. I'd want that even if I was in perfect health." He smiled and kissed me. I remembered something then and said, "Hey, Happy Valentine's Day, by the way. I have a present for you, fortunately it was in my pocket when we got swept up on this road trip." I stood up and stuffed my hand in the front pocket of my jeans, then pulled out a little object awkwardly swaddled in red tissue paper and way too much Scotch tape. "Sorry that this looks like it was wrapped by chimpanzees."

"Should I open it now?" When I nodded, Shea put down his coffee and worked his way through the tape and wrap, finally revealing a little steampunk brass heart made out of tiny gears and watch pieces.

I tried to find the words to explain the gift to him. "I wanted you to have my heart. I mean, you already have the real one, but I wanted you to have this one, too. I made it during my first semester at Sutherlin. It's always been special to me because it represented a new beginning after my first attempt at college. I carried it in my pocket every day that first year and took comfort in it at a time when I was feeling really vulnerable. I guess...I guess I'm hoping after I'm gone it'll comfort you too and help you find a new beginning."

Shea grabbed me in a tight embrace, a tremor going through his body. "Shit," I murmured, "sorry. I didn't mean to make this depressing. I just wanted you to know the story behind it."

His voice was rough when he said, "You didn't make it depressing. It's perfect and incredibly beautiful. Thank you." He let go of me and hastily wiped his eyes with the back of his hand. "Your present's in my backpack. I'll give it to you later, okay?"

"You didn't have to get me anything." He shot me a look and I offered him a little smile. "But thank you."

We finished our coffee, then decided to go for a walk. There was a ramshackle gazebo at the highest point in the vineyard and we made that our destination. A lot of kissing led to making love on the dusty pine floor of the small structure, hidden from view behind the drooping half-walls. I finished in Shea first, then he eased himself into me and finished in me as well.

As we got dressed and he pocketed the compact container of lube he almost always had with him, I said, "I wonder if that's Zandra." She and her boyfriend were flying up from L.A. for the wedding. In the distance, a white rental car was making its way down the long dirt road leading to the farmhouse, kicking up a plume of dust.

"Probably," Shea said as he tucked in his t-shirt. "Let's go say hi."

*****

We spent the day visiting with our friends until it was time for the ceremony. Nana had spent all day alternately cooking and pulling together some last-minute decorating with the help of Jessie and Joshie, who made a couple trips into town. When the wedding official arrived, Nana directed all of us to go out back, where she'd spun a little of her magic.

While the color scheme in the living room was pure Valentine's Day, apparently she'd second-guessed that idea for the ceremony. The little lawn area off the back deck was surrounded with clusters of blue and white flowers, all of them placed in or on found objects, like the basket of an old bike and the seat of a rusty patio chair. That was so Skye. A white vine-covered arch had been turned into a focal point with daisies woven into it. A lot of white twinkle lights added some sparkle.

When Skye stepped out the back door, his eyes got misty. "It's so pretty," he murmured.

"It's absolutely perfect," Dare agreed, taking his fiancé's hand.

Skye's mom took her place of honor on a padded lounge chair with Draco the cat on her lap and the mouse beside her in its carrier. The rest of the guests gathered around in a half-circle, including Benny the dog, who sat beside me wagging his tail and panting happily. The wedding official stood with her back to the arch, and River and I (and the dog) flanked the couple. Both grooms wore jeans and blue t-shirts. It was all exactly right somehow, so totally my best friend and the man he loved.

The ceremony was short and sweet, and when the two were pronounced husband and husband they kissed passionately. Nana signaled to Jessie and he started playing music on his phone, which came out through a series of speakers hidden around the garden. While Chance circled at a distance and snapped photos, the couple held each other and had their first dance right then and there, staring adoringly into one another's eyes. Since dance was a huge part of Dare's life, it was really fitting that this was a part of the ceremony.

As soon as the romantic instrumental song concluded, Lady Gaga started playing and Skye let out a delighted yell. All the wedding guests started dancing on the lawn. Tina's boyfriend picked her up and spun her a few times, cat and all, before kissing her and settling onto the lounge chair with her on his lap. Draco looked unimpressed.

Sometime later, Joshie and Jessie helped Nana set up the huge Italian buffet she'd prepared. When it was ready, Shea filled plates for both of us and we sat in the living room. I tried to pick up one of the forks that he'd set down on the coffee table, but I just couldn't quite manage it. "How do you want to do this?" he asked gently.

I considered the question as I assessed the plate of food and finally said, "If you put the finger foods in my hand for me, I can probably take it from there. I won't be able to manage the salad or pasta, though." He picked up my hand and turned it palm up, then balanced an appetizer on my fingertips and gently curled them around it.

A tear fell, soaking into my jeans, and Shea asked me what was wrong. "It's going to get so much worse than this," I whispered.

"So, we'll deal with it."

"I love you so much. I wish I didn't have to be such a burden."

"You're not a burden, sweetheart. Not at all."

I sighed quietly and we continued the meal. After I ate the appetizers, he fed me carefully. It was kind of awkward. "All your food's getting cold," I told him as he picked up some pasta with my fork.

"I don't care."

"But I do. Please eat something. I know you're hungry." He hastily ate a forkful of salad, then tried to go back to feeding me. I wrapped my hand around his and said, "This isn't going to work if you sacrifice your own health and well-being for me, baby. Please eat your lunch."

"But then yours will get cold."

"So, we'll stick it in the microwave."

He frowned at that, then compromised by feeding me and himself in turn. It took a long time, but eventually we got through the meal. "Will you come with me?" he asked as he got to his feet. "I want to give you your Valentine's Day present."

After dropping our plates and silverware off in the kitchen, where Hawk's kids had somehow been coerced into teaming up on the dishes, we went to the bunkhouse. I slipped my arms around Shea and held him for a long moment. He felt strong and solid, just like he always did. It was so reassuring.

He led me to his bunk and pulled his backpack out from underneath it. "Okay, this first part isn't your Valentine's Day present. It's your Christmas gift, actually." He put the comic book he'd been making for me in my hands. "This took so much longer than I anticipated. Sorry about that."

"Thank you," I said, hugging it to my chest. "I can see why it took some time. You've been devoting every spare moment to me and to the art center."

I started to fold back the cover, but Shea said, "Hang on. Before you do that, I want to give you your real present." He took a silver charm out of a black jewelry box. It was a beautifully rendered abstract representation of two hands holding a heart that was wearing a crown. "I found a metal artist to make this for you. I wanted it to represent both of us, traditional and modern at the same time. It was inspired by a Claddagh ring. I love you, Christian, and I wanted you to have a symbol of my love."

I threw my arms around him again, the comic book sandwiched between us. "Thank you, baby. I love it."

"Is it really okay?"

"It's perfect. Could you help me with this?" I pulled the black leather cord out from inside my shirt, the one with my dad's pendant on it, and Shea added the charm. The two pieces were roughly the same size and contrasted really beautifully. After he put it on again, I pressed my hand over it, holding it to my heart. "Thank you so much. It's wonderful."

He rested his forehead against mine and smiled. "I'm so glad you like it."

Next, Shea turned the pages of the comic book for me and explained each illustration. They didn't need explanation, but I thought it was cute that he did that. "This turned out amazing. You've produced an incredible work of art," I told him when we reached the end. "Please tell me you'll keep pursuing drawing."

"I will, somewhere down the road," he said, looking away.

I reached for his chin and turned his face toward me. "I know you're going to have your hands full now that I'm getting worse, but please, Shea. Promise me you'll make time for yourself and for your drawing. This is important."

"I'll try." I kissed him softly, and he slid his hand around the back of my neck and deepened the kiss. We ended up making love for the second time that day there in the bunkhouse, switching off again, which was becoming our norm.

When we were dressed, I finger-combed my hair and said, "Come on, baby. There's a party going on and I feel like celebrating."

I really did, too. I'd been on such a roller coaster of emotions lately, wonderful events in my life contrasting sharply with the fear and sadness of becoming ever more helpless and realizing my days were numbered. I kept reminding myself of what Nana had said, though. *You think I'm going to squander even one day by sitting around fretting over how much time I have left?*

Today was an absolutely wonderful day. I'd gotten to be best man and watch my best friend marry the love of his life, and I was spending Valentine's Day with the man of my dreams and my closest friends. What could be better? I picked up Shea's hand and smiled at him, then led him out into the sunshine.

Chapter Twenty-Four

June.

"Hell no. Tell him to leave."

I sighed in frustration and pushed my hair back from my face. "No, Dad. He's not leaving. You sent him away the first four times, but this time it's for real. Gianni's taking over for me, starting today. Shea and I are on our way to Palo Alto because the clinical trial starts this afternoon. You know this!"

"Why can't Skye bring me groceries until you're done with the drug study? It's just for eight weeks."

"He and Dare are leaving on their belated honeymoon tomorrow, now that Skye graduated."

"Did he finish his sculptures in time?" Zan asked, fidgeting with the drink in his hand.

"Quit stalling."

"I'm not. I really want to know!"

"Yes, he finished. He got the last pieces on the day before he had to turn them in."

"I want to see. Surely you took pictures."

I rolled my eyes, then shot Shea a look. He was leaning against the kitchen counter with his arms crossed over his chest. "Could you show him please, even if he is just stalling?"

Shea grinned a little, pushed off the counter, and crossed the room to Zan. He took out his phone and flipped through a few screens before handing it over. Skye really had done an amazing job on the three dancing figures. It was his best work, no doubt about it. He'd then floored me by asking if they could find a home in the big music room in the art center. I told my dad this, and he beamed at me. "Perfect. Music and dance were always meant to go together. What's going on with Zane, by the way? Did you get that scheduling conflict ironed out?"

I'd ended up calling it The Zane Center for Art and Music, but most people just called it Zane. That name had always represented both Zan and me, so I was happy with my choice. I told my dad, "I didn't have to get the conflict ironed out. Hillary did it. That's why I hired her, to run things for me."

Over the last few months, I'd conducted countless interviews and hired a great administrative staff and teachers (funded by an insanely generous grant from my father), and brought in scores of volunteers. I worked closely with Sutherlin, recruiting students and alumni to develop and teach classes, and a local symphony orchestra to build the music program. To make sure it wasn't too stodgy, I'd also found a local rock band whose members were friends of Jessie's, and they taught music classes as well. Those classes had the longest waiting lists.

Student turnout had exceeded all my expectations. Skye and Dare volunteered to go around to every grade school in San Francisco, Berkeley and Oakland to do art demonstrations and hand out fliers. The day doors opened for enrollment (which was free, of course), over three hundred and fifty kids and their parents lined the sidewalk.

That was when I knew Zane was going to be a shining success. It had gone from an empty building to a community. I was incredibly proud of what I'd begun, and I just knew it was going to flourish well into the future.

A door banged open. "Enough already!" That came from down the hall. I could hear Gianni stomping toward us. Suddenly he appeared in the doorway, looking more than a little flustered. "I'm out there getting heat stroke and fending off yellow jackets! *Yellow jackets!* This is ridiculous! I'm not going to let that man send me back to the city again without so much as meeting me!"

Zan glared at the intruder. "There. I've met you. Now bugger off, I was talking to my son!"

Gianni put his hands on his hips and squared off against my father. "Your son needs to be at the other end of the Bay Area in just a couple hours. It's time to face the facts, dude. Christian and Shea will still come for visits, but you're stuck with me for the rest of it."

Zan turned to me and said, "Dude? You found someone who calls me *dude*? And I'm supposed to trust this person to buy me food?"

"You only eat five things," Gianni snapped. "It's not that hard."

My dad ran his gaze up and down his new caretaker. "He looks like a rich, spoiled party boy. What are his qualifications?"

Gianni raised a dark eyebrow at him. "For buying groceries? *Seriously?*"

"I hate to butt in," Shea said, "but we really do need to get on the road. We're going to be late for check-in."

"Dad, stop being an ass and come here and say goodbye to me," I told him, holding my arms up. I'd been in a wheelchair for about six weeks. It was such a basic thing, just putting one foot in front of the other, so when my coordination failed and I became unable to do that it was a shock. All I could do was deal with it though, with Shea's help.

My father sighed and crossed the room to me, then clutched me in a tight embrace. "I love you, boyo. Now remember what you promised."

"We remember. Shea will call you every single day and let you know how I'm doing." We'd made the same promise to my mom, who we'd visited that morning. We'd been meeting her and my stepdad once a week for lunch over the past few months, and all of us had grown closer. She'd been in tears this morning, but it seemed like my stepdad was going to be a good source of support for her. He was doing well with his sobriety and I was glad he'd gotten it together in time to help her through what was going to be a difficult few months, both during the drug trial and beyond.

"Sure you don't want to back out?" Zan asked.

"This is important, Dad. I've told you why I need to do this."

"I know. I'm just worried."

I kissed his cheek. "When the eight weeks are up, we'll come see you right away. I won't be allowed to go anywhere until then." He nodded, still holding me tightly. "Give Gianni a chance. Please? You need him and he needs this job."

Zan straightened up and ran his thumb underneath his lower lashes. "Why? What happened to his last job?" When I broke eye contact, he asked, "He has had a job before, right?"

"Well, no. But he did complete nearly three semesters of nursing school," I said.

"Oh, nearly three semesters, brilliant! And no job ever! Well, with qualifications like that, surely I'm in good hands!" My dad's accent ramped up with his temper.

"I know why you're really upset, Dad, but this is going to be okay."

"You don't know that. You don't know if it's going to be okay." He turned to Shea. "Don't let them hurt my boy. Please, laddie? You'll look out for him, won't you?"

"I'm going to do everything I can for him, Zan," my boyfriend promised.

When we finally said our goodbyes and Shea wheeled me down the long hallway to the side door, I could hear Zan and Gianni bickering again and smiled. It was going pretty well. My dad was staying and engaging instead of locking himself in the bathroom. That was what he'd done the last four times we'd brought his new caretaker to meet him.

Shea steered me around Gianni's white BMW, the wheels of the chair crunching over the gravel. When we got to the Jeep, he swung the passenger door open and lifted me effortlessly. Just like every time, he paused to kiss me and rub his cheek against mine before putting me in the car and fastening my seatbelt.

The bright June sunlight didn't do much for my migraine, and I squinted as I fumbled to get my sunglasses into place. Shea helped me, guiding my hands gently. My doctor had cut my meds back to just the essentials in order to get me ready for the clinical trial. Without the large doses of pain killer I'd been relying on, migraines were now a fact of life. I tried not to let the pain show as I gave Shea a smile. He always knew though, there was no fooling him. He cupped my face between his hands and whispered, "You're the bravest person I know, Christian," before kissing me again.

We were both quiet on the long drive from Marin to Palo Alto, his fingers laced with mine on top of the stick shift. The trials were going to be occurring at an offshoot of Stanford Medical Center. Since the researchers were trying to control as many variables as possible, right down to diet and exercise, I'd be living on-site in what was basically a cross between a miniature hospital and a dormitory. Shea had rented a small apartment nearby. I'd only be allowed to see him during visiting hours every afternoon, between lunch and dinnertime. It was going to break my heart to be away from him. We'd become completely inseparable over the last few months. He'd even taken a leave of absence from his job and devoted himself to my care.

When we reached the medical center, Shea held me for a long time when he lifted me out of the car, his face pressed into the space between my neck and shoulder. I wanted to tell him it was going to be okay, but we both knew I had no idea what these next few weeks would have in store for me. Instead, I told him I loved him again and kissed his hair as I held him tightly.

When he wheeled me into the lobby, I burst into tears. My friends were waiting for me. I'd said 'goodbye for now' to all of them over the last couple days, but they'd decided to come down for a final send-off.

Chance reached me first, grabbing me in a hug before pressing a little, worn teddy bear into my hand. "The bear's just a loan. Bobo got me through some hard times as a kid. He'll help you through the next few weeks." He slipped a stretchy bracelet lined with amber beads on my left wrist and explained, "This is to keep. They're called worry beads. In Greek culture, some people believe they guard against bad luck. They also help you pass the time or relax. Usually you hold them, but I knew that'd be tough so I made them into a bracelet for you."

I ran my right hand over them and said, "Thank you, Chance. That was incredibly thoughtful."

All of them had something for me. Trevor and Vincent had brought me an accessible iPod set up to accept voice commands, loaded with music and audiobooks. Skye and Dare had brought an orchid (so I'd have something pretty to focus on, they said), and a thick, fuzzy robe and slippers. They also passed along a gift from Zandra, a frame containing several pictures of me with my friends. Nana stepped forward, slipped an engraved silver flask in my pocket and gave me a big wink. I wouldn't actually be able to drink alcohol while the study was going on, but I thanked her graciously.

Suddenly, Shea's brother burst through the doors. "Oh good, glad I didn't miss you," Finn said, catching his breath. He thrust a package into my hands and said embarrassedly, "Look, it's no secret I've had my doubts about you, but I think you're doing a pretty cool thing here, Christian. So, um, I brought you copies of some of my brother's favorite comic books. I thought they might help you pass the time. I know if it was me, I'd go pretty stir-crazy stuck in here. Also, you know, this way you'll be able to see some of what makes Shea, Shea." He seemed to run out of steam then and stepped back, looking embarrassed. "Anyway, good luck." His brother grabbed him in a hug.

A man with an ID card clipped to his shirt pocket came into the lobby with two nurses and said, "Welcome! All participants in the Sangene study, please follow me for orientation."

"Well, this is it," I said, turning to my boyfriend. I stood up carefully and took him in my arms.

"See you in forty-four hours, sweetheart." That was when visiting hours would begin.

"I'll call you as soon as I'm settled in my room," I told him, and he kissed me. "I love you, Shea." My voice broke a little.

He rubbed his cheek against mine and told me, "I love you too, Christian, with all my heart." I had to force myself to let go of him. When I sat down again he picked up my duffle bag and put it in my lap, along with all my presents.

A red-haired nurse of about forty came up to me with a friendly smile and gestured at my chair. "Want me to give you a hand?"

"Thanks, that'd be great."

I turned to say goodbye to my friends, and they swooped in for one more round of hugging, kissing and well-wishing before I was wheeled through the double doors. As we followed the group of about twenty people making their way past a series of offices, she said, "That was quite a send-off. You're lucky to have such good friends."

"I really am."

*****

What followed were eight of the toughest weeks of my life. I spent the first two violently ill. The drug-induced nausea was compounded by my intense headaches. I lost a lot of weight and became weak because I couldn't keep anything down. My doctor nearly pulled me from the study group, but finally the nausea dialed back. Once I could eat, I started to rebuild my strength. The headaches remained so

428

bad that I spent a big part of each day in my little room with the lights off and an icepack on my forehead.

My friends came to see me, but soon realized I needed my daily visiting hours to be all about Shea, so they switched to texting and writing instead. Skye got in the habit of writing long, hilarious letters with lots of illustrations. I got at least three a week. One of the nurses, a middle-aged father of three named Alonzo, always offered to help me with the texts and letters because he said my friends were a riot.

Their gifts were such a comfort. I spent a lot of time wrapped in that thick robe, an arm curled around Chance's little bear with my dad's and Shea's pendants in one hand and the worry beads in the other, eyes focused on the white orchid or on the photos in the frame on my nightstand. On days when I felt well enough, I'd play music, listen to an audiobook or read a comic and that helped pass the time, too.

All of that was wonderful and helped keep my spirits up, but Shea was what really got me through those two months in Palo Alto. He was right there, every single day, from the minute visiting hours began until they kicked him out when they were over. He'd give me updates on Zan (doing fine though constantly feuding with Gianni) and the art center (running like clockwork) and our friends. When things were really bad, he'd reassure me and kiss my tear-streaked cheeks. Sometimes, he'd softly sing my dad's songs to me, rocking me gently when nothing else would soothe me.

Most importantly, he held me, and that was the best thing in the world. We'd spend most of the handful of hours we were allotted each day with me on his lap in the green upholstered chair in a corner of my little room, arms wrapped around each other. That more than anything kept me going when the pain and nausea wore me down to almost nothing. No matter how bad things got, I had that time with Shea to look forward to.

Even though I knew he was worried, whenever we were together he was calm, reassuring and positive. He was my strength when I couldn't find my own. I loved him like I'd never loved anything or anyone, more than I ever realized it was possible to love someone. The love he gave me in return was the most beautiful, amazing gift, pure and true and steadfast. I was so incredibly thankful for it, and for him.

I tried to tell him how much he meant to me and how grateful I was for him. Words completely failed me. Just saying 'I love you' didn't begin to cover it. But maybe Shea knew anyway, in that way he had of always knowing what was going on with me. I really hoped he did.

Chapter Twenty-Five

August.

Those eight weeks eventually passed. The trials ended with a whole battery of tests. I'd had blood drawn and CAT scans and MRIs at the start of the test period. All of that was repeated at the end, with follow-ups scheduled every two weeks for the next three months.

The day of my release, we went directly to Doctor Halpern's office for a scheduled appointment. The tests were repeated since he wouldn't have access to the data collected by the drug company. He ramped up all my meds again, administering a dose of narcotic pain relievers while I was still in the office, though he warned me that eventually my headaches would stop responding to the pain pills as the tumor spread. For now though, they took the edge off and made it bearable.

When we finally got home, my boyfriend carried me straight to our bed and we made love urgently. I couldn't get enough of him, my mouth tasting his as Shea's cock filled me, my hands clutching his body to mine. I had no idea how I'd survived for two months without feeling his skin on mine and the reassuring weight of him on top of me. Once he came, he eased my cock into him and rode me until I came too, crying out, hugging him to me with the last of my strength.

We stayed in bed the rest of the day, even eating dinner there (pizza, which I'd sorely missed). In the morning, he rushed out and bought groceries, then made me a big breakfast. I didn't have much appetite but with Shea's coaxing, I ate what I could.

Once we both got cleaned up, we went to visit my dad. He was thrilled to see me. After I told him all about the last few weeks and assured him I was okay, the complaints started. "That Dombruso blighter is going to be the death of me," Zan ranted. "He's the most stubborn little shit I've ever met! And such a prima donna! Everything has to be his way. Please tell me you and Shea will take over for him now that the clinical trial is over."

"We really can't do that, Dad. Shea already has so much on his plate trying to take care of me and you know I'm just going to keep getting worse. We'll still visit you of course, but Gianni has proven that he's reliable so he'll keep bringing you the things you need." That, of course, resulted in a lot more grumbling.

We spent most of the day with my dad, then went to visit my mom and stepdad before meeting our friends for dinner at Nolan's, Jamie and Dmitri's bar and grill. Skye brought along his laptop and set it up on the table so our friend Zandra could Skype with us from L.A.

When Chance arrived, he kissed my cheek and I returned his bear to him. "Thank you, he really helped. So did these," I said, indicating the beads I still wore on my wrist.

"I'm sorry to make you give Bobo back," he said embarrassedly. "That's probably pretty cheesy."

"Not at all. It was sweet of you to lend him to me. He was a good buddy while I was stuck in that place."

"Are you okay?"

"Yeah."

"What did the drug do to you?" he asked.

"No idea, aside from making me puke my guts out." I looked at Chance closely and picked up his hand. He looked paler than usual and his blue eyes were underscored with dark circles. "Are you alright?"

"I'm fine."

"No you're not. What's going on?"

"Nothing." He absolutely refused to open up, no matter how much I prodded. I sighed quietly and pulled him into a hug. Trevor and Vincent arrived then, looking tan and happy after a vacation in southern California with their son, and Chance went around the table to visit with them.

I turned to Skye, who was seated on my left, and asked, "How's postgraduate life treating you?"

"I miss Sutherlin, more than I thought I would. I really loved being a student. Not that I don't also love volunteering at Zane, mind you. That's a hell of a place you founded. You need to come by soon and take a look at what you started."

"Oh, we will. So, what's it like being a professional sculptor?"

He grinned at that. "I wouldn't know. So far the only prospects I have are through friends. Christopher told me he'd feature a couple of my pieces in his gallery, assuming I make something small enough to fit in the door."

"You made me that great tabletop sculpture for Christmas, you can totally do small-scale." He'd rendered one of my murals, two boys running and holding hands, as a miniature three-dimensional figure.

"True. Also, Nana commissioned me to make a sculpture for her backyard. I don't exactly work quickly, though. Those three things could take me the next year. Fortunately, my husband has money coming in from his dance classes, so I can just be a big leach and live off him." He shot Dare a smile, and his husband leaned in and kissed his forehead.

"You're not a total leach," his brother River chimed in from across the table, his arm around his boyfriend's shoulders. "You're also helping Cole and me with our business."

Skye nodded. "Oh yeah, that too. I have a pity job as a cater-waiter. It's a damn good thing I have friends and family, or else I'd be taking the whole starving artist thing really literally."

"No one's starving on my watch!" River pushed a basket of garlic bread toward us and said, "Both of you, eat! Christian, didn't they feed you in that place? You look thin enough to slip through the floorboards."

Nana and Jessie burst in the door just then, both of them flushed and excited. Gianni trailed a couple steps behind them, looking more than a little irked. Nana rushed over to me and kissed my cheeks, then complained that I looked thin and practically force-fed me one of the slices of garlic bread. When they all sat down, Shea said to her, "Should we even ask what you've been up to, and was law enforcement involved?"

"They just jumped a guy on Market Street," Gianni told us.

"What? Why?" Shea asked.

"He was wearing a t-shirt that said 'homosexuality is a sin' so they pulled over and Nana got in his face. After a yelling match, she pulled the shirt right off him and dove back into the limo with it. Jessie sped away like they'd just robbed a bank," Gianni said. "I swear, these two are going to end up in jail."

"I've been to jail," Nana said proudly, straightening the lapel of the demure blue suit she was wearing. "It's not so bad. You meet some nice people." She gave Shea a wink as she set her big handbag on the table in front of her.

"Okay, well, what if that asshole with the t-shirt had become violent? What then?" Gianni asked her.

Nana rolled her eyes, flipped open her handbag and pulled out a huge .44. "Bring it on, baby!" she yelled.

This was followed by a lot of chaos as Gianni and Shea both leapt up and tried to disarm her. Nana waved it around along with a laminated sheet of paper and told them, "It's fine! I got a permit to carry concealed! See?"

Skye and I both burst out laughing and I leaned against him as I said, "God, I missed you guys."

*****

When Shea and I got home that night, I pulled my phone from my pocket and realized I'd forgotten to charge it. He plugged it in for me and said as the screen came up, "You have a couple voicemails, want me to put them on speaker?"

"Sure. Thanks, baby," I said as I started to change for bed.

The messages were both from Doctor Halpern, who sounded slightly more animated than usual. "I need you to come back to the office first thing in the morning," he said. "We're going to run some more tests."

"Ugh, what now?" I grumbled, falling back onto the pillow. "Between Halpern and the final round of tests at the center, I've had so damn much done to me in the last couple days."

"It could be important though," Shea said, sitting beside me on the bed and brushing my hair back.

"I know. I'm planning to go, I just wanted to complain about it first." I gave him a smile and pulled him into my arms.

"I'm so incredibly glad you're back, Christian," he murmured as he nuzzled my cheek.

"Me too. I missed you so much."

He kissed the tip of my nose and asked, "Are you glad you participated in the study, though?"

"I am now that it's over. I knew my tumor was fairly uncommon, but I found out I was the only person in the study group with that type. That made me feel like it was doubly important for me to be there." I brushed my lips to his before asking, "So, what did you do to pass the time while you were staying in Palo Alto?"

"I got a two-month gym membership, I watched a lot of Netflix, and I drew. Mostly though, I just sat around missing you."

"You were drawing?"

He nodded as his fingertips lightly brushed my bangs aside. "I really wasn't up to going anywhere, so I just sat at my kitchen table and filled sketchpads."

"What were you drawing?" I'd gathered one of his hands in both of mine and held it to my heart while his free hand tenderly traced the outlines of my face.

"I was working on ideas for a gay superhero. I was thinking maybe I could publish a comic book series independently someday." I beamed at him delightedly and he said, "Don't get too excited. It's just a side project, no big deal."

"It *is* a big deal. You're going to do great with it."

He grinned and said, "Thank you for always believing in me. I was used to people in my life always telling me what I couldn't do. But not you."

"They were all wrong. You can do anything you set your mind to." I kissed the hand I was holding and said, "Hey, I was thinking. Do you want to go camping next week? I think we could both use some time in the fresh air, and you can bring your sketchbooks." We'd gone for the first time in late spring, and when I saw how happy it made Shea, we'd gone back twice more.

"You want to?"

"Sure."

His grin got wider. "It's sweet that you humor me. I know it's not your favorite thing."

"My favorite thing is being with you." I smiled at him and added, "Even if it does mean freezing my ass off in a tent."

"It's August now, your cute little ass is safe from freezing." He slid a hand down my back and cupped it gently.

That was all it took to jump start my libido. I leaned in and kissed him deeply. Within minutes, we were both totally worked up, and he slid his cock into me. I sighed with relief.

*****

We went back to my doctor's office the next morning as requested. The fact that he met us there on a Saturday and accompanied us to the imagining center was odd. I endured yet another MRI and when I asked him why we were doing it again, he said, "I need to verify an anomaly in the images taken yesterday." That basically told me nothing, but he said it was 'premature' to say any more. He had me schedule an appointment for the following Tuesday.

*****

Tuesday morning, we were his very first appointment. He looked more excited than I would have thought possible, which is to say he was mildly excited. "Your tumor responded to the test medicine," he told me. "I really didn't expect such dramatic results."

"Responded in a good way or a bad way?"

"It shrank approximately eight percent when compared to the images we obtained prior to the clinical trials."

I leaned back in my chair and blinked at the doctor as I reached for Shea's hand. "It shrank? That never happened before, not with any of the treatments we tried."

"No, never. That's a significant change in just two months. I really don't want to raise false hope, but this to me is extremely promising."

I took that in for a moment before saying, "But...the drug is still in testing. It won't make it to market for years. By then it'll be too late."

"True. However, I'm on the advisory board for Sangene and was able to meet with the head of their research and development department yesterday. He'd already noted your results in the preliminary data from the clinical trial. You were the only participant with this type of tumor, and you showed the most improvement out of any of the test subjects."

"So, what did he say?" Shea asked.

Halpern slid three grey plastic bottles toward us that had been sitting on the left side of his desk. "This is a six-month supply of the drug at twice the dosage you'd received in the study. Normally, the company wouldn't be willing to alter protocol like this, but study participants in advanced stages with your particular type of tumor are extremely rare. I made the case that the data obtained from you could be extremely valuable, but if we waited until the Phase Three trials began officially we probably would lose you as a test subject."

"Because I'd be dead by then," I murmured and he nodded. "Is this legal? Won't you get in trouble for giving me an unlicensed drug?"

"Sangene is allowed to file an addendum to their Phase Two testing protocols. They're going to stipulate a longer testing period for subjects in advanced stages. Their lawyers will undoubtedly have you sign a fresh set of waivers, similar to the ones you signed at the start of the clinical trials, and I will of course remind you that there are potential risks associated with this. I also can't guarantee that this will help, but at this point, I'd say it's by far your best option."

"If my tumor continues to respond to the drug, then what?"

"When you first came to me, surgery was already impossible because of the size of your tumor," Halpern said. "It had sent branches deep into your brain by that point, to such an extent that attempts at extraction would have killed you. Those branches are responding to the drug and that's promising. Best case scenario: if you continue to progress in a similar fashion, extraction might become a possibility. Keep in mind I said *if.* There are no guarantees, of course. But honestly, at this point we have nothing to lose."

As we drove home from the doctor's office that day, the three grey bottles lined up on my lap, I studied Shea's profile and said, "I'm not sure what to think about any of this."

He glanced at me and smiled before turning his attention back to the traffic. "I know you've always been afraid to get your hopes up, but this is exciting."

"It's possible nothing will come of this."

"But what if it does?"

I rested my hand on top of his and said gently, "Won't it hurt more if you get your hopes up and still end up losing me?"

"No. Losing you is utterly devastating no matter what precedes it, so I'm going to go ahead and get my hopes up for both of us."

Chapter Twenty-Six

February.

It was hard to open my eyes, but someone was calling my name. I felt like I was swimming toward the sound of the voice—Shea's voice—through murky water. Finally, I broke through the surface and managed to force my eyelids open.

"Hi sweetheart, welcome back." My boyfriend was smiling. I blinked a few times and looked around me. We were in a hospital. Everything was pale yellow and way too brightly lit.

Doctor Halpern approached me. He was smiling, too. I wasn't sure if I'd ever seen him do that before. "You're still feeling the effects of the anesthesia," he told me. "I'll come back tomorrow and brief you when you're more awake. For now, I just want to let you know the surgery was a success. I was able to do a clean extraction. We'll still follow up with chemotherapy as a precaution to be certain nothing remains, but it's looking extremely positive, Christian."

I tried to process that. A couple nurses were moving around me. There was an IV stand, tubes, lots of machines...too much to take in.

After they left, Shea leaned over me and caressed my cheek. "Did you hear that? It was a success. He got the tumor."

"What...what does that mean?" My voice sounded raspy and my mouth was so dry. Everything was still hazy, not quite in focus.

"It means you're going to live." Shea's voice caught.

"I am?"

"Yes, sweetheart."

I wondered if I was dreaming.

*****

By the time Halpern came back the next day, I was propped up in bed and feeling a lot more lucid. Shea held my hand, his thumb gently caressing the back of it. My friends, mom and stepdad had left a little while ago, after deciding they were probably tiring me out. Shea had been checking in with my dad every couple hours, too.

Halpern answered Shea's questions while I just took it all in. "There's no way of knowing at this point if the damage that was done will be permanent," the doctor said at one point. "Christian might regain some of his lost motor skills or he might not. We'll have to wait and see."

When Doctor Halpern left sometime later, Shea moved from his chair to perch on the edge of my bed and told me,

"The human brain is capable of some pretty remarkable things, and I bet you're going to regain much of what you lost. But even if you don't, I'll be right by your side to help, just like always."

"You've been amazing throughout all of this," I told him. "I'm so grateful for the way you put your entire life on hold and cared for me. It couldn't have been easy for you."

"I was happy to do it."

"I wouldn't be here now if it wasn't for you. I wouldn't have made it through those first few weeks of the clinical trials and found out what the drug could do for me if you hadn't been there to support me."

"Yes you would. You're much stronger than you give yourself credit for, Christian."

"I know I'm capable of dealing with a lot, but I also know I'm so much stronger with you at my side."

He smiled and told me, "That's right where I'll be, always."

"Ever since I was first diagnosed, almost four years ago now, I stopped thinking about the future. I just learned to live day by day. I never asked myself where I wanted to be in five years, or what I'd do when I finished school, or any of those things people normally think about. All of a sudden, my future's been given back to me and I don't know what to do with it, because I stopped asking those questions a long time ago." I raised my hand, trailing the cords from an IV, and touched his cheek as I looked in his eyes. "There's only one thing I know with absolute certainty. Whatever I do, wherever I go, I need you right there with me."

"You have me, Christian, for as long as you want me."

"I want you forever, Shea. Will you marry me?"

His face lit up with a breathtaking smile. "Of course I will." As tears spilled down my cheeks, I pulled him to me and embraced my future.

The Beginning

###

Thank you for reading!

For more by Alexa Land, please visit
http://alexalandwrites.blogspot.com/

Find me on Facebook
And on Twitter @AlexaLandWrites

Books by Alexa Land Include:

Feral

The Tinder Chronicles

And the Firsts and Forever Series:

Way Off Plan

All In

In Pieces

Gathering Storm

Salvation

Skye Blue

Against the Wall

The Firsts and Forever Series will continue
as Christian and Shea get married,
Gianni finds the love of his life,
Chance seeks his happily ever after,
favorite characters are revisited,
and new characters join the Firsts & Forever family!

Made in the USA
San Bernardino, CA
27 June 2016